Circulate

By K. R. Smith

ISBN: 978-0-646-53776-4

'Circulate' first published October 2005
By Eclectica Press
eclectica@optusnet.com.au

'Circulate' 2nd ed. 2010
By K.R. Smith
onaya3@yahoo.com.au

~Acknowledgments~

Sorry everyone. I'll try to keep this shorter than a Cuba Gooding Jnr Oscar's speech. But there are just a few necessary things I feel I ought to say...

Thanks Mum and Dad, for giving me free reign of my creative abilities early on in my life and supporting the decisions I made (even if they were bad ones).

And thanks to UWS Nepean, where I spent the best part of my life. To the lecturers; to the friends I made in my subjects; and to my flatmates when we all lived together on campus who continue today to offer their friendship and support; Paul, Karen, Pete, Jane, Nathan, Liz, John and Greggor. Their advice and readership when writing this book became invaluable.

Then to some of the best years I had in the work force at Starbucks in Parramatta; Darianne, Nicole, Karen, Brenda, Sera, Rebecca, Elite, Suzanne, Patrice and Paula... you made me look forward to every shift just to be in your presence.

I'd also like to say a BIG thank you to Gaylynn & Brenden. I went through an awful time in my life, but it was with their friendship and hospitality that I survived. They picked me up off the ground, shook the dirt off, and invited me in for pizza and videos. Watching horror flicks and trying to predict which character will be the first to 'cark' it has never been so much fun...mwahahaha! (evil laugh)

Thank you Darran Jordan and Eclectica Press for publishing me in the beginning. Rather than hiding Elisha on a hard drive, you sent her out into the big scary world on the printed page.

A huge thank you to Isabel de Sequera for your wonderful illustrations. Seeing Elisha for the first time on the cover was to me, seeing her for the first time in solid form. It actually made writing this book finally a reality to me.

- K.R.Smith 2005

~ Contents ~

Hamilton's College:
Making a Mark in Time

A Prospectus

Hamilton's College is a unique institution that helps gifted children to prepare for the challenges of the fast paced environment of the western world. It is in a college environment that offers subjects at secondary school level as well as a curriculum that even branches out into University level learning.

At Hamilton's our broad multi-cultural spectrum includes students that speak English as a first and or second language from a wide range of countries. The ages of our students range between 16 to 19 years of age, and upon occasion we have also accepted applicants as young as 14 years old.

During school semester there are no more than 70 students at a time attending college which provides our students an individualistic approach to their welfare and education. There is a full time school counselor that works one on one with the students to ensure that we are crafting our education directly to their needs.

At Hamilton's College we are more than just a boarding school. We offer our students their own individual bedrooms that supply a heater, bed, closet, draws, mirror, book shelves, desk and chair. From our experience we have found that students who have their own rooms can study better and fully apply themselves to their chosen courses in life. The Dormitories are on the ground floor, first floor and second floor, with each floor one teacher is assigned as Den Mother or Den Father. There are approximately 22 bedrooms per floor, with two bathrooms, one for girls, one for the boys. Our dormitories are co-ed, with a communal recreation room that has a TV and VCR, as well as a smaller, second library in the school.

All of the meals served in the Cafeteria are selected by a certified nutritionist. We also cater for special dietary needs such as diabetes, vegetarian and Kosher. Once a week on Saturday nights there are 'fun nights' where students can choose to eat either hamburgers, hot dogs, French Fries etc. and this is the only night of the week where soda, or 'soft drink' or chocolates are served.

In the cafeteria, meals are served five times a day:

- Breakfast   7:30   AM
- Morning Tea   10:30   AM
- Lunch   12:30   PM
- Afternoon Tea   3:30   PM
- Dinner   7:00   PM

Our school year is roughly based on the Canadian school year, where first semester starts approximately* the 1st of September and up until approximately to the 20th December where school closes for Christmas and New Years Holiday. Then the second semester is from approximately the 20th of January to approximately the 30th of June. **

* Approximately is used as dates may change due to the calendar cycle.

** Students have a week off class during April over Easter, but since the holiday is so short, international students may not have the chance to return home during this time.

Class times during the school semester are:
- 8:30 AM to 10:30 AM
- 11:00 AM to 12:30 PM
- 1:30 PM to 3:30 PM

What Hamilton's can offer:

- Olympic Size Sports Oval
- Indoor pool
- Indoor gym
- Nearby Lake where students can Kayak in summer, ice-skate in winter
- World Heritage protected natural Forrest which students are taken on hiking trips
- A theatre for drama productions, musicals and once a semester dances.
- Two Libraries
- Greenhouse
- Two Recreation Lounges, both with TV's and VCR's and table tennis
- Hospital Wing with a qualified M.D in practice

Hamilton's College is just 20 kilometres outside of the township Brownsville, Manitoba. It has a population of under one thousand, and where many of our gardeners, cleaners, chef's and administration staff come from. The town has a small airport and heli-pad, a country hospital with a Dentist where we take our students for check ups or appointments, Fire Station, RCMP station, cinema and a hotel. Brownsville is located on the edge of Lake Laura, where Hamilton's College is just on the other side of. Hamilton's College has a good relationship with the township of Brownsville. On occasion the Royal Canadian Mounted Police on their days off, volunteer to take the students walking in the World Heritage Protected Pine Forrest that surround the college and township, as well as teaching the students how to Kayak in summer and ice skate in winter on the lake.

The college campus is made up of four main buildings: Alpha, Beta, Gamma and Delta.

The Alpha Building is comprised of:

- Classrooms
- Library
- Teachers Offices

The Beta Building is comprised of:

- Dormitories for both the teachers and the students
- Recreation Room
- Second Library

The Gamma Building is comprised of:

- Cafeteria
- Greenhouse
- Theatre
- Recreation Room

The Delta Building is comprised of:

- Hospital wing
- Gymnasium
- Indoor Pool
- Guest Cottage

TO: mbaker@hotmail.com

FROM: ebaker_hamiltons@evers.com

SUBJECT: I'm all right, what's going on?

DATE: 09/ 10/ 00

Mark, it's me, Elisha. I'm alive. I'm alive...

I don't know what you heard from Dad or anyone else, but I guess you know I tried to do it. I cut myself and took Dad's stash of sleeping tablets. I am so embarrassed! It didn't work! Now everyone thinks of me as the freak who tried to kill herself. I can only imagine what Dad thinks. I guess he found me, in the bathroom. But how the hell did I get over here? Did he call you? Has he told you why he's sent me away?

I'm in a hospital bed, typing this from a laptop they gave me. I'm in a hospital wing, it's small with only six beds. From the window next to my bed I can see mountains with snow on the tops, and pine forests, and a huge lake. I'm in fucking Canada, can you believe it? Somewhere called Ontario, or is that the state and not the place? I don't know... I still feel a little groggy. I've been here for 3 days apparently.

I woke up yesterday and there is this female doctor and a female nurse who is looking after me. I'm in a kind of boarding school...? I don't understand... I think it might be some kind of mental hospital/boarding school or something. Because apparently there are other kids here around my age, in class somewhere. I'm told I'm the only

Australian they've had in a couple of years. They get kids here from all over the world, so they say.

So what happens? As soon as a kid tries to off themselves they get sent here? I don't know what's going on... I need your help. I know I'll owe you big time, but can you call and ask Dad what's going on? How angry is he with me to send me away like this? And ask when I can come home. I miss Angela. I wish she was here. I'm going to send her an email next. I wish I could call her, but I'm too scared to ask if I can use the phone to make an overseas call. I don't know where my stuff is or how to pay for the call.

If Dad was going to send me away somewhere, why couldn't I have just stayed with Angela? I'm sure her parents wouldn't have minded. I really get on well with her Mum and stuff. She never minds when I crash at their place on weekends.

I wish it worked. I don't want to be here. Not just here here, but alive. I know you hate it when I talk this way, but it's how I feel. I don't want to be here anymore... and I feel like such a loser that I even stuffed up my own suicide. I couldn't even do that right.

Bye.

===

10/ 10/ 00

Dear Diary,

I know it sounds kind of sucky, but that's how I always began in my old diary, when I was writing it down, and not typing on this laptop they gave me. Speaking of which, how weird is that? The laptop they gave me to let me email in the hospital wing, they told me I could keep, to use for my assignments and stuff. It's still officially school property I think though. But if I want I can take it to class and stuff. Man, I'm only in Year 10 and I already feel like I'm about to start University!

I'm not in the hospital wing anymore. It wasn't really a wing or whatever you called it, it was only a hospice which was on one of the floors of one of the four buildings on campus. I'm in my dorm room now, which is on the top floor of Beta Building at Hamilton's College.

Hamilton's College seems to be like a combined mental hospital - slash - boarding school. But it calls itself "Hamilton's College: Making a Mark In Time," in the brochure, which I found on my desk when I was shown to my dorm room. Also in my room were two suitcases full of my stuff. The room comes with a desk, chair, wardrobe, mirror, built in oil heater, bed and two blankets. I found out Dad had packed my suitcases for me, with Angela's Mum's help. So she knows why I'm here. I was kind of hoping that the mere fact of me trying to end my life might have escaped her attention. It didn't. I also got a good telling off from Angela too.

I don't know why she got worked up over it though, she completely blasted me in her email. It's not like I stabbed her in the back or anything, I think it's ironic that the only stabbing or cutting that anyone got was myself! So why is everyone else acting completely offended? Maybe it's like that scene in the movie "Flying High" where that guy who talked all the time was so boring the people who got stuck sitting near him kept trying to kill themselves. Maybe they think I was so bored I tried to kill myself to get away from them?

Anyway I unpacked my two suitcases this afternoon and I saw more of Mrs. Jay's influence than Dad's. I can't imagine he would think of packing my stereo and tapes and CD's and Walkman. The rest were two sets of sheets and pillowcases, two towels, toiletries and clothes. I wonder if Angela helped too? Someone knew enough about me to pack my favorite black velvet singlet top and my silver antique jewelry. I didn't get all of my clothes sent to me though. I had to buy some more in town this afternoon.

They were winter clothes because it's October here and it means winter is coming here in Canada. It's already cold even though technically it's only Autumn here. Right now it feels like a Sydney winter and I saw earlier other kids still walking around in T-shirts! Also what was packed were my two pairs of jeans, Doc Martins and Mum's old brown suede jacket. Now that reeks of Mrs. Jay's influence, I can't imagine Dad noticing what I call my favorite clothes. And once she told me she liked my jacket too. So when I was taken into town by Nell (she was the nurse in the hospice who is apparently also the school's counselor I have to meet once a week) I bought three woolen turtle neck jumpers one black, white and red, black mittens, woolen socks, a white scarf and some stationery stuff for schoolwork and a new school bag.

Brownsville is a very small country town with nearly all the buildings made out of wood. The small department store where I bought my stuff from is also the post office! And there are no police stations, just a RCMP station which immediately reminded me of that TV show "Due South". Remember the one with the cute Mountie? There is a small cinema though and Nell told me that once a fortnight students are allowed to go see a movie. That's good. I don't think I could cope with no movies! This place feels isolated enough as it is! And the General store where people buy their groceries also has a small video rental section. I asked Nell about movies being rented out by the students and she said it isn't usually allowed by the Juniors or Sophomores because our grounds privilege depends on being taken into town by one of the teachers. Man that sucks! I must have looked angry or something, because then she added that every weekend they have a video night run by the teachers anyway.

Brownsville only has one main street with a bar, a diner, a chemist (or Drug store as they call it here), the department store (where they have a puny music section and pitiful fashion sense) and a small motel. On the outskirts of the town is the small country hospital with it's own helipad for transporting serious injuries. And the dentist is in the hospital too, where students have to get a check up twice a year. Hamilton's is 10 km's away from Brownsville (man, what a name. Is it called that because all the buildings are made of brown wood?) and there is a huge lake that you have drive around to get from one to the other. Nell tells me that at night, the town can see the lights from the school in the distance, and the school can see the lights of the town. Surrounding us is huge, thick, pine forest, and the mountains to the north and south. Apparently nearly all year round they have snow on the top (snow! I've never seen snow before in real life!) and in winter we can ice skate on the lake and sometimes go on ski weekends (of course, taken by a teacher).

Nell seems nice. She is the third person I've met here so far. I've also met Dr. Knight, who was the Doctor in the hospice, who supposedly also teaches Chemistry, Biology and Mathematics here at the school. How freaky is that? A doctor who treats you and then teaches you fractions? And I've met the school principle, Professor Stephen Hamilton, who will be my Literature, History and Philosophy teacher. He came to see me when I was in the hospice and introduced himself and welcomed me to his college.

I've probably made a bad impression already, I wasn't very friendly or polite. I demanded that he tell me how did I get here without waking up after THAT day and fly me all the way to Canada. He seemed a bit elusive, and yet direct at the same time... I don't know how to explain it. His eyes just drilled into me, he seemed to take me in and assess me and accept me all at the same time. He spoke calmly and told me that I had been accepted to Hamilton's under scholarship (but Nell told me Dad will also direct credit my bank account with a monthly allowance - she told me that when we were shopping and I had my purse back) sorry... I got off track. I basically accused him of kidnapping me! He seemed to... deflect it? (I heard Nell use that word) and patiently told me that he recommended to my father that his college could help me more than my school was supporting me now. So they flew me on over.

Or basically Dad couldn't wait to get rid of his second child as well and now he has the house to himself. But why is he giving me a monthly allowance? I remember last month I forgot to hang out his shirts the way he liked so they would dry wrinkle free and he didn't pay me my pocket money for that week! Then I couldn't go to the movies with Angela that weekend! And now with me on the other side of the world and doing no chores, I get paid? Maybe I'm getting paid to stay away? I still don't know what's going on... but I know the situation isn't as simple as some people are trying to make me see it. This is too bizarre and surreal to be true. Girl attempts suicide. Girl winds up on scholarship to private school in middle of nowhere? YEAH, RIGHT!

==

TO: angiepevensie@ihug.com.au

FROM: ebaker_hamiltons@evers.com

SUBJECT: Met some sane people at last!

DATE: 10/ 10/ 00

Hey Angela,

Everyone came back from dinner in the cafeteria and I met two people whose rooms are next to and across from mine and who'll be in my year. Their names are Nelson and Pat. Nelson is from America and Pat is Irish! Or Northern Ireland as he repeatedly told me. Nelson is from somewhere in the country apparently (or 'the mid-west' as she calls it), she grew up in a small town whereas Pat grew up in Belfast. He doesn't have a laptop in his room but a bigger desktop computer. He does carry a laptop to class with him though, so he says. Genevieve, sorry, Nelson as she prefers (her last name) asked me if I smoke, and I immediately jumped at the chance. Thank god this place isn't going to be such a concentration camp as I was worried it would be!

As we were walking down the hall towards the stairs a teacher I hadn't met yet, Miss Inez stopped us and asked us where we were going. Nelson told her we were going to the library. So she said that it was a good idea to show me around a bit, but reminded us not to get lost behind any of the buildings. Pat gave her this funny smile and said to her, "would we ever do that?" and Miss Inez reminded him that he does it nearly every day. We got away with it and as we went down the stairs I found out from Nelson that Miss Inez is our Music, Art, Drama and Gym teacher (I think that's what they call PE over here) plus she's also our Den-Mother on our floor of the dorms. She, like Nell, look pretty young. I think definitely in their twenties. I wonder how they wound up here in the middle of nowhere to teach around four subjects to kids who are nuts?

Anyway, we got outside and started crossing the oval that's in the center of the grounds, with the four buildings, Alpha, Beta, Gamma and Delta around it. We started heading towards the Alpha building where Pat said the biggest library is and where the classrooms are. It's the biggest of the buildings, but in my opinion they all look pretty big… and old. They all look like stately manors that should be in an English period drama or something… but I can't work out why they're here in the middle of nowhere? And with a shitty little place like Brownsville next to them, instead of a proper town or city or something?

When we reached the building, instead of going up the couple of stairs and inside the doors, we walked around the side of the building and stood just around the corner of the back. Both Nelson and Pat each pulled a packet of their own out and Pat offered one out of his to me. I thought I could use this opportunity to ask them some questions about the school.

I asked them how they got their cigarettes as I noticed when I went to the shops today that a sign said the legal age limit is 21. They told me there's a Senior student in one of the bottom dorm rooms that gets them for them. Cool, I'll have to check that out. Next I asked them how they got here. Apparently Pat also tried to kill himself in Belfast, and his family were approached by Stephen Hamilton to come here, like what happened to me. Nelson shook her head at us and told us we were a pair of freaks. So I asked her what she did to deserve to come here? She said she would have been sent here or to Juvenile Court, but wouldn't tell me anything else. Pat has been here for a year already, and Nelson started last month. Then I asked them if anyone had ever run away? Pat shrugged and said he'd heard stories that kids in the past had tried it, and managed to hitchhike out of here, and some of them ended up coming back of their own free will. I laughed and asked why, when Nelson said something that now bugs me and makes me wonder.

"When there's no home to go to, what do you run from?" with that she threw her cigarette to the ground, stumped it out with her foot, then turned around and left before Pat and I had finished. I guess all of my questions had somehow offended her.

This can't be true. I mean, if all the misfits and outcasts all come here, there would surely be more than 60 students attending at a time at Hamilton's, right? So where are all the other kids who have tried killing themselves? Or have criminal records? It doesn't make sense.

"Basically life here is pretty good. There is some disciplining, but basically the teachers let us just get on with it. You'll notice there are no curfews or lights out, you just go to bed when you feel like it. The only thing is if you're a Sophomore, which you are, you have to have supervision when you leave school property. Welcome to Hamilton's School of Headcraft and Heterodoxy. There must be something special about you for you to be here." Pat said to me.

Was he complimenting me? Was he hitting on me? Why does there have to be something special about me to be here? I thought it was just because I tried to kill myself.

We finished our cigarettes and came out from the back and then he offered to actually show me the library as he had to get some books. I said thanks, but no thanks, and went back across the oval towards the dorms, or Beta building as everyone else calls it. I went back to my room and I noticed Nelson's door was shut. I guess that was it for any more conversations with her tonight.

So I'm sending this email to you Angie. It's 10:30 PM. I better go to bed soon, breakfast is at 7.30 tomorrow morning, then I have my first class. What time is it in Sydney at the moment? What's the weather like? Here, there is a cold wind outside. I shivered so much I nearly dropped the cigarette!

I may not have a home with Dad but at least I've got you.

Night night.

==

11/10/00

Dear Diary,

I had my first three classes today! And tonight will be my fourth, which we do at night because it's Astronomy! There are only three classes a day here, can you believe it? Well, except for Wednesdays, which are four because the fourth subject is Astronomy... But the bad thing is they go for two hours! Two hours of Math... eeww! Pass me the razor... just kidding! No seriously, I found out more about this place today.

My day started with me getting up at 7 AM and going to breakfast at 7.30 with these two people I met last night, Pat and Nelson. Pat is a 16 yr. old Northern Irishman who is tall, skinny, with dark blonde hair and glasses. Nelson is a pretty, black haired, green eyed American who has this cool black leather jacket that she wore today, like I noticed she was wearing last night. I wore Mum's old, brown, suede jacket today, over my new black turtle neck jumper. Pat has this really cool Irish accent, and he told me I looked like I was dressed for winter already! But I'm cold already! He's walking around in cargo pants and T-shirt! No jumper, no jacket or anything like that, or a 'sweater' as Nelson calls it in her American accent.

We went into Gamma building for breakfast, where the cafeteria is. Did you know this place also has a greenhouse? It's attached to the

Gamma building. There was lots of yummy food on display, like fruit, yogurt, toast, cereal, bacon, eggs, grilled tomato, hash browns, baked beans... it was like the time we stayed at that resort overnight at the Entrance when I was 12, when the full buffet breakfast was included in our stay.

Anyway, I looked around at everyone dressed casual (we don't have to wear uniforms which feels kind of strange because now I have to worry about what to wear everyday!) and I asked Pat what years were all here? He said there were Freshmen, Sophomores, Juniors and Seniors taught here. He said that this school has one of the highest rate of University accepted students, more than any other private schools in the northern hemisphere!

Wow! So what am I doing here then? It reminded me of something that Pat told me last night over a cigarette, that only special people are chosen to come here or something, and maybe not just the nutcases (by the way, I have to find out what the word heterodoxy means). I found out there are 15 people in the year below me, the Freshman year, 20 people in my year, known as Sophomore, (well 21 now with me here), 15 people in the year above called Junior year, and 10 people in the year above that called Senior year. And at any time that it's not a school assembly or meal times in the cafeteria, there are no more than 10 people per class. Cool. I like that idea. I always liked it when in class we broke off into smaller groups, especially when it got me away from certain people in the classroom.

Soon after I had finished eating breakfast a bell went off at eight o'clock and Nelson said that it was the class bell. Everyone stood up to leave and I followed Nelson and Pat outside. We went over to Alpha building where my classes were. My first class was Math, and Pat went into a separate classroom for another subject, I think Philosophy.

"He's a level higher than us. That's why he's got the bigger computer in his room. He's the brainiac with all things mathematical, technical and scientific." Nelson told me as we sat down. So that explains why he's in a different class. But then guess how we sat down? Our class sat down at a huge circular table! Then our teacher came in, Dr. Knight. She took her seat at the table as well and everyone immediately took their notebooks out of their bags. They also took a textbook out of their bags and then Dr. Knight passed one over to me that she told me to keep.

Dr. Knight seems very nice and laid back. There was a white board behind her but instead of standing up and looking down on us, she seemed more comfortable sitting down and talking to us face to face. She asked everyone to go around in a circle and introduce themselves to me. I was so nervous I forgot half of their names already! No one else in my class was from Australia, so they seemed interested in me because of that. There were two Chinese girls, whose names I've already forgotten, one Japanese guy Yuichi, and Indian guy Raj, a Pom called Peter, an Egyptian girl named Jordon, a cute Canadian guy named Zack, and the other two Americans, a guy and a girl I've forgotten as well.

During class I noticed the cute Canadian, Zack, look at me a few times. He was pretty open about it. At one point he even smiled at me! I smiled back I think, I just hoped I didn't blush as well! That would be so embarrassing!

Math wasn't as bad as I thought it would be. Dr. Knight can read people like she can read the book of fractions in front of her though. A couple of times I looked lost, and she stopped and explained it in a different way that I did understand without making a big thing out of it. And she never said or made a point of me and only me not knowing what she was talking about, but she said, "I can see some confusion, let me try another method." Or she would just say, "So, another way to look at it is..." and once got out of her seat and used the white board to draw her example. I think she was the best maths teacher I've ever had! But she did set us homework unfortunately and asked us to not do them in our notebooks, but on separate pieces of paper to hand in.

The bell went and we all stood up to leave. I was right behind Nelson when Dr. Knight asked me to stay a minute or two. She had a quick glance at my notes and commented on how many I made. I got nervous again and asked if that was a bad thing, and she smiled at me and said no, that it was a good thing. It was how I learned, by writing things down and visualizing them. She also said that it's good for her to know that, so she can 'cater to my learning development', quote unquote. Then she let me leave and I came outside to find that Nelson hadn't waited for me. Great.

So I walked back towards the cafeteria in hope of seeing Pat again when Zack approached me. He was waiting outside the cafeteria, talking to Peter, and when I walked past, he said, "So lets hear your Ozzie accent!"

I think I blushed again! How embarrassing! I tried to hide it and said, "what do you want me to say?"

"What do you think we want you to say?" Peter teased back in his English accent.

"What's it like?" Zack asked me.

"What is what like?" Peter teased him.

"Australia you dumbass, what do you think I meant?" Zack elbowed Peter.

"Warmer," I told him.

"So you have all those beaches, huh?" Peter asked me.

"No, I live in the Blue Mountains, two hours away from the beaches," I told them.

Peter has dark brown curly hair and dark brown eyes and wore dark green or grey army kind of clothes. Zack was wearing jeans and a sports jumper. Diary, get this, he has brown hair, blue eyes and dimples in each of his cheeks, no joke! Isn't that the poster boy kind of thing for American apple-pie-boy-next-door kind of thing? I was worried that might make him up-himself or a F.I.G.J.A.M. or something, but I ended up sitting in the cafeteria and talking to them during morning tea break. And he was nice! Well, actually, he was a bit shy and Peter did most of the talking.

I asked them when did they start here at Hamilton's. Peter started just last month (as did Nelson), and Zack said he's been here for three months. Now this confuses me a bit, I thought school semesters here go from the beginning of September to the end of May or June? So he was here during the three-month school holiday? Zack nodded and said there were summer classes, but the main idea was just getting him away from home and occupied with something else. Peter ran away from home all the time and did drugs to get landed here. Zack froze up a bit and said he was just having trouble at home, and said no more than that.

Before I could get any more out of them the bell rang again for our next class. Zack asked me what I had next, and I told him it was Ancient

History. He said he and Peter had that too and they showed me where the classroom was. Then I remembered who my History teacher would be... Professor Stephen Hamilton. Shit. I was worried I'd already made a bad impression on him, from back in the hospital wing. I was hoping I could just sit at the back of the class and make myself look small, but when we went inside, I found it was another circular table and Pat and Nelson were already sitting down. I asked Zack and Peter if we could sit next to Pat, and they didn't mind. I didn't even say anything to or look at Nelson. I don't think she likes me very much, and the way she's treating me, soon it will be mutual.

Class started by Professor Hamilton arriving and sitting down at the table and he immediately asked if I knew everyone. He seemed friendly, like he didn't have any bad feelings from the hospital wing. There were three new faces that I didn't know, and he made them introduce themselves to me and me introduce myself back. They were Sally from Scotland and Numu from Kenya and Maya from India. I loved Sally's Scottish accent! I know I've been going on and on about the accents around here, but they are so different to what I've been used to. I remember when Dad used to tell me off when I was little for not telling the time the way he liked. I couldn't say 11:40 AM, I had to say "it's twenty to twelve". Now here are all these different people just doing their different thing and saying different things in different ways.

Professor Hamilton asked us to open our books (and I got another new text book - damn!) and we opened to the chapter on Pyramid building in Ancient Egypt. But then Professor Hamilton started talking about something I hadn't heard before, except on those TV documentaries about those Inca and Aztec temples in South America, how the pyramids in Egypt also have certain alignments to the calendar and yearly cycles and magnetic forces that baffles scientists today. And how and why they actually built those pyramids are still under debate by some scientists. This history lesson almost seemed more like an 'X-File' than the boring old reading from a text book!

Then he pulled down the blinds on the windows and showed us slides of computer graphics of how some scientists believed Thebes (or Cairo as it is called today), looked thousands of years ago, and how the pyramids were 'in all probability' built.

Then Pat spoke up and said, "that's what I love about the academic field, you can say 'in all probability' when really you mean, 'I'm only fucking guessing.'"

I couldn't believe he said that! The whole room burst out laughing! I put my hand over my mouth to try and stop myself from joining in, waiting for Professor Hamilton's reaction. He even chuckled!

Then he said, "But I hope by now Patrick that you have enough faith in me to know that I wouldn't tell you something that wasn't true?"

"So I guess you just jumped in your time machine and went and had a good look?" Nelson crossed her arms and glared at Professor Hamilton.

"Who needs a time machine when time has preserved enough evidence for us to have a good look for ourselves?" Professor Hamilton answered evenly.

Then the bell went and it stopped our discussions in the dark room. I was actually disappointed that the class was over, can you believe it? None of my other history lessons back at my old high school were ever that interesting!

Nelson packed up her stuff quickly and took off again, this time not waiting for me or Patrick.

"What's with her?" I asked Pat as we walked out of the room.

Pat shrugged. "She's like that."

I grabbed a sandwich and bottle of juice from the cafeteria and went to sit outside in the sun to eat it with Sally and Maya. We ended up sitting on the oval, out on the grass. It wasn't windy and we were trying to absorb what little heat there was from the sunlight, when Peter and Zack ended up joining us as well. I noticed Pat and Nelson disappear in the distance around the corner of Gamma building again for a cigarette. I was tempted to go over and join them, but I thought I'd better not.

"Elisha, what class have you got next?" Maya asked me, checking her timetable.

Zack had noticed what I was watching and shook his head at me. "You're not a smoker too, are you?"

"Sometimes." I tried to shrug it off, before answering Maya's question. "I've got Computer Studies next."

"Same here," Zack nodded.

"Nup, Gym for me," Peter answered.

"Yeah, the same," Sally said. "You get to meet the next one."

"Next who?" I asked her.

"The next teacher, Dr. Quentin Myles. If you thought your teachers were, ah, 'different' up until now... wait till you meet this one." Sally smiled at me.

"Why?" I asked, intrigued.

"He also teaches Gym, Astronomy and Physics." Maya informed me. "We have our Astronomy class tonight after dinner, how about you?"

"Yep." Sally, Zack and Peter confirmed.

"He's also a black belt, I hear," Sally told me.

"So? He teaches it sometimes in Gym," Peter shrugged.

"He's got tattoos, and wears his head shaved," Sally continued.

"So, who cares? The way you're carrying on, you make him sound like an ex-con who's breaking his parole by being near children!" Peter laughed at her.

"Well, not many of my teachers in Glasgow looked like him!" Sally retorted.

"You need to get out more," Peter threw a bit of grass at her.

The bell went and I got up and followed Zack, Sally and Maya to Computer Studies and Peter went off somewhere else, it looked to be the Delta building for gym. The Delta building was where I woke up in the hospital wing when I arrived here. But that's another story, and I'll stick to this one at the moment. I'm typing this on my laptop in the library. It's 6:34 PM already and I started this entry at 4:45 PM. If I don't hurry up dinner will start without me! I just want to get all this down first then I'll worry about my Math homework after dinner. Damn it, I have Astronomy after dinner tonight! I'll have to do it after then.

Anyway, our Computer Studies teacher was a hunk! He was built-up, head shaved, and had a tattoo of some kind of symbol on the back of his neck! He wore jeans and a long sleeved T-shirt and his voice was really deep and husky. Thankfully I didn't get any more text books in this class, but he handed out CD's with programs on them and walked around the room telling us what to do or what we should be seeing on our computer screens.

Pat wasn't in this class, he must be in a class higher than me, but Nelson was there. I noticed that in this class she actually seemed to participate more, and she didn't speak up, she just sat back and watched Dr. Myles. Or it was probably more 'checking him out'. I didn't sit with her this time, and the computer lab had the tables running around the walls of the room with no round tables this time. I think I'll sit with Maya and Sally all the time now. Maya is really nice. She saw I was still on a screen behind everyone else and leaned over and helped me. I think Zack was having as much trouble as I was, because Dr. Myles had to come over and help him with the command codes we were supposed to be using.

For our class exercise we were building HTML pages to put on the Internet. How cool is that? I'll have my own web page where I can put up pictures of the 'X-Files', Dan Paris (which reminds me, I'm going to have to ask Angie to tape some episodes of 'Neighbours' for me!) and Kevin Sorbo! Speaking of which, my room looks pretty lame. It's too bare without all of my old posters! I haven't talked to Dad since I got here, I wonder if it would be wrong of me to ask him to send my posters over?

When class finished, Maya, Sally, Zack and I went to the cafeteria again to get some arvo tea. There's still a pretty good lot of food between the three main meals of brekkie, lunch and din-dins. They have fruit, fruit salads, frozen yogurt, little packets of dried fruit and nuts, sandwiches and bottles of water or fruit juice. I had a banana and choc chip muffin and hot chocolate with marshmallows! Yum! Then Maya suggested we go to the library and do our homework.

I get the impression Maya takes her studies very seriously. But I thought it was too late for me to go and find Pat and Nelson for a cigarette, so I ended up agreeing with her. I've been here ever since, typing on you instead of doing my Maths homework. I've never been able to concentrate properly in a library, all the other people distract me. When Zack tried to talk to me, Maya shooshed him! Can you believe it? I would call her a nerd but she has been nice to me today.

It's dinner time now. I'll have to do my Math homework after Astronomy. I better not skip it, I don't want to make a bad impression too soon. I wonder what Dad would do if I ever got kicked out of a place like this? I mean, he just sent me here without even talking about it! If this place wasn't not so bad, I think I would think about running away too.

==

TO: mbaker@hotmail.com

FROM: elishabaker_hamiltons@evers.com

SUBJECT: Thanks for the offer

DATE: 13/ 10/ 00

Hey Mark,

Thanks for finding out that stuff from Dad. I owe you one big time! And thanks for your offer. It's really nice of you, but so far this place isn't that bad, so it's OK. Also I know living with you I would end up having to pay rent and groceries even if you did cover me for a while, but I'd like to finish high school first before getting a job. Also you would have to ask your flatmates if I can come and live with you, so don't worry about it. I'm OK here, really.

So anyway, how freaky is that? They just showed up at the hospital like that and offered the scholarship to Dad? Almost like the Grim Reaper showing up and spiriting away the children! But I have met Professor Hamilton and he's actually not that bad. And all of the teachers are pretty cool. This school isn't that bad either. The food is nice, I have my own room and the kids here are okay.

I've found out that not all of the kids here are emotionally fucked up, only 40% or something like that have been sent here by their parents for emotional disturbance. The rest are like normal boarding school kids who have relatively normal families who they visit over the holidays, but other than that their parents are paying for them to come here. I have some friends who I hang with, Zack, Peter, Sally, Maya and Pat. Out of all of them, only Sally and Maya come from the normal families! And Zack, Peter, Pat and I are the ones with the weekly counselor appointments from our 'troubled backgrounds'.

Pat is Irish and tried to kill himself - won't say why, Peter is English and got into trouble with drugs. He reckons his parents don't care about him and it started when he was very little because he always had Nanny's and stuff while his parents traveled a lot. And Zack hates his Mum and says she's weak and she lies but won't say what about. There is a girl here, Nelson, who I met on my first night out of the hospital wing but hasn't talked to me since, who said she was nearly sent to Juvenile court but wound up here instead. They're the nutzoids I've met so far.

This afternoon after my last class I had to go back to Delta Building to the hospital wing. The nurse and counselor there, Nell, took my stitches out and then we went into her office for my first weekly session with her. She asked me lots of questions on what it was like at my old school and if I had many friends, then she started asking questions about Dad. I told her that I missed you not living with us.

Now don't drop dead in surprise Mark, I know we fought a lot and I hated living with you most of the time… but… well, I don't know how to put this. When you and Dad were fighting it made me feel a little relieved… because when he was yelling at you he wouldn't be yelling at me. If you were doing something wrong, it would take his attention away from me. I never realized this before, but it came up with Nell. She was really nice and understanding. She did take notes in a folder though, but kept looking up at me and saying "hmmm," or "uh huh". I think she was much better than that stupid school counselor I had back at Blaxland High School, the one I had to speak to when Mum died. That one kept telling me how I should be feeling instead of actually asking me what I was feeling!

I'm glad it's Friday night. Did you know classes go for two hours here? Even if there are only 3 classes a day (except on Wednesdays when my fourth class is Astronomy after dinner) it's pretty intense. Our classes are only 10 people big, well, 11 now that I'm here, and so the teacher has the time to almost go around each of us to make sure we're working and understand everything. But I'm relieved I don't have any homework tonight (I'll do it Sunday). But there are two movies showing tonight in both of the recreation rooms, one is "The Mummy" and the other is "She's all that" with that cute actor Freddy Prinze Junior.

Tonight in the cafeteria for dinner they're serving hot dogs and hamburgers and soft drink, or 'soda' as they call it here. I can't wait! They only do movie nights and 'fun night' (that's what they call serving 'junk' food) once a week. Normally it's on a Saturday night, but the Seniors are going away on an excursion for a couple of days tomorrow, so they're doing it tonight.

I'm going to go meet Zack, Peter, Sally and Maya in the cafeteria for dinner now, so I have to go. I think we're all going to see "The Mummy" tonight. You know how I love horror movies! Maya wanted to see the other one, but ended up deciding to see this one because we all wanted to. But I really have to go now. I'm going to borrow a cigarette from Pat and have it before I eat.

See ya!

==

13/ 10/ 00

Dear Diary,

It's past 2 AM and I thought I might as well catch up with you. Truth is I can't sleep - I think I drank too much coke at dinner and then during the video. Too much coke and too much chocolate... my stomach feels like rat shit. Also I'm jittery and restless as all hell from the caffeine!

Well I've just finished my first week at Hamilton's. It wasn't too bad. Well, I only had three days of classes - Wednesday, Thursday and Friday, today.

My last class today was English with Professor Hamilton himself. In class we got to go into two teams for a debate on the use of mysticism and Christianity, using "The Chronicles of Narnia" and "Harry Potter" as our examples! I'm on the Narnian team of course! Zack is on my team, and so is Sally and Maya and Nelson. Peter, Pat, Yuichi and the Chinese girl Soong are on the Potter side. We got to leave the classroom and go into the library where the Narnians were on one side, and the Hogwarts team were sitting in the other corner of the room. We get two classes to prepare so next Friday we do the actual debate. I can't wait!

Sally thought it would be a good idea to take some notes tomorrow while watching "The Lion, The Witch and The Wardrobe" and I asked her how were we going to do that? She says she has the Narnia videos in her room! Excellent! So over dinner tonight before the movie Sally, Maya, Zack and I all planned to meet in Sally's room tomorrow morning to watch the video. Apparently she even has her own TV and VCR/DVD player in her room! I guess that's what you get when you're not mentally fucked up and you voluntarily come to Hamilton's. Then your 'nice' parents spoil you for getting good grades.

While we were planning this, Nelson overheard us while she was sitting with Pat. She shook her head at us and told us to get a life. Maya got a bit offended and told her that since she was on our team she should be supporting us because the grade affects us all. Nelson gave her a dirty look, stood up, gave her the finger and left!

Nelson was nowhere to be seen when we were all watching "The Mummy". But I had a blast sitting between Zack and Sally. Peter kept making all these sarcastic, but funny comments every time something scary happened, and he teased Maya for getting scared and putting her hands over her eyes. Sally threw one of her chocolates at Peter and told him to shut up, then he threw some popcorn back at her!

FOOD FIGHT!!!!

Our whole row ended up getting in on it! This Senior guy told us to stop it and to clean it up and Peter threw some food at him and then ran out of the room. So when the movie finished, guess who were the only four made to clean it up? Pat was nowhere to be seen, he left before it began, probably to go find Nelson. Zack was a bit shitty for cleaning up Peter's mess. I didn't care really.

The recreation room where the movie was shown was in Beta building, so we just went upstairs to our rooms afterwards. Zack and Peter's rooms are at the beginning of the hall near the stairs and my room is all the way at the end of the hall. So I said g'night and went to my room. I think I had popcorn in my hair and I wanted a shower. I felt disgusting after eating so much junk!

When I went to bed I couldn't fall asleep. So I opened my door to be met with the familiar sight of Pat with his door open, working on something on his computer. So far, every time I go to bed, he's on his computer with his door open. Last night when I had to use the toilet at around 3 AM, he was still up and on his computer. Doesn't he sleep?

"You're always on your computer, what do you do on it?" I came and sat on the floor of his doorway in my pajamas.

"At the moment I'm downloading some trance for Peter. Otherwise I'm either on the net or working on some homework."

"Trance?" I asked him.

"Yeah, you know, Trance... it's music. Kind of like Techno, only better." He turned up the speakers connected to his computer and played some of the music for me.

"Hey, that's cool." I liked it! "Can I have a copy too?"

"Yeah sure." He pulled out a blank CD from his desk draw and put it into his CD-ROM. "Any other music you want?"

"What else is there?"

"Everything. Don't rely on the radio stations up here, it's all Country Music, unless you like that. You have to depend on the Internet to hear anything decent," Pat warned me.

"What, no 'Top Forty'?" I asked him.

"Have you heard anything on your radio that sounds remotely like the 'Top Forty'?" he asked back.

"Bugger. What kind of shit hole has my father sent me to?" I kicked his door.

I noticed Pat was looking at my wrists, which made me nervous and I pulled down the sleeves to cover the scars.

"Did you get the stitches out today?" Pat asked me. "Is that why you had to go to the hospital wing after English?"

"Yeah. Nell took out the stitches and then I had my first session with her." I told him.

"Weekly sessions?"

"Yeah, every Friday afternoon I have to see her."

"I see her Sundays," Pat said. "The scars are going to be purple for the first month."

We didn't talk much after that, I told him I was going to bed.

When I stood up I thought I saw Nelson's door close, like it may have been open a little bit. It made me wonder if she heard our conversation. Like Pat's door is always open when he's not asleep or changing clothes or at class, Nelson's door is always closed. Just like her really.

===

15/ 10/ 00

Dear Diary,

It's a lazy Sunday arvo here at Hamilton's school of Headcraft and Heterodoxy. Finally found out what the word means; "Heterodoxy - not in accordance with established or accepted doctrines or opinions, esp. in theology." Well that explains Hamilton's very well! There's nothing established about this place except the buildings... which I still don't get. How and why would a person just build four huge, beautiful, white stone English style mansions in the middle of nowhere in Canada? From the looks of them anyone would think that these buildings were here longer than any white settlement.

Maybe the natives beat Columbus to it - they rowed over to Europe in their canoes, took one look at 'white' architecture, then rowed back and built their own? So when white man came to 'discover' and conquer, they were stumped to see someone had beat them to it? That would make a funny short story... maybe I should write it and hand it in for my English essay that's due next week? Or is it more of a historical story? Who knows... I'm sure Maya does. I'll ask her later.

After lunch today I went to the library in Alpha building with Maya and Sally and we did our homework. I also used the chance to look up the meaning in the dictionary here. Well, one of them, because they have so many! Almost one for nearly every language spoken here on this planet! This library is bigger and older looking than my old school library, with heaps of leather-bound books that look and smell old. I've always loved the smell of books, I don't know why... there's actually something homey and comforting about them.

At the moment I'm typing on you in one of the big leather chairs in the afternoon sun, now that I've finished my homework. It feels nice sitting here, in the sunlight and not in the cold wind outside. It's getting colder, apparently it could even snow soon! It's only October right now and it could start snowing next month! Can you believe it?

Outside Zack and Peter are playing Baseball on the oval with some other students and Dr. Myles is the coach or umpire or whatever you call him. Aren't they cold? I think it's because Maya comes from southern India and I come from Sydney where neither place snows or gets such cold winters, which is why we find it harder to adapt. I guess how Peter's from England, Sally from Scotland and Zack from somewhere else in Canada it gets colder, much colder and they've seen snow before. Maya agrees with me, she thinks it's freezing and she's sitting at the table in the middle of the room doing more studying. I don't know what else there is to study... we did our homework hours ago! That girl is a study-maniac!

I got in trouble with Miss Inez last night. Pat introduced me to this guy whose dorm room is downstairs on the ground floor, who's a Senior. Anyway, this guy is the one who gets their cigarettes for them, and I bought a packet from him yesterday. It was really cold last night, so instead of going outside and behind a building like Pat and Nelson do, I closed my bedroom door, put my window up a fraction and had it in my room. Next thing I know Miss Inez is knocking on my door and catches me! I don't know how, her bedroom is all the way down the other end of the hall, so she couldn't have smelled it? She tells me to put it out immediately, don't do it again and confiscates my packet from me! Then she starts lecturing me about bloody lung cancer and stuff!

Sure lady, take the packet away from me, that's bad enough, especially when I just opened the fucking thing, but don't start acting like you care if I drop dead!

Now I wish I had said that. Instead I didn't look at her as she raved on, I crossed my arms and stared at the wall behind her, wishing she would just finish and go away. She did after five minutes of health warnings, and Pat whose door was open (as it normally is when he's working on his computer), and whose room is right across from mine, heard the whole thing. As soon as Miss Inez was gone he started laughing at me!

"Come on, it was pretty stupid!" Pat shook his head. "Here," he chucked another packet at me.

"What? Why?" I was surprised. Why was he giving it to me?

"I have another packet. Keep it, but don't lose it!" he waved his finger at me.

"Thanks." I came and sat on the floor of his room, leaning against his door. "I mean, I don't get this place... they don't have a curfew on lights out, but they rib us for smoking in our rooms? And they know we smoke behind the building."

"It's a responsibility thing. Officially they can't condone it because of legal rights and responsibility of care." Pat told me. "They know we do it, but they have to show to our parents and the authorities that they don't support it." Then he added, "also, smoking IS supposed to kill you one day."

"Did you just get caught again?" suddenly Nelson showed up in his doorway.

"Nup, it was Elisha this time," Pat told her.

"Don't worry, after midnight they never bother you about it," Nelson told me. "C'mon, I'll show you something."

I got up and followed her to her room. She opened the door and let me in and then closed it again immediately. Her room was... black. She had black linen on her bed, a black lamp on her desk that didn't light up anything that much, and all of these black and white gothic posters on her walls. But what I noticed immediately was that her room stank of cigarettes!

She knelt down and pulled out a huge, over stuffed ashtray from under her bed. "I smoke in here all the time. What time is it?"

I looked at my watch. "It's 10:30 PM."

"Sit and hang out if you want. It should be safe at 11:30."

Wow, what a change of heart. I sat down and looked at her posters. "I like your room. I don't have anything on my walls."

"Then use the computer lab. Just go on the Internet and download the stuff you want and print it. That's what I did." Nelson told me.

"Cool, I will," I nodded.

"So, are you and Zack going out?" Nelson asked me.

"No." I gave her a funny look.'

"Why not?"

"What do you mean, why not? We're just friends."

"He wants more than that." Nelson sat on her bed and I sat on her desk chair.

I didn't know what to say to that, so I just shrugged. "I thought he was just nice."

"Men are never 'just nice'."

"Pat is, and you hang with him, don't you?"

"Pat is interested in somebody else," Nelson stated matter-of-factly.

"Who?" I asked, interested.

"Can't say. It's his secret, not mine to share," Nelson also stated.

"Come on, I won't say anything," I promised her.

"If Zack asked you out, would you?" she changed the subject.

"I don't know!" I blushed - again. I hate my face sometimes, it always gives me away.

Needless to say diary, that our conversation ran around in circles until 11:30 when we finally lit up. But I got to learn more about her. I don't think of Nelson as a complete bitch now... but more as just an up front and confronting kind of person. I think she's been hurt badly in the past, and possibly by a male, so I guess she's really skeptical now about trusting anyone.

It's 4:30 in the afternoon and the sun is setting. Baseball has finished and I can see Zack coming towards the Alpha building, probably to see if I'm still here. I don't know if I like him more than a friend, or if I want a relationship right now... but he is pretty cute, and he does have nice eyes. I haven't said anything to anyone else about what Nelson told me. I think I'll just see what happens.

==

TO: angiepevensie@ihug.com.au

FROM: ebaker_hamiltons@evers.com

SUBJECT: Please please pretty please!

DATE: 18/ 10/ 00

Hey Angie,

Gees I hate missing episodes of 'Neighbours' and 'Home and Away'. Can't you tape them for me? I mean, I know you can't tape every single one for me and keep sending them over, but what about taping and sending the odd few now and then? Yeah I know I can check out the official website for episode details and stuff, but I miss watching it! The good thing about this school is although it may be away from a lot of TV channels, we do get satellite TV. So I can watch re-runs of Simpsons and even some Goodies and Astroboy now and then!

Hey, you know how your Mum helped my Dad pack some of my things earlier... do you think your Mum, or even you, could go back and pack my 'Buffy' and 'Angel' DVD's? I miss them and my friend Sally has a TV and DVD/VCR player in her room and says I can come and watch movies any time I want. She has lots of 'Monty Python' and even the 'Chronicles of Narnia' in her room on video! Remember the 'Narnia' TV series that was on the ABC? She's got it! I watched 'The Lion, The Witch and The Wardrobe' in her room last night after dinner.

Oh guess what, Zack came and watched the movie with me. He says he never saw it or read it before and came and sat on Sally's bed next to me and watched it. He didn't care that he was watching a kid's movie. We were sitting kind of close together with our shoulders touching. He's really cute, have I told you about him? I don't always hang out with Pat and Nelson because I don't smoke as much as they do, but sometimes between and after classes I hang with Scottish Sally, Pommy Peter, Indian Maya and Canadian Zack.

Zack could be a poster boy for wholesome apple pie kind of thing... he has blue eyes, short cropped dark hair and he even has dimples when he smiles! He keeps hanging around me too. When I eat, he wants to sit next to me in the cafeteria. When I eat outside, he eats outside. When I do my homework in the library, so does he! But then last weekend on Sunday afternoon when I sat in the library to write in my diary he didn't follow me then, he played Baseball with some students on the oval.

I'm not used to guys being so obvious. Remember at the last school disco when Brian liked me he didn't do anything? He just watched me dance with you guys and never came and danced with me? I guess he was afraid of being obvious, and having people talk about us. But here a lot of the kids don't give a 'rat's ass' (thanks to Nelson for that saying!) about what the other kid is doing.

I guess here the kids are more wrapped up in their studies or their own personal problems. And the good thing about this is, there is no fashion police! You can wear whatever you want! It doesn't matter if you wear Nike or Reebok or even no brand name at all! There are quite a few Goths around here (Nelson is one, only she doesn't paint her face, she just wears black all the time) and there is the grunge look and there is the 'whatever' look. At first when I found out this school had no uniforms I was worried about what I would wear all the time, now no-one cares if you've worn the same jumper more than once! Pat practically wears his black denim jacket nearly every day, as does Nelson her black leather jacket. So I've been wearing my Mum's brown suede jacket every day too, and my Doc Martins.

I can't wait for the 31st of October. They celebrate Halloween here! I mean technically it will be a school night coz it's Tuesday, but the teachers are organizing something special! It will be 'fun night' with junk food and one recreation room will have horror movies playing, and in the theatre there will be 'club night' (nightclub in reverse, get it? D'oh!) where it's basically a school disco! There were signs up in Alpha building where we go for classes and a sign up in Gamma building where the Caf is and where the 2nd recreation room and theatre are, where the party will be!

It's not dress up or anything, but it's a chance to wear something different! Thanks for packing my black velvet singlet top, I'll wear that with my black long velvet skirt I got from 'Valleygirl' when we went shopping in Penrith last month. Or will that look too black? Or even too slutty... Maybe I'll wear my red top? With the black crystal drop earrings? The outfit I wore to the last disco? Or is it too try-hard? Maybe that's why Brian never asked me to dance, and how he kept talking to his mates while they looked at me. But you said I looked all right, so I might wear it again.

Anyway, gotta go. I have to get ready for my Astronomy class that's after dinner tonight. Say hi to your Mum for me.

===

TO: mbaker@hotmail.com

FROM: ebaker_hamiltons@evers.com

SUBJECT: No Joke!!

DATE: 19/ 10/ 00

Well I've just found out what's wrong with this school, it's bloody haunted!

I just saw the ghost! I'm serious! A real live ghost! I'm for real! A ghost! And if you don't believe me Nelson and Pat were with me when I saw it! When we saw it, is what I mean.

We were in the Alpha Building in the computer labs, downloading stuff off the Internet. I was printing out pictures of David Boreanaz, Kevin Sorbo and Sarah Michelle Gellar to put on my walls in my room.

We went over at 9PM as Pat said the labs are usually unlocked at night since the teachers knew the students liked to use it for homework or whatever, and since we're in the middle of nowhere, who's gonna come and steal the computers? There's nobody around! Well, nobody alive anyway... then around 11PM Nelson and I went outside for a cigarette and when we came back, we heard footsteps coming down the hall. We thought it was either a teacher or a student or even a cleaner, we didn't care about it.

After a couple of minutes, I complained how it seemed colder in the lab than it was outside. Pat said that the heaters in the building should be on until midnight and he got up to check the thermostat. He said that the thermostat said it was 22 degrees Celsius, and I told him it was not because I was freezing!

Just then we heard the footsteps again, as if they were walking right past the doorway of the lab. So Nelson got up and said she'd see if it was a cleaner or someone we could ask about the heat. She gets up, goes to the doorway and then freezes... I mean, totally not moving. Pat and I quickly got up to see what she was looking at, and we see the back of a woman in an olden day dress walk through a wall with a window!!!!

No, she didn't go out the window, she went through the wall!

The window was still closed and it wasn't broken or anything! It may have only happened in just a couple of seconds, but I know what I saw... what we saw! We quickly grabbed what we had printed and then we ran out of there! We ran out of the building and then Pat stopped running when we were halfway across the oval, and Nelson and I were yelling at him to hurry up. I think he was looking back to where the wall with the window was, then he turned around and we all ran again back to Beta building.

In Pat's room later on, Nelson said what made her freeze was this feeling inside that what she was seeing... wasn't natural. Pat has been here the longest, and I asked him if he had ever seen anything like this before. He said yes, but then he seemed to change his mind. Nelson and I pressured him to tell us what he was thinking of.

He said that a few months ago before the summer break he saw one of the rooms in Alpha building light up with a bright white flash in the middle of the night once. It was a room on the top floor, that lit up very brightly, then went black. He thought it was just something else until now. I asked him if it was the computer lab, and he said 'don't be stupid' since it was on the top floor, and we were just in the computer lab on the second floor. So Nelson asked him which room was it, and he said it was Professor Hamilton's office.

I swear to you Mark, just as he said that, a cold chill ran down my back! I think I blurted out something about how I think Professor Hamilton is related somehow to what we just saw and Pat immediately told me to shut up and don't be so stupid. Then Nelson told him to shut up and to let me speak.

I told them how I think we should find out how old this school actually is and how old the buildings actually are, as I just had this feeling this wasn't quite right. That this whole situation isn't quite right as to why we're all here. Then I reminded Pat of what he said that first night I met the two, when he said there had to be something special as to why I'm here.

"She's right. Why are any of us here? It's like somebody has hand picked us to be here for a reason." Nelson said, staring at the floor. I thought she was about to say something else then, but she seemed to be struggling as to how to say it.

"What is it?" I asked her.

"Nothing," she shook her head.

"Come on, we've heard from Mulder over here, now it's your turn Scully," Pat said sarcastically.

"Fuck you Paddy." Nelson got up from the bed and left back to her room.

"Nice one!" I glared at Pat and followed Nelson out. I tried to go into her room with her but she slammed her door in my face! Great! I really wanted to know what she would have said. So I went back into my room and slammed my door too.

It's 2AM here at the moment, and I've just left Pat's room. Mark, if your offer is still on the table, I might just accept it soon. I have to find out how weird this place is. Fuck you Dad for sending me here!

==

20/ 10/ 00

Dear Diary,

Wow, what a week. I did a class debate for English this afternoon, yesterday I finished my HTML page to put on the Internet for Computer Studies, and the day before that was getting my part as the First Witch in Macbeth for Drama class. Oh yeah, and I found out my school is haunted... Just another week in my life that was supposed to end a little over two weeks ago.

I'm fighting with Pat at the moment over this ghost business. And to top it all off, Nelson seems to be avoiding the both of us! I don't know why she's avoiding me. But I can understand the Pat part because he was a total dickhead about it all!

What happened was, we were in the computer lab downloading stuff off the net when the temperature dropped, and we heard footsteps, and then we saw a ghost of a lady wearing olden day clothes walk through a wall!

Then when we ran back to Pat's room, we learned from Pat that he's seen something strange from Professor Hamilton's office too. He said he saw a strange bright light in the middle of the night. Nelson was going to say something else, which I think it was going to be important about this school or something. But then Pat says something really mean and she walks off!

Now she's not talking to either of us, so I'm not talking to Pat.

Since Thursday night, in class or in the cafeteria, I've been sitting between Sally and Maya, or Zack and Peter, so I can avoid Pat.

Actually, talking about class, Nelson has been acting strangely there too.

She kept asking Dr. Knight in Math's and then in Biology all these really weird questions. Like in Biology she asked Dr. Knight what kind of creatures could be classified dead even if they appeared to be alive? Or what were the symptoms of death besides no brain activity or heart rate? Or something like that... I think it has something to do with what we saw last Thursday night. I wish I knew what was going on with her.

I've just finished my session with Nell that I had this afternoon. She said I seemed preoccupied with something and asked if I wanted to talk about it. I didn't want her knowing about Thursday night and how I'm going to try and investigate the school. So instead I brought up the topic of my Dad again and spent the last 40 minutes bitching about him.

The good thing about this weekend is we can go into Brownsville. Tomorrow morning a shuttle bus will take us Sophomores into town for the day so we can either shop in the department store, hang out at the diner or go the movies in that tiny little cinema that they have. I'm going to use this chance to ask some of the locals about the history of Hamilton's. Maybe there are rumors about it? Small towns usually have rumors or stories, don't they?

Zack asked me if I wanted to go see a movie with him, but I don't know... I don't think he's asked anyone else. When I asked him who else is coming along, and he looked uncomfortable and said he didn't know, he hadn't thought about it! Oops. I probably just stuffed up his plans. Oh well, maybe he can help me with mine instead... I'm thinking of telling him and Sally and Maya. I think they'll believe me, and then it will be great to have a brainiac like Maya onboard to help me unearth the history and secrets of this place! I'll tell them tonight after dinner. But before then, I'm going to try and make another attempt at talking to Nelson.

===

TO: angiepevensie@ihug.com.au

FROM: ebaker_hamiltons@evers.com

SUBJECT: Guess What?!?

DATE: 20/ 10/ 00

Hey,

You're not gonna believe what I saw two nights ago... a ghost in Alpha Building!

I was in the computer lab with Nelson and Pat when the room got really cold, then we heard footsteps in the hallway. And when we went to go and have a look, we saw the back of this lady wearing olden day clothes disappear into a wall at the end of the corridor! She looked all see-through and really bright, like she was made out of light or something.

Actually Nelson saw first. Tonight after dinner I went into her room for a smoke and I confronted her to see why she's been acting so strangely since we saw it (actually Pat has been acting pretty strange too, acting like he never saw it and doesn't want to talk about it either). Anyway, Nelson told me that she saw the front of the ghost, and she recognized the face. She said it looked exactly like Dr. Knight, our Math's and Biology teacher!!!

I didn't know what to say... I don't know if I believe her or not. I mean this school is weird enough with out the idea that our teachers are the undead! Hang on, aren't the undead vampires? OK, let me rephrase that... it's hard enough being here in the middle of nowhere with out wondering if you're being taught by the dead and restless. That sounds better... actually, that would make a cool short story for my English assignment!

So anyway, I told Nelson that I told Zack, Sally and Maya about what we saw over dinner tonight and that they believed me. Well, two of them did. Zack told me that Peter told him ghost stories that a Senior had told him, and Sally seemed really up on all things supernatural (another thing we have in common) and she said that the temperature drop and footsteps were trademarks of hauntings. Then ole booknerd and know-it-all Maya said it sounds a little too characteristic and asked if I had any proof. So I turned around and told her that with her help of looking up stuff, we can find the proof we need.

Zack asked me heaps of questions, like what did the ghost look like? I told them that the kind of dress that she was wearing looked to be in the same fashion that I saw in a Mel Gibson movie, called "The Patriot". Sally instantly knew the movie I was talking about, and said that that was around the 1700's. I wandered out loud if these buildings here are that old and Zack said that we would find out. Then we all looked at Maya to see if she was in or not. Maya said "not", because she has her schoolwork to concentrate on, then she got up and walked away.

"Don't worry, she's not the only one who knows how to read a book you know." Zack joked and nudged me. "We'll help you find out this stuff. Did you want to do it after the movie tomorrow, or skip the movie?"

He looked a bit worried or something, so I looked at Sally, then back at him and said afterwards, which he looked really relieved about. Sally suggested we meet at the Diner afterwards in the town. She knows the owner a little and reckons we can ask her some questions about Hamilton's.

I asked Nelson if she wanted to meet us at the Diner, but she shook her head and said she'd wait to see what I find out. She seems a bit paranoid lately, now that she thinks she saw the ghost of our Math's and Biology teacher. Maybe she's scared of this school now, and of all the teachers here. She's always looking over her shoulder or hanging out in her room. I mean, she already did this and never talked to the other students here much anyway, but she's doing it even more now. I wonder if she's cutting us all out in a way to protect herself somehow?

Patrick isn't much help. Nelson used to hang with him, but since he's been a dickhead with this whole haunting thing, I think his attitude has made Nelson even more introverted. Since she can't talk to him, somebody who was there when she saw this, maybe she feels like she can't talk to anyone? I have to take a bloody crowbar to her to get anything out of her now. It's kind of a pity, because I really like her, even if she is bitchy sometimes.

I know what you'll say Angie, I'm a glutton for
punishment! Remember our Math's teacher Mr. Soames said
that in class, when I didn't do my homework and he gave me
all those detentions? Some kind of masochist that keeps
hurting herself. Oh well, as long as I enjoy it, right?
Just joking!!

So, does Mr. Soames know I'm here? Who knows I'm here? Do
they know why? What do they say? You're probably thinking
I'm nuts and this whole ghost stuff is another sign of
this. But if I'm a nut for being here, at least I know I'm
not the only one in the packet!

==

21/ 10/ 00

Dear Diary,

It's Saturday night and instead of watching some movies in the Rec
Rooms with Peter, Zack, Sally and Maya, I'm typing this in Nelson's room.

For dinner in the Caf tonight we had a combination of Mexican and
Japanese. So basically they served sushi and stuff and if you didn't want
to eat raw fish, you had tacos instead. I ate with Zack and Maya and
Sally, then I saved some food and I brought it back for Nelson. She said
she wasn't hungry, but she still ate what I brought. It makes me think she
only said she wasn't hungry so she wouldn't have to leave her room. I
told her what I found out today about this school.

Today was 'Brown Day', not very original I know, but that's what it's
called when we can leave the grounds on supervision and get driven
into Brownsville. After I saw the movie "The Mummy Returns" with Zack,
we then met up with Sally and Peter in the Diner. Peter didn't want to sit
at the counter and eat, so we ended up getting a booth. But after we'd
eaten, Sally and I went up to the counter to pretend that all we wanted
to do was to order some more cokes. But on the sly Sally asked this girl, I
think her name is Lee-Anne, who works there, some questions about
Hamilton's.

This Lee-Anne, who looked like she was only a couple of years older than
us, wasn't buying it. She gave us this weird look and then she said

something like; "What's wrong? The private school your Daddies sent you to not working out for you?"

"What do you mean?" I asked, surprised.

"Look, go get your manicures somewhere else and stop wasting my time." She said coldly, then she walked off and picked up some dirty plates and took them into the kitchen.

"What was that all about?" I asked Sally.

Then this guy who I think is Lee-Anne's brother (because I think this place is family run), comes over to us looking really angry.

"What did you say to my sister?"

"Nothing! All we did was ask some questions about Hamilton's!" I exclaimed.

"What about that place?" he seemed to get defensive too.

"How old is it?" Sally shrugged. "How long has it been a school for?"

He just looked at the two of us, then shook his head and walked off too.

Sally and I just looked at each other, wondering what this was all about.

"I thought you said you knew the owner." I said to her.

"Yeah, I think it's their Mum or something. I guess she's not working today." Sally shrugged defensively. "But the last time I was in here she was really nice and talked to me when I was feeling homesick."

"Hey, what's up?" Peter and Zack came over to us.

"They acted like we just insulted them or something." I said quietly. When I looked back over to the kitchen door I saw Lee-Anne standing there, watching us. "Lets just go." I got off the stool and started to leave.

When we went outside suddenly Lee-Anne was right behind us and she stopped us.

"Why do you want to know about Hamilton's?" she asked us, as if she had a change of heart.

"Because it's haunted." I blurted out. "I want to know about the history, that's all."

Sally rolled her eyes at my lack of subtlety and Peter burst out laughing at me!

"Haunted? What is this crap?"

Lee-Anne looked hesitantly at Peter, then looked back at me.

"What do you know?" Sally asked her.

"We've heard ghost stories, sure." she shrugged. "The school is old, older than this shit-hole of a town that's for sure." she kicked at the dirt. "There are rumors about what goes on there, why it's so exclusive and all."

"So exclusive?" I inquired.

"Yeah, why my brother and I and all the other kids here can't get in. Sure, you hire us for your cleaning, gardening and office work... but the kids aren't good enough to go there, are they? How much money do you pay to get taught there?" Lee-Anne asked us.

Now this really shocked me. "I'm there on scholarship." I told her.

"Same here." Zack admitted.

"Hey, my parents would pay anyone anything, to take me off their hands." Peter scoffed.

"I don't know what my parents are paying..." Sally answered.

"So what's so special about you to get in there for free?" Lee-Anne asked me.

This stumped me, I hadn't a clue! "Good question." I shook my head. "Absolutely nothing. I thought the school was a funny farm and that's why I'm there."

"Lee-Anne!" came from inside, and we looked and saw it was her brother calling her back.

"I gotta go." she started back but I stopped her.

"Could you ask your Mum some questions for us? How old is this place? Have there been any deaths there?"

"And what do I get out of this?" she asked me back. I must have looked taken aback or something, because then she added, "all right, come again next weekend, I only work weekends."

Then she was gone, leaving us all looking at each other, wondering... We had no idea that Hamilton's was so exclusive. Exclusive, why? Keeping us out of the world for a reason? Or keeping the world from getting in?

"What is this? The 'Famous Five'? Fucking 'Poirot'? Why do you want to ask about the hauntings?" Peter asked Sally and I.

"Because she saw the ghost, you dickweed!" Zack punched his arm.

"You?!" Peter looked at me and laughed. "What did it look like? Headless? A mascot for a boarding house, by any chance?"

I turned around and walked off with Sally and Zack, leaving Peter laughing behind us.

So tonight during 'fun night' I skipped the videos in the Rec Rooms and went straight up after dinner to Nelson's dorm room and told her. She's on the Internet on her computer researching ghosts and smoking as she does it. I thought not to be rude or anything, that while I type on you I may as well join her.

She did ask me heaps of questions about the movie with Zack though. Like, did we hold hands? I told her we didn't, but we did share a popcorn and coke, and our hands kept bumping when we were trying to get the popcorn out of the box at the same time. She seems surprised that he hasn't made a move on me yet. But secretly I'm glad. I'm not ready for anything yet. My life is too fucked up right now, and the scars are still pretty obvious.

Besides, this ghost business has really freaked me out and sometimes I wonder if the attempt worked or not. Where am I? Is this place somewhere between life and death? Maybe that's the secret why this place is so exclusive...? Only those who are not quite living may attend here. That explains me and Nelson in a nutshell.

===

22/ 10/ 00

Dear Diary,

It's 1am. I'm supposed to be getting up in six hours for breakfast then class, but I don't care. I'm still so angry!

I was in the library after lunch. I had already done my homework so I was researching more ghost stuff. Nelson was helping me. I managed to convince her to leave her room and go to the Caf for lunch, then to the library with me afterwards.

Then Peter walks up, snatches the book off me, then laughs and yells out to everyone in the room that we're seeing dead people! And everyone in the room laughs with him... at us.

Nelson just loses it, I mean, really loses it. She lunged at Peter and punched him in the jaw! And she kept hitting him! Then Peter hit her back! He gave her a split lip and I think she's going to have a black eye tomorrow.

I tried to drag Peter off her, when he elbows me in the face and my nose starts to bleed!

Zack walks in the room, sees me bleeding and still trying to stop Peter, then he goes ape shit and he attacks Peter!

"You bastard! You hit her! You fucking bastard!" Zack yells and he goes for his best friend (or I thought they were bestfriends) and I was the cause.

"No!" I tried to stop Zack, but he pulled Peter off Nelson and threw him across three tables! Oh my god! I've never seen him like this! He just completely went off!

People scatter, there's yelling, and a couple of Seniors try to stop Zack from kicking the shit out of Peter when Professor Hamilton and Dr. Myles arrive!

Dr. Myles pulled Zack up and pinned him to one of the tables and yelled at him to calm down as Professor Hamilton helped up Peter, who then received a kick in the balls from Nelson!!

"That's enough!" Professor Hamilton yelled. Then he told a Senior to help Peter up again and take him over to the infirmary and to ask Nell to come to his office with a first aid kit. Then he took Nelson to his office.

I tried to stop them by trying to explain that it wasn't Nelson's fault, but Professor Hamilton completely disses what I say and tells me that right now it was his business to talk to Nelson.

They leave and Dr. Myles tells two of the Seniors to oversee the cleaning up of the library. Then he dragged out an enraged, kicking and screaming Zack, presumably to another office somewhere. I tried to follow behind them, but then Dr. Myles yelled at me to stay behind!

I felt like this was my fault and I'm not the one being dragged off. And when I tried to tell them, they completely ignored me! This is so fucking typical! All these teachers here... they try to come across as your friend and different from other adults, but in actuality they're exactly the same! They don't listen and they don't care.

Maya came over and offered me a hanky to put on my nose, but I pushed her hand away and left too.

Everyone was staring at me, probably thinking it was all my fault too. I had to get away, but I didn't know where to go. I couldn't go back to my dorm room, not if Pat is there. With his open door policy I still find it hard sometimes to close my door on him which shows something is wrong.

So I just kept walking.

I walked past Beta building and past some of the trees and I found this incline that led down to the back fence and then the lake after that.

I sat down on a log and stared at the lake and the surrounding woods and mountains. I could just make out the town of Brownsville across the lake, which I think is like, 10 km's wide? I had my bag with me, and my ciggies in that. So I lit up and took some long drags. I didn't care if a teacher came and found me like that. I think I would have dared them to expel me with the mood I was in.

The sun soon set and I looked at my watch. It was too cold to sit outside and it was close to dinnertime. I thought everyone should be in the Caf by now. So I walked back up the hill to Beta building.

When I was unlocking my door, I found Pat was still in his room though, in front of his computer as usual.

"I heard what happened." he managed in before I could quickly close my door behind me.

"So?"

"Drop this ghost business Elisha. It's not good for anyone." he said flatly, not looking at me, but still at the computer screen.

===

23/ 10/ 00

Dear Diary,

It seems I wasn't immune from yesterday's incident. I was called in early to see Nell after class today instead of just my usual Friday afternoon sessions. She started by asking me my version of events and what I thought happened.

All I could do was shrug and say I didn't know what set everyone else off. I said that Peter started it, but I don't know why he had to act like such a dickhead about it all. I told her I think Nelson is sensitive about what people think about her, which probably triggered her. Then I said I had no idea why Zack got all over protective of me.

She said Zack likes me, and I scoffed (more like a half laugh, half scoff) and I said I knew that. Then she told me that something in Zack's past (she wouldn't say what) made me some kind of symbol to him, like the way he's trying to protect himself from whatever bad happened to him was making him protect me. I didn't get it. So she explained that he feels he is trying to protect me the way he wishes someone could have or should have protected him in the past. Oh. But Nell wouldn't tell me what happened to Zack, which now I'm dying to know, to see if I can help him somehow.

She said all we can do is offer our friendship and support until he feels ready to discuss it, and to do the same with Nelson. I told her I thought I was already doing that, and she agreed. She urged me to keep trying, because before my arrival Nelson was a lot more introverted.

Then Nell asked me if I knew why Nelson and Pat aren't talking anymore. I told her I didn't know, but Nell saw right through it. She asked me if it had anything to do with the night we saw the ghost. I tried to hide my surprise, and she said she knew about it for a while, as Pat mentioned it. I forgot he still has meetings with Nell... so I asked her why has he been acting like a wanker about it all? Then she started telling me how everyone handles a shock or a surprise in different ways and some other psychobabble and how some people like myself, want to talk about it, and other people, like Patrick, don't want to.

I thought I'd use this chance to ask her some questions. I asked her first if she believed us, which she said yes. Then I asked her if she knew who the ghost was? She said she had a fair idea from stories and rumors, before she changed the subject to psychoanalyze me and my interest in the supernatural. She asked me if it was related to my depression and stuff. We ended up discussing this for the rest of the session. I think she thinks it's related to the time I tried to die, as if it's a morbid obsession to see what would have happened if it had worked.

I don't know about that. Ever since I was a little girl I've been interested in that kind of thing. I remember before I was 10 years old and "Poltergeist" was on TV. My parents sent me to bed, but I hid in the hallway where I could still see the TV so I could watch it. It scared me shitless, and I couldn't sleep afterwards, but I remember the thrill it gave me.

Those were good times then. Mum was well, Dad was happier, and we had lots of bar-be-cues and entertaining of family and friends. I remember when we had dinner parties, the adults would be in the lounge room talking all night, and the kids would get together in either Mark's or my bedroom (usually mine, because his room was always messy) and we would play 'Murder in the Dark' over and over.

I reminisced about all of this, as Nell just sat back and nodded and listened. Then just before I left at the end of the session, she said something to me, something I'm still thinking about. "Did you know when you talk about your father in your earlier memories, you talk about him differently."

"Differently?" I wondered what she meant.

"It's not angry or resentful." She smiled at me. "Maybe in our next meeting we could talk about when things changed."

"I can tell you the exact date when things changed... 20th April 1997. When Mum was diagnosed with the cancer." I said flatly, and I opened her office door and left.

==

TO: angiepevensie@ihug.com.au
FROM: ebaker_hamiltons@evers.com
SUBJECT: School life...
DATE: 23/ 10/ 00

Hey,

So the whole school knows, huh? Great, I'm considered
freakish across two continents now! So it was rumors going
around? Who started the rumor? Who else but you knows what
happened to me? I guess somebody could have heard some of
the teachers talking about it, hey? Remember when we found
out what happened to Douglas Talbot when you and I had to
report to the teachers staff room to start our detention?
Now I'm the new gossip. Great.

I feel like I'm the subject of gossip here too. Two days
ago there was a huge fight with three of the guys I've
mentioned to you before, Peter, Nelson and Zack. No, we
all weren't fighting together, but each other. Well, three
of us against Peter, but he started it! He said something
stupid, Nelson retaliated, he hit her, I tried to pull him
off her, he hits me (now I'm not sure if it wasn't
accidental) and Zack goes ape shit and beats the crap out
of him for hitting me (which could have been
accidentally).

Peter is walking around with half his face bruised and
he's limping a bit and I think his ribs are sore. Nelson
has a cracked lip and a black eye. Zack and I are the only
ones relatively scott free. I did have a bleeding nose
when it happened, but that's long gone.

There also seems to be a strange division of who is
sitting with who now in class and in the Caf for meals.
Nelson, Zack and I are sitting on one side of the table in
class, with Peter, Pat, Maya and Sally on the other side.
At lunch Sally came and sat with us though and told us
that she wasn't taking sides. She wasn't in the library
when it happened, but she told me what Maya told her, who
saw it happen. But by the way Maya explained it, it's as
if Nelson is about to be posted next on the FBI's Most

Wanted list! Considered unarmed but extremely dangerous...
I'm starting to really not like Maya now.

Nelson is acting like she doesn't care, but I know she
does. She got up and left the Caf at recess after
exchanging death glares at Peter and Pat, and then she
didn't show up at our next two classes. I think she's gone
back to hiding out in her dorm room again.

Zack has been following me everywhere I go, even offering
to carry my books for me to one of our classes together!
He's still acting so overprotective of me, I'm starting to
get the feeling like I'm going to suffocate soon! He's
sweet, he's good looking... but there is something missing
from him. When he and Peter were mucking around together
they were a funny team and he looked like he could lighten
up now and then. Now that he bashed up his best friend,
he's all over me, listening to my every word, going where
ever I go. If I asked him to rob a bank I think he might!

After my session with Nell this afternoon, I found he was
even waiting for me outside of Delta Building! He asked me
if I wanted to go to the library to do our homework
together. But I didn't want to make an appearance in there
again, not with the guy who nearly trashed it over me. So
I said I wanted to go back to my Dorm room, and he
followed me there as well.

I sat at my desk and pretended to be really interested in
my computer studies assignment on my laptop, as Zack sat
on my bed, doing BOTH of our math's homework! Well, he
didn't write down the answers because Dr. Knight knows our
handwriting, but he was telling me the answers so I could
put them down.

Nell told me that Zack is bonding to me because of a past
childhood trauma or something. I can understand that, but
this level of bondage is driving me insane, and I don't
know how to tell him this. So I turned around and tried to
talk about Peter with him. I told him Peter may have
accidentally hit me in the nose with his elbow when he was
fighting Nelson. Zack just shut off and said he didn't
want to talk about it anymore.

Bugger.

Then the bell went off for dinner in the Caf and I knocked on Nelson's door to see if she was coming. There was no response, so I knocked again. I knew she was in there because I could smell cigarette smoke.

Suddenly from inside, we heard a massive "FUCK OFF!!"

...OK... Zack and I looked at each other and then left her alone to her sulking.

Don't you just wish you were here instead of me? At least when I went to school with you it was only a day thing and we could go home afterwards... away from the school! Not here it's like 24 / 7.

==

TO: angiepevensie@ihug.com.au

FROM: ebaker_hamiltons@evers.com

SUBJECT: Peace Talks...

DATE: 24/ 10/ 00

I know I'm supposed to feel lucky that a cute guy likes me. I know I always used to complain that I could never get a guy I liked. But I don't know if I like Zack like that... I think I just want to be friends with him. And I told him so.

It was at lunch and I didn't want to eat in the Caf, I wanted to have some alone time with Sally, so we decided to have lunch outside in the sunshine against the wall to get out of the wind (you wouldn't believe how cold and windy it's been! And this is only Autumn!). Zack said, "OK, I'll just get something to eat and I'll join you."

I must have flinched or something, because he asked me what was the matter. I told him I wanted to talk to Sally about something private. Then he went off at me! He asked me why I'd been acting so funny lately, kind of distant, and I couldn't help myself, but I laughed! I told him considering I'd only been here for two weeks or something, how would he know what "I'm normally like"?

Zack walked off and I called after him to apologize, but he kept walking.

Damn it. I knew I could have handled that better. I felt so guilty, I mean it was only yesterday Nell told me that Zack had problems, and encouraged me to help him.

I went and sat outside with Sally and told her what happened. She was really nice and listened to me and pointed out that it would have happened eventually. I guess she's right, but after the fight and everything, I wish I held it in now.

In class afterwards Zack didn't come and sit next to Sally and I, he was sitting next to Patrick of all people! Then two people down, there sat Peter. I noticed Peter was giving me daggers all through class. If this was an X-File episode I'd have probably gone up in flames from the death stares he was giving me! At least Nelson came, even if it was late, and she took the seat on the other side of me. It almost became a boy against girl thing, with Pat also giving me and Nelson funny looks. I got sick and tired of this shit, and when Professor Hamilton's back was turned, I gave them the finger! Not Zack, but at Pat and Peter.

After class Sally and I went back to Nelson's room, where Nelson and I immediately lit up. We couldn't wait till 11pm. We opened the window a bit and Sally got some incense that Maya gave her and burnt it to help cover up the smell.

Nelson's window as well as mine doesn't face the oval, but overlooks the lake and mountains. I happened to be sitting on her desk next to the window when I looked out and I saw Zack walking by himself towards the incline and the back fence. I put the rest of my cigarette out and told the two that I would be right back. Then I ran downstairs and outside and went to catch up with him.

I found him sitting on the log that I sat on a couple of days ago when I needed to get away after the fight.

"Are you OK?" I asked him.

"Isn't this enough space? I'm not even practically on the school grounds anymore! Do you want me to go even further away?" he looked like he'd been crying, so I didn't take what he said personally.

"I don't want you to go away!" I sat next to him and put my arm around him. "I'm sorry if I hurt your feelings, but I just don't want to be in a relationship right now. I want to be your friend though, if you want."

He looked at me, and I wasn't sure what he was thinking. "Friends?" he rolled his eyes, but he didn't seem that angry.

"Yeah." was all I could say with out blurting out how I was really feeling.

"What?" he asked me, I guess he could sense what was on my mind. "Go on, tell me. You may as well, you've been honest all day."

"I just still feel freaked about being here, you know?" I shrugged, taking my arm back. "I'm not even supposed to be here... not just at this school, but here..."

I think he thought it was his turn to put his arm around me. "I know."

"And my head is still spinning... it was so surreal waking up in that hospital bed, not even in my own bloody country anymore! For the first day I thought I had died!"

"I know." he hugged me tightly. "You don't have to think about that now. You're here, you're safe now. Nothing is going to happen to you anymore."

I think this was what Nell was talking about. I don't know what he was going on about, but it stopped being about me. For some reason Zack thinks my suicide attempt was to run away from something, something bad. Like the reason why he's here maybe?

===

TO: mbaker@hotmail.com
FROM: ebaker_hamiltons@evers.com
SUBJECT: Party Time!
DATE: 29/ 10/ 00

Hey,

Congratulations on your promotion! That is so cool! So, what are you going to do with the extra money? Spend it on your little sister perhaps? LoL! Just kidding.

So tell me about Patrice. What does she look like? How long have you two been going out for? No, I'm not going out with anyone at the moment. Zack and I have agreed to be just friends. He's a really nice guy. It's like at my old school I never hung out with guys before, and here there are two guys that hang out with us, Pat and Zack. That almost rhymes, doesn't it?

Pat was the guy who acted like a dickhead about this ghost business. But he apologized to Nelson and I and asked if we could just hang out with out talking about all this stuff anymore, and Nelson seemed quite happy to. So I guess we've just dropped it and now we're just concentrating on... you know... nothing much anymore. I am a little relieved to be honest, it's hard fighting with someone whose room is exactly opposite to yours and his door is always open. He downloaded all this cool music off the Net for me and I've been listening to the CD on my stereo. Sally gave me this spare blank tape that I could record it on so I can also listen to it on my Walkman too.

One of our teachers, Miss Inez, whose also our Den Mother, recently busted Nelson for smoking in her room. Now there are all these signs up warning against smoking in our rooms and saying you'll get an instant week's worth of detentions. Nelson's detention was washing dishes in the Caf for 7 nights! Well, not actually hand washing the dishes, but after dinner she was rinsing them and loading them into this industrial dishwasher or something.

Nelson's been given extra sessions with our counselor Nell lately for missing classes too. It's almost like at this place they don't want to be strict, but they will if they have to be. They'd rather talk it out of you. Like a couple of days ago when there was this huge fight in the library, no-one was given detentions, but everyone had to go see our school counselor, Nell, about it.

In two nights time there is going to be a Halloween party! There have been signs up the last week broadcasting it. In the theater will be 'Club Night' and in the Rec room also in the Gamma building, horror movies will be shown. So it's a chance to get dressed up! Also it will be naughty night, which is what we call 'Fun Night' when they serve junk food and chocolates and chips and stuff. They only do this on Saturday nights normally (and the rest of the week is all healthy food).

I'm going to wear my black velvet singlet top and borrow Sally's long purple velvet skirt for it. You know the top, it's the one you lent me money for. Nelson's going to lend me her really cool gothic, black-beaded choker and in exchange I'm going to let her wear my long black velvet skirt.

Pat and Zack had a good laugh at us. When we were in the library today, supposedly doing our homework, Sally, Nelson and I were arranging the swop. Then Zack put on this camp voice and started to do the same with Pat!

"I'll wear your black skirt Sweetie, and you can wear my Calvin Kleins."

"No, I'll wear your Calvins, and you can wear mine, Darling!"

"And don't forget the rouge, sweetie-darling!"

"And I'll wear 'Forever' perfume."

"Is that Calvins too, sweety?"

"Oh yes Darling."

I burst out laughing! It was hilarious! Sally and I nearly cacked ourselves when Maya, forever the nerd, told us to shoosh and not to disturb the peace.

Then she said something really mean, "If you're always
going to be disturbing the library, why don't you go to
the other one and mess that up a bit?"

She was referring to the fight I mentioned that involved
Zack and I in the library. I gave her the filthiest look I
ever gave anyone in my life, and she turned away and went
back to her homework. Lately she's been hanging out with
the two Chinese girls, Soong and Wong, and the Japanese
guy Yuichi. I guess because they always seem to be
studying like she is. But after that remark, I wouldn't
want to hang with her again.

===

01/ 11/ 00

Dear Diary,

Last night was the Halloween bash, and what a bash it was! Even the
teachers dressed up for it. Pat did an hour of DJ'ing with the other Senior,
Steve, I think his name is, with some of the music they had downloaded
off the net and remixed. Everyone danced, ate, and danced some
more and we didn't have to stop the music till 2 AM! Well, nearly
everyone. Everyone except Zack, Sally and me.

As soon as classes finished that afternoon, we all rushed back to the
dorms to try and get our showers first. I was halfway through shampooing
my hair when somebody started banging on the door telling me to hurry
up! Then as we were getting ready, Nelson, Sally and I were running
between each others rooms to lend/borrow the clothes and make-up
and stuff. It was funny, Sally kept screaming, "Don't look! Don't look!
We're not ready yet!" and slammed my door in Pat's face!

"Freaking hell! I'll meet you guys at the Caf then. I'm going for a
cigarette." Pat shook his head at us, but I think he was trying not to
laugh. He caught Zack just as he was leaving his room and took him with
him, warning about a couple of shrieking banshees running wild at the
end of the corridor.

Even Nelson got into a girlie mood. She did her make-up in my room and then after doing her eyes with black liquid eye-liner, she did mine for me too. Sally raced in with this color of lipstick she reckoned went well with the purple velvet skirt I was borrowing from her. Nelson and Sally then started fighting about what kind of music to play as we were getting ready, and they finally compromised on U2's, 'Rattle and Hum'. I turned up "In the Name of Love" really loudly and we three started jumping up and down on my bed. Then Sally started teasing Nelson about her crush on Dr. Myles and joked that she should ask him to dance tonight!

'Club Night' started at 7.30 PM after dinner and was in the theater in Gamma Building, where the Caf is. We three skipped dinner and turned up at 7.30. We saw that with the theater they had folded away all the chairs and lined them all along the walls, and darkened the place with the lights that usually lit up the stage, now flashing around the room like we were in a real night club or something! There was the senior guy, Steve, DJ'ing from the stage, and at the back of the room there was a table in the corner offering punch and cans of soft drink and some nibblies.

Pat and Zack were already there, waiting for us. I noticed Peter was there, hanging out with the two other Americans in our year, Brett and Sophie. He gave us a dirty look and whispered something to Brett, probably about us, and they laughed. I tried to ignore them and grabbed Sally and we started dancing. Zack and Nelson joined in, and Pat seemed really uncomfortable. Nelson asked him what was up, and he said he couldn't dance.

"So? That's not stopping Zack!" I teased and Zack tickled me!

I noticed Jordon and Raj and Yuichi come in and just stand around the refreshment table, looking a little uneasy themselves. I pointed them out to Sally and we went over and asked them to join us. Jordon and Yuichi looked relieved and agreed, but Raj shook his head and said he was waiting for someone.

After a little while of more dancing, I soon found out who... Maya arrived, looking quite conservative but still very pretty. Raj immediately gave her a glass of punch and tried to engage her in conversation. She looked over to where we were dancing, but I looked away and pretended I didn't see her. She said something mean the other day which I'm still annoyed about.

Everyone seemed to be enjoying themselves, including the teachers. Nell, Dr. Knight and Professor Hamilton looked on happily at the turn out, as they stood to the side and talked. And Dr. Myles even took Miss Inez out onto the floor for a spin!

"I think they're dating. Steve, the DJ guy, told Pat that he saw Dr. Myles take Miss Inez out to lunch at the Diner last Sunday." Sally whispered in my ear.

I looked over at Nelson, who was looking at Dr. Myles. She was still dancing, and when she noticed that I noticed, she turned her back to him and got on down with Pat, who was still moving very awkwardly. He reminded me a little of a robotic scarecrow the poor guy! Then paired with Nelson who looked like she was doing the lambada or something... I tried not to laugh!

Around 10 PM I went outside with Nelson and Pat for a smoke, and when we were finished, I told them I wanted to use the bathroom and I'd meet them inside the theatre.

When I went down the hallway, past the Caf, I heard voices coming from around the corner. I stopped before going into the Ladies and listened. I recognized one of the voices as Peter's. He was talking to someone else, another guy from the sounds of it, something about money...

I peered around the corner to see Peter putting something in his pocket, and another guy, a Senior called Paul who I buy my smokes from, put money in his wallet. I didn't know Peter smoked... he never joined Pat or Nelson and I. I turned around and went into the Ladies.

When I came back to 'Club Night', it looked as if Peter had returned the same time as I did. He went over and whispered something to Brett and Sophie, and the three then turned around and left. I watched them go, but something didn't feel right about this. I nudged Sally and indicated the three leaving.

"Good riddance." Sally shrugged.

"No, I think something bad is going to happen." I said to her.

"What the fuck are you talking about?" she shook her head at me.

"Come on!" I grabbed her arm and pulled her with me.

"Hey, where are you going?" Zack called out after us, then followed us too.

We three hid in the doorway of the building as we watched the other three walk around the oval and go into Alpha building. Once they were inside, I then dragged Sally with me as Zack followed behind just to see what the hell it was that I was doing. I couldn't explain it, I just had this growing feeling inside me that something bad or something big was going to happen.

When we reached Alpha building, all of the lights were turned off, even the library and computer lab were all turned off.

"What the fuck are we doing here? The party is in the other building!" Sally whined.

"Shh!" I nudged her again, and walked very slowly and quietly inside, trying to listen to any footsteps or voices that might tell me where the three went. Then I heard it, footsteps that sounded like they were going up the stairs.

I pulled Sally with me, and Zack came along anyway, and we three crept inside the hallway and then slowly up the staircase. Once we had reached the first floor, I stopped us so I could listen for anymore footsteps.

Then I heard them. They were slow, but they were loud, and it only sounded as if it was one person making them. They must have known we were coming and split up. I may as well follow the one, since I don't know where the other two went, so I pulled Sally up some more stairs.

"Would you let fucking go of me!" she said angrily, snatching her arm back.

"Shh!" I hissed back at her.

I went up the next few stairs to the second floor and looked down both sides of the darkened corridor. It was totally black, with no lights, or even emergency lights on. I thought this was weird, even the EXIT signs were off.

Zack came and stood next to me. "I can't hear them anymore." he whispered to me. I shook my head to let him know that neither could I.

"This is the teachers offices. What are we doing, following them up here? You think they're gonna get high of Hamilton's own desk?" Sally scoffed.

"What makes you think they're gonna get high?" I asked Sally. Then I realized that that was what Paul sold to Peter. "Shit, maybe that's it."

Then we heard voices coming from the bottom floor, and Zack and I leaned over the railing for a better look, but we couldn't see anything.

Just then Sally started pulling on my arm.

"Ah, guys... I think you should see this."

"What?" Zack asked, then he stared, and I could see him stare, because there was a blue light on his face.

I turned to see what he was staring at, and what I saw was the source of the blue light. It was coming from under one of the teachers office doors. And it was getting brighter and brighter.

"Shit! Somebody's in there! Lets run!" Sally started back down the stairs.

"But all of the teachers are in Gamma building! We saw that!" I yelled back at her in a whisper.

Suddenly the blue light flashed into a blinding white light. Then it was gone, leaving us blinking blindly in total blackness again. But all the hairs on our arms and on the back of our necks started standing up, and suddenly the temperature was freezing cold!

"Oh shit! Lets go!" Zack grabbed my arm and started running down the stairs, with me being practically dragged behind him!

Then Sally, who was running in front of us screamed and stopped, and Zack and I ran into the back of her, nearly knocking her down.

She had run into Peter on the first floor who had given her another fright.

"What the fuck are you doing here?!" We all exclaimed at each other.

"Where's Brett and Sophie?" I asked him.

"Pissed off they did. Thought they heard a teacher upstairs." Peter said indignantly.

"That wasn't a teacher, that was us. Or maybe that was a teacher as well..." Sally tried to think.

"But all the teachers are in the Gamma building! It wasn't a teacher in that office!" I said defiantly.

"What the fuck are you talking about? Seeing dead peeeooo..." his voice trailed off, as he didn't get to finish his sentence.

We noticed a new blue light coming from the window at the end of the corridor.

The temperature dropped here as well, and the hairs on our arms and necks started to stand on end again. We all watched, as if in slow-mo a figure of a man in a short skirt and armor, wearing a helmet, slowly materialize from the window at the end of the hallway. The same window that Nelson, Pat and I had seen that lady disappear into.

"OK, time to go." Peter announced.

He grabbed Sally, Zack grabbed me, and we bolted down the rest of the stairs and out of the building.

"Now do you believe me?!" I shrieked on our way down.

As we all poured out of the front door, we were in for another surprise! Professor Hamilton and Dr. Myles were standing outside, as if they were waiting for us. Myles grabbed Peter as Hamilton yelled at us to stop.

"Would you mind telling us what you were doing here?" Hamilton asked, looking at us individually.

"This is my first guess." Myles pulled a small plastic bag with some white powder out of Peters pocket.

"What?!" Sally exclaimed. "You WERE going to get high? I was just joking!"

"There's enough in here for a little party for four." Myles handed the little bag to Hamilton.

"No way! There is no way that we were going to do that stuff!" Zack said indignantly. "I don't even smoke! Tell them Peter!"

We all looked at Peter.

"They're clean." he said.

"But you're not, are you Petie? You were planning another party with some other people, weren't you?" Myles patted Peter on the back - hard.

"Did you know Sophie is on medication at the moment? If she took this as well, she would have overdosed!" Hamilton lost his temper and yelled at Peter.

"Hang a minute! How did you know?" I asked Hamilton.

"You don't have to have three doctorates to work out what three teens, one with the goods, are up to when they leave a party to go into an empty building to start their own." Hamilton said. "Now you three either go back to Gamma building, or to the dorms." he ordered Zack, Sally and me.

We quickly left, not to the dorms, but to Gamma building.

After what we had just seen tonight, I think we all wanted to feel the safety of numbers. We didn't go into the theater again though, we went into the Rec room where the horror movies were shown. We sat on a lounge in the corner away from everyone else, and then just looked at each other, wondering what to say.

"There you are! What have you been up to?" Pat asked as he and Nelson came over, carrying some drinks.

We three all looked at each other, not knowing where to start.

On the TV screen it was showing the movie "House on Haunted Hill". You know the one, where all the characters are locked up in an old funny farm and are slowly being killed off, by the past inmates. At that moment it was the scene where the character Sarah was running around the maze of hallways and corridors, chasing a ghost.

I pointed at the screen and then looked at Pat challengingly, daring him to disbelieve again.

==

TO: angiepevensie@ihug.com.au

FROM: ebaker_hamiltons@evers.com

SUBJECT: Elvis never left the building

DATE: 07/ 11/ 00

Well, what to say? Everyone and everything seems to appear normal on the surface. But underneath… well, what to say...?

I told Nelson and Pat, what Sally, Zack, Peter and I saw. I told them about the blue light coming from one of the teachers offices, like what Pat saw when he first arrived here. How it was exactly the same as the blue light from the window we saw the ghostly Lady disappear into. And now the man in armour and a short skirt appear out of.

Pat didn't say anything mean this time. He's keeping silent on the whole matter, but I know there's something up with him. He admitted to seeing the blue light first, and now that three other people saw it, I'm surprised he doesn't feel justified at having his phenomenon witnessed, but rather maybe he's terrified? He seems worried about something, that's for sure. I think he's keeping another secret from us.

The first question out of Nelson's mouth was if the see-through guy in the armour and short skirt looked like any of the teachers? I said no, at first, but now I wonder about it. I mean, when it happened, I wasn't exactly concentrating on the guy's face, if you know what I mean.

But then I noticed something a little bit different about school the next day.

There was a guest lecturer for our history class on Friday, here to talk about the Roman legions. We've left the topic of Egypt behind, now we're concentrating on Ancient Rome. Then slap, bang, onto the wall, a picture of a Roman Centurion goes up.

Sally, Zack and I all exchanged stares... that was the guy in the armour and the short skirt that we saw! Peter didn't look at us, he started scribbling something down in his book. In fact, in this class he seemed very unlike himself and actually paid attention and kept his mouth shut. Or maybe it's because he is in Professor Hamilton's bad books over that drug bust...

We all thought Peter would get kicked out for sure over that drug thing. But instead they've put him on a months detention of cleaning duties! Not only does he have to wash the dishes after dinner, but he also has to mop the floors and wipe down all the tables, and even on weekends he has to clean the bathrooms in all the buildings! Ha ha! Sucked in! But he's not the only one doing all of this... so is Paul, the senior who sold the stuff to him. Only I think Paul's punishment is worse, he has to do it for three months or something, and he has to start work earlier, coz when I lined up to get my food, he was one of the people serving the stuff!

Damn it.

I think this is going to affect our supply line of cigarettes.

==

07/ 11/ 00

Dear Diary,

We were in the library doing our homework after dinner when Peter came in and sat at the table we were at. He tossed us over his notes from history and then started with, "from the guy we saw, the kind of armour he was wearing, I'd say we're looking at a ghost from around 100 BC. But what I can't work out is, why a ghost from Ancient Rome is hanging around Ontario? From the types of hauntings I've researched, there are two types of ghosts, one that died in the area, even when the building wasn't even built yet and it can interact with people years later; or it's a kind of recording, one that seems to be imprinted in the surroundings. But that doesn't explain what Roman soldiers are doing in a country which wouldn't have been discovered yet."

Sally, Zack, Nelson and I just looked at him, throwing our own daggers at him. "NOW you're interested? Bugger off Peter."

"How is the cleaning going, Pete? You look a bit hot and flustered there." Zack said coldly. That was true, he stunk of bleach.

"And doesn't that perturb you in any way? The way Hamilton and his crony just showed up, perfectly timed?" Peter leaned forward. "And what about the timing of our guest lecturer? He arrives magically, to talk about Roman Legionnaires, right after we've seen one? And how did our guest lecturer arrive here, may I ask? Did you guys notice any new looking cars parked in the staff carpark outside of Alpha building? Or did he just helicopter in, using the prestigious Brownsville hospital helipad?"

"So what are you saying, you saw our guest lecturer arrive in the middle of the night, bathed in blue light? Wow, I should become a poet." Nelson said sarcastically.

But that did make me think what he was saying may have been right. "You know what, I have been thinking about this a lot. You know how Hamilton caught us and said to Peter, 'with the type of medication she was on, she would have overdosed?' He didn't say 'could have', he said 'would have', like it was a forgone conclusion. Like he knew it was about to happen."

Zack just looked at me, then he turned to Peter. "What exactly was it you and Brett and Sophie heard that night? That scared Brett and Sophie away."

"Footsteps. Lots of them."

"That could have been from us." Sally looked at Zack and I.

"No, I mean LOTS of them, the kind that sound like it's Piccadilly Circus in rush hour. They thought it was all of the teachers and probably all of Brownsville, come back from partying early, because it came from upstairs where the teachers offices are."

"That's strange, we didn't hear anything." Zack said. "And we were right outside the teachers offices."

"Which office was it that you saw the blue light?" Peter asked us.

"How do you know we saw a blue light?" I asked him back.

"I heard Hamilton talk about it. He knows we know." Peter sung warningly.

"So? What's wrong with that?" Sally shrugged dismissively.

"Girlfriend, buy a clue! Pat saw a blue light coming from his office once, we have a guest speaker from 100 BC, and Hamilton knows when his students are about to drop dead from overdosing! What do you think?" Nelson snapped at her.

"So, which office was it?" Peter asked me again.

"I don't know, I've never been up there." I shrugged.

"Well, there's no time like the present." Peter stood up. "Come on, show me."

"What? Now? But it's cold outside." I whined.

"We should find out." Zack stood up too.

"Come on." So did Nelson, and she looked at Sally. "Don't you wanna know? Or are you too scared?"

"Fine!" Sally huffed and stood up.

"Bloody hell. Can't this wait until morning? When it won't look so strange, on our way to class?" I refused to stand up.

"Good idea." Sally quickly sat down again.

Then they all sat down again.

"And we don't all need to go. Let's keep them guessing just a little bit, shall we?" I pointed out. "They mightn't know we all know."

"Know what? Our teachers are ghosts?" Nelson said flatly.

==

(THE FOLLOWING PIECE WAS WRITTEN ON SCRAP PAPER BY ELISHA BAKER AND PASSED ON TO NELSON, PETER, ZACK AND SALLY AT 8.15 AM THE 8TH NOVEMBER 2000, DURING DR. KNIGHT'S MATH CLASS)

Left breakf. early so could go to class early to check out Alpha. Light did come from Prof. H. office.

==

TO: mbaker@hotmail.com
FROM: ebaker_hamiltons@evers.com
SUBJECT: About your offer...
DATE: 11/ 11/ 00

Hey Mark,

Congrats again! You and Patrice moving in together is a big thing. What did Dad say? I'm glad you two are talking again. I bet he's happy that one child of his has got his life straight.

I talked to him last night, from the school counsellor's office. Nell kept nagging me to do it. She said that she can't just keep giving him progress reports on my settling in and grades and stuff, that he does care and worry about me rah rah rah. So finally, she handed me the phone and then left her office to give me the privacy to make the call.

I thought I might as well, I have been here for a month now. I guess I do miss him now and then, especially now. I wish I was home with Angela, doing a sleep-over/video night at my place. Dad would let us order pizza. At least he was always cool to let me do that whenever Angela spent the night. And he always let us use the big TV in the lounge room, while he we would watch the news on the little TV in his bed room or read a book.

So anyway, I made the call, and he answered the phone.

At first I didn't know what to say, and he must have thought I was a prank caller, because he sounded angry, "hallo? hallo? Who's that?" Then suddenly his voice softened and he said, "Elisha?" All I could say was, "yes Dad."

He asked me heaps of questions, and I started crying. I suddenly felt so guilty about the idea of him coming home and finding me like that, in the bathroom. He asked me if I was feeling better, and I think he was talking about if the scars were healed over yet, so I said yes. He asked me what the school was like, was I making friends, what the weather was like... I was so emotional all I could manage out were short answers, like "yes", "no" or "it's OK".

He also asked me if I needed anything? Did I need more money, or would I like him to send over more of my stuff, and man, when he said that, I just bawled! He was acting so nice! It made me feel even more guilty.

Then when it was time to hang up, he said he loved me, and so I told him I loved him too. He also added that I should behave myself and study hard, because he's actually heard good things about this school. I wanted to ask how he heard these things, but he cut short the call by saying "this call is probably costing a fortune. I'll go now, but call or write soon. Bye now."

I wish I knew how he heard these things. I need more information on this school, and whenever I ask the locals about it they act all funny. But anyway, I cleaned myself up from all the crying, and I opened the door to go find Nell to let her know she can have her office back. Then I saw her talking to Professor Hamilton.

I wouldn't call myself nosy. But I guess from what's been going on lately and from the way Professor Hamilton was talking to Nell so quietly, it did make me suspicious! So I quickly ducked back in and hid behind the doorway, trying to hear what they were saying.

Whatever it was, it certainly was secretive, because they were practically whispering to each other! I only made out a couple of words, like "should we use medication or should we continue counseling?" Then something about a new rule, that the school was soon going to impose a curfew or something to "stop 'them' going into Alpha Building so freely around midnight".

Suddenly the talking stopped, and Nell reappeared, making me jump in fright!

"How did the call go?" she asked me.

"It went well, yeah." I nodded. I was about to walk past her and get away so I could tell the others what I just heard, when she stopped me.

Oh shit, I was worried she knew I heard. But instead she plucked another tissue from the box and wiped my cheek with it and smiled kindly. "You missed a spot."

"Thanks." I took the tissue, and tried to leave again.

"You know, the phone is always available when you want to use it. I'm sure your father will appreciate it. I'm sure you'll end up appreciating it too."

"Thanks." I said quickly, and this time, I was successful. I ran down the stairs and outside and across the oval.

It was 5.30 PM, and I wondered where the others might be.

I went to the Rec Room in Beta building, and there they were, watching a video of a "Dr. Who" episode of Sally's.

"How was your session?" Zack asked me. "Hey, are you all right? You look like you've been crying."

"I was, but that's not what's wrong. I heard Hamilton talk to Nell. I think it was about us, unless there are other students going into the Alpha building at night. They were talking about maybe drugging us, or even putting a curfew on us."

"What?" Pat sat up and looked at me as if I'm nuts.

"Take a chill pill and then tell us exactly what you heard." Peter told me.

"That's not funny! I think that's what Hamilton's thinking of too!" I turned on him.

"OK, this is ridiculous. First our school is haunted, then our teachers are the ghosts, who, I understand it are psychic and know when a student is about to die, and now, we're all going to get drugged? Get fucked!" Pat stood up and left the room.

"That's right! Keep walking and don't come back!" Nelson lost her patience with him. He gave her the finger back just before disappearing up the stairs to go back to his room.

"Drugging us? That can't be legal." Sally shook her head.

"If Nell the certified counsellor and registered nurse, under the supervision of the medical doctor, Dr. Knight, decide they want to, on the students who are already their patients, I think it's very legal." Peter said.

"Exactly what did they say?" Nelson pressed me.

"Professor Hamilton asked Nell if they should try medication or keep using counseling." I answered.

"And what did she say?" Zack asked.

"I didn't hear that part. But he said they'll bring in the curfew very soon." I said defensively.

"Well I'm safe, because I'm not even getting counselling!" Sally announced.

"Good for fucking you!" Nelson turned around and left, not upstairs, but outside for a cigarette and some fresh air.

So Mark, as you can imagine, it's been a little tense around here of late. As Pat said, first our school is haunted, then it's our teachers who are the ghosts, and now this...? And Dad said that he's heard good things about this place???

If the offer still stands… I know you've just moved in with Patrice and it might get a little crowded… but if they do try anything on us, can I crash at your place? It will just be for a little while. You know how you're getting more money from your promotion, is it enough for a one-way ticket back to Sydney?

===

TO: angiepevensie@ihug.com.au
FROM: ebaker_hamiltons@evers.com
SUBJECT: I might be coming home sooner than I thought...
DATE: 15/ 11/ 00

Hey,

The subject title is right, I might be coming home sooner than you thought. If I do, I'll stay with Mark for a couple of weeks till I work out what to do. He lives in Leichaardt, which is in the city somewhere, so you and I can still see each other.

I overheard the headmaster talk to the counselor about drugging us... the ones that know their secret. We think that the teachers are the ghosts coz two days after we saw the second ghost, we think it was the same guy who was our guest lecturer in our history class! And if you think I'm nuts, ask Nelson, Peter, Zack and Sally, they're my witnesses! And Nelson thinks Dr. Knight is a ghost also... which still kind of confuses me. Ghosts are usually dead, right? Then how come at night they go all see-through and walk through walls, but in day time they're regular people, teaching class? I see them eat food... drink coffee... it doesn't make any sense.

Today we had a school assembly in the Theatre after classes were finished for the day. Professor Hamilton said that from tonight onwards there will be a curfew. For weekdays, Monday to Friday, the Alpha Building would be closed from 10 PM till 7am, and from 11pm to 9 am on weekends. So that means from 10 PM or 11 PM onwards we all should be in Beta building, and nowhere else, unless it's Saturday night, and 'Fun Night' and we are watching movies in Gamma Building.

I feel like they're closing in on us.

At least I've got Mark who can fly me out of the country, or in the very worst, he will come and get me if he has to. But poor Nelson, she doesn't have a loving family environment with her parents, and she doesn't have any older brothers or anything. She says she'll just run away, that she knows how to survive. I wonder if she's lived on the streets or something? We were talking about this in the Caf at dinner.

Dinner, what a laugh! I took my plate of food (it was Indian night, so it was Basmati Rice and Lamb Korma - once a week they serve food from a different country) and I just sat and stared at it. Peter was scoffing it down, he said he hadn't eaten curry this good since he left England (Maya who was sitting at the table next to us, gave him a funny look when he said that!). So I watched him for a couple of minutes, then I said, "how do you know that the drugs aren't in the curry?"

Everyone just looked at me, and Peter burst out laughing!

"Hey man, shut up. She was right about the curfew, wasn't she?" Nelson gave him a dirty look.

Suddenly everyone else at our table wasn't hungry either, well, except Peter.

"More for me." he grabbed my plate and Naan bread and started munching on that next. Bastard. I was hungry too.

"Don't worry, I've still got a Snickers Bar from last 'Fun Night'." Zack pulled it out of his bag and handed it to me. It was warm and squidgy, probably from being crushed at the bottom of his bag. I thought that it was so sweet of him to give it to me.

"No, it's yours, you have it." I smiled and gave it back to him.

"No, I've got others." he pushed it back towards me.

"Hey, I'll have it!" Nelson tried to grab it but Zack was too fast for her. He put it in my hand and I instantly ripped it open and ate it, with the whole table watching me now.

"I've still got some junk food in my room." Sally said. "I'm going to go get it." She got up from the table to leave.

"I'll come too. I didn't think I would be living on chips and chocolate again, otherwise I would have grabbed more of them." Nelson stood up and left with her.

When we got back to Beta building after Astronomy tonight we all met in my room and pooled together what junk food we had been hoarding. I felt guilty, because I hadn't been hoarding any (I like only eating chocolate once a week -

good for my skin) and Zack offered to give me two more chocolate bars. But I said thanks, but no thanks. I'll keep doing what I have been doing so far, only eating the Caf food in tiny amounts. If there are any drugs, I'd only been getting them in small doses. And if I am being drugged, then they'll know because they'll see any changes in me.

===

TO: mbaker@hotmail.com

FROM: ebaker_hamiltons@evers.com

SUBJECT: Drug free

DATE: 17/ 11/ 00

Hey Mark,

I just want to say thanks for believing me and nearly flying me back to Sydney. I feel like such an idiot. I think everyone else here thinks so too. I am so embarrassed! Shame, man, shame!

I had my weekly appointment with Nell as usual this afternoon after class. I was quiet and I didn't really want to talk to her, in case she would jump up and jab me with a syringe or something. She remarked that she and all of my teachers have noticed a change in me this past week. I haven't spoken up in class and my homework has either been late or of sub-standard, like a rush job. I told her I'd been a little pre-occupied with stuff. She asked me if it had anything to do with the conspiracy theory that she and the teachers would be soon drugging their students in one massive attack or something, and I didn't know what to say.

She must have known I overheard them talking. She looked like she was trying not to laugh and asked me if I had any other thoughts that the students weren't safe in this school. I asked her what she meant by that, and she asked me this really weird question on whether I hear things, like hidden messages on the TV or radio or music I listen to on my Walkman. Now it was my turn to laugh and I said no, I didn't. She seemed a little relieved by that, then asked me if I saw 'things', weird things, in my day to day routine. And I replied "besides weird lights coming out of teachers offices and people walking through walls? Not really." Then for the rest of the session she brought up my depression and asked me how I was coping with living away from home.

I realized that she thought all of this was some home-sick, depressed ploy to go back home. She even flat out asked me if offered a plane ticket, would I want to go home, or stay here a little longer till I can make an informed choice. She also told me that her conversation with Professor Hamilton was about an unnamed student who did suffer paranoid schizophrenia, where sometimes when counseling isn't enough, Doctors do have to use drugs as a way to treat the patient. I could see what she meant by that, because there was a student in the year above me at my old school who did go schizo and they dragged him off in an ambulance. Then after some time away, he came back, heavily medicated. Whenever he acted up afterwards, the teachers would ask him about his medication (yes, another overheard conversation when I was standing outside a staff room waiting for another detention).

So then I asked her about the curfew thing. Was this to stop me, Nelson, Sally, Zack, Peter and I from going into Alpha Building at night and from seeing the phenomenon? Nell sat back in her chair and looked at me long and hard.

"With students abusing the trust given to them, to use the computer lab and library in the building at night, but instead they skulk around and get high in the dark, unused areas of the building, what do you think, Elisha?"

"But we don't do that!" I retorted. "Only Peter did!"

"But Peter wasn't the only one who did it, was he? What about the student who sold him the cocaine in the first place? You think he would only sell it and not try it out with his friends as well?" she raised her eyebrows and did the stern teacher look on me.

Fine. I sat back in my chair as well and crossed my arms and gave her a long stare back. They are doing the typical teacher routine... one student stuffs up and we all pay. At least I know I can eat properly again. I'm not looking forward to telling the others though - they're probably starving by now! They're going to kill me when I tell them!

Shame, man, shame!

```
===============================================
```

TO: angiepevensie@ihug.com.au

FROM: ebaker_hamiltons@evers.com

SUBJECT: The trouble with living at school...

DATE: 19/ 11/ 00

I really hate Peter. At dinner tonight Peter ate a handful of his fries, then instantly pretended to start choking on them and even over dramatically fell off his chair and writhed on the floor as if he'd been given poison or something. What else do they want me to say? I said I'm sorry! I already look like an idiot! Do I have to slit my wrists again to prove it or something?

Pat has been hanging out with Brett, Sophie, Maya, Soong, Wong, Raj and Yuichi lately. He saw what Peter was doing from his table and whispered something to Brett and they laughed. The whole school looked at me. Apparently everyone knows that I had spread the rumor about drugs in the food or something. I noticed Sophie wasn't laughing though. She must think I'm schizo or something, because when I bumped into her coming out of the bathroom in the Dorm this morning, she instantly backed away, ducked her head, and almost ran back to her room! I scared her out of going to the toilet, can you believe it?

At least Zack and Nelson haven't given me a hard time. When Peter went off at me after I told them after my session with Nell, Nelson and Zack stuck up for me. Zack reminded him that we still don't know properly what's going on with this school and Nelson threatened to destroy his other testicle (you know when they fought in the library, she kicked him in the balls, right?).

I'm a bit let down that Sally didn't stick up for me. She didn't rib me out for it like Peter did, but she didn't say anything either. She did say she was relieved she could eat properly again. She hasn't said much to me since, either. She's probably thinking that it might be a good idea to spend less time with me too. When I went to the library this afternoon with Zack and Nelson to do our homework, we knocked on her door to see if she wanted to come too, but she said she'd rather do it in her room instead. That was weird, because she's never said before that she didn't want to do something with us. But then two hours later when Nelson, Zack and I were packing up to go back to the dorms, Sally walked in with Maya and Pat to study with them! And Maya even smiled and whispered something to Sally and Pat as they walked right past us and got the table in the corner. I think she was gloating that she got her friend back or something, and was trying to make a point of it to me.

"Come on, we don't need them." Nelson said quietly to me and put her arm around me and we three left.

Then when Sally came and sat with us at dinner, Nelson gave her the cold shoulder as punishment. And then Peter does that thing at the table over dinner with the fries and I noticed Zack and Sally try not to laugh. At least Nelson stuck up for me when she asked Peter if he wanted some more fries for embellishment and tipped the rest of hers as well as a whole bottle of ketchup on him!

I really am an idiot, and everyone here thinks so.

I don't want to go to class tomorrow. I can't be bothered sitting across from Pat and Maya and now maybe Sally, with us all giving each other death stares all day. I'm so over Hamilton's, I'm really ready to go home now. Maybe I can call Dad and say I'm cured and ask to come home. But then, I don't want to go back to my old school... not with everyone knowing I'm the loser who couldn't kill herself properly.

I'm a loser in two schools now.

===

20/ 11/ 00

Dear Diary,

I didn't want to go to any of my classes today. I stayed in bed this morning and when Miss Inez, our Den Mother came and checked on me, I told her I wasn't feeling well. She said that she would send Nell to come and check up on me. Great. This whole place is so like a school 24 hours a day, 7 days a week, complete with a Nazi squad checking on truancy! I can't even chuck a sickie in peace and quiet anymore!

I laid in bed with my Walkman on, high volume. I didn't hear Nell knock on my door. Anyway, she just walks into my room, opens my curtains and tells me it's a beautiful day outside and I should be outside enjoying it before it starts snowing soon. I felt like saying, "oh just go away, will you?"

Gees this woman is annoying. She sits down on my chair, moves it next to the bed and tells me she knows why I'm in bed today. I couldn't be bothered being polite, and I think I was hoping for some kind of expulsion too, so I asked her sarcastically why she thought I was in bed?

"Come on Elisha, snap out of it. You're too smart for this." she says.

"Smart for what?"

"Lying in bed all day, hiding."

"Didn't you get the memo? I'm the dick who couldn't kill herself right."

"Don't start feeling sorry for yourself. It's not productive."

"And neither is this." I retorted.

"Then what do you want me to say? Promise you no one else will tease you or make fun of you over this drugging business? We don't condone bullying at this school. But we hope that our students can tell the difference between bullying and the odd joke here and there. You're teenagers, and you as a teenager, should expect it a bit laughter and jabbing now and then. If you would prefer, I can have a word with some of the students and ask them not to mention it again..."

"No, don't do that." I said flatly.

"You have to admit, it is a little bit funny. Professor Hamilton and Dr. Knight found it quite amusing." Nell giggled. "Can you imagine us putting that in our brochure? The reason why have such a high success rate at getting our students into the top universities around the world is because we put drugs in the water."

The way she said that, I have to admit, was funny.

"I saw that! No point frowning again, because I saw that smile escape! You might as well let it out now." she leaned over and gave me this huge grin, and she kept doing it and doing it, which made me laugh.

Then she turned slightly serious again. "Elisha, I know you've been through a lot these past two months, all of your teachers and friends here do. We know it is a serious issue when a person chooses to end their life. We brought you here because we honestly believe we can help you. There is a special quality about yourself that you don't know about yet, but we brought you here because we know we can show it to you."

I didn't know what to say to that. She said it with such warmth and sincerity... I could see now why Nelson finally left her room and started going to classes again. Sometimes Nell has this way that she can not only see through you, but the world as well and your place in it. She can make it seem special or more real.

"OK." was all I said.

"Good. Now, it's 10:15 AM, so if you get dressed and ready now, you can join your friends for recess. Are you ready?"

"Yes." I said. I would have preferred to stay in bed for longer and snooze, but I didn't want anymore attention on me.

So as soon as she left I got out of bed and dressed and did my hair. I could hear the bell go off so I went downstairs and crossed over the oval and went into Gamma building.

"Hey!" Zack waved me over to his, Nelson's, Sally's and Peter's table in the Caf. It was nice that he spotted me and waved me over so enthusiastically. He even got up when I came over and asked me before I sat down, "Are you all right?"

"Yeah, fine." I shrugged it off and sat down.

"Well, you missed Sally's stellar performance in drama as Lady McDuff." Peter said dryly and Sally turned around and hit his arm.

"You haven't learned your lines yet either, so shut up!" she said annoyed, blushing slightly.

"What happened?" I asked them.

"We had to stand up and do these theatre sport exercises, right? And we had to quote some of our lines while we did them." Nelson told me. "Sally got caught out quoting Midsummer Nights Dream instead of Macbeth."

"Really?!" I burst out laughing. "Nice one!"

"Well, what have you learned so far?" Sally asked me.

"Bubble bubble, toil and trouble..." I started.

"That's unfair! Everyone knows that line!" Sally exclaimed.

"Fire burn, cauldron bubble!" Nelson and I finished in these high pitched, witchy voices.

"I wish I was a witch. Why do I have to be a Lady?" Sally complained.

"What, you're a man? Oh god, that night, in the janitor's closet..." Peter pretended to be embarrassed.

"What, now you complain? You weren't doing that last night, in my closet!" Zack put on his camp voice again and Nelson, Sally and I laughed harder.

It felt good mucking around with them again. And I'm glad Sally was there for it, I guess I haven't lost her to the dark side of Maya yet. Maybe I have been taking things a little too personally or seriously. I guess it doesn't always have to be about 'us and them', does it?

===

25/ 11/ 00

Dear Diary,

Guess what! It started snowing today! Real live snow! It's soft and cold and wet. Today was another cold rainy day, and when Zack, Sally, Peter and I were sitting in the Diner, I noticed that the rain looked a bit strange. When I commented on this, Zack laughed and told me it was snow! It was 'Brown Day' which means the Freshmen and Sophomores got to pile into a mini-bus and get driven into town for a couple hours of freedom.

We all went and saw 'Scooby Doo' in the cinema and then we went to the Diner afterwards for hamburgers. I also wanted to see if this girl, Lee-Anne was working there today to ask her some more questions about Hamilton's. Now that Peter's on the investigative team he kept telling Sally and I what questions to ask her. He's getting quite bossy actually. Sally told him to shut up or we would kick him out of the 'Mystery Machine' just like they did to 'Scrappy Doo' in the movie we saw. LoL!

When Sally and I went up to the counter to pay for our food, Lee-Anne was on the cash register. I asked her if she had a break coming up and she said she'd meet us outside in 10 minutes. So we four waited out the front for her, and I started to smoke while we were waiting. She came out and pretended to talk to us by asking me for a cigarette, which I gave her. She lit it and then we started asking her the questions.

"So, has anyone died there?" Peter asked her first.

"No, no-one. A few years ago a gardener had a heart attack when he was mowing the lawns, but your doctor who teaches there, revived him long enough till he was taken to the hospital here. Then they flew him out to a hospital in Thunder Bay and he had some kind of triple by-pass surgery." Lee-Anne answered.

"What about the stories you've heard about the school." I mentioned.

"What about them?" she shrugged.

"Well, what are they?" I asked her.

She shivered and pulled her jacket around her more tightly. She seemed to hesitate before telling us, as if still trying to make up her mind if she should or not. "Strange lights are seen coming from the school."

"From the main building?" Peter asked her.

"Yeah. From across the lake we see strange, bright bursts of lights, like when there's supposed to be no-one there during summer holidays." she answered.

"Blue lights? White lights? What kind of lights? Coming from the windows?" Zack asked next.

"All of the above." She shrugged. "I've seen them. One night I was in the woods with my brother and his friends. We even climbed over the fence on a dare. It was summer and there was supposed to be no-one there. But then there was a bright light, and then all of these people were walking around this building, like they came out of nowhere. One minute it's dark and quiet, the next minute it was all lit up with all these shapes of people walking around."

Just then I got a cold chill down my spine and I shivered.

"That's like what we saw and heard." Peter said to the rest of us.

"We didn't see a group of people." Zack interjected.

"But I bloody well heard them!" Peter retorted. "And it happened when you guys saw the light."

"So it's true, huh?" Lee-Anne asked us.

"Don't worry, feel fortunate that you're not there." I said to her.

"Hey Lee-Anne! Break time's over!" her brother suddenly opened the door and yelled over to us.

"I gotta go." she sighed and stumped out the cigarette. It was only half finished too, and I almost regretted the waste of a good cigarette with my supply running so low. I think she saw my reaction. "What's wrong? Running out?"

"Yeah." I said.

"For $20 my brother can keep you in supply." she said simply.

"$20? What a rip off! A packet costs only $7!" Peter replied before I could.

"$13 commission. Take it or leave it." Lee-Anne shrugged.

"Fine." I got my purse out.

She took my money and went inside, then we had to wait another 10 minutes until her brother came out this time and tossed the packet to me.

"See you next weekend?" he asked me, suddenly a lot nicer than the last time we spoke.

"I guess so." I shrugged.

"It will be $20 again, and the time after that as well, capiche?" Then he went back inside, leaving Peter, Zack and Sally staring at me as if I had just bought a broken down car or something.

"Sucker." Peter teased.

"Who else is going to buy my cigarettes? My last supply line was given a 3 month detention, remember?" I shrugged again.

It's been snowing all afternoon and most of the evening. I hope it snows all night, then maybe tomorrow I can make my first ever snow man! It's been pretty cold, I've had the heater on constantly in my room. I've had to, it's this annoying old oil heater that takes at least half an hour to warm up when you first switch it on!

Tonight for Fun Night we got to choose between hamburgers and tacos. I had the tacos. The two movies showing afterwards were "Perfect Storm" and "Event Horizon". I chose to watch "Perfect Storm". Remember when you made me go see that other movie in the cinemas? I still think that is the scariest movie I ever saw! Peter made Sally go see it with him while Zack saw "Perfect Storm" with me... and after about 45 minutes Sally came and sat with us instead, she hated that movie too! But Nelson loved it. She ended up staying and watching it with Peter. Pat watched that movie too, apparently, but he sat away from Nelson, I think with Soong and Wong.

After the movie finished (we were in the Gamma building Rec room) Dr. Myles came in and rounded up all the students and made sure we all left back to our dorms coz the curfew was about to start soon. I think it was about 5 minutes till 11 o'clock or something... but I thought he was being extra pushy about it. When we were walking back across the oval to Beta building, I looked over at Alpha building. I nudged Zack and pointed.

Dr. Knight, Nell and Professor Hamilton were watching us all from the library window on the second floor.

"What are they doing there?" Zack asked me.

"Good question." I thought out loud.

Just the way the three of them were standing there, watching us, made me feel a little uneasy, and definitely curious. I know they're hiding something. I know they think we suspect. And I know this curfew business isn't just to stop students from breaking the rules.

==

TO: angiepevensie@ihug.com.au

FROM: ebaker_hamiltons@evers.com

SUBJECT: Twilight Zone in Northern Hemisphere

DATE: 26/ 11/ 00

Hey. I found out yesterday when I went to the Diner with Zack, Peter and Sally that even the locals have seen strange lights and people appearing out of nowhere. Great, that just makes me feel so safe and cozy inside. Also have made a new contact to get my cigarettes from in future, but it will cost me $13 commission every time. Even better. I think Nelson was more interested in hearing my news about the guy who works in the Diner will buy our cigarettes for us than about the locals thinking we're being schooled in a haunted house. I had to lend her 10 cigarettes till our next Brownsville weekend.

See Angela, I'm not nuts. I'm not the only pistachio that's realized it's been put in the wrong packet with the other peanuts. It's not only the whacked out students, but it's the wacky towns folk who've seen what we've seen. I'm guessing that if we keep asking, we're bound to find even more people out there.

==

TO: mbaker@hotmail.com

FROM: ebaker_hamiltons@evers.com

SUBJECT: Thanks again!

DATE: 30/ 11/ 00

Mark, sometimes you are the coolest oldest brother ever!

Thanks for the mobile phone! So I can text you there in Sydney whenever I want? Cool! Thank you thank you thank you! It's just nice to know that I don't have to keep using the phone in Nell's office if I suddenly had to call you or Dad or someone else. Angela has a mobile too that she was given for her last birthday, so I can send her text messages too! Yes, I know I'll be paying my own bills, so don't worry about that. I know how to behave responsibly... sometimes!

It was nice receiving the package in the mail. When our Den Mother Miss Inez was handing out the mail, all my friends crowded around to see what I got. I practically hadn't even taken it out of the box yet when Peter snatched it off me and started playing with it.

Nearly all afternoon we've all been playing Snake and seeing who could get the highest score. No idea how to play Bantumi though, the damn phone keeps beating me! So far Zack and Peter have been hogging it the most, they keep passing it between the two of them, I haven't even been able to pick which ring tone I want! But I love the cover! Metallic yellow, it's so... me! Finally Sally snatched it off them and helped me pick the picture I want on the screen. Now I have flowers on my display. I love it!

Thank you so much!

===

TO: ebaker_hamiltons@evers.com
FROM: angiepevensie@ihug.com.au
SUBJECT: RE: Twilight Zone in Northern Hemisphere
DATE: 03/ 12/ 00

Hey Elisha,

I never said I didn't believe you. I just don't think you should try to find out all this stuff about the school. I think you should just concentrate on getting well and come home.

If you keep trying to find out all this ghost stuff, then
the teachers are either going to think you're crazy and
keep you there for longer. Or if it's true and the
teachers are weird, you shouldn't let them know that you
know or they'll try to keep you at College to keep you
where they can keep an eye on you. Either way, I really
think you should drop this ghost business and ask your Dad
when you can come home.

Your best bud,

Angie

==

03/ 12/ 00

Dear Diary,

Wow, I can't believe Christmas is only in 3 weeks! I can't believe I've
been here for nearly two months. I can't believe it's snowing! I can't
believe I'm going to have a white Christmas. Now all I need is Santa
Clause to drop down the fireplace in the library and tell me he'll grant
me a wish. Then *bing* I can have a white Christmas with Mum.

The school has been buzzing a little more than usual. I mean, lets face it,
we're a school full of geeks, nerds, rejects and retards, with 40% of the
population in therapy. 60% of the school is looking forward to going
home for two weeks over Christmas to see their families over the festy
season, while the other 40%... well... probably looking more forward to
reaching for the prozac and/ or valium.

The bugger about all this is if I were back in Australia I'd be enjoying a
month and a bit off from school. But not here, I only get two weeks off.
But I am looking forward to going home. Mark text me on my new
mobile he gave me that he's going to be home for Christmas as well, so
we'll have a semi-family Christmas, of me, him and Dad. I am a little
looking forward to seeing Dad. I have been talking to him once a week
on the phone in Nell's office every Sunday night after dinner in the Caf.
He has been pretty nice most of the time I'll admit, always asking if I
have enough money. I think that's the way he can communicate his

affection for me, by trying to provide for me. I remember when I was little he did it by carrying me on his shoulders everywhere.

It's a bit like Zack actually. He hasn't made another move on me since I told him I wanted to be friends, but he always acts protective of me and is always asking me if I'm OK. I haven't forgotten him trying to provide for me by feeding me his snickers bars when I thought the school was going to try to drug us or something.

Speaking of Zack, since this Christmas month began and people started talking about going home for the holidays, he's been acting edgy of late. He's not talking about going home, and when I asked how he was getting there (he lives in Ontario somewhere near Ottawa or something) he just suddenly packed up his things and left the library. All I said was, "are your parents coming to pick you up?" and whoosh, he was gone. I looked at Sally as if to say, "what did I do wrong?" and she just shrugged and went back to her homework.

Homework. Homework. Homework.

We have so many bloody assignments due at the moment that the last thing I want to think about is the math's test looming up. Maybe I'll pull a Zack and tear up the library. Then they'll give me extra counseling and not make me have to do all these bloody things.

Got an email back from Angie this morning. She told me to stop with the conspiracy theories and just concentrate on getting well again. I never noticed this before, but I'm starting to realize that my own best friend may think her best friend has gone insane. Now that really makes me feel better...

===

05/ 12/ 00

Dear Diary,

Yesterday Zack didn't want to talk to Peter or myself. At breakfast when I asked him if he was all right, he ignored me and went off to class early. Then at recess when Peter asked him, he ignored him too. So last night after dinner when nearly everyone else was studying in the library, I knocked on his door to see if he wanted to talk. He seemed surprised to see me, but he let me in.

It's the first time I've seen Zacks' room actually. It smelled just like a guy's room, a little bit like a combination of dirty laundry and aftershave (I always thought Marks' room stunk because I think there was rotting food in there too!). Zack shoved his laundry off the bed and asked if I wanted to sit down, so I did. I noticed there were no books out on his desk or anything, and I wondered how much studying he was getting done.

"Where's your homework?" I asked him.

He looked like I'd just caught him with his hand in the money jar or something. "I haven't done it."

"What about your history assignment? It's due tomorrow!" I reminded him.

"I know... I just.." he faltered.

"And we're supposed to be studying for the biology test at the end of this week." I said again. I know I sounded like Maya right then, but I was worried about him.

"Is this why you came? To bug me about homework?" he asked me.

"No, I came to see if I can help you." I said. "What's bothering you?"

"Nothing, why can't people just leave me alone?" he growled and turned his back to me by looking out his window.

"What is this? 'The Young and The Restless'?" I teased him and stood up, then put on a mock accent; "Victor, I love you!" then another mock voice, "No Ashley, I love you!" and I turned my back to him on one side, then I turned my back to him on the other side. I made him laugh, and I kept at it. "People will never understand you like I do, Victor." "I understand you too Ashley."

"You know what's really scary, is that you know their names." Zack fell on his bed, chuckling.

"You know what's even scarier? You know that I know the names on that soap opera!" I teased him. "So how would you know that the names are correct?"

"Oh shut up. My Gran watched it when she used to mind me." he tickled me.

"And you know what's even scarier than scarier? That we even remembered -" I started.

"Their names!" Zack finished and we laughed harder.

"And what you saw Ashley and Victor doing when you were like four or something, if you turned on the TV now, they'd probably still be doing it. Or even better, I loved it when Victor's daughter Victoria grew up 10 years in like, 6 months!" then I impersonated another character.

Suddenly Zack grabbed me and pulled me down onto the bed with him and he kept tickling me. My jumper was riding up with all the wrestling around as I tried to get off the bed. Then Zack took my actions as play fighting.

"No, hang on, hang on... HANG ON!!"

His hand had accidentally, or so I thought, grabbed my breast, but then his other hand grabbed the crotch area of my jeans as his lips tried to plant themselves on mine... and that was it.

"HANG ON ZACK!"

I jumped off the bed as fast as I could and grabbed the door handle to leave.

"Sorry! Sorry Elisha! I am so sorry Elisha, please don't go..." he instantly got up too, looking like a kicked puppy or something.

I have to admit Diary, my heart was pounding and for a moment there I had actually liked what nearly happened on his bed... but I didn't know if I wanted to be more than friends with him, which staying in that room with him then would probably mean.

"I better go." I quickly left.

I nearly went to the library to find Sally, but I decided to go back to my room instead. I think I was in shock. I tried sitting back at my desk and picking up my Biology textbook, but the words just seemed to blur together. I ended up just sitting there for half an hour, spinning on my chair.

I felt confused. I had always thought of Zack as a friend, you know. But now I liked what nearly happened... I even started daydreaming about what might have happened if I had stayed in his room! I didn't know what to do, so I went to bed.

When I woke up this morning, there was a note under my door. It was from Zack,

Elisha,

Sorry about last night, I promise it won't happen again if you don't want it to. I know you're still recovering so I will keep my distance until you want me too. I didn't mean for last night to happen. I love you so much that it sometimes hurts me inside and I make a mistake. Please don't be angry with me, I would hate it if we stopped being friends as well.

I think it's kind of sweet that he wrote me a sorry note. So I decided not to hold a grudge, and when I saw him for breakfast in the Caf, I still sat with him and Sally. Then we three sat together in class afterwards.

It's kind of a relief having a good friend like Sally who gets along with Zack as well. Sometimes I use her as a third wheel, or a 'chaperone' I admit so I don't have to be alone all the time with Zack. But since the three of us get along so well, we're just friends hanging out. So I hope I'm not giving out any confusing vibes to Zack whether I'm interested or not.

==

TO: angiepevensie@ihug.com.au

FROM: ebaker_hamiltons@evers.com

SUBJECT: I'll be home for two weeks in nearly a week!

DATE: 10/ 12/ 00

It's official! I talked to Dad this evening and the tickets have been bought. I'm flying home on the 17th! I'll arrive sometime in the evening of the 18th. Dad will be picking me up from the airport, if you wanna come as well.

I can't wait! I'm so excited! And I found out that my Uncle Peter and Aunt Gabby with my cousins Tina and Jenny will be spending Christmas with us! So will Grandma! She'll be driving with Uncle Peter up from Wollongong. And Mark and his new girlfriend Patrice will be there. Wow, those two have only just moved in together and she's already doing a family Christmas with us, that's pretty serious, huh?

I think my excitement has pissed off Nelson some how. I came back from Nell's office after talking to Dad on the phone and I was jumping around when I was telling Sally. Nelson then walked past us, so I grabbed her and told her too. Then she gave me a dirty look and walked off! So I knocked on her door to see what was wrong, and she ignored me. Sally told me not to bother, but I felt bad. If I did something wrong, I want to know.

Then Pat, with his door open, as usual, speaks up.

"So, you're going home?" Pat asks me.

"Yes." I said coldly, not wanting to talk to him.

"Nelson isn't, just like a couple of other kids here who aren't. You might be fortunate enough to go home to a loving family, but some other kids here aren't." then he closed his door on me. It's the first time he's ever closed his door when he wasn't changing clothes or sleeping. It looks like I pissed off more than one person tonight.

Sally and I just looked at each other, and she shrugged. "Come on, lets go to the library and finish up our Drama Journals."

Then just as we were leaving, Zack opened his door and saw us with our coats and bags and asked us where we were going.

"Just to the library." we told him, and he said he'd come too and grabbed his stuff and we left.

When we were walking across the oval we told him what happened with Pat and Nelson. Zack was quiet and didn't reply. Then Sally asked him again if he was going to be picked up by his parents, or how he was getting home.

"I'm not." he said flatly.

"But you live in Canada, right?" I asked confused.

"I turn 16 in two weeks, that means I'll be legally allowed to leave home. I'll never have to step one foot in that place again." Zack stated.

Sally and I were surprised. I mean, we knew he hated something about his parents, but I didn't know how severe it was. I knew he was here at Hamilton's on scholarship. But if he's left home on bad terms, who sends him money to finance our trips to the movies or Diner on 'Brown Day' weekends?

So we dropped the subject and just went to the library to actually do our homework for a change, with very little talking and mucking around.

You know how I mentioned we were going to do a play called MacBeth? Well, with so little people in our year we had to perform just small tableaus from the play instead of putting on the whole thing. To be honest, I was relieved. The only people who saw us perform were each other and

some of the teachers who came for a look. I was worried
that we might have to had to perform in front of the
school, but thankfully we didn't. But just like our Drama
class back home, we had to keep a Drama Journal.

Now in just one night I had to remember and bull shit my
way through twenty entries when I was supposed to be
writing them down for homework through out the term. Oh
well. Isn't it nice to know I still haven't learned my
lesson after so many detentions with you for not doing our
homework? Anyway, reporting all those lunch times to the
teachers staff room always gave us that chance to
eavesdrop on the teachers and student gossip, hey?

I wonder if this thing with Zack, with whatever bad
happened to him and his hate for his parents are the same
thing? I guess they would be, wouldn't they? I wish I knew
what it was. And I wonder why Nelson and Pat won't be
going home? I think Nelson once lived on the streets at
one stage of her life. Was it when she was nearly sent to
juvenile hall just before she came here?

===

15/ 10/ 00

Dear Diary,

I met Zack's parents last night in a way I guess you could say was 'not in the best circumstances', not for Zack anyway. But I guess I know now what the secret he's been hiding. And it's not a very nice one.

After our last class, which was Art, Dr. Knight came to meet Zack just as we were about to leave and head towards the Caf. She asked him to come with her to Professor Hamilton's office. He looked pretty surprised at this, I think he was worried that he failed badly on one of his exams or something.

So Sally and I went to the Caf with out him. Then afterwards, when we were about to go to the library to do our homework, Nell came and found me. She told me I had to come with her to Professor Hamilton's office too. Now I was worried about what I had done wrong!

My heart started pounding and I felt really nervous.

When we were outside of the building, Nell walked closely beside me and started to talk to me very quietly, so no passing students could hear us.

"Zack's parents are here to see why Zack doesn't want to come home for Christmas. We think it would be a good idea if you're there. I think he needs your support right now." She said to me.

"Really?" I asked, shivering. "What can I do?" I felt a little relieved it wasn't about my test scores or something, but now I was worried about this instead. I didn't know what they expected me to do to help him.

"Just be there for him." Nell put her arm about me, noticing my hands were shaking a little. "It will be all right. We're going to do everything we can to help Zack, but your presence will help him even more, OK?"

"OK." I said.

So we went inside Alpha building, up the three flights of stairs to Hamilton's office, and even before we went entered I could hear yelling going on. This made me hesitate before going in, and Nell could sense it. She gave me her usual big comforting grin, squeezed my shoulder, then opened the door to let me in.

As soon as I walked in and Zack saw me, I could see he looked relieved to see me. He was standing between Professor Hamilton and Dr. Knight as these two strange older man and woman stood across from them. I guessed they were his parents.

"You can't just kidnap him like this!" the man took a step closer to Hamilton in a confrontational kind of way.

"Zack will be of legal age to leave home in one week. It is his decision that he doesn't want to come home for Christmas." Hamilton replied in his customary, calm way.

"You're brainwashing your students! I'll call the police! I'll contact the Board of Education!" his father ranted and raved.

"Call the police? Yes, you do that. What a good idea. I'm sure they would like to know the reason why Zack doesn't want to come home." Dr. Knight said coldly. I'd never seen her angry before, and she had her arm about Zack in a protective manner. It was kind of like the same way Nell was with me.

"And what do you mean by that?" Zack's father turned on her next.

Zack's mother turned and looked at me for a moment, then back to her son.

"Zack, honey. We don't understand this. We sent you to this school because we thought it was what you wanted. Are you punishing us?" his mother asked him tearfully.

"You know why I want to stay here!" Zack yelled at her.

"No I don't!" she cried, and her husband put his arm around her.

"I hope you're proud of yourself Hamilton, for breaking up our family." The father glared at the principal.

"With your kind of family, we feel very proud, actually." Dr. Knight glared at him. "It was just a perk of the job."

I think Dr. Knight was going to say more, but Hamilton put his hand on her shoulder in a nice way to tell her to lay off for the moment.

"In OUR kind of family?" the father spat back at her. "I beg your pardon! What insinuations are you trying to make here? We did everything for our son! We gave everything we could to him!"

"Yes, but we won't go into too much detail about HOW you gave it, will we Mr. Reece? Otherwise the topic of the police might have to come up again." Dr. Knight said in a snide manner.

Zack's face went bright red and he was staring at the floor. He was making sideways glances at me, and I wonder if he was wishing I wasn't here now. Hamilton saw this and redirected the conversation.

"Mr. and Mrs. Reece, we understand Zack has some very good reasons why he doesn't wish to return to your home. He has fit into our school very well and made some very good friends. His grades are steadily climbing and he has come to feel at home here at Hamilton's. We are fully prepared to extend his scholarship for the next two years as well as offer some income support for miscellaneous expenditure. After

Wednesday next week, if Zack does not wish any further contact with you, we can legally arrange it."

"The hell you can! Zack! How can you just stand there and let this man talk like this to us?!" Mr. Reece turned red as well, but it wasn't with embarrassment.

Nell left my side now and walked towards Zack. She positioned herself directly in the middle between Zack and his parents and she spoke to him in a warm, comforting voice. "I can imagine that this moment is very uncomfortable for you right now Zack. In fact, it's downright horrible. This is something that the nightmares have been about, haven't they?"

Zack couldn't look at her, and I saw now that he was crying. He was trying not to shudder as the tears started to fall down his red face. He looked so vulnerable I wanted to run up and hug him and protect him some how.

"What you say, here and now, doesn't have to leave this office. No-one has to know if you don't want them to know. You can ask Elisha to leave if you would like, and she won't be offended. But she does want to help, and so do we. You want everyone to know, don't you Zack? It's what's been pent up in you for so long, that occasionally it escapes and you lose control, isn't that right?" Nell kept talking in a soothing voice. "We're here for you. We will protect you. You are safe now. You are safe now. Look at Elisha. She's here for you. She's your friend and she wants to help you. We're all here for you Zack."

"No! Shut up! Just shut up! Stop it! How can you? How could you? How could you!"

For a moment then I think we all thought he was yelling at Nell, when suddenly he pushed Nell aside and confronted his father and mother.

"You - you - you used me! You abused me! You fucking abused me!"

His father looked flabbergasted as his mother looked horrified.

"Zack..." His father began but Zack shut him up.

"You touched me! You touched me in ways that weren't allowed! I found out! I went to school one day and they did a lecture on sexual assault and child abuse! And what they said... the things you weren't allowed to do... you were doing them! To me! I'm your son! You're supposed to protect me! You hurt me!"

"Zack, what are you talking about?" Mr. Reece turned white as his mother began to cry harder.

"Zack, please, just come home and we'll talk about all of this..." his mother reached out for him but he backed away from her.

"I tried to tell you! I tried to talk to you! You wouldn't listen!" he yelled at her next. "All those camping trips, all those presents, all those holidays by the lake... the way you kept telling me you loved me, that I was 'your' boy, 'your' boy! I'm not 'your' fucking boy anymore! You can't touch me anymore! You can't do those things to me anymore!" Zack exploded at them.

Then suddenly he looked like he was about to lunge at his father with his fists outstretched, when Professor Hamilton stopped him and pulled him back.

I felt repulsion, or I think it was repulsion. It was the strongest feeling of disgust and hate I had ever realized, and it was directed towards the strange man and his wife who had molested my friend. And I felt powerless to stop all of this from happening, because I could see that this was hurting Zack even more.

"It's OK, Zack, it's OK. He can't hurt you anymore." Professor Hamilton held him with Nell.

"I suggest you leave now and pray that you don't have the police knock on your door in the next few weeks, or even the next few months. Don't contact Zack again, or legal proceedings against you will follow. There's the door, just be careful you don't slip over and fall on your asses on the way out, the steps are quite icy at the moment." Dr. Knight walked over to where I was still standing and opened the door to let them out.

"Zack... please." His mother was bawling her eyes out, but his father, now very quiet and not meeting any of our eyes, escorted her out.

The man who molested my friend walked right by me and all I could do was glare at him, and I'm not even sure if he even saw that, since he was now trying not to look at anyone.

Dr. Knight followed behind them, I guess to make sure that they left with out any more disruptions.

Zack collapsed into an emotional heap onto the floor, with both Nell and Hamilton kneeling beside him now.

"I meant what I said before Zack, you're safe here. You don't have to worry about any sort of contact with your parents again if you do not wish it. You can stay here at the College as long as you need to, but if you decide to leave, we can arrange something else for you too. Don't worry about your future. You will be taken care of." Professor Hamilton said in a serious tone of voice, which kind of surprised me. I've only heard him use this tone of voice once before, and it was when he caught Peter that night with the drugs.

Then Hamilton got up and crossed over to me. "I think we should let Zack use this time alone with Nell to help go over the issues that were raised today. So how about you go over to Zack and tell him you'll catch up with him later."

"OK." I said, still feeling nervous. I guess I was wired from all the emotion that had been flying around the room. So I did what I was told and I went over and knelt down and said as nicely as I could. "Hey Zack, I'll see you later in the Dorms, OK?"

"No, don't go." He grabbed me and hugged me. Really tightly too, it almost hurt.

"I'm not going anywhere. I'm just giving you and Nell some time to talk. I'm going to be in my room back at the dorms, waiting for you, OK?" I squeezed him back.

"OK." He sniffed and wiped his eyes, trying to stop crying. He hadn't let go of me yet, and he looked at me with still that vulnerable expression that made me want to hug him back even more.

I kissed his cheek, to his surprise, then I quickly got up and left.

To my further surprise Professor Hamilton then escorted me out of the building.

"Thank you Elisha. We appreciate what you just helped us do in there." Professor Hamilton said to me.

"But I didn't do anything." I said back, confused. "All I did was stand there. And I wasn't even there for very long."

"You let us use you as emotional back up for Zack in there. You showed your support for him. Your presence in that room helped him in a way we couldn't." Hamilton told me.

"Really?" I asked him.

"Zack has never spoken before about what had happened to him, it was only until this day that his teachers and counselor could confirm their suspicions. It was with your help that Zack could finally confront his past and change his future. That's why I think what you did in my office was an exceptional thing to do."

He smiled kindly to me as he opened the main door of the entranceway.

Now it was my turn to be let out. So I crossed the snow covered oval and went inside Beta building. My head was spinning with what just happened in that short 20 minutes of finding out somebody's darkest secret that they tried to hide. But I'm not ever going to tell anyone else about it. I think I'll leave that to Zack to decide.

As I was walking down the hallway to my room, Sally had her door open and when she saw me she popped her head out. "There you are. What was the emergency in Hamilton's office?"

"I'm sorry, I can't talk right now. But can I ask you a favor?"

"Sure." She said in surprise.

"I'm gonna sit in my room and wait for Zack. But could you please bring me back a plate of food from the Caf after dinner?"

"Sure." She nodded.

I unlocked my door and went inside my room to wait.

===

17/ 12/ 00

Dear Diary,

Zack did come to my room that night after talking to Nell in Hamilton's office. His face was red from crying and I think he wanted to hide from Peter in my room. He had been talking to Nell for two hours, while I had been waiting. I received a knock on my door from Peter, wondering where Zack was.

"So, do you know what's wrong?" Peter asked me.

"What do you mean?" I played dumb.

"Why he and you were sent to Hamilton's office!" he rolled his eyes at me.

"Oh, we were just telling his parents to get stuffed," now I tried to shrug it off.

"Brilliant." He chuckled. Then he leant in closely to ask me quietly, "so, did you find out what was up with him?"

I thought this was really nice of Peter to be concerned over his friend, but it wasn't really my secret to share. So the actress/liar in me replied, "not really. I think it's just over worrying about going home, which he doesn't have to anymore." I think my acting/lying needs more practice, because I sensed he didn't believe me but he left it at that.

"When you see him, tell him I'm looking for him, OK?"

"Sure." I shrugged, then closed my door on him dismissively.

An hour later Sally came and knocked on my door with a plate of food from the Caf, which I gratefully accepted, and then I closed my door on her too, apologetically though.

After I'd eaten, I turned my computer on. But I couldn't think properly enough to do my Astronomy assignment. So I did what was soon becoming an art form - spinning on my chair and listening to music. Then I heard a third knock on my door and I knew it was Zack.

As I let him in, Pat sitting at his desk in his room opposite to mine, gave us a good stare. He was probably wondering why, or trying to guess why, we were acting so secretly when I quickly let him in then instantly shut my door again. We probably looked a bit suss.

"Are you OK?" was all I could say as he sat on my bed.

"I don't know." He mumbled. Then he looked at me with that vulnerable look on his face again. "I was hoping you would never find out."

"Why?"

"So you wouldn't think I'm a freak." He looked at the floor.

"You're not a freak!" I tried to laugh it off, but it didn't cheer him up so I stopped. I sat beside him and held his hand, and I tried to put it in the most politically correct term I could think of. "It's not your fault. Your father is the sick fuck!"

"So am I!" he pulled his hand back and put the both of them over his face.

"Why? No you're not! Why do you say that?" I put my arm around his shoulders, trying to be sympathetic.

"Because until I met you... I... I can't say it." He violently shook his head and shrugged off my arm.

"What?"

"Until I met you I thought I was gay!"

I tried not to laugh and covered my mouth with my hands.
"Why?" I ended up letting the giggle out. "There wouldn't be anything wrong if you were gay!"

"But I didn't want to do to any thing with a girl that was being done to me..."

"Zack, you shouldn't feel that way. You should never feel that what was done to you, you should do to someone else." I turned serious again.

"But I do!"

"Why?"

"I want to do those things to you... I want to touch you!" he turned to me. Suddenly he was blurting out all these things that I didn't think I wanted to hear. "I've never been interested in girls before. I had a fake girlfriend back at my old school, but all we did was kiss on the cheek and hold hands. But I want to kiss you all the time, hold you all the time, and to touch you... please let me touch you!"

Then he grabbed me again! And he tried to kiss me! I swear to God that I didn't want to be mean and hurt him even more, but I pushed him away and jumped off the bed. Plainly put, I panicked.

"Zack! Remember your letter that you wrote to me? I think you should remember it right now!"

"We don't have to go all the way! But can't we even kiss?"

"Zack... I don't even know if I feel that way about you..." I squirmed, trying to find the right words.

"We'll try it now." He stood up in front of me. "I'll kiss you and you can tell me if you feel something."

"Really? Right now? Can't we just start off slowly or something? Like a date?" Suddenly I felt really nervous and I think my whole body was shaking.

"We've already been on a date."

"When?"

"The movies, remember?"

"That was a date? I thought that was just hanging out!" Now my hands grew really sweaty.

"We'll try it right now, OK?" He leaned in towards me, but I ducked away.

"Sorry! Sorry! I wasn't ready!" My face was burning and I think I was bright red. Great, at that moment I was probably a bright red, shaking, sweating, ugly thing.

"OK, how about now?" this time he cupped my face (in romance novels they call it cupping - but I think in reality the guy only does this so he won't miss this time) and he put his lips on mine. He started off gently, then his lips parted mine, then he stuck his tongue in, but not in a gross way, but a shy, little way.

This was my first real kiss! I can't wait to tell Angela! My first real kiss and it's with a great looking guy! Sure, I mean, he's a little fucked up from a messy childhood... but... And I didn't even know if I was doing it right, there was no romantic music going in the background like in the movies, and my Trance mix CD had finished playing. I guess Zack thought that it was working, because then it felt like he had his whole tongue in my mouth and his hands started grabbing my breasts!

"OK! That's enough." I pulled away.

"Well?" he looked at me hopeful.

"The first part was good, but then you..." I didn't know how to say it. "Can we stay friends a little longer?"

I don't know if he was angry or hurt, or both. But he didn't stay in my room much longer to tell me. His face went red again and he opened my door and he left with his head down. And that was a couple of nights ago, he hasn't said much to me since either.

Bugger.

===

(THE FOLLOWING NOTE WAS WRITTEN BY ELISHA BAKER TO ZACKERY REECE THE MORNING OF HER DEPARTURE FROM THE COLLEGE FOR CHRISTMAS HOLLIDAYS)

Dear Zack,

Please don't be angry with me about last night. I don't think you're a freak. I'm trying to be your friend and help you. I know something bad happened to you when you were little and it's made you confused now. I want to help you and be there for you. It's just that sometimes I get a little freaked out and want to take things slowly, OK?

Have fun over the holidays, and I've written down my email address on the back of this piece of paper in case you want to email me.

===

TO: ebaker@yowser.com.au

FROM: zreece_hamiltons@evers.com

SUBJECT: How's it going?

DATE: 23/ 12/ 00

Hi Elisha,

How's the family gathering going? How's your Dad? Do you like your brothers' new girlfriend? Have you seen all your old school friends?

It's been snowing really heavily the past couple of days. We had a blizzard last night and this morning they've had a snowplough clearing the roads. It was cool! We nearly got blown away just going to dinner in the Caf! It's really thick on the ground. Nelson kept swearing as the snow was knee deep and she fell over getting to breakfast this morning. She says hello by the way.

All the teachers are still here. They've been trying to keep us busy with all these extra-curricular activities, like self-defense classes, art classes, music classes, quiz nights… but Nelson and Peter haven't been in to anything much of what they've offered, except the self-defense classes. Nelson and Pete seem to have stopped fighting for the moment and have been downloading music off the net of early 80's English punk rock bands and stuff.

Pat came into Pete's room last night when we were hanging out and Nelson told him to f**k off. He came in, as he said to 'see if we're doing it right' as sometimes it can save as a corrupted file, but Nelson didn't want his help. Then when she wasn't looking, Peter nodded and winked at Pat as if to say, 'check back later'.

It's a lot quieter here with half the school missing. I miss you and Sally not being your loud and happy selves to liven the place up a bit. This place is a lot more boring, especially when you're stuck with people who only want to smoke and hang out in the dorms. Maya's still here, did you know? I'm even tempted to go and see if I can be on her and Raj's team for the quiz night tonight. That's how bad it is here. But I guess your having a party where you are right now with all your old school buddies, right? Well, I better go. I can hear Nelson start to get loud again, I think she and Pete are about to get into another fight.

I miss you.

===

TO: zreece_hamiltons@evers.com

FROM: ebaker@yowser.com.au

SUBJECT: Sunny Christmas

DATE: 24/ 12/ 00

Hi Zack,

Gees it sounds cold there at the moment. But I think I must have been slowly adjusting to Canadian weather coz right now I'm finding it really hot here. Patrice, Mark's girlfriend, teased me how white I looked when I put on my singlet and shorts when I got home from the airport. So yesterday arvo I went over to Angela's to see her and we sunbaked in her back yard by her pool. Dad told me to take the sunscreen, which I did just to get him off my back, but I didn't wear it. Now I'm really sunburnt and he told me off for it. Now Patrice is laughing at me for looking like a big tomato when she put moisturizer on my burnt shoulders. Can't win, can I?

Dad hasn't changed. I can tell he's trying to make the effort to be nicer and act chatty and friendly, especially around our guests, but he's still the same underneath. He took me shopping and bought me heaps of new summer clothing and then took me out to a nice lunch and we sat by Nepean river and ate it. But then he snapped at me last night over the dishes and this morning he bit my head off for not making my bed.

At least Aunt Gabby and Uncle Peter and my cousins Tina and Jennifer have been nice and easy going. It's great to see them again. They arrived yesterday afternoon from Wollongong. They asked me heaps of questions about Hamilton's and Canada and stuff, like they're really interested. My cousin Jennifer is sharing my room with me, and last night I told her about the ghosts. I even freaked her out! She told me to shut up coz I was giving her goose bumps! Jennifer and I used to be pretty close when we were growing up. I see her nearly every Christmas and we always have fun. I think I'll email her too when I come back to school.

I haven't really seen my old school friends yet, only Angela at the moment. Angela says it's because half of them are on holidays, but what about the other half? I wonder if they even know I'm back in the country? Believe it or not, I'm actually missing Hamilton's a bit. I can't wait to get away from Dad again and have some independence… where Miss Inez doesn't care if we make our beds or not, or how late we stay up, or even if our rooms are messy.

==

30/ 12/ 00

Dear Diary,

It's been weird being back home again. Dad is trying to be nice and easy going. He is letting Mark and his girlfriend Patrice sleep in the same bed in Mark's room, even though I know he secretly doesn't approve. He even took me shopping yesterday to get some new summer clothes. But last night he still bit my head off for not washing up something properly after dinner. I feel like every time I let my guard down and start to relax around him, he suddenly yells at me for something. At least he can't really ground me like he used to do all the time coz I'm not here long enough for it.

I can't even relax around Angela properly either. She was there to meet me at the airport, which was nice, but all I kept hearing was about was what she's been up to with the ole gang at school who I haven't seen yet. I was given the goss on who's going out with who, who's broken up with who and blah blah blah. But I get the impression none of my old friends has really asked about me and that they don't care that I'm back in the country. I suggested that maybe we could all meet up for a movie night or something, and then Angela gave this weird, dead-end answer that half the people are away on holidays. Well, what about the other half? Can't I catch up with them as well? I even called one of my old friends up on the phone last night to say hallo. She sounded so shocked to hear from me, it's almost like she was getting a call from the dead or something! We didn't talk long, she said she had to go coz her dinner was ready or something. She said in this really vague way, "oh we should catch up before you go back", but she didn't say when or where, so I guess I shouldn't hold my breath and wait for her call.

I feel like I am dead in this place. Maybe my old friends don't want to be associated with the freak who tried to kill herself and was sent away. Maybe Angela's even ashamed of me, and doesn't want to be seen with me. So far it's just been hanging out at my place or hers. Even her Mum has been acting weird around me. Her Mum used to be really nice and crack jokes with us all the time, but now...

So since Christmas Day I haven't called Angela and she hasn't called me. But Aunt Gabby and Uncle Peter and my cousins Jennifer and Tina have been staying with us which has been pretty good. It's cool hanging out with Jennifer again, we never have a problem catching up when we see each other every Christmas. She's been sharing my room with me. I told her about the ghosts we saw at College one night, and she didn't disbelieve me like Angela did, but she did tell me to shut up because I gave her goose-bumps!

Aunt Gabby, Uncle Peter, Tina and Jennifer have to drive back to Wollongong tomorrow. I wish they were spending New Years with us, but they say they can't. So Dad, Mark, and Mark's girlfriend Patrice and I are going into the city to see the fireworks this year. That should be pretty cool. Then I fly back to Hamilton's two days after that, and to be honest I'm looking forward to going back. I miss Zack and Sally and Nelson. I miss my independence. I miss talking Nell.

==

TO: ebaker@yowser.com.au
FROM: s_parson@snailmail.com
SUBJECT: HAPPY NEW YEAR!!
DATE: 01/ 01/ 01

Hi Elisha,

Just thought I'd drop a quick note, since I'm going to see you again in only a couple more days! Anyways… HAPPY NEW YEAR! Sorry I haven't written sooner, had lots of family commitments but you know how it is. Having a good time? I've been pretty busy catching up with all the rells. But you'll be please to know I got plenty more DVD's for you to watch when I get back! It's bloody freezing here in Glasgow, but I suppose you're having a ball on a beach somewhere in Oz, eh? Catch you soon sweetie darling!

p.s. isn't good to get away from all that supernatural nonsense even if it is for a little while?

==

07/ 01/ 01

Dear Diary,

Man, it's good to be back at Hamilton's. Zack was so pleased to see me, that when I was getting off the minibus, he raced outside and hugged me and picked me up and swung me around! He insisted on carrying my suitcase for me to my room and kept asking me if I had a good time.

"Not really." I shrugged, not wanting to talk about it.

I said hallo to Nelson who was in her room reading a book. She seemed a bit blasé about me being back, so I continued on to my room. Zack followed me in and told me not to worry. He said that when I was gone that she said she did miss me. Then Nelson poked her head in and asked if I had any cigarettes on me and if I wanted to go for one. Zack let out this really loud moan and banged his head on my door! I guess he wasn't exaggerating in his email.

Sally came into my room with her arms full of DVD's to show me that she got for Chrissie. Then I opened my suitcase and showed her my videos and DVD's that I brought back too. We were arranging a swop & borrow when Peter then came into my room. He closed my door so Pat couldn't hear us from his room, then he started with; "So, who wants to know what we found out while you were away?"

"OK, what?" I ask him.

"On Christmas Eve before curfew we borrowed the electromagnetic field detector from the science lab." Zack told me.

"The electromagnetic field detector?" Sally gave them a funny look. "What do you want that for?"

I immediately guessed. "So they can scan for ghosts with it."

"Yep." Peter nodded.

"Ghosts leave an electromagnetic field?" Sally looked at us as if we were nuts.

"Kind of, they can generate one. One book I read while you were away was that ghosts possibly use portals to move inside our world and out again. These portals usually create an electrostatic charge in the room." Peter continued his lecture.

"It could explain why a Roman Centurion is in Canada." I shrugged in agreement. "Maybe these portals link countries like it links points in time."

"When we scanned the outside window where the lady and the Roman soldier were sighted," Peter told Sally and I, "the readings went off the scale."

"Really?" I asked in surprise.

"Yep. Now all we have to do is try it on Professor Hamilton's office." Nelson stated.

"And how are we going to do that?" Sally laughed at her. "It'll look a bit suspicious!"

"Maybe when they're at dinner?" Nelson shrugged.

"Or when they have a staff meeting. They meet in the teachers lounge in the Delta building every Friday night. Why not then? And it's before curfew, so Alpha building won't be all locked up." Zack suggested.

Peter looked impressed. "Zack, I never knew you could be so devious mate."

"Wait!" Sally objected. I think she was still uncomfortable with all of this. "We should use the process of elimination, just for science's sake. Did you test the electromagnetic fields on any of the other buildings? What if the reading is just coming from the computer labs, or a high electrical reading from something else?"

"Not the readings we got, love! Yeah, we tested the equipment first, we're not complete amateurs! But with the readings we got... the dial went crazy!" Peter laughed at her.

"Look, if you're too scared shitless, don't bother." Nelson sneered at her.

"Would you shut up?! Just because I don't want to get kicked out of this place, you don't have to rib me about it all the time!" Sally snapped back.

To be honest with you diary, I don't want to be kicked out of this place either. Now that I know that home isn't a haven for me and I don't have any real friends back there either. I could definitely see Sally's point. But as I think I mentioned earlier, I am a glutton for punishment. Or maybe it was just a case or morbid curiosity?

===

TO: ebaker_hamiltons@evers.com

FROM: angiepevensie@ihug.com.au

SUBJECT: Thanks a lot!

DATE: 08/ 01/ 01

Thanks a lot for leaving with out saying goodbye! I mean, what happened to you after Christmas? You just stopped calling me and you could have arranged a time to catch up one more time before you left. Thanks Elisha, thanks for letting me know how much our friendship means to you!

Just because I'm not into all of these conspiracy theories and I'm not one of the Lone Gunmen to follow your Mulder around, it doesn't mean that I don't care. And now it's like that you don't care about me or my life either. Everything doesn't evolve around you, you know. You just shut me out because I didn't like you obsessing about this ghost business and I want you to get well again and come home and to stay home.

You've always been like this. As soon as someone does something you don't like you just shut them out. Fine. Shut me out if you want, but just so you know, this isn't healthy and you need to change.

===

09/ 01/ 01

Dear Diary,

Got an email from Angela yesterday. It wasn't a very nice one. It upset me pretty bad.

I don't understand, I mean, if she wasn't acting so distant and unhappy to see me when I was home for the holidays, why is she acting so angry with me for not saying goodbye? Why didn't she even call me? Why was I the one who had to keep calling her all the time?

So I said this in the email I sent back to her.

Nelson noticed I looked a bit upset over dinner last night and asked me what was wrong. So I told her, and she got angry too and said I should just tell her to fuck off. Sally even agreed with Nelson for a change.

But I can't do that. Angela and I have been best friends since we started school together in Yr. 1. We even planned to go to University together!

I just hope this blows over and we can stay friends.

==

TO: jeni_B@goggleyes.com
FROM: ebaker_hamiltons@evers.com
SUBJECT: Plan of action
DATE: 13/ 01/ 01

Hey Cuz!

It was so good catching up with you again over Chrissie. Enjoying your school holls? I bet your going to the beach or pool a lot, huh?

It's freezing here. And apparently it won't even stop snowing until end of Feb - mid March! They have snow plows that clear the roads nearly every day. And you wouldn't believe how many layers of clothes I have to wear! I'm wearing a thermal long sleeved singlet, thermal long johns, jeans, skivvy, woolen turtle necked jumper, leather jacket, woolen mittens and a scarf. Oh yeah, and two pairs of socks! That's when I'm out doors, when I'm indoors no leather jacket or mittens or scarf.

My friends, Nelson, Zack, Sally and Peter all have a good laugh at me sometimes. I mean, sure the buildings are heated, but there are a lot of high ceilings since the buildings are pretty old and I still don't feel warm enough. They say I look like the "Stay-Puff Marshmallow Man" from the movie 'Ghostbusters' with all the layers

I've got on! Since they all come from colder climates they're used to it and wear less than I do. They all tease me that my room is like an oven too, as I have the oil heater constantly on high.

The good thing about this school is that they let you take in cups of coffee or tea or hot chocolate into class with you. So it's not just the teachers who have this luxury. The other day in Math's I sat there in a huddle at the table, still with my scarf, jacket and mittens on, clinging to my mug of hot chocolate to steal the warmth from it. Dr. Knight, my teacher had a chuckle at me and asked if I wanted her to turn up the thermostat.

With all this cold weather, there's not really a lot of people outdoors. Today Dr. Myles with this Mountie from the local RCMP station, were handing out ice skates and supervising students ice skating on the lake. There were only twenty or so people out there, trying it. Zack took me out and tried to teach me the basics, but I got pissed off from falling over so many times that I skated back to the edge and just watched him instead. He and Peter kept trying to knock each other over and pull each other down, so I started throwing snowballs at them! Then we three got told off by Dr. Myles and got kicked off the ice.

Tonight is 'fun night' which means we get to eat junk food and watch movies in either of the two recreation rooms. Peter suggested we use tonight to scan outside Professor Hamilton's office with the electromagnetic field detector as he's going to have to return it soon to the science lab. But Sally kept saying that we should wait until Friday night when we know all the teachers will be in the staff room in Delta building for their weekly meeting. I think she's scared of us getting caught. I think really she's scared of getting kicked out and what her parents would say.

Oh yeah, did I tell you? I guess I didn't. We're going to scan the teachers offices in Alpha building for electromagnetic field readings. With all the weird stuff going on, when I was home for Chrissie, Peter, Zack and Nelson scanned the window where we saw the two ghosts and the readings went off the scale! So we're going to scan Hamilton's office where the blue light and temperature drop came from. Well, not inside his office, coz it's locked, but the outside of it. I'll email you and let you know more.

===

16/01/01

Dear Diary,

Guess what! The readings we got from Professor Hamilton's office were just as high as they were on the second floor window! So tonight, after dinner in the Caf, we all met up in Peter's room to plan our next tactic of investigation.

We all sat on his bed. Well, Nelson, Sally and I did, while Peter and Zack stood up. Peter seems to have taken charge of this whole thing, which I don't really mind. But every time we think he's getting too bossy, at least we know Nelson will put him in his place! LoL!

Anyway, Peter pulled out this small digital camcorder that his parents sent him for Christmas and told us his idea. This Friday night, when the teachers are in their staff meeting, we leave his camera somewhere hidden on the third floor to record the teacher's offices over night. Then Nelson suggested that we should do that too with the window that we've seen the ghosts come and go through on the second floor. Peter said we could do that tomorrow night, when Astronomy finishes, since our classroom is already on that floor where the window is.

To test that the digital camcorder is working, Pete started filming us on his bed. Then in this 'Austin Powers' accent, he asked us to do something naughty! Nelson pretended to stick her tongue in my ear as Sally got all shy and jumped off the bed and threatened to leave. Nelson ignored her as she then pretended to neck me.

I think it's because Sally is really self-conscious about her weight. I mean, she's not fat, but she is a little plump. But she has the most beautiful long, curly blonde hair. I don't know why she's so self-depreciating, I mean, in the renaissance time from what I've read and seen in the pictures, she would have been the attractive one, with Nelson and I the skinny, dark, drowned-rat types.

So anyway, then Zack jumped on the bed between me and Nelson to 'get jiggy with it', and Pete puts down his video camera and jumps on top of Nelson... and then Sally left.

She threw open Peter's door and slammed it shut behind her.

"Stop it! Wait!" I tried to sit up but Zack kept pulling me back down again, I think he thought we were still joking around.

Finally I threw Zack off me and ran after Sally... But she slammed her door on me. Luckily she hadn't locked it, so I opened it and went into her room.

Sally was sitting on her bed, crying. I sat next to her and tried to put my arm around her shoulders, but she shrugged it off immediately. So I just sat beside her, quietly, waiting for her to tell me what was wrong. It couldn't just be a weight issue.

"He likes her, doesn't he?" she sobbed.

"Who?" I asked her.

"Peter."

"You mean Peter likes Nelson?" I asked in surprise. I hadn't thought of it, actually. I had always thought Patrick had a thing for her. "Why? Do you like Peter?" I asked her.

No reply. So I tried to make her feel better. "At least you've never kicked him in the balls." I smiled at her and she let out a laugh. "You've got that going for you. And you're blonde, don't gentlemen prefer blondes?"

"She's a bitch! And guys usually fall for the bitch! Especially the fucked up ones!" she spat out. "And the thin ones! They go for the bitchy, thin, fucked up ones!"

"Look, I can tell you now that Nelson doesn't like Peter that way." I said flatly. "And she's not really a bitch... she's just... up-front."

"That's the politically correct term for bitch."

I sighed. I didn't want to get in the middle of this and I wasn't going to bitch about one friend to another. I've been down that road in the early years of high school. It didn't work out then, in fact, it ended quite badly. So I didn't want to go there again.

"Shhh. Come here." I hugged her to show her my support but I didn't say anything else.

==

TO: jeni_B@goggleyes.com

FROM: ebaker_hamiltons@evers.com

SUBJECT: Results

DATE: 21/ 01/ 01

Well, we have two separate results from two investigations, one you know about. That sounds so 'X-Files', doesn't it? Only we've started calling them the H-Files.

We put Peter's little digital camcorder in the hallway, facing the window last Wednesday night. When we watched for the results, there weren't any. No lights, no people, no nothing. Then Friday night we left the camcorder in the hallway where the teachers offices are… and the results we got from that!

Once we saw that all the teachers were in Delta Building for their staff meeting, with only a few Seniors keeping an eye on things in their place in the Dorms and Library, we got to work.

Peter and Nelson went upstairs to the offices with the camcorder, Sally and I pretended to study in the library to keep an eye on the Senior there and to be a diversionary tactic, and Zack waited on the steps between the two floors, in case Sally and I called out our signal that the Senior was coming and he had to warn the other two upstairs.

They positioned the camcorder on Prof. H's office door, hidden behind a statue of Socrates or whatever famous Greek statue head was standing in the hallway.

Then after breakfast yesterday morning we all waited in Peter's room as Peter went to Alpha building to get his camera back, on the pretext of going to the library and borrowing a book for our history assignment that's due tomorrow.

So anyway, he comes into his room, plugs his camcorder into the computer, and all of our eyes were glued to the monitor.

First of all we didn't see anything. So he made it fast forward for a while. I have to admit, it wasn't a very good picture. It was so dark, we could just barely make out the door frame to the office!

"Wait!" Zack tapped Peter on the shoulder. "Notice how dark the picture is?"

"So? The whole bloody thing is dark!" Peter said.

"Go back 3 minutes." Zack told him, and Peter did.

Then we all saw it. When before you could see the door and the door frame, suddenly it got darker and you could barely make anything out. It was like a light had gone out, or clouds had just blocked out the moonlight.

"I bet the Exit light went out again." Zack announced to everyone.

"So?" Peter shrugged.

"The Exit light isn't supposed to go out. But it was out the night Zack, Sally and I were upstairs in front of Hamilton's office, the night of the Halloween party." I told Peter and Nelson.

"Yeah…" Sally remembered.

"Now play it slowly, like on half speed or something." Zack ordered Peter.

Peter did as he was told and then suddenly everyone started to lean forward even more.

A little light under Hamilton's' office door was glowing, and getting steadily brighter.

"What's the time index?" Nelson asked Peter.

"0333. So it's 3.33 AM." He answered.

"I know 24hour time you know." She retorted.

"I'm sorry, I guess I wasn't sure if you're small town hick brain could handle it." He replied.

"Shut up and watch." Zack quickly put in before the two could go at it.

Then, just as before, the light turned into a brilliant flash, which caused static on the screen for a couple of moments. The static was probably caused by the electrical interference we scanned before. Then there was nothing for a couple more minutes, before the Exit light turned back on.

"Woah… you guys saw all this? What was it like?" Nelson asked Zack, Sally and I, impressed.

"Cold. The temperature dropped just like when we saw that first ghost, and the hair on our skin was standing up." I told her.

"Caused from the electrostatic charge, no doubt." Peter stated, turning to us.

"Shut up and look!" Sally pointed back at the monitor, her eyes wide and her hand then covered her mouth.

Professor Hamilton suddenly appeared from inside his office, as he opened the door to let himself out.

"Shit." Peter breathed.

We all watched, stunned, as he re-locked his office door behind himself, then turned and walked down the hallway and left back down the stairs.

"Was he in there when you guys were up there?" Zack asked Peter.

"Of course not! He was in the staff meeting! You fucking saw that!" Peter said back. "There was no-one in that fucking room when we were outside of it."

"Not unless they like sitting quietly in a dark, locked room for a long time. Look at the time index! It was 8.30 PM when we left that camera there! No-one had a chance to go in with out being on camera!" Nelson said defensively.

"And he just suddenly appears in his own office, and walks out of it. How hard would it be to climb in through his window?" I turned to Zack.

"I couldn't do it." Zack shook his head. "Three floors up and all smooth walls with no edges or cracks to hold onto."

"Well he could have forgotten his keys and had to climb in..." Sally shrugged. "Maybe he used a ladder."

We all just turned and looked at her as if she was the one who was crazy.

"We don't have a ladder on the grounds tall enough. I once asked Pat about it." Peter said flatly.

"Why would you ask about a ladder?" I asked Peter.

"To break into the hospital wing for the pharmaceuticals."
e said plainly.

"What?!" Now we all looked at him as if he were the crazy
one.

"Look, it was my, 'I'm going to try to get kicked out of
this school just like all my other school's' phase." Peter
shrugged like it was just another day in the week of
trying to piss off the parents.

So Jen, that's all of it for now. I tried to remember as
much as I could to tell you. But what's not included is
the bit where Nelson said we should break into Prof. H's
office to have a good look around. Sally freaked when she
said that, and even Zack looked nervous. I know these two
really don't want to get kicked out of Hamilton's, with
Zack he has good reason not to.

I guess I don't really care. Sometimes I still get angry
with the way my Dad just sent me here when I was
unconscious and had no say… I just woke up and I'm here.
But I'm not exactly thrilled at the idea of returning to
my old high school. Not since I've seen some of my
friends' reactions just over my home coming over the
holidays, so I wouldn't want to experience a real return.
Still, there's something inside of me that's egging me on
to know, to find out, to ultimately understand.

==

TO: mbaker@hotmail.com

FROM: ebaker_hamiltons@evers.com

SUBJECT: It's official, we're not insane!

DATE: 22/ 01/ 01

Guess what… we caught on tape one of our teachers
appearing out of nowhere… and it wasn't just me, it was
five of us who saw it.

We put Peter's camcorder in the hallway outside the teachers offices at 8.30 PM and caught Professor Hamilton leaving his office at 3.33 AM. No, he wasn't in his office for that long, in fact, when we put the camera there he wasn't in his office at all. So he managed to get inside of his office without getting recorded on tape, which is on the third floor with no way to climb through the window with no ladder tall enough. And even before he appeared, we recorded the strange flash of light coming from his office!

And you know what they say… the camera doesn't lie!

So we're planning another investigation, but this time this one may be a little more illegal. We're thinking of breaking into Hamilton's office to see what we find there. Peter and Nelson have seen the inside of Hamilton's office before from being sent to see the principal, and they tell me there's a huge filing cabinet in there. Peter is betting that we can find more answers in that filing cabinet, although I'm not completely sure what ghostly business could be kept in there.

We're planning to do it soon, probably next Friday night when the teachers have their weekly staff meeting in another building. Nelson is pretty confident that she can pick the lock, and since Sally's really nervous about this whole thing, we put her on watch. That way she can say that she was just passing by with out getting into trouble since she's so paranoid about getting kicked out.

I doubt that we will get caught, but I thought I'd just let you know. I wonder what punishment they would inflict on us? Expulsion? I'm not thrilled at the idea of going back to live with Dad again, or going back to our old high school. But I want to know what's going on in this place, and why there are so many weird things going on.

Don't worry Mark, I'm not about to inflict you with my presence either, if anything did go wrong. I can see you and Patrice are pretty happy together, alone. I won't crash your party, I promise.

===

27/01/01

I don't know how to say this, or how to write it down. But something extraordinary and almost unbelievable happened on Friday night of the 26th of January, 2001. I say it's ALMOST unbelievable because if anyone else read this they probably wouldn't believe it. But since it's only me, and it happened to me, how can I doubt myself? Everything else I'm doubting... my life, my existence, even my very own reality. And Dad... how could I ever explain this to Dad? Or even Mark or Angela or Jennifer? They would never believe me. The only people who can believe me are the ones going to this very school, because it's happening to them too.

Haunted... how accurate a term. Everything that I had ever known right up until Sunday... the world is round, there are 12 months in a year, man can't travel at light speed... even the very nature of time itself has changed. Not even Death is a constant anymore! I'm still trying to grasp what they said... I'm trying to keep calm, keep my cool, accept what they've told me, and not to shit myself thinking about all this!

I always thought my depression was an isolated thing. When I felt depressed, and I couldn't handle reality anymore, when I even thought the world had changed, and that I was the only one had noticed this, I was right! Well almost right, the people at Hamilton's noticed the same thing, that's why they're here. That's why I'm here, I understand this now.

I used to think Dad was punishing me for sending me here. Now I don't know how to explain it back to Dad, or even if I will explain it, this truth I've been told. I don't think the outside world would understand this. It's almost become an "Us and Them" routine around here. We all know something they don't... and it's something big.

Where to start...? Friday night? Of course. It started Friday night, or rather, it happened on Friday night. Zack, Peter, Nelson, Sally and I broke into Professor Hamilton's office when he was out with all the other teachers in the Delta building for a staff meeting. We watched them go into Delta building and then from the window (the staff room is on the ground floor) we saw them all sit down and start. Even some of the Senior students joined them so we thought they were planning the next school excursion or something.

So then when the coast was clear, we walked across the oval to the Alpha building. At first we pretended we were going to the library to work on our history assignment. Pat was in the library studying with Maya, and then in front of Pat (since he's been acting strangely lately we didn't trust him) Peter said loudly that we should go to the computer lab to download some pictures off this web site for our assignment. So we all 'agreed', but we didn't go to the computer lab, we went up the stairs to the third floor to the teachers' offices.

It was dark with all the lights turned off, but Zack had a torch in his backpack that we used. He shone the light on the door so Nelson could see as she took out these two ragged metal strips and picked the lock. I guess she was an expert since she was nearly sent to jail or juvenile hall or whatever they call it in the states.

"Are you sure there are no alarms?" Zack asked Peter.

"No! How many bloody times do I have to tell you?" Peter shook his head. Peter knew, because remember he was sent to the principals office for the drug bust? I guess we were all pretty nervous, well, Zack, Sally and I definitely were.

When the door opened, we all went inside. Except Sally who was on watch, she went back down the hall a bit to keep an eye on the stairs. She stood at the top of the stairs, looking down, and also listened for anyone coming our way.

Hamilton's office had an antique desk and leather chair, but everything else in it looked pretty modern. It was hard to act stealth like or anything in the huge winter jackets we were wearing. It was cold in there, and I didn't like taking my mittens off. We started checking his shelves and desk draws first, and Zack had a fit over the filing cabinet.

"Damn it! A fucking electronic lock that you need a code! You didn't mention that one!" Zack yelled at Peter in a whisper.

"Move over you amateurs." Nelson came over from the desk and pulled out her strips of metal again.

"Well, you must have been a real cat burglar around your old town!" Peter laughed at her, I think he was impressed. "Do you have a tight suit and a whip?"

"Fuck off and come on your own time! And don't just stand around and watch! There are other things to do!" Nelson snarled at him. I tried not to laugh and took over where she had been looking in the draws.

I didn't find much, just stationery stuff. There was a weird looking calculator in his second draw though, I think it looked like some ultra modern ipod or something. I was about to turn it on and see what was on it when Nelson cracked open the second lock and the draws opened.

All four of us practically jumped on the cabinet. I guess the first things we took out were our files and fought over the torch light so we could read them. I was a little curious to see Zack's file, but he turned away and read his by the moonlight coming in the window. So I did the same with mine.

It seemed pretty basic at first, it had a copy of my last school report and a school photo, and then behind it was a dossier with my personal details like my birthday and Dad's address and Mark's address, and what year Mum died. Then when I turned the next page, there was a psychological report written by Nell. I thought this was a little weird. Aren't doctor/ patient conversations meant to be private? She diagnosed me as suffering depression, well, I knew that one. But then she also adds I have very strong empathic abilities when I decide to use them that can be further trained and honed. Huh? What does that mean?

Then I turned the page and there was another report written by Dr. Knight on my 'struggle to grasp mathematical and physical formulas in the environment around' me but 'as many people with the talent, can understand and see the physics rather than calculate'. Then there was another report by Dr. Miles and then Miss Inez and so on about all my other subjects. Dr. Miles commented how I may have difficulty with calculating the math involved in Astronomy, he is impressed by my 'ability to see'.

My 'ability to see'? That's been mentioned a few times now. What does that mean?

"Hey guys, what does it mean, my 'ability to see'?" I turned around and asked them.

"How the fuck should I know?" Peter snorted. Then he shook his head as he read his file. "What the fuck are they talking about? See the fuck what?"

"It's in my folder too." Nelson slammed hers shut. "I think they've sent us to a funny farm. And we're not the funny ones."

"Oh yeah, they're bloody hilarious." Peter put his file back, and so did Nelson. Then she took out Pats.

"Hey, what are you doing? We can't read Pat's file!" Zack tried to stop her but Nelson got away from him.

"I don't trust the bastard." Nelson opened it up, then she froze again. She completely froze, not because of the cold, but it was like when she froze when we saw that first ghost three months ago.

"What is it?!" We all converged around her and Zack shone the torch down so we could all see.

There was a black and white photo of Patrick that looked like he was much younger, like 13 or something. That wasn't what surprised us, but it was what he was wearing... olden day clothes. Peter quickly turned the next few pages over till we got to his personal dossier. Birth date: 2nd

February, 1918. Parents: Deceased, Father died in First World War, Mother was arrested and hanged for role in the I.R.A.

"Oh my god..." Nelson muttered, before handing the file over to Peter and going to sit down on the desk.

"This must be some kind of joke." Zack shook his head.

"Let's get another file out and see." Peter gave the file to Zack and went back to the filing cabinet. We checked Sally's, it was normal. We checked Maya's, it was fine. We checked Yuichi's, his was OK. Then we checked Soong's...

There was another black and white photo with Soong looking the same age as she is now, but she and her mother were wearing old customary Chinese dress.

"Check the date of birth!" Nelson almost yelled, she had tears in her eyes, like she was about to break down or something.

Birth date: 14th January, 1951

"Raj! Check Raj's date of birth!" I urged.

His file came out next, and his was completely normal.

Then I had a realization. "Check some of the Senior's files!"

We all put our files back into the draw and then opened the next draw down. We handed out five each and immediately started flicking to their date of births.

"1967!"

"Normal one here."

"I have one for 1958!"

"Normal. Normal. Normal. Wait, the next one says 1942!"

We didn't care about being loud any more, we were calling them out by this stage.

"Hey, what's going on here? You guys are being pretty fucking loud!" Sally stuck her head around the door and yelled at us in a whisper.

We all just looked at her, not knowing how to say what was happening.

"Check the teachers." Peter looked at Zack who was standing the closest to the cabinet at that stage.

We all jammed the folders in, not caring if they were in alphabetical order anymore, and we opened the bottom draw.

Zack was rummaging through the files with his torch for a while.

"Hurry up!" Peter knelt over to see what was taking so long.

"I can't find them!" Zack said, he sounded stressed.

"What's going on?" Sally asked me.

"Umm." I tried to start, and I looked at Nelson for help. She turned away and went to go stand by the window again.

"You'll find the folders with the teacher's dates of births in another building. Would you like me to show you?"

The light switched on and we all jumped to see Pat and Professor Hamilton now standing in the doorway!

I was so scared, it was my turn to freeze.

"Stay away!" Peter pointed at Hamilton and ran behind the desk.

"What is this place?" Nelson asked him. "Why have you brought me here? Why me? What the fuck are you people!!" Nelson practically ran over and pushed Hamilton hard in the chest.

But he didn't react to Nelson, instead he said in a softer voice, "I will answer all of your questions. If you come with me to the staff meeting room, I can explain to you there."

"We're not going with you anywhere!" Peter yelled at him.

"What the fuck is going on?!" Sally yelled at all of us.

"They're the ghosts!" Peter pointed accusingly at both Pat and Hamilton.

"What?!" Sally nearly laughed. Then she saw the look on all our faces, and her smile was wiped off. "Are you for real?"

"I am not dead, I am perfectly well. Feel my heart beating..." he took Nelson's hand and put it on his chest again.

But she snatched it back and started backing away from him slowly. "But how old are you? How old are you, can you answer that?"

"I'm 45 years old, and I was born in 1785." He answered her, then looked at all of us. "Pat was born in 1918, and he is turning 17 in two months time. He came here when he was 13 years old."

We all looked at Pat, who was just standing there, almost casually, with his hands in his pockets.

"I told you I came here when I was 15 because that's the usual age students are brought here to Hamilton's. Truth is, I was 13 years old, and I was brought to this school in this decade." Pat announced.

"Why?" I asked. It just came out of my mouth with out me realizing it. I was still in shock.

"Because the truth is, at some stage in all of our futures, we ask Stephen Hamilton to help us, and when to help us. That's how he knew to come and get me just after my mother's hanging, how he knew where to find you when you were hiding on the streets," he looked at Nelson and then he looked at me, "and when to tell your father to come home when you slashed your wrists."

"He came home early?" I uttered. "You told him to leave work early?" this new fact hit me hard. I didn't care if I looked like a whimp, I started crying. Now I know I would have died if my father had come home from work on time... I wasn't sure whether to feel relieved or disappointed. I had always thought that I had done it wrong, but now I knew I had done it the right way. The right way to die...

"There are a lot of facts that I can explain to you tonight. I've summoned a meeting for all sophomore students in the staff meeting room. They're all waiting there now." Hamilton looked at all of us long and hard.

"What, the whole year?" Peter asked him disbelievingly. "What about the whole school?"

"The rest of the school knows." Pat stated. "Well, except most of the Freshmen."

"Oh." I uttered. "So while Nelson and I were ghost hunting and trying to find stuff out, you put us down for it! You already bloody knew!?" I yelled at him! "You fucking bastard!!" (Or so I thought at the time)

"I was trying to put off the hard truth to let you live in happy dreamland till Professor Hamilton saw otherwise." Pat said coolly.

Now I was about to beat his face in when Professor Hamilton put out his arm to stop me and said to the group, "Come on, confrontations can come later when you have more information. You do want to learn the truth now, don't you?"

We all looked at each other. Nelson was the first to make the move and she left the room, followed by Sally, then Peter, and then Zack and myself. Zack put his arm around me, and kept it there as we walked out of the Alpha building and then towards Delta building. He didn't say anything on the way, which I'm glad of. We just walked. I was feeling pretty upset, my feelings of confusion, shock, anger and sadness in the last 10 minutes were taking a while to get over.

We went inside and true to his word, the rest of our classmates were all sitting around the long table in the staff meeting room. The teachers and five of the seniors were standing up around the sides. There was a fire going in the fireplace and the warmth of the room made me feel a little better.

Zack made sure we got to sit together and then he held one of my hands in his lap. I think he was trying to be supportive of me, even though he was going through this too. I thought it was really sweet, and I squeezed his hand back.

"Thank you all for coming. Your teachers and I had initially planned to have this meeting with you at a later stage, such as the beginning of next semester when you reached the next grade. But in light of recent events, and of the many questions now being asked, we thought we should have this out." Hamilton began and he came to stand beside Dr. Knight.

"You were all invited to come here to this college because each of you in this room has a very unique talent that not many other people in this world have. If anybody else in this world had this talent like yourselves, they would be invited to this school too, or would have already been trained here. It is not genetic, and what we have noticed, is that in each century there are no more than a hundred people across the globe that receive it."

Besides Zack, Sally, Nelson, Peter, Pat, Soong and myself, the rest of the table of people started looking pretty confused right then.

"This talent that I am talking of, as some of you may have guessed in their own way, is of being either able to see through or to manipulate time." Hamilton announced.

"What?" Raj had a funny look on his face.

"But that's impossible!" scoffed Brett, the other American in my Math's class.

"Is this going to be our next drama production?" asked Yuichi, confused.

"I am not kidding, nor am I trying to trick you. You have been invited to this college so we can hone your talents and show you what has been taught to us." Hamilton continued. "I was borne in 1785 AD by a colonial family who just acquired land when the United States was only an independent country for 9 years."

"My English family title is Lady Dunmore, I was borne in 1726 to an Aristocratic family, who believed that educating a woman was only to show her status in society." Dr. Knight announced to the room. "I am 39 years old."

"I have no title, my family name is the same, Inez, and I was borne in a Catholic colony in Brazil, 1826." Miss Inez said next. "I am 28 years old."

"I was borne on the 14th of February in 1926, and I am 32 years old." Dr. Myles said plainly.

"Hi everyone. I know this is a little hard to grasp, but to those who don't know me, my name is Nell Kennard and I'm the counselor and nurse here at Hamilton's College. I have the boring birth date of 2nd of July 1971, and I am 29 years old."

"But how...? If they're older, like much older... how can you...?" Peter asked.

"That is what we will also be teaching you in your studies here." Hamilton told us.

"What? How we don't have to age and we can pass up the ole Oil of Olay?" Darianne scoffed and half the table laughed, but it wasn't our half. Pat, Nelson, Peter, Sally, Zack and myself were dead silent.

"What we are going to teach you here at Hamilton's, besides the odd bit of Shakespeare, and some Math's in between, is that time is not a constant. Time is only relevant to whoever experiences it. We will teach you how to see through the layers of time as you would with a reflection in a pond, and for some of you, how you can move through it as you would as if you would walk into a new room, or an old room. Literally." Hamilton said.

Just as he said that last sentence, "as if you would walk into a new room, or an old room," a huge cold chill ran down my spine and made me shudder.

"The hauntings!" I blurted out to the room. "There are hauntings where people walk into a room and see it as it looked a hundred years ago, or two hundred years ago! Is that what you mean? And the hauntings where you see mindless ghosts repeat the same action over and over and over again, like video recordings, is that like it too?"

"Ah, now that's a good question. Yes to the first question, with the second question, that one will come up in one of your classes some day." Hamilton nodded to me.

"So you're going to teach us how to walk into rooms a hundred years in the past?" Peter asked, I'm not sure if he was skeptical, or still in shock. I don't know if he knew either.

"Or two hundred years, or three hundred years, or even five hundred years. But why the past? Why not the future?" Dr. Knight asked the group. "I know I enjoy the future a whole lot better than my past. I can be a doctor and it depends in what country I'm in, I am also treated as an equal."

"So where is the time machine?" Zack asked the teachers.

"You don't need a time machine, man, that's what we're saying." Dr. Myles spoke up. "What we're trying to say, is that this talent is in you already, with no construction required. All you need is a little practice... and it's almost away you go."

"Almost?" Peter now became skeptical.

"We do have a few warnings and caution signs, of course." Miss Inez told him. "Such as it's not always a good idea to tell people who don't have this gift, for the risks involved."

"You mean they try to lock us away?" Abdul, the Arabian guy in my Computer Studies class, said sarcastically.

"That's right. And I can speak from personal experience on how hard it is to try and leave a jail cell when there are no mirrors or glass windows." Dr. Myles chuckled to himself and shared a smile with Hamilton, Knight, Inez and Kennard.

"And if you're thinking about going back and changing events in time, like the sinking of the Titanic, or taking a machine gun with you to the American colonies war of independence... well, that is never recommended and this matter will be discussed in your classes as well." Dr. Knight looked at us as if she just read somebody's mind.

"Trying to avert disasters is not always a good idea. It hardly ever works either." Miss Inez added.

"Why did you mention glass or mirrors? Are they the doorways?" Nelson asked.

"Yes, but before you go charging at any of the windows here on campus, I suggest you get your instruction manuals first. Dr. Knight and Nell here have a lot of experience at stitching cuts and pulling out glass, and it hurts like hell, trust me." Dr. Myles turned around and lifted up his jumper to show us a long scar down his back.

"I can't believe this, I can't fucking believe that you're all sitting here and taking this in!" Abdul suddenly stood up and turned on us all sitting at the table. "This is fucking horseshit! Why are you even listening to this crap?"

"Because it's true Abdul." Pat spoke up.

"How can you fucking prove to me that this shit is true?" Abdul turned on him.

"I don't know, how about I take you back to 1931 when my mother was hanged and just before they dangle her from a fucking rope she can point at me and tell you I'm her fucking loving son!" Pat said angrily.

"It's true Abdul. We just saw the files." Zack said plainly.

"What files?" Maya asked us.

"Files on all of us, in Hamilton's office." Peter said flatly.

"It has all of our birth dates and everything. There are some people here that were borne in the early or middle of this century." I said to Abdul.

"So what? Who cares if who comes from what part of this century. At least that's not the fucked up part! It's better than not saying they were born in 1898 or some shit like that!" Abdul retorted.

"Take a good look at Soong, man. Looks pretty good for a 49 year old, doesn't she? It must be all those secret Chinese herbs and spices, ay?" Peter snapped back at him.

Abdul looked at Soong, then he looked at Peter, then Sally, Nelson, Zack and myself, one by one, to confirm all of this. I think our expressions said it all.

"But why here, why now? Why bring us all to this time frame?" Brett asked Hamilton now.

"Well I was borne in this time frame!" I interrupted. "I was borne in 1984!"

"He meant everyone else, you stupid bitch!" Abdul turned on me next.

"Call her that again, and I'll drown your dirty mouth and face in detergent!" Zack immediately leapt to my defense.

"OK, now we all need to calm down here, people. I know this is a great shock to a lot of you, I felt the same way when Dr. Hamilton first told me. But name calling and threatening violence isn't exactly helping the situation, is it?" Nell stepped forward. Everyone at the table didn't look happy. Aside from the small group of us, some people looked skeptical, like this was a sketch for candid camera, and the rest looked completely shaken.

Nell continued. "Please understand that we know this can be upsetting to all of you, and we are trying to make this transition for you as straightforward and gentle as possible. Remember, you are not alone in this, and that everyone in this room went through this moment, or is going through this moment right now. So if we can talk about this in a calm manner, myself, Dr. Hamilton, and all of your teachers will certainly answer any and all questions that we know you need to ask, because we had to ask them too."

Abdul and Zack still exchanged dangerous looks, but Dr. Hamilton took Abdul's attention away for a moment as he answered Brett's question.

"Now that's a good question Brett. All of us here decided that the turn of the Millennium was a good time in history to train the minds of our students. The educational means of the end of the 20th century aid us with our teaching methods, with the use of computers and other technology. And since a lot of our students come here before there were computers or televisions, we thought this time frame was an excellent gateway. From the millennium onwards, humankind will make even greater steps forward in both technology and space travel. We decided that training your minds at the end of the 20th Century and the beginning of the 21st Century, would enable you to be fully equipped with the knowledge of the past so that it will help you deal with the future."

"So basically, students who come here from time zones where there was hardly any technology, come here and learn our technology. Then they can move into the future if they choose and be better trained with what they find there." Dr. Myles added.

"How many students have come through Hamilton's?" Giselle, the French student, asked.

"So far, since we've started... 399 since 1455 AD when our predecessors began a college such as this." Hamilton answered. "Not all of them at this campus, in Canada, but in schools such as this from all around the world."

"Who were the predecessors?" Darianne questioned, now interested.

"Some historical figures you may have heard of, and others, you would not have heard of." Dr. Hamilton said elusively.

"Come on, can you give us some names?" Peter pried.

All of the teachers exchanged looks, before Dr. Knight answered. "There was one famous man you all probably have heard of... Nostradamus."

"Yeah right..." Abdul just shook his head and rolled his eyes disbelievingly.

"No, it makes sense. In our files it mentioned something about 'seeing'... now this Nostradamus guy was famous for his 'seeing'." I nodded. "And don't forget nearly all of his prophecies about the future were right."

"All except the end of the world one." Maya said dryly, "or is that one going to happen too?"

Professor Hamilton continued to talk in a calm manner while he walked around the table to look at us individually.

"Nostradamus could see through the layers of time, but he didn't have the ability to travel between them. He taught the first of us from his home in France and then those students taught new students, and then those began this college. Leonardo Da Vinci was another. He also could see, but not travel."

"What, you were one of the first?" Maya guessed.

"That's correct." Professor Hamilton answered. "There have always been people like us through out history, but it was only during a certain point in time that many of us came together to form the first of the Circulate."

"Circulate?" Sally asked.

"We disperse and alternate through the rotation of time." Dr. Knight announced.

"That's what you were doing when we saw you that night... dispersing yourself?" Nelson asked her directly.

"That's exactly right Genevieve." Dr. Knight said.

"What night?" Sally asked again, her head turning left and right so fast as she was looking from person to person I wondered if her head was going to snap off soon.

"She was the ghost I saw back in October." Nelson said, almost proudly, as if to say to everyone in the room, 'see I'm not nuts!' and then she gave Pat a filthy look.

"What about the olden day dress? Why were you wearing that?" I asked Dr. Knight next.

"Would you turn up to dinner with your parents who live in the 18th century wearing late 20th Century clothing?" She arched her right eyebrow, amused.

"So your family doesn't know about this?" Maya asked surprised.

"No. They think I'm living with relatives in Scotland. I do visit them once a year though." Dr. Knight smirked.

"Hang on..." I put my hand up. "If you can move through time... and you change clothes and stuff before you go... how are some of you the ages that you are and qualified teachers of 4 subjects and medical doctors and stuff?"

"The gift of moving through the layers of time also comes with the talent of manipulating time around you. When you realize the idea that time is only relative, you can slow it down as well as speed it up internally and externally." Professor Hamilton told me.

"Lets just say that among the staff, we don't celebrate birthdays every year anymore." Miss Inez said quietly, and shared a smile with Dr. Knight.

"There were points in our lives where we individually decided to slow down our aging process. We can't stop time, but we can slow it down internally." Dr. Knight added. "So far, I have lived for what the customary time line would call 200 years."

Our whole year let out a gasp at that and stared from Dr. Knight to each other, trying to digest all of this in.

"Look, you guys, we know what a big shock it is for you, because it was for us as well." One of the Seniors, I think his name is Jack, spoke up at last. I was starting to wonder if they were around for decoration. "But you'll learn that the lessons here are pretty intense because what Professor Hamilton told you tonight, all the teachers here try to prepare you for it. And they're not going to just pat you on the head and send you on your way... those frequent 'excursions' you see us go on... lets just say that they're not all just in this time period."

"So where have they taken you?" Jordon the Egyptian student asked him, still skeptical.

"Egypt 1288 BC, Greece 450 BC, and we're planning the next trip to Rome 53 BC." Jack told her. "They're training us how to Circulate by ourselves by our own free will."

"But what about the glass problem? They didn't have glass in some of those times!" Maya the booknerd exclaimed, who would probably know about this stuff already from studying it somewhere.

"There are other ways to Circulate." Dr. Myles nearly laughed at how worried Maya looked. "But you'll learn that later."

There were more questions and answers, as we stayed in that meeting for over two hours. I can't remember them all now. Perhaps if I wasn't so shocked, afterwards I could have written all of this down. But as we stayed in that room, asking our questions, I think we were all trying to work out what was wanted or expected from us.

When the 'meeting' was announced to be over, we all with Miss Inez in tow, were lead back to the Dorms.

Peter, Zack, Sally, Nelson and I walked back as a group. We were quiet but there was a slight feeling of semi-solidarity. Everyone else in our year who walked back was looking at us strangely now. We should have felt justified at being right, that our suspicions had been correct... but now, all I felt was another pressure had been heaped on my shoulders. I was supposed to be this amazing person when all I felt like was a freak.

We five wandered into the recreation room instead of going straight up the stairs to our rooms so we could talk one more time before the night was over.

"So, do you believe all of that shit?" Peter asked us all.

"Yeah, yeah I do." Nelson stated, not looking at us though.

"It explains a few things." Zack kicked at the floor for a moment, then he looked back at Pete.

"Like what?" I asked him, but I already knew.

"Coming to Hamilton's... it isn't the first time I've seen a ghost. Well, I thought it was a ghost at the time. I guess now it wasn't, it was something in the past that other people didn't see." Zack said honestly.

"Why didn't you say so before?" I asked Zack.

"I bet you've seen stuff in the past, stuff that you haven't told us." Zack replied.

"Yeah..." I said uncomfortably, not wanting to talk about it now. "I wanna go to bed." I said plainly and yawned. I felt physically and emotionally exhausted.

"That's a good idea." Sally now spoke up and instantly turned and left for the staircase.

"We should meet back in my room, yeah? Tomorrow." Peter said.

"I don't know. Maybe in a couple of days." Nelson told him, as we all started for the stairs.

"We should talk about all of this!" he insisted.

"Right now, I'm gonna sleep on it." Nelson said dryly.

Just then she nearly walked into Pat, who had returned and was heading in the same direction as well.

The two glared at each other for a moment, before Nelson turned and kept walking.

"Thanks for trusting us enough, man, for not telling us." Peter said coldly to him as he overtook him going up.

"Would you all have believed me?" he called back as we all hurried past him going up.

When I reached the top floor I went to my own door and unlocked it. Zack was still right behind me. I was tired, after all it was 12 AM now, and I wondered how to ask Zack for some space so I could go to bed.

I looked at him, about to say it, when he must have guessed.

"Can I sleep on the floor? I don't want to be alone tonight." he said.

I looked at him, a little undecided. I think I was nervous he might try something. So far we have been pretty weird, like on-again-off-again in a non-existent romance. What the hell... he is a good friend and he has been nice to me tonight.

"Yeah, sure." I agreed and let him in.

True to his word, he slept on the floor and he stayed on the floor. I had the heater on all night to make sure he didn't get cold since I didn't have any spare blankets. I did give him my pillow though and I put my head on my Pound Purry as a make-shift pillow.

That was last night. Now it's close to 12 AM again and it's time to finish and go to sleep. It's taken me 4 hours to write all this down, and I can't believe how much I remembered of who said what in the teachers meeting room. But I guess it certainly was an unforgettable night.

A night etched in time, my time.

==

28/ 01/ 01

Diary,

Things are changing around the school. Even the people are changing. Everything's changed. From the lessons we're learning to why we are learning them, how we perceive the teachers who are teaching the lessons to us, to even if we want to learn the lessons anymore.

Even Sally has changed. She seems quieter, more reserved, or is that more introverted? The morning after the meeting in the staff room Peter wanted another meeting with all of us to talk about whether we completely believe what they told us. So we all convened in his room again, Sally almost unwillingly.

"So, what do you think? Are they being straight with us or what?" Peter looked at Zack, Nelson, Sally and I.

"It makes sense with what they said to what we've seen." Zack shrugged.

"I believe it." Nelson stated. "Coz last night reminded me of something that happened when I was a kid."

"You still are a kid." I pointed out.

"When I was younger you dick." Nelson rolled her eyes at me. "When I was like 8 or something, I went to the bank with my Mom as she was running errands. I saw a cowboy walk into a crowded bank, pull a rifle on a bank teller, shoot him, then run out of the bank again with a bag full of the goods. Then I realized that I was the only one who just saw this."

"Really? Wow." I said in surprise.

"Yeah, the same shit happened to me when I was younger." Peter said next. "I was sent to my first boarding school when I was 12. It was some Church of England boys' school that was once a monastery that got trashed by Henry the 8th. We had to go to services every Sunday morning. And I saw a monk dangling by his neck at the end of a rope from the church rafters. It didn't take long to realize I was the only kid who saw it."

"Yeah? Well my story is different." Zack told all of us. "I saw a reflection in the window of my Grandma's upstairs spare bedroom of this little girl in old clothes playing dolls. And I saw her pretty regularly, almost the same time of the day, in the afternoon when the sun was setting. You know how when it's darker outside than it is on the inside, and the window becomes almost a mirror? Only I didn't see my own reflection, I saw the little girl's."

"That's almost what happened to me!" I nearly jumped up and down excitedly, remembering. "I was 12 and my Yr. 6 class did a school excursion to old Government House in Parramatta Park. Before we did the tour inside the building, when I looked inside one of the windows, I saw a formal dinner party going on with everyone wearing olden day clothes! I could even hear the laughter. Then when we went inside, there was nothing there!"

Then we all looked at Sally for her turn. But she didn't seem to want to join in with our soul sharing revelations. She seemed really uncomfortable.

"Well?" Peter asked her.

"Well what?"

"What happened to you in your childhood to wind up here at this school?" Peter demanded.

"Nothing, OK? Nothing happened. I shouldn't even be here!" she said angrily, jumped up from his bed, then flounced out of his door for a second (and I was later to find out for a last) time.

Later on that afternoon after arvo tea I knocked on her door to see if she wanted to talk about what was bothering her. But she wasn't in her room. Then at dinner she didn't come to the cafeteria either. I was getting really worried about her.

Finally I found her in her room again, but she was packing up all of her stuff.

"What are you doing?" I asked her in shock.

"What does it look like I'm doing? For a school for the gifted, people ask a lot of stupid questions around here." She glared at me and continued with what she was doing.

"Sally please don't go. Don't you even want to talk about this?" I asked her.

"I've just spent two hours in Hamilton's office talking about this. I want to go home." She said coldly.

"What did he have to say about you going?" I asked her.

"He tried to talk me out of it. But I think he wanted to make sure I wasn't going to go blabbering about all this to the media. He kept telling me that this was a gift. What a laugh!"

"Why? Aren't you exhilarated, or even curious, to learn what this thing we've learned we can do, do?" I sat on her bed.

"No. I came here because I thought that this school was a place where top grade students came to get into the best colleges around the world. I didn't come here to join in a 'Dr. Who' episode."

"Chickening out I see." Nelson suddenly came to stand in her doorway. She'd just come back from the Cafeteria too. "Why aren't I surprised?"

"Nelson! Not now!" I growled at her, but Sally had had enough. She walked up, shoved Nelson backwards out of the way, then slammed her bedroom door shut in her face.

Then this morning I saw Sally off on the mini-bus to be driven to the local airport just outside of Brownsville. As the driver was loading Sally's suitcases in the back, I made Sally promise me something. I made her promise that she would at least email me occasionally so I would know she's all right.

"Yeah, sure, I'll email you." She gave me a hug, then became tearful. "Look Elisha, I loved meeting you. But this just isn't my thing. I was never a good 'Ghostbuster' and I certainly don't think being a 'Timelord' is my thing either. See ya, OK?"

Then she got on the minibus. But the bus didn't pull away immediately, and I soon saw why. Both Sophie and Abdul were leaving too. They both came down in tow with their luggage and friends to farewell them.

Brett was helping Sophie carry her suitcases and I tried not to obviously watch them say their farewells, as Jordon and Numu saw off Abdul. Wow, from our 21 students, we were going down to 18 of us left. I wonder how many others are thinking of leaving now?

Then the minibus started up its engine, and away it went, with Sally inside.

I waved as it drove around the oval and up the driveway to the main gate. Then it was gone, hidden by snow covered pine trees. I sighed and turned, about to go back inside Beta building.

Brett charged in front of me and pushed in first.

"What are you looking at?" he glared at me when I opened my mouth to tell him off.

What a dickhead!

As I went back to my room, I walked past Nelson's room as usual, and I heard two voices coming from inside. One of them had an Irish accent. Well, I guess she and Pat are on speaking terms again.

My room felt too lonely, and classes had been suspended for the past 3 days, so I wasn't sure what to do. So I went looking for Zack to hang with. I knocked on his door, but he wasn't in. I knocked on Peter's door, but he wasn't in either. Maybe they were in the library, which I didn't want to go to right now. So I went back to my room and played some music.

Oh yeah, I guess I didn't tell you. Classes had been suspended for today, yesterday and the day before so the teachers and Nell could have one on one appointments with us students to make sure that we could handle what they told us. To make sure we wouldn't go schizo or into shock or whatever. Like Sally, Sophie and Abdul did. Like their refusal to accept such things. Like their determination not to be involved in this.

I miss Sally.

==

07/ 02/ 01

Diary,

Everyone here seems to be working harder. They all seem to be paying more attention in class and raising their hands more to ask more questions. It's like there's this new sense of purpose, almost like a new meaning in our lives.

Now instead of Sally dragging me to the library, it's Nelson. Instead of Sally being the one who's done her assignments first, it's Nelson. It's not Sally who occasionally helps me with my Math, it's Nelson (and one night Pat too - since we all know his secret he's been sharing it's like he's hanging out with us again). Even Peter has been paying more attention, and showing off his intellect that had been hiding for months under his sarcastic and rebellious exterior. But Nelson can still kick his butt when a question is asked in class, I never knew that Nelson was actually this really smart person. She's a brainiac! She even corrected Maya in Biology class yesterday.

Now, today, I noticed Nelson wasn't in my Math class. When I asked Zack if he'd seen her, Dr. Knight answered the question for me by announcing that Nelson has been put in the other Math's class, Pat's class. That made Zack and I share a surprised look. I have to admit, I'm starting to feel lonelier in that class with out her. But at least I know Zack isn't going anywhere coz he has as much trouble with Math as I do. Actually, all my classes are the same with Zack, we both get average grades. At least I'm not alone here at the bottom.

Peter has less problems with Math's than we do, but he has trouble with English (funny about that when he's English himself - sorry, couldn't resist!). Zack told me last Sunday that Peter is dyslexic, he sees words back to front. So maybe I can make a deal with him, he'll permanently help me with my Math now that Nelson's moved classes, and I'll help him with his English essays.

Tonight when we were in the library doing our homework after dinner, I was asking Peter about the deal, when suddenly Brett pulled up a chair and sat down at our table.

"I'll help you with your Math's if you like." He said to me.

Zack and Peter looked at him incredulously. Peter and Brett had stopped talking the night of the drug bust, when Brett accused Peter of telling Hamilton on him and Sophie, which Peter didn't. Zack and Peter actually looked like they were about to jump up and punch him! So before they could start anything, I spoke up first.

"What do you want?"

"I heard you. If you're having trouble with Math, I'll help you." He shrugged as if nothing was amiss.

"She didn't ask you." Peter glared at him. "So why don't you sod off?"

"I really don't think that a person who got 71% on his last exam is in any kind of position to give private tutorials, do you?" Brett replied.

"Then what did you get Mr. Genius?" Zack challenged him.

"89%" Brett said coolly, then he looked at me again. "Do you want my help or not?"

"Not. She didn't ask you, remember?" Zack said icily, putting down his pen. I could almost see another library throwing match occurring.

I guess so could Brett. He was about to get up and walk off when I asked him again, "What do you want, Brett?"

He paused for a moment, about to say what it was, but then he seemed to change his mind. "I just offered my help. I mean, we're all in this together now, right?'

I guess he's right. We are all in this together now supposedly, learning of something that we can all do, a commonality that binds us all together like a woven woolen scarf. And to be honest, lately that woolen scarf has been feeling awfully tight around my neck.

"Fine. Sit. Do your homework with us." I shrugged.

Peter and Zack looked at me in surprise.

"Who made you judge and jury to acquit him of being an arsehole?" Peter asked me.

Just then Nelson and Pat walked in with their books to join us. Nelson saw Brett and immediately her defensive guard went up. "I'm sorry, no pets allowed in the building." Nelson greeted him.

"Hey, that's a good one! Why didn't we think of that one?" Peter laughed.

"This is so not worth it." Brett stood up to leave.

"I invited him." I told Nelson. "Brett, sit down."

"Sit Brett, sit!" Peter chimed in. "Roll over! Good boy!"

Brett turned around and walked out.

"That was uncalled for." Pat looked at us all in disapproval. "Since Sophie's gone, he's been feeling pretty alone."

"Serves him right. He was an arsehole." Nelson shrugged dismissively, sitting down and getting her books and pens ready.

Pat looked like he was about to follow after Brett to see if he was all right, but I thought I should be the one to offer the olive branch. I could understand how much he was missing Sophie, as I was missing Sally as well. I wouldn't like to be in his position and have no-one to talk to.

"I'll go." I stood up and packed up my things.

"You've got to be fucking kidding me." Peter shook his head and Zack looked up at me in surprise.

I ignored them and walked out. But by the time I got downstairs, I found Brett was already across the oval and entering Beta building. I ended up knocking on his bedroom door. I almost didn't though - I was half paranoid that he'd open it, see me standing there, then slam it shut again. But he didn't, thank god.

"Sorry about those guys." I greeted. Then I didn't know what else to say. I think I just stood there looking like an idiot.

"Forget about it. I have." He shrugged again, trying to play it cool.

"Maybe if you apologized or something, like officially.... " I suggested. "Then they'll know it's for real and be less skeptical."

"Me? Apologize?" he scoffed. "What for?"

That was it. I rolled my eyes and was about to walk away when he stopped me. I guess he sensed I was ready to just completely walk away for good.

"Fine. I'll officially apologize." He said, then smiled at me.

Wow. He smiled at me. He actually showed a sign of civilized human expression! So I left it at that and went back to my room. I felt like I'd made the first gesture, now it was his turn to make the next one.

==

(TEXT MESSAGE FROM MARK TO ELISHA DATED 13/02/ 01)

Hey, r u all right? Long time no hear. U didn't get sprung doing Hamilton's office did u? Call or text me back, OK?

==

(TEXT MESSAGE FROM ELISHA TO MARK DATED 14/ 02/ 01)

Hey it's me. Am OK, just busy. Everything OK.

==

14/ 02/ 01

Diary,

I got a text message from Mark yesterday asking me if everything is all right. So I lied and sent him back one saying yeah, everything is OK. I wouldn't know what or how to tell him what is really happening in this place. The same goes with Jen, I got an email from her two days ago asking the same thing, and how it went with Hamilton's office break in. I haven't replied to her yet, coz I don't know what to say.

I've been feeling pretty snowed under lately, literally and figuratively. I'm already so over with the winters here in Canada, it's just too damn cold! I'm tired of feeling cold all day and only properly warming up in a hot shower. I hate how there are no bathtubs here, I would kill for a lovely long hot bubble bath right now. I mean, yeah the buildings are heated and all, and I have enough warm clothes, but my feet are always cold! I'm sick and tired of them always feeling cold! I think it's because they get cold as I trudge through the snow between the buildings between breaks and classes and meal times, and going to the library of course. But then they never defrost properly till I have my hot shower at night.

There is a nice big fireplace in the library in Alpha building with a huge fire going in winter which is nice - but I hardly get to sit in front of it coz the other students (mainly Seniors) get there first. They take up the four chairs and lie on the rug in front of it and study before I can even get there. Sometimes I hate the Seniors, they act like they know everything and they treat the school like it's theirs and theirs alone. And they boss us around when the teachers are in the staff meeting room.

I've been studying less in the library and more in my room the past week. This way I can have a hot shower early in the evening straight after dinner (when I don't have Astronomy that is) and stay warm in my room, in my flannel pj's. I put my feet up on my heater and get out the ole homework and off I go. The only bummer about this is my Math's homework. I really need help with it right now, but everyone else seems preoccupied with their own stuff. Like, I asked Nelson if she could study in my room with me two nights ago, but she said she had already made plans to study with Patrick in the library. She didn't even offer me an invitation to come along either. Since she's made up with Pat and they're now in the same class, it's like I'm not even in the picture anymore. It's almost like they don't even see me as on the same level anymore, Math's or otherwise!

Zack offered to study with me in my room, but Peter won't coz he says my room is too hot and stuffy in there for him. But Zack can't really help me coz he's having as much trouble as I am. Remember the one time I mentioned how he offered to do both of our Math homework after the fight with Peter? Well he got half of the answers wrong and Dr. Knight got suspicious that we both got the same answers wrong and even where we went wrong in the calculations. So I told Zack to go study with

Pete in the library. Then Zack offered to come back afterwards and show me the answers, but I thought that would really look too suss, three people having the exact same answers and calculations so I thanked him and said no.

Zack is so sweet, and he's still trying to get us together. As you may tell from the date, today was Valentines Day. When I came down for breakfast in the Caf this morning, Zack pulled out a box of chocolates out of his bag for me! He'd bought them secretly at our last 'Brown Day' weekend and hid them in his room since. He said he wanted to buy me some roses, but they wouldn't keep that long until he could give them to me. But that was the only good thing that happened today.

The rest of the day for me just went downhill from there. In Math I realized I only got one of the problems out of the 10 given to us for homework correct, then Dr. Knight wanted us to hand in the sheets of paper so she could see them. I panicked! I didn't know what to do, show her that I'm an idiot, or lie and say I hadn't done it? But I was too chicken to do that, so I handed the bloody thing in. As we were leaving class, I could see her flicking through the papers, then pause and look right at me right as I was leaving. I almost ran down the hall so she couldn't call me back!

Then I had a good History lesson. Professor Hamilton handed back our assignments from last week and I got an A on Roman Citizenship and Politics. Yes! And Nelson only got a B for it! Ha! Sucked in! I felt like getting up and doing a little dance and singing, "I'm not that stupid after all!" But lucky I had kept my mouth shut, coz in Computer Studies next, we also got our assignments back and I got a C minus! I had just barely passed! And Nelson got an A plus! Pat helped her with it, that was what he was doing in her room that day when I heard him in her room, and he didn't even to offer to help me with it! I almost felt like she cheated, but in a way I knew she didn't, she did do most of the work on her own. I guess I'm just stupid with Computers and Math. Come to think of it, Astronomy as well.

After dinner when we went to Astronomy, we had to do this calculation on space-time to demonstrate Euclidean space time or whatever. Man, I had no idea what Dr. Myles was going on about! I mean, can't we just look at pictures of stars and galaxies and learn about volcanoes on Venus or the black hole in Cygnus X-1 or whatever? Why do we have to use calculations? Zack seemed to be enjoying himself, as he, Peter and Nelson were getting right into it. I just sat to the side, quietly, no idea what was going on. They may as well had been talking in Martian to me!

I wonder if they've made a mistake picking me to be here at this college? What if I'm so stupid that the time I did see back in time was just a once off lucky chance occurrence? Maybe it won't happen again? And why is Math so important to learn anyway? Didn't they say it themselves, that we don't need to build a time machine? That this ability is inside of ourselves? It's not like we need to have the technical know-how to build the time machine. So why the emphasis that we do?

What am I doing here? Maybe Sally had the right idea in leaving. Maybe I should leave too.

===

18/ 02/ 01

I feel so isolated. It seems like everyone is advancing full steam ahead without me. I can't keep up. I don't even want anymore to try to keep up.

Maybe I've just been in shock for so long since that night in the teachers' staff meeting room, that it's just hit me now what they said to me. I woke up this morning, and it hit me... what the f**k am I doing here? I don't belong here!

I came down to breakfast and sat with Pat, Nelson, Peter and Zack as usual, and they were talking about doing more study in the library that day. I felt like I didn't belong there. Not with them, not at this school, not here in general. I felt like I wasn't even there properly. Zack turned around and said something to me, and I couldn't even hear him. I saw his lips moving, but I had no idea what he said.

So I got up and left back to my room.

I wasn't hungry. I didn't want breakfast, then I didn't feel like any lunch either. I put my stereo on loudly and swung on my chair, staring out my window. The mountains and lake looked so peaceful, and yet, so surreal, like I wasn't even really looking at them, but at a postcard or something. Like it was my last time I was ever going to look at them and I wanted to burn the scalding hot image into my mushy brain.

I just don't see the point of staying any longer. I wondered what to say to Professor Hamilton. But then, I didn't know what to say to my Dad either, and the idea of living with him again didn't sound exactly appealing. I certainly don't want to go back to my old school... I suddenly felt trapped and scared. I can't go forward in this place, and I can't go back to the old place.

Zack came to my room this afternoon. Peter had shown him how to solve the latest Math problems we had for homework, and he had come to show me. But I told him I wasn't interested and that I just wanted to be alone. Then he walked into my room, ignoring the blatant hint, sat on my bed and asked what I wanted to do instead?

I lost it, I mean really lost it. I yelled at him to get out and leave me alone! I mean, why does this guy always have to act like the human version of cling wrap? Can't he find another person to stick to? Why can't he leave me alone? Everyone else here is!

He just sat there silently and took it, before he stood up and left, slamming my door behind him as his form of protest.

==

20/ 02/ 01

Diary,

Dr. Knight asked me to stay after class today to discuss my recent homework, or lack of it lately. I haven't been doing it (or my Astronomy or my Computer Studies) coz I'm tired of putting myself through the trauma of looking like an idiot. Looking like a rebel is much more preferable. But I didn't tell her this. Instead, when she asked me if I'd been having trouble understanding the work lately, I gave her some smart-arse answer that landed me a week's detention. So for the next 7 nights I'll be washing dishes.

...yay... (drip drip with sarcasm).

So tonight after dinner I had to stay back in the Caf, go into the kitchen and rinse over 100 dishes and stack them into the sanitizer and take them out again and put them away. I had to do the same with the cutlery, glasses, dessert bowels... you get the picture. It took me nearly two hours.

I am so over this bloody school.

When the detention was over, I went back to my room. I showered and changed into my flannel pj's, and went back into my usual routine of swinging on my chair and listening to music. I looked at my homework sitting on my desk. I had finished my English essay before dinner, only my Math homework remained. There was no way I was going to do it, so I turned the page over face down and instead picked up my History text book.

Then there was a knock on my door.

I groaned and nearly banged my head on my desk in a maddening way, expecting to see Zack behind door number 1. Since our fight (well, it was me who did the fighting) we hadn't been sitting together (in fact I'd been sitting alone quite a lot lately). But I got up and answered it, expecting me to be telling Zack to bugger off again.

There stood Brett and Maya, holding books and pens and looking back at me.

I didn't know what to say, so I stood there dumbfounded.

"Maya and I thought we'd try and do some studying in your room tonight. The library is getting a little crowded. Do you mind?" Brett asked me.

"Ah, yeah... sure." I said in surprise, and they came inside my room.

I closed my door again to keep the heat in as Brett took a seat at my desk and Maya timidly sat on my bed.

Maya and I just looked at each other.

"I heard you got an A on your history exam." Maya said to me.

"Yeah." I shrugged.

"I only got a B plus." She told me.

"So?"

"I'll help you with your Math if you wouldn't mind reading over my English and History essays." Maya said a little shyly, probably expecting me to smack her down or something.

I looked at Brett, knowing he had a hand in this somehow.

"What about my Astronomy and Computer Studies assignments?" I asked them.

"I can help you with those too." Maya agreed.

"I have to warn you now, I'm an idiot. I don't think I should even be at this school." I told them. "I may even leave."

"Idiots don't get A's in History, English or Drama." Brett said casually. "And besides, you might be even better than this time circulating thing or seeing through time than we are. After all, you are the one who decided to follow Peter, Sophie and me into Alpha building that night, aren't you? You suspected something was up, right as Hamilton and Myles showed up. That means you felt a ripple in the time line."

"What do you mean?" I gawked at him in surprise.

"Sophie was going to overdose that night on the drugs Peter bought for us, but because we heard you, then Hamilton and Myles showed up, she didn't. Hamilton knew from the timeline that Sophie was going to overdose, so he knew to show up and when. He changed the timeline to stop and interrupt us before we could do the coke that Peter bought.

You sensed the timeline change, and you showed up as well." Brett told me.

"But how do you know all of this?" I asked him, in further shock.

"I heard Hamilton talk about it to Dr. Knight two weeks ago." Brett shrugged.

"How did you know?" Maya asked me.

Now it was my turn to shrug. "I don't know, I just knew."

Then Maya looked timid and shy again, and looked to be struggling how to say something.

"Elisha, I owe you an apology. When you first told me about this ghost business, I thought it was all in your head. Now that I've learned it's not, I would like to offer you my sincerest wishes. It would be my privilege to help you with your homework."

Wow... I was totally thrown by this gesture.

"Sure, no worries." I said, not knowing how else to take it.

Then we three looked at each other, not knowing where to go now.

"It's nice and warm in here." Maya took off her scarf and jacket and settled onto the bed into a more comfortable position. "I still feel cold in the library sometimes."

"Really? Same here!" I said in relief that I wasn't the only one. "I have to have a long hot shower and hole up in here with my feet on the heater till I feel human again."

"Boy, it really must be a lot warmer where you two come from." Brett chuckled, taking off both of his jumpers till he was just wearing a T-shirt with his jeans. "So where are you up to?" he half asked me as he picked up the piece of paper on my desk with the Math problems on it. He saw that they were unanswered. "We better get started."

So I sat on the bed with Maya as these two showed me how to do the calculations for homework. Afterwards, I let Maya read my English essay as I read hers and gave her some advice, which she actually took to heart. Then Brett helped me with my Astronomy, then Maya helped me with my Computer Studies. It was midnight by the time we had finished, but I wasn't even tired. I suddenly understood a lot more than when the day started, and it wasn't just homework.

===

26/ 02/ 01

Diary,

Tonight when I had just finished my sanitizing duties, to my surprise, I found Dr. Knight waiting to talk to me.

She made both of us a cup of hot chocolate in the kitchen before motioning for us to sit at one of the tables in the empty cafeteria.

I sat and waited, almost cringing, waiting to hear what she had to say. I think I was worried that she would bring up my behavior over the past few weeks. I wasn't far wrong, but what further surprised me, was how she wanted to discuss it.

"Your homework has picked up. I guess your study sessions with Maya and Brett are helping." She smiled at me.

"Yes." I said flatly, not wanting to go into it with her.

"It's OK if you can learn better in a smaller group. That's what we've tried to provide here at this college. But I just want you to know that if you ever need more help, you can always come to me. There's nothing wrong with asking for help, Elisha." She said seriously. "My room is on the bottom floor of Beta building, I don't know if you know that or not. Most evenings I'm free. If you or Zack would like to come and ask me any questions, I'm certainly not going to turn you away."

"OK." I said plainly, still feeling a little uncomfortable.

"I also need to know where you get confused, or need help. There's no point you sitting in class, lost, while the rest of us go on without you. You'd be surprised to know that you're not the only one who feels left behind sometimes. But I need to know where you get lost, before I lose you behind me, so it won't be hard for you to catch up."

I didn't say anything and I just stared at my marshmallow melting in my drink.

"Even if you don't want anyone to know if you're having difficulty, come and knock on my door in the evening if you can't do it in class. I'd like to help you as much as I can." She continued, trying to catch my gaze.

But there was something else weighing on my mind, which I thought I'd try asking her instead.

"What were you and Professor Hamilton talking about a few weeks ago when you were talking about me? About the night Peter was sprung for the drugs?" I blurted out.

"The night of Halloween?" she asked back.

I nodded.

"We were talking about your ability to sense what Peter, Brett and Sophie were going to do, and what may have happened. We suspect that you sensed the ripple in time when we changed the time line and prevented Sophie from using the drugs and ultimately overdosing. We also suspect that was how you sense the ghosts, when you sensed us moving through time. Are we correct?"

"I don't know." I shrugged and looked down again. I thought I might as well say it and say it now and get it over and done with. "I think you've all made a mistake about me."

"In what way?"

"I don't know... that maybe I can't do all of these things that you think I can. I'm pathetic at Math's, I'm hopeless at calculating space-time in Astronomy and me stumbling upon you as a ghost going through time was pure coincidence! Me seeing the Roman soldier was sheer luck! Me sensing what Peter, Brett and Sophie were up to was a dumb guess!"

Dr. Knight sat back and looked at me quietly for the longest moment before speaking to me again.

"When you saw back in time at Government House in Parramatta Park, when you were 12 years old, that wasn't the first time, was it?"

"How do you know about that?" I asked her in surprise.

"A few years from now you tell me. You also tell me about the time you knew your mother would never recover from cancer, even before she was diagnosed. You also tell me about the strong feelings of deja vu you would receive when walking down the street and looking at a building you've never been to or seen before, or your way of just knowing about something you've never even heard before. Professor Myles has told me that you do struggle with the calculations in his class as well, but if he told you that space was green and not black, and which galaxies have black holes inside of them, that you would just nod as if you had already known that. You can see space time in effect Elisha, it doesn't matter if you have difficulty working out the quantum mechanics in your head. We simply teach these principles because there are students here that want or need to understand the nuts and bolts of what they can do rather than just do."

"Really?" I looked up at her.

"You simply know. You can see. You don't need to pull it apart to see the grand picture. You don't need to know what exact colors they used to paint the picture. And you have the ability to walk through the canvass with out cutting it first with a pair of scissors." Dr. Knight stated.

"Can I ask you a question?" I asked her again. She smiled and nodded, taking a sip of her drink. "Is traveling through time, how we go all see-through, is that because our molecules are speeding up, and we can dissipate and rotate through the layers of time that way? Is time like this huge circle, with lots of other circles inside of it, like layers in an onionskin? And we move through the layers that way?"

Dr. Knight just looked at me.

"Did you get one of your 'guesses' from this?" she asked me.

"Yeah..." I slumped back into my chair, wondering if she must be thinking I'm talking rubbish.

"That is exactly right, Elisha." She stated. "When did this idea come to you?"

"In Astronomy when we were talking about light speed and the Maxwell Water Ripple example."

"And this theory gave you another sense of deja vu?" she asked me and I nodded. "Then Elisha, how can you have any doubt at all that you belong here?"

"Because I may be able to 'see' all of this crap, but I can't explain how I see it. And when somebody tries to explain the mechanics of seeing it, I have no idea of what they're talking about!" I said frustratedly.

"OK." She sat forward. "I'm going to bring this up at our next teacher's meeting. We will try to revise our teaching methods to explain the basics to you, and see how you go from there."

"No, don't do that! Everyone will know I'm an idiot!" I said, going bright red.

"As I said before Elisha, you're not alone in this. I can think of at least four other students who are in the same boat as you. They can also 'see' and will become some of our most important Circulators. I think it's more important that we cater our teaching to their learning techniques."

"What do you mean, 'your most important Circulators'?" I asked curiously.

"As we mentioned that night in the staff meeting room, there are students here at Hamilton's who will be able to circulate through time, and there are others who will be able to calculate. Those who can see and calculate, work in a special place where they can monitor any changes in the timeline in not only just our planet but in the universe. Then there are those who are able to see and to circulate through time. Interestingly, not many of those who can Circulate can accurately use quantum mechanics with their seeing, which is much more than mere understanding. But in fact only a third of our community can actually manipulate time rather than just read it, which we call Circulators. All of the teachers here can manipulate time, only our counselor cannot, she can see through time."

"So you have Circulators and Calculators?" I asked half jokingly.

"That is correct." Dr. Knight stated. "Though we do call our organization of people the Circulate. In the Circulate, we all hold our members prized and esteemed. We are democratic community with elected council members."

"What about the Roman soldier, and when you were going back in time to visit your family… you may have been traveling through points in time, but what about points on earth? How did you travel from 2000 AD Canada to 1700 AD England?"

Dr. Knight looked a bit hesitant to tell me at first, or was she trying to find the words to explain it?

"As you said before, when traveling through the layers of time our molecules and electrons speed up and dissipate. Now, on our own, we can travel freely through time. But using future technology that won't be invented for another 100 years, that technology is able to catch our matter and transport it to another location. While that future technology can only move matter from one point to another, using our own ability we also change the time frame." She told me.

"So is that like using wormholes or portals or whatever?" I asked her.

"No, because stable wormholes or portals have fixed locations or points. This is more like a fax machine that can send our dissipated matter to an unfixed location where it doesn't need another fax machine to print us out again. Imagine yourself fishing from the ocean, but with technology so finely tuned that you know how to detect where the fish will be, and when the fish's matter dissipates, you collect their electrons and molecules in a special net. Then you put that matter and molecules back into another point in the ocean, and the fish reform into fish again, just at a different time and place." Dr. Knight used the analogy to explain to me.

I could almost see those fish going all see-through in my mind. And that would be me one day? A see-through fish being scooped up and put into another country and time? Wow... that thought is just too weird.

"But what if you just want to travel through time and not country?" I ask her.

"Then you travel through time." She shrugged, taking another sip from her drink.

"But how will the machine know that you don't want to change countries?" I asked her worriedly.

She let out this really loud laugh and looked back at me. "The Calculators operating this machine will know."

"So they know what we're going to do before we do?" I asked in surprise again.

"Not all the time, but they do have a 99% success rate. As I like to remind them, that another famous man once said, 'the future is not yet written in stone'." Dr. Knight smiled at me.

Then a thought struck me. "What about Sally? Did a Calculator see her leaving this college?"

"Perhaps." She said elusively.

"So what's going to happen to her?" I asked Dr. Knight. "What was she going to be? A Circulator or a Calculator?"

"Sally is going to be a Calculator. Just as Abdul will be, and then Sophie will be a Circulator, like yourself."

"She will be?"

"Sally will one day decide she wants to learn more about this ability she has, and she does join the Circulate." Dr. Knight said confidently, as if she was stating a simple fact. "So does Sophie, and so will Abdul."

"So I guess you've seen this happen." I watched her face to confirm this.

"Of course. Elisha, all of your teachers met you long before your father or even yourself ever heard of this college."

"In the future?" I asked her.

"Yes."

"How far into the future are we talking about?"

"Now that I can't tell you."

"Why not?" I leaned forward, impatient to know.

"That one you'll find out for yourself eventually. I can't give away everything right now. All I wanted to do was to assure you. You're one of us Elisha. You are special, and you are in the right place right now."

===

TO: ebaker_hamiltons@evers.com
FROM: jeni_B@goggleyes.com
SUBJECT: Plan of action
DATE: 13/ 01/ 01

Hey Elisha,

Long time no email, so I thought I'd drop you one instead
to see if you're still alive.

Did you get my first email I sent a couple of weeks ago?
Did they catch you coming out of Hamilton's office? What
happened? Find out anything interesting?

I hope you're OK. Email me back and let me know everything
is OK. Otherwise I'll come over there and kick your arse!

Cheers, Jen xoxo

==

TO: jeni_B@goggleyes.com

FROM: ebaker_hamiltons@evers.com

SUBJECT: Probably not what you were expecting...

DATE: 02/ 03/ 01

Hi Jen,

Sorry I haven't written in so long, it wasn't intentional.
Things around here are a little full on at the moment and
the work load is just getting heavier and heavier. It
feels like I'm constantly doing homework and I've just
finished a week of washing dishes for detention.

I can't talk about the Hamilton's Office expedition, but
all I will say is that is certainly a night that will go
down in the history books.

I hope it doesn't sound like I'm giving you the complete
brush off, but I do hope you are well and I can't talk
much more. I will send a longer email in the not too
distant future. Say hi to your parents, Aunty Gabby and
Uncle Peter for me. xoxo

==

03/ 03/ 01

Diary,

Got an email from my cousin Jen a few days ago and sent her a reply back yesterday. I'm afraid I sounded a little short with her, and I hope she doesn't think I'm being rude or anything. But how the hell do I tell her what's happening in my life right now? How do I try to explain what I am and how different that is to her now?

"Hey Jen, I'm Wonder Woman, and you're squat. See ya and have a nice short life... as I may be able to live as long as old father time..."

I can really see that happening...

Closed in. That's what's happening now. We re all bonding together so closely over our secret. The secret the rest of the 99.9% of the world's population can never know or share...

The secret Sally or Sophie couldn't bear. A secret even Abdul couldn't let himself believe. A secret that weaved itself around us so tightly that even made the remoteness of our small little school community seem even further away from the rest of the world.

Woven. Close. Knitted together. We are now apart of something, chosen to be here for a reason. To learn you're not insane, but special; not just plain different but preciously unique; wanted; invited; welcomed; appreciated.

That's what the teachers here have been trying to show us all this time. But in our tempestuous teenage state we couldn't recognize it. They want us here, they want to show us why we're here, they want to invite us into their future; that the school is only a doorway into a much larger picture, an almost limitless domain.

Hamilton has created a new home for us. The Circulate is a new state of being. We are all connected, one action can result in another, a chain of events ripple through space-time and then, ultimately each other.

===

04/ 03/ 01

Diary,

Last night I thought I should make peace with Zack. After dinner in the Caf, instead of going straight to one of the Rec rooms to watch videos, I went looking for Zack. I was surprised that I didn't find him watching "The Mummy Returns" with Peter, Nelson and Pat in Gamma building. But I knocked on his door and found him in his room instead.

"Hi." I smiled nervously, almost scared at what his reaction would be. Thankfully there weren't that many students left on this floor right at this moment, so if he did want his revenge and yell at me, I wouldn't be humiliated by too many witnesses.

"What do you want?" he asked.

"I came to apologize. Can I come in?" I asked, feeling awkward standing in the hallway.

"You just apologized. You can go now." He nearly shut his door on me when I put my hand out and stopped him.

"Zack..."

"Look, you're not interested, you've never been interested... fine. Let's leave it at that." he tried to close his door again, but I put my hand out again and stopped him.

"Zack, please..." I became tearful. I didn't mean to, they just welled up and threatened to really embarrass me by trickling down my cheeks. "I'm sorry, I didn't mean to be such a bitch. I was depressed..."

"We're all depressed, you don't see us going on about it."

"You're not all depressed! And I do see you going on about it, about your studies and your own lives with out me! That's what I got annoyed about."

"What are you talking about? I tried helping you!" he raised his voice.

"I know, that's why I'm standing here apologizing, remember?"

We just looked at each other.

"Fine, come in." he stood aside to let me pass.

I came in and stood in the middle of his room. I noticed his room looked a lot messier than the last time I saw it. But I have to admit, I loved the smell of his aftershave or deodorant or whatever that was that I could smell.

"Have you had a girl in here?" I tried to joke. "Something smells nice."

"That's not funny." He glared at me, crossing his arms.

I didn't know what else to say after that. I suddenly felt very self-conscious standing there. In fact, the old feelings that I looked like an idiot standing in that bedroom, started up again.

"Look, I just came to apologize. So I'm sorry, all right? OK, bye." I said and started to walk past him again to the door when he grabbed my arm.

"Why do you like him and not me?"

"Like who?"

"Brett! He treated you like crap when Sophie was here! He even laughed with Peter behind your back! And the next thing I know you're sucking up to him!" Zack vented out his frustration.

"I'm not sucking up to him! He apologized! He offered his help! And it wasn't just him, it was Maya too!" I defended myself, snatching my arm back.

We ended up standing there glaring at each other again.

"Fine, whatever." He walked over and opened his door to show me out.

I walked over to the doorway, letting myself being shown out this way, when suddenly I felt really guilty. This wasn't the way I wanted our friendship to end. I didn't even want it to end! Zack has been a rock for me here at Hamilton's. I may have lost Sally temporarily, but I didn't want to lose him too.

Instead of keeping on walking, I stopped in my tracks when I came to stand next to him. Then, with my eyes meeting his, I leaned over and kissed his cheek softly. I was about to kiss his other cheek, when suddenly he grabbed my shoulders and pushed me against his cupboard!

"No! You can't keep on doing this! You can't just use me like this!" his face was flushed and he looked really angry!

I was about to open my mouth to apologize again, suddenly scared of what I'd done, when suddenly his mouth covered mine! He kissed me so hard, his tongue going right into my mouth for the longest time, I nearly suffocated! I had to push him back a little just to get some oxygen.

As we were kissing, his hands were grabbing at my breasts, my arse, my waist, my neck... it was almost like he couldn't make up his mind what he wanted the most of or that he wanted all of me at the same time. It didn't take long for them to reach the zipper on my jeans that let me know what his real intentions were.

"Zack, your door..." I murmured.

He kicked it shut and as soon as did, he fell backwards onto his bed, pulling me down with him.

It was a bit difficult trying to get undressed lying down, especially when you're wearing as many layers of clothes as we were. I couldn't even kick my shoes off properly! And I didn't feel particularly sexy wearing long thermal underwear. I felt like the romantic spontaneity was leaving as quickly as it had come.

"Zack... Zack wait." I sat up, half naked and rumpled.   "This isn't working."

"What? Why?" he asked in surprise.

"I can't even get my clothes off properly!" I think I was blushing, my cheeks were so hot that they spread to my ears and I think even my ears were red.

"Come here." He got up off the bed and sat me on the side of it.

Then he knelt down and untied my Doc boots, and took them off, then meeting my gaze again, he put his hands on the top of my jeans and slowly pulled those off as well. Then as he did the same with my long johns, I think my cheeks went from red to pink at the tenderness he showed me right then. I lifted up my arms so he could take off my thermal long sleeved singlet and soon I was sitting there in nothing but my bra and undies.

Zack lifted up his arms for me to take off his two T-shirts that he was wearing, one long sleeve and one short sleeved, and he took off his own jeans himself.

I have to admit, I was surprised at how well toned his upper body was! I knew he was a sporty kind of person, but by the looks of this he must have been doing push-ups in his room every night. I reached out my hand kind of shyly to touch his stomach and then his chest and shoulders, which he grabbed my other hand and made it do the same thing.

He parted my legs and pulled me closer to him so that it was only the fabric left of our underwear keeping us apart. His eyes were trying to hold onto mine as I think we were both so nervous both of our hearts were pounding and our hands were shaking! I think I was trembling more than he was though. At least I know I'm not the only virgin here, which was reassuring.

"I've dreamed of this... every night. I dreamed of doing this with you every night. I love you Elisha."

I didn't know what to say! I mean, I supposed this is what every lovebird wants to hear... but I don't know if I love Zack. I mean, I do think he's good looking, and I love his company most of the time... I kissed him back so I wouldn't have to say anything. Then pretty soon there was no fabric keeping us apart.

Afterwards we laid in his bed for a little while. I liked the feeling of lying in his arms, and of the way he kept stroking my back with his fingertips. I stared at the cupboard, looking at the dents in the wood, wondering if we had put any new ones in it tonight. Then Zack brought up his childhood.

"I remember like it happened yesterday, the day I went to school. It was a Wednesday, and I thought it would be like every other Wednesday. Classes all day, with football practice in the afternoon. Then in our last class for the day, Health class, they brought up sexual abuse and sexual assault. And I remember, sitting there... as the teacher went on and on about child sexual abuse, thinking, 'this can't be happening'. Nearly every fucking thing the teacher mentioned... my father was doing to me..."

It made me uncomfortable him talking about it right now. Why does he have to talk about it now? Did I just abuse him or something? I don't want to hear about it now when we've just had sex for the first time.

It made me feel a bit dirty. I suddenly felt weird and self-conscious lying naked in his bed. So I got up and got dressed.

"Hey, where are you going?" Zack sat up.

"I'm going to go shower and get in my pj's before everyone comes back all at once from fun night." I made an excuse.

Suddenly there was a knock on his door and somebody turned the handle, trying to come inside!

"Hey Zack, you in there?" Peter's voice came from the other side.

"Shit!" I dove into bed again, half dressed.

"Wait a minute!" Zack called back out, jumping up and putting his jeans on again. Then he opened his door a crack to speak to Peter. "Now's not a good time, I'm getting changed for a shower."

"Did I just hear another voice in there? Hey Elisha, is that you?" Peter called past Zack, laughing. "What have you guys been up to?"

Oh shit… I really didn't want the whole world knowing what we just did… I groaned and put the pillow over half of my face.

Just then I saw Zack's arm suddenly jut through the crack and I gathered it would have grabbed Peter's shirt in a warning gesture.

"NOT NOW, OK PETER?" Zack said through gritted teeth.

"Sure man, sure." Peter suddenly sounded apologetic.

"And not one word…" Zack seethed.

"No man, no." Peter agreed.

Then Zack closed his door again and sat on the side of his bed and took the pillow off my face.

"It'll be OK. He won't say anything." Zack promised me.

I thought that was very chivalrous and gallant what he just did, so I sat up and kissed him then gave him a smile. "Thank you."

He hugged me back tightly.

That was last night. It was my fourth most memorable night since coming to this school. And yet, life hasn't changed that much since.

I had always imagined that once I lost my virginity, bells would ring somewhere and that birds would sing. But since it's winter and the birds have all migrated... maybe they're singing somewhere else, where there actually are bells ringing. Meanwhile here at Hamilton's'... it's just homework and trying to sexily undress out of long johns.

===

05/ 03/ 01

Diary,

Today was unlike any other school day we had so far, because our whole year was restructured. And a new teacher came to start teaching at this college. He's a Circulator as well. In fact, he's the same guy who was the Roman soldier we saw, and did the guest lecture on the Roman army. I can tell that our schooling at Hamilton's will be completely different now. I mean, since that night in the teachers staff meeting room things have been different, but now I think things will be more so.

At breakfast this morning in the Caf, Professor Hamilton asked all Sophomores to remain behind instead of going off to morning class. Then he introduced the new teacher to the rest of the school. His name is Dr. Rufus Kell, and he will be teaching Math, Ancient and European History and some Astronomy as well.

So as the rest of the Freshmen, Juniors and Seniors went off to their classes, we Sophomores stayed behind to hear the second part of the announcement.

"From now until the end of the semester, there will be three classes instead of two, and some of you will find Dr. Kell taking half of your classes from now on. Now I'm going to call out names from a list, and when you hear these names, I want you to stand up and go and sit at the table with Dr. Kell." Professor Hamilton announced.

We all looked at each other in surprise, and Zack squeezed my hand under the table. I exchanged a glance with Zack, and squeezed his hand back. I hoped that we wouldn't be separated.

"Jiunua Wong, Jordon Rah, Numu Kamah, Peter Kensington, Zachary Reece, Elisha Baker."

Pat and Nelson watched as we three, Zack, Peter and myself, get up from the table we had been sitting with them for breakfast and go over to the table where Dr. Kell was seated.

Then Professor Hamilton explained what was happening to the rest of the year.

"As you may all recall at the meeting in the staff meeting room that took place on the Friday of 26th of January, we told you that there would be people in this year who would be able to see through time, and that there would be people who could travel through time. After much consideration, the teachers here at this college have decided to make adjustments to your learning schedules. From now on, until the day you graduate from Hamilton's, you will be taught in two separate groups, the seers will be taught how to Calculate, and the travelers will be taught how to Circulate."

Nelson put up her hand to ask the first question. "Is that group the ones who can see or who can travel?" she implied Peter, Zack and I.

"This group of people will be Circulators." Hamilton answered her.

"You mean they're the only ones who can travel through time? That's only a small group... what do the rest of us do?" Jose didn't bother putting up his hand to speak.

"While all of you will have certain limitations on how far you can see through time, the rest of you will learn the exact science on how to Calculate with time. You will learn to recognize patterns in human evolution, forecast planet wide contingencies, and then to ultimately foresee universal phenomenon. In a metaphorical sense, you will be the watch keepers and overseers to the Circulators, calculating how, when, where and why they travel through time and in some instances, keeping them out of harms way." Hamilton explained to everyone.

"Then we won't be traveling through time at all?" Giselle asked a little disappointedly.

"You will, and quite frequently. But with the help of a Circulator." Dr. Kell suddenly spoke up. "You see, in the not too distant future here in your education at this college, you will be shown a sort of Headquarters, or a base camp where the Circulate has set up shop. From this foundation you will see technology that hasn't been invented yet, that helps a Circulator not only move through time, but to different locations on this planet, and even this solar system or galaxy. Calculators can travel with Circulators, using this technology and sort of being piggy-backed by the Circulator."

"Great, so if we pissed one of these guys off, they could leave us in the Dinosaur age or something." Brett half joked.

"It wouldn't happen. If something were to happen to injure or strand a member of the Circulate in a point in time, then a Calculator would see it and another Circulator would be dispatched on a rescue mission. We have only lost one member of our organization." Dr. Kell continued.

"What, only one?" Paulo from Uruguay asked in disbelief, in his strong accent. "What if a member in your organization harmed another?"

"That has never happened. As we watch the world fall into numerous wars, as we see countries tear each other apart, why would we want to emulate such destructive behavior? The once I speak of was from an incident when the said Circulator brought it on themselves, kind of like drink driving, but we call it, phasing under the influence." Dr. Kell answered.

"In the Circulate we value knowledge over power. We want of nothing, we have material gains but we don't cherish these by-products of greed. We simply use money to finance our goals." Professor Hamilton said simply.

"All of you, right now, being here at Hamilton's and learning what we have to teach you... you have joined the Circulate. Whether you choose to become an active member once you graduate from your studies, or need to fulfill your own personal experiences first, we know from the future that we work side by side with you in years to come." Dr. Knight told us.

Everyone looked at each other feeling impressed and a little intimidated at the same time.

"Usually we don't separate you into the two groups of Calculators and Circulators until your Senior year. But this year has been an extraordinary one of not following protocol..." Hamilton half smiled at Peter, Zack and I..." where students are rushing ahead at their own speed. So after a discussion with all of your teachers, and the Circulate Council at our Headquarters, we have moved this process forward."

"Is the same thing going to happen with the other years?" Darianne asked the teachers.

"With the Juniors, yes. But the Freshmen will remain the same." Hamilton nodded. "Basically many of your classes will stay the same, but only in the manner that we teach them will change."

"Why?" Giselle put up her hand again.

"Because Calculators and Circulators see differently. There are some Circulators who can Calculate as well as Circulate, but the majority of our organization is divided into two. As there are many of you who can calculate quantum mechanics and space-time theory with ease, there are some of you who can see the larger picture and feel inundated by the finer details. But by the time all of you graduate, you will be surprised at how close the commonality is between the two of you." Dr. Knight answered her question.

Then there was a moment of silence, as most of the room was mulling all of this over, trying to digest this new information. For a second life altering experience for a bunch of 16 year olds, I think we were taking it quite well. And it wasn't too long ago, like in the space of less than two months ago, that the first life altering experience happened and that we learned how we were different from the rest of the human race.

"Then lets get started." Dr. Kell stood up from sitting on top of the table.

"Right." Professor Hamilton agreed. "For the rest of you who were going into Math with Dr. Knight, please follow her to your classroom. Those of you in English with me, we'll go to class now. The students at Dr. Kell's table will now be escorted to your new class."

"Follow me, if you dare." Dr. Kell chuckled evilly to we five, who exchanged one more look with each other. The look said it all... what have we gotten ourselves into now?

So we followed our intrepid teacher out of the building, across the snow covered oval in the same direction as the rest of the sophomore students, and into Alpha building. Only we didn't head straight into a classroom, we followed him up the stairs two levels to the teachers offices. There he unlocked a previously unused office and motioned us all inside.

The room was cold, with an old, scratched up desk by a small window, and near by the door which we came through, was an old scratched up coffee table with six small leather chairs around it.

"Sit, sit!" he said boisterously, to which we all obeyed.

We sat down a little uncertainly, unsure which books to take out of our bags first.

"What class are we having first, sir? English, or Math?" Numu asked, holding her bag in her lap.

"Neither. This class will be induction to time travel, class numero uno." he sat on the last empty chair. "I'm sure you all have plenty of questions to ask me. So lets get into it."

I watched Peter, Zack, Numu, Jordon and Wong all exchange uncertain looks, not knowing where to begin or how. I felt slightly ahead of them, I have to admit. I'm guessing I have been the only one up until this point Dr. Knight has had a one on one with.

"So we're going to be the 'Timelords' while the rest of them will be the 'Daleks'?" Peter started.

"While the rest are going to be what?" Dr. Kell asked bemused.

"'Daleks'. Robots on wheels. It's from a TV show called 'Dr. Who'." I said.

"Ah, 20th Century popular culture. Love it! Good analogy Peter. I supposed that's what you think 'Daleks' are? Calculators on wheels?"

"Exterminate! Exterminate!" Peter did his impersonation and we all laughed. It felt good having a laugh, I think it broke the ice between everyone in the room.

"Well, you could look at their position that way I suppose... the same way the other students can see you as a human 'Tardis'. But how about we talk about instead how your classes will be changing and indeed, your very first school excursion through time?" Dr. Kell sat back into his chair and looked at us all individually.

"Really?" I asked excitedly. "Back in time? Can I wear a long dress?"

"So much for women's liberation. All you want to do is get tied up in suspenders and a corset!" Peter teased me.

"You will all with another teacher or myself, be offered the chance to be sent into any period of time for your first assignment." Dr. Kell announced. "How the process works is, that individually, with either myself or another teacher here at this school, you will be sent through time. This way it will introduce you to the process."

"Do we get to choose which period in time we want to go to?" Zack asked him.

"As long as the destination is safe, that is correct." Dr. Kell nodded, taking a sip of his coffee he brought along with him from the Caf.

"What do you mean, if it's safe?" Jordon asked him nervously.

"Well, we're certainly not going to let you go to France in the middle of World War 2 now, are we?" he raised one of his eyebrows.

"Damn." Peter said sarcastically. "That was my first choice."

"So we can go anywhere in the past or future? For how long?" Zack asked him.

"A school excursion will go no more than 12 hours. Yes, you can go anywhere in the past or future, as long as it is safe." He answered, repeating himself.

"Wow..." Zack looked shocked. "I think I'd want to go the future!" he looked at me. "Where do you want to go?"

"In England's past. I'd love to wear an olden day dress and go to a dinner party or ball or something!" I told him.

"I want to see Ancient Babylon!" Numu announced to the room.

"I would like to see Ancient Egypt." Jordon spoke up. This didn't surprise me. Jordon is Egyptian, and I guess that she'd love to see her country in the glory days.

"Ah... Egypt during the New Kingdom is a sight to behold." Kell stretched and yawned, then looked back at us all. "So you all know where you would like to go?"

"Yeah!" we all nodded in unison.

"Then let us discuss how I am going to structure your learning development to help you get to these places." Kell picked up his folder of notes and opened it.

Then Numu put up her hand again.

"Yes?" he inquired.

"Sir, when we graduate from this college, will we be permitted to explore time on our own?" she asked demurely.

"You will."

"And live in which time period we decide?" she continued.

"Yes."

"Then what does this Circulate want from us?"

The whole room went silent on this issue, waiting for his response.

Dr. Kell was quiet for a moment or two as he collected his thoughts and I guess, was trying to choose his next words very carefully.

"Ours can be a lonely gift. We can travel backwards and forwards through time… but even a traveling salesman can tell you that after too many nights in a hotel can make a person wish for home. With an ability like ours, long life can also come part and parcel with the manipulation of time. It is very sad to watch one's wife age before your eyes and leave you left in this life alone. When I was first taught this ability, I spent many years wandering alone. Sure you make friends with the people you encounter and you can splurge on the fruits you taste, and believe me, there are many fruits to be had. But it is also nice knowing that there are people out there that share this gift with you. So when you are out there exploring the galaxy, they can and do offer some kind of home environment to come back to."

We were all silent again, pondering on these sets of words. I like the way he uses his words, and the mixed accent he has behind them. It sounds like a combination of English, French and even Italian.

"So it's a support structure?" I asked.

"Exactly." He pointed his pen at me enigmatically. "Now, who here is ready to board the train for certain adventure and new knowledge?"

"I am!" we all cracked up laughing at him.

So anyway, in that first class we had with Dr. Kell, he outlined how we would be taught Math and Astronomy differently to the other students. We would only have him for these two subjects, and he would teach English and History to the rest of the students in the school. So we would still have our other classes the same as we always had, only our Math and Astronomy would be different.

===

23/03/01

Diary,

Life here at Hamilton's' has become so much better lately. Dr. Kell is teaching us Math and Astronomy in an easy and understandable manner. Every time we have these two classes the five of us meet in his office. He's recently moved a white board into the room and uses a projection screen attached to his laptop to show us illustrations of all the theories he's trying to teach us. And I'm relieved to say, that we don't have to use so many bloody mathematical problems now for homework and we don't have to calculate anything anymore for Astronomy. It's almost like the way he's teaching us and showing us pictures of the nearby stars and other solar systems, he's giving us maps. The only thing we still have to do is to learn how to calculate space-time, but the good thing about that is, he's teaching us to use space-time as a sort of compass.

A lot of the time our Math and Astronomy classes seem to blur together. The main topic always under discussion is time, but with the theory and less of the calculation of space-time brought up. But what I have discovered, which didn't surprise me when he first brought up the analogy, is that time is like water in a perfectly circular pond, with the layers of depth being the layers of time. And being perfectly spherical, when you start at the beginning, travel through the middle and arrive at the end, you find yourself at the beginning again. Basically, when we learn to Circulate, we will be phasing through these layers.

What some people called a type of haunting a 'time slip', where a room they enter looks completely different one minute, than normal the next, I learned differently in my classes with Dr. Kell. I have learned that it is a naturally occurring time displacement. When an everyday Joe accidentally stumbles into a room in either the past or the future, it is brought on by atmospheric conditions in the environment that can be triggered by electromagnetic charges. This can be brought on by a combination of causes, resulting from solar winds, or even the build up of geometric electrostatic charges from the Earth itself. When these time warps happen, it sends displacement waves through the pond of time like little ripples in the water, and then a temporary hole in time is formed. Then when we phase between the layers of time, we create momentary holes in time, often using mirrors and windows to focus on and use as temporary gateways between the layers of time.

In class today Dr. Kell had put a large mirror on the white board, and a second large mirror on the back wall next to the door, and made it that the mirrors were facing each other.

"Elisha, if you could stand up beside me please." Dr. Kell motioned, as he stood before the mirror on the white board. I did what I was told, as everyone watched me, and soon I was staring into my reflection. "Now tell me, what do you see?"

"My reflection." I shrugged.

"And anything else?"

"A reflection of my reflection." I implied the second mirror behind us.

"Very good." he turned around and sat with the rest of the class. "Now, everyone, what you will learn in today's lesson is how useful a mirror can be. It is the simplest device, either of a highly polished metal, or a refractory sheet of glass. But what lies beneath this simplistic device, is a very interesting principle. Now Elisha, I want you to stand there, with out me, looking into the reflection of the reflection for a few moments."

"What? Why?" I suddenly felt self-conscious standing there alone.

He waved his hand at me to just do it, so I turned around and did what I was told.

I stared into the reflection of the reflection of the reflection, and after a few moments, soon I could do it with out blinking.

My eyes glazed over and mystified slightly, as the reflections warped and changed. At first the reflection of the reflection seemed to expand... and I could no longer see the boarders of where each mirror ended. Then the reflections of the reflections didn't look two dimensional anymore, and when the boarders disappeared, I felt like the view seemed to get temporarily brighter as the view seemed to be in four dimensions. Soon I didn't see the reflection of the reflection of the reflection of my teacher and classmates anymore, I saw an empty room with no furniture!

It startled me, and my eyes went back to normal as I took a step back.

"What did you see?" Dr. Kell asked me.

"The room changed!" I told him.

Peter snorted, about to laugh at me when Dr. Kell gave him an icy glare and he immediately shut up.

"How so?" Dr. Kell asked me, standing up again.

"There weren't any people or furniture." I said.

"Excellent." Was all he said with out explaining why to me. "Peter, you're up."

So Peter stood up and went to go look in the mirror as I took my seat beside Zack again. We all waited to hear what he would have to say next. But it seemed to take longer with him. He kept fidgeting, not looking into the mirror properly, and adjusting his stance.

Finally he concentrated, and we heard him let out a long held breath.

"Yes?" Dr. Kell asked him.

"How did you do that?" Peter turned and asked him.

"Do what?"

"They're just mirrors, right? So how can you change the picture?" Peter asked him.

"Peter, what did you see?" Kell asked him.

"This woman sitting reading a book in old clothes or somethin'."

"Thank you, now take a seat again." Kell waved his hand again and then turned to the rest of this.

"Mirrors, like the surface of water, or even looking through a glass window, can collect, distort and refract light. It can concentrate it, and it can dissipate it. You've all seen how Polaroid sunglasses work, haven't you?" he asked us and we all nodded. "Mirrors can also refract laser beams and energy particles. What you will learn is how to use a mirror so not to reflect your particles, but instead how to dissipate them as you phase between layers. Using mirrors and glass windows will be your first step to learning how to Circulate."

"Then what was that looking glass exercise we just did all about?" Peter asked Kell.

"A normal human being would not have seen anything different in their reflections. When first learning to see through time, mirrors and windows are useful tools to use to catch the reflections of time, which you all have the ability to see through. The different time periods that you two saw... if you had concentrated any longer you could well have stepped through the mirror and remained in that frame of time." Kell stated. "Congratulations. You just officially made your first step towards Circulating through time."

===

31/03/01

Diary,

I didn't feel like having dinner and watching the movie for 'fun night' tonight. I was too wrapped in writing my Astronomy assignment on Ley Lines, Circular Stones and other landmarks and their position towards the stars and the universe. I think this kind of stuff is absolutely fascinating! So far my classes with Dr. Kell are a little on the kooky side, but I love how he blends into understanding Math, Astronomy and their part in History.

I had a nice surprise tonight. As I was working on my essay, Pat came in with some Mexican food they had served in the cafeteria. He had saved me a plate and brought it in for me.

"Thanks." I smiled at him, then immediately started stuffing the burrito into my mouth. I hadn't realized I was hungry.

"How are your classes going?" he asked me.

"Pretty goo'." I said with my mouth full. "Yours?"

"Yeah, same ole, same ole." He picked up my note book and started perusing through it. He paused at my diagrams of spherical space-time and at the layers of time in a pond analogy. "We're actually working on the same thing at the moment."

"Yeah, but while you're doing the calculating of the phenomenon, we're just getting the basics." I said. "But we have got to use examples where we've actually seen through time."

"No way." He looked up at me in surprise. "We haven't even got that far yet!"

"Yeah, but our classes are on the practical side, remember?" I reminded him before taking another bite.

"Yeah, I guess." He put my book down again.

"At the end of the semester, we're going to go on our first excursion through time." I told him.

"Really?" he asked impressed. "Which time period?"

"Any." I guess. "Whatever we choose I guess."

"That would be cool." He agreed.

"Hey Pat, can I ask you a question?" I asked him after a moment.

"Yeah." He shrugged.

"What was it like for you when you were 13 years old and Hamilton appeared and offered to bring you here at Hamilton's? Into the future?"

He was quiet for another moment, before saying, "it was a surprise. I mean, my father had been dead for six months, my mother had just been hung and only moments before I ran a knife across my wrists. I was about to pass out when this strange man approached me, spoke to me, picked me up and the next thing I knew, I was in the hospital wing at this school."

"Really?" I asked surprised. "That's almost the same way it happened to me! Then what happened?"

"Hamilton and Dr. Knight told me where I was and offered to let me stay here." He said.

"Did you need to think about it for a while?"

"Nup. I mean, I didn't have much of a future staying where I'd come from. I thought I'd give this time frame a go instead. I certainly had nothing to lose."

"I guess not." I saw his point. "I think that's the way how I felt too."

"Can I ask you a question?" he asked me next. I nodded and he continued. "Why do you always write in your diary?"

"I don't know. My mother first gave me a diary when I was 12 years old. It just caught on, that's all." I answered.

"Sometimes, watching you, it's like you're documenting this time frame now, for later on in the future." Pat said to me.

"That's kind of true." I shrugged. "But do you ever get the feeling that none of this is real? That you're not really here? Well, putting my thoughts onto paper, or hard disk as it were... it's kind of like leaving my mark on reality. To show that I was here, that I existed."

"I always thought that you wrote in your diary because you were marking down how you perceived your existence." Suddenly Nelson showed up in my doorway.

"Well, that too." I confessed.

Nelson came into my room, shut my door behind her and put my window up a tiny bit. Then we all took out our cigarettes and lit them. We hadn't done this all together in what felt, a very long time. It felt good getting together again.

"How are your classes going?" I asked her.

"Good." she shrugged. "How about yours? Little Miss Circulator of 2-0-0-1?"

"Good." I shrugged again. "But there is one thing I'm a bit nervous about."

"And what's that?" Pat asked me.

"Well, when we Circulate, dispersing and rotating through the circle of time, our bodies actually dissipate into energy, or light waves. How am I physically dispersing myself into light waves? It just sounds impossible right now." I pointed out.

"Well, you saw Dr. Knight go all through see-through, I guess that's how." Nelson said. "Her molecules speed up in the process."

"Have you guys studied the Friedman model yet? How gravity is so strong that space is bent around itself, making the universe with all the galaxies inside of it like a sphere? How space is 3 dimensional and time is the 4th dimension?" I asked them.

"Yep. Covered that in Astronomy two weeks ago." They nodded.

"Do you believe it?"

"Well, since they, the teachers, know what it's actually like in the future, do you think that they would teach us something that's incorrect?" Nelson raised her eyebrow at me.

"I've got a question for you." Pat looked at me as he exhaled smoke. "That night you, Sally and Zack followed Peter into Alpha building on Halloween. How did you sense what was going on?"

"You're like the fifth person who's asked me that, and the answer's still the same. No fucking idea." I said annoyed.

"Well here's one. Space and time are dynamic quantities, so like when a body moves, or a force acts, like a reverberation, it affects the way in which other bodies move or other forces act. Space and time not only the effect but are also the affected. You felt the change in the time line, like a reverberation." Pat explained.

"Oh yeah. I think that's what Dr. Knight was trying to point out to me. That goes with the ripple effect in the pond of time." I nodded.

"Hey, I want you to promise me something." Nelson suddenly grabbed my arm.

"Yeah? What?"

"When we've finished at this college, that you'll take me to New York in the 1980's." she said.

"What? Why?" I asked her, nearly laughing.

"I'd love to be apart of that disco, punk, retro thing and live in a Fifth Avenue apartment. Didn't you ever see the movie, 'American Psycho'?" she looked at me.

"What, you wanna become the psycho and kill everybody?" Pat laughed at her.

"OK smart ass, where and when would you wanna live?" Nelson turned on him.

"The future. After World War 3 when the whole planet goes through its second Renaissance." Pat stated.

"You know about World War 3? When does that happen?" I asked, shocked.

"You'll learn about it in History in Senior year." Pat stubbed out his cigarette.

"Is it in our life time?" I asked him, suddenly worried about my family... Dad, Jen, Uncle Ben and Aunt Gabby... even Mark.

"Chill out. You'll find out later." Pat wouldn't say anymore than that. "Well I'm gonna go downstairs and watch the movie."

He opened my door and closed it behind himself.

"Well, that's a cheerful note to end the conversation on." I grumbled to Nelson.

"Fuck the world. Human kind has always been a disaster waiting to happen. Now, tell me about what's new with you and Zack..." Nelson poked me in the ribs.

```
=================================================
```

TO: s_parson@snailmail.com
FROM: ebaker_hamiltons@evers.com
SUBJECT: Hallo, how are you?
DATE: 29/ 04/ 01

Hi Sally,

How are you? I haven't heard from you since you left school, so I thought I'd send you an email instead. Did you get my text messages? Your number is 01199 614326 isn't it? My phone number is the same, 61402 216323.

Are you enjoying living with your family again? Are back at your old school? Have you been sent to a new school? I hope this email reaches you.

Life here is OK. As you can imagine, things have changed since THAT night, but in a good way. Classes have been restructured, we have a new teacher called Dr. Rufus Kell (you've met him - you may remember him best dressed as a Roman Centurion) and we're even planning our first excursion!

I can't say anymore, not until you email me back anyway so I know this email has reached you OK.

Please write, or call, or text or whatever… I miss you, so does Zack and Maya.

```
=================================================
```

TO: ebaker_hamiltons@evers.com
FROM: s_parson@snailmail.com
SUBJECT: Hi
DATE: 01/ 05/ 01

Hi Elisha,

Thanks for your emails. Yeah, I got your text messages, sorry I didn't text you back though. It has just taken me a while to get over that place, you know what I mean?

Yes I'm back living with the family and attending my old school. I'd forgotten how bitchy going to an all-girls school can be! But it's a nice change being able to go home at the end of the day and getting away from it all (especially from girls like Nelson!).

I'm glad to hear you're enjoying yourselves. What do you mean by your first excursion? Is it what I think it means?

Say hi to Zack and Maya for me.

===

TO: s_parson@snailmail.com
FROM: ebaker_hamiltons@evers.com
SUBJECT: Life imitating Art…
DATE: 03/ 05/ 01

Yep, it is exactly what you think it means. In a couple more weeks time when end of term has reached us, my class will be taken on their first Circulation. Zack, Peter, Wong, Jordon, Numu and I will be each taken separately on our first trip with a teacher. The excursions will only be for 12 hours, but we can go anywhere, anytime… it's our choice.

You know how we monitored the electrostatic charge at Hamilton's office and the window on the second floor where we saw Dr. Knight in olden day dress and Dr. Rufus Kell as the Roman Centurion? It's because our phasing in and out of the time frames when our molecules are speeding up and we look see-through, causes an electrostatic charge. The charge in the atmosphere can effect temperature changes as well makes our hairs stand on end, which is why we felt all cold and tingly those nights.

We are learning to use mirrors, windows and even some doorways in a building. But what we've learned is that while we have more control over Circulating using windows and mirrors; there are some doorways in buildings that are natural holes in time we can use as well. You know how in our research we came across stories of hauntings where people walk into a room and it looks completely different, like in the past or the future, but then the room goes back to normal? These are natural holes in the layers of time. In class at the moment we are learning how to sense and use these doorways. But unlike Circulating, these doorways and holes in time have only fixed locations in time, but when we Circulate, we can control which time frame we want to go to.

Also with these doorways, they're not just limited to buildings, but can occur outside as well. It's because 90% of these doorways aren't fixed, but they're almost like bubbles. They float around, and are called displaced time. It has something to do with interaction between the Earth's rotation and it's magnetosphere, solar winds from the sun, our magnetic poles, electrostatic and electromagnetic consistencies in the atmosphere... blah blah blah, you get the idea. But the other bad point about these doorways, is you may move forwards and backwards in time, but it's in that same location only. With Circulating, there is a futuristic technology I haven't seen yet (only heard about in some Headquarters somewhere looked over by a Council of Circulators and Calculators) that enables us to move between different locations on Earth as well as in time. So, as our molecules speed up and our body matter dissipates to disperse and rotate through time, this machine can move our matter to another geological point. So as Dr. Knight did, she left Canada in 2000 AD and reappeared in England in the 1700's AD.

Here's something that would interest you, it's about the British Isles and some of the Islands in the Pacific and even the pyramids in Egypt and South America and Asia. I've just learned this in my astronomy class, even though Professor Hamilton also mentioned it in our History class... that this even involves Leylines. The first of the Circulate who were either High Priests or Shamen or Witches or Druids in either or all cultures, who could see and Calculate, were the ones who in their culture, instructed the creation of the landmarks. You remember how the Great Pyramid in Egypt was built in a way that aligned itself with certain astronomical and magnetic forces? And the South American temples with the exact amount of steps as there are to days in a year? And the positioning of the altars to the movement of the Earth to the sun? I know that you know about Stonehenge and it's positioning to the sunrise, sunset and at night certain stars in the sky. But the circular symbols engraved in the rocks, even in many of the other stone circles around the British Isles, are a testament to the Wheel of Time. And guess what the Wheel of Time is a testament to? Circulating, and the rotation of time. Even the Ancient Circulators and Calculators saw, or suspected that space is round, and that space is in three dimensions, with time the fourth dimension.

Leylines were created to mark the magnetic forces on the planet, and to track the movements of displaced time. The Druids foresaw that the bubbles of displaced time, even though they happened sporadically, there were certain geographic marks in the environment that sort of attracted them, or pulled on them. That's probably why there are many stories in your culture, Celtic Mythology, on how people walking along a road at night could be in danger of accidentally walking into the Fairy Kingdom, for they walk into displaced time momentarily, see either the past or future, panic, then run away again.

I hope I haven't massively freaked you out. I just wanted to let you know what we're learning, and to pass it on to you. I still feel like you're involved in all of this somehow, so I just want to keep you updated. If you like I can email you my class notes and assignments?

I told everyone that I got an email from you at dinner in the Caf last night. Peter asked me how you are, and I told him that you're good. Brett and Maya have been sitting with us a lot lately, and Maya told me to say hi again. We all miss you very much. Even Zack himself said that he missed the three of us mucking around like we used to.

Do you reckon if you asked your parents if you could come back, they'd let you? Hamilton could arrange it. He could tell your parents that you could be offered some sort of scholarship or whatever. Don't worry about money, Sally, we'll sort something out.

So, what do you think?

===

TO: ebaker_hamiltons@evers.com
FROM: s_parson@snailmail.com
SUBJECT: Thanks but no thanks
DATE: 10/ 05/ 01

Thank everyone for the well wishes. Thanks for the History lesson. And thanks for the invitation.

But no thanks.

I left Hamilton's College to get away from that kind of stuff, remember?

Take care of yourself Elisha, and good luck flying through time and the universe.

===

06/ 05/ 01

Diary,

I think I frightened Sally off again. She replied to my email, and then when I told her what we've all been doing lately... she just ran in the opposite direction... again.

I told Zack about it last night when we were hanging out in my room. We skipped the videos after dinner last night and just laid on my bed, listening to music. He held me in his arms again, running his hand up and down my back. I like it when he does that.

"Do you think Sally is ever going to come back to this college?" I asked him.

"I dunno. It doesn't sound like it." He shrugged.

"But Dr. Knight said that in the future Sally does become apart of the Circulate."

"Did she say when?"

"No."

"Maybe she does when we've all left College or something. Like, maybe when we're like 30 years old or something." He thought out loud.

"Yeah, I suppose. But it's a long time away." I sighed.

"Not really. Not when you don't think of time in a linear sense. You can always fast forward to that point you know." Zack reminded me.

"Don't you mean, phase to that point?" I smiled at him.

"Yeah, that too." He leaned in and kissed me.

Then we were quiet for a few moments, but I could tell he was thinking about something else now.

"What?" I propped my head up so I could look at him.

"What?" he asked me back.

"What are you thinking about?" I asked him.

"Well, you know how they say that we can slow down our aging process? That we can live for almost four times longer than the average human being in the 21st Century?"

"Yeah...?"

"What if you and I got married? Then we would never have to worry about outliving our partner. We could almost stay together forever." Zack looked directly into my eyes.

"Yeah, but, we want to live in different eras. Like, you're all for the future, and I want to explore the past." I pointed out.

"We could take turns. We could live in the era you want, then we could check out the era I want." He offered.

I pulled away from him as I sat up and moved towards the edge of the bed.

"I don't know..." I faltered.

"Why?"

"I don't know... I guess I was just thinking of what Dr. Kell told us. Exploring on our own, sampling different cultures, you know, just finding out who we are and what we want by ourselves." Zack looked hurt, so I quickly added, "but there's always each other and the Circulate to come back to."

He looked up at me with that vulnerable/ kicked-puppy expression on his face again and said softly, "I bet you think I'm just some desperate loser who is so wet in love he can't think of anything else."

I smiled at him and tried to make a joke of it. "You mean it's not true?"

"You want some time apart, don't you?" he sat up dejectedly.

"No. What, you mean right now or in the future?" I asked him.

He shrugged.

"Zack, right now, here at Hamilton's, this is our time. I have no idea about us and the future... well, yeah, I do." I joked again. "But lets just enjoy this moment, OK?"

Zack didn't say anything else, but he leaned over and kissed my neck softly, then wrapping his arms about my waist, he pulled me back down onto the bed.

07/05/01

Diary,

In our first class of the day with Dr. Kell, he handed out these kind of ultra-modern ipod things (like I found in Professor Hamilton's draw that night we broke into his office). As we turned them on, we found that they had detailed information and pictures of the eras we each wanted to travel to for our first excursion. We also found out which teachers would be taking us through time as our guides/ baby-sitters.

I found out I would be taken to London in the summer of 1755, to a large Aristocratic Ball.

I got so excited reading over this, I started giggling!

"What are you so happy about?" Peter asked me, and tried to snatch my ipod thing off me.

"I've got exactly what I asked for." I gloated. "And you?"

"Yeah." He shrugged.

"Where are you going?" I asked him.

"To a certain music festival in America during the 1960's..." he gloated back.

"Woodstock?!" Zack and I exclaimed.

"How did you land that?" Zack grabbed his ipod to look at it for himself disbelievingly.

"I have my ways..." he said simply, then let out an evil laugh.

"Well it's not like they're going to let you do drugs or anything, so don't get your hopes up." I pointed out.

"As an English rogue once said, 'ways and means old girl, ways and means." Peter said smugly.

"Zack?" I asked him next, looking at his ipod.

"I'm going to a Zero-G Football match in the year 2083 AD."

"To watch or to compete?" I asked him, already guessing.

"I'm going to compete." He tried to sound modest, but he suddenly attracted everyone's attention in the room at once.

"To play?" Jordon asked him, impressed.

"Yeah." He told everyone.

"What is a Zero-G Football match?" Numu asked us, puzzled.

"Zero Gravity." Peter told her.

"So, Jordon, did you get Egypt?" I asked her.

"Yes. 1200 BC." Jordon nodded.

"Numu? What about you?" I asked her next.

"No. I'm visiting the Babylonian Empire in 590 BC." Numu replied.

"Wong? Where are you going?" Zack asked her last.

"Beijing in 1370 AD, during the Ming Dynasty." Wong answered.

"OK everyone." Dr. Kell now called everyone's attention back to him. "In your next few classes with me over the next four weeks, we will be going over your information disks thoroughly. Also on Saturday and Sunday mornings of the next four weekends we will be adding extra classes. Some of you will be learning the basics of a new language, all of you will be learning off by heart detailed histories of the eras you have chosen, and you will all be learning how to immerse yourselves in a new culture. You will each be assigned a teacher who will be your guide. Tonight, you will be meeting your teachers to discuss your plans. Peter and Numu, you will both have Professor Hamilton as your guide. Zack, you will have Dr. Myles, Wong and Jordon, you will both have me. Elisha, you will Dr. Knight. Now, are there any questions?"

Numu put up her hand. "Sir, what happens if something goes wrong and we are separated from our teachers?"

That caught all of our attention, and we all went quiet to hear the answer.

"Then your teacher will find you again. You may have been taught as a child a simple rule to follow if you are separated from your parents... stay where you are and try not to keep moving about. If in some circumstance you are unable to, try not to panic. Not only will your teachers be watching over you, but the Circulate will be as well. Your excursion back through time will be over seen by a Calculator." He assured us.

"So in this Headquarters where the Circulate is, our time traveling habits are always being monitored?" I asked Dr. Kell.

"That is correct." He answered.

I don't know if I like that idea. It's like Big Brother watching over us all of the time... this both freaked me out as well as made me feel safe in a comforting way. Freaked and comforted... I wondered if this is what my future would hold? I exchanged looks with Peter and Zack and saw that they felt the same way.

In a way it's like we have almost limitless freedom with this ability we have, but then, with the Circulate, we could almost be tied to a leash.

===

13/ 05/ 01

Diary,

So far I've had six classes preparing me for the Aristocratic London social life of 1755. Then when I'm not doing homework for my classes, I'm studying Aristocratic English culture. Zack, Peter, Nelson and Pat say they couldn't think of anything more boring... but I'm having a blast!

Just looking at the pictures of the clothing they wore, the powdered wigs, the jewels drooping from their ears and necks... the wine, the dancing, and even the romantic intrigues that were simmering below the surface! Marriages were very much political and made upon a person's position in society and how much money they had in their bank accounts, but even if you didn't love your husband (or wife) there were the affairs, or to borrow the term from one of my favorite Michelle Phieffer movies, 'dangerous liaisons'. As long as these remained secret, as long as the rumors remained rumors and 'one was never discovered', you could almost have as many lovers as you want!

Dr. Knight will be reprising her title of Lady Dunmore and will be my 'chaperone' to introduce me into society. They will call this 'my first season'. Normally in that era a young lady enters the London season to look for a suitable marriage. I'm just coming along for the ride!

My title will be Lady Elisha Durrant, I'll be a Scottish relative of the Dunmore family and my social identity has ties to the Bruce clan (but according to Dr. Knight most clans have ties to each other anyway from such a long history) and my money has come from principally owning vast amounts of land in the Colonies (the U.S. before it's War of Independence).

I don't expect to have much romantic intrigue or any marital offers on my first excursion out... but I am still excited about it. Excitement... and nervous you could say my mood is at the moment. I've noticed it in Zack, Jordon, Numu and Wong as well. We're excited about the destinations that have been given out to us, but we're all nervous about the journey. This will be our first phase.

Dr. Kell thinks this is all highly amusing, our fear of walking into glass. So far in class we've been using the mirror exercise so we can actually see our destinations, also with the help of the geography relocator in Circulate Headquarters. This helps us to see the different location, as we can see back in time. Next week we will move onto windows. But actually phasing our bodies into light waves so that we can 'cross over' to another period of time is still pretty scary to think about It's almost like going on your first sky-dive and being told you don't need a parachute!

I haven't told anyone this, but last night, I decided to stay in my room and study more for my first journey instead of watching any movies in the Rec rooms. After a while of reading, I turned off my light and pulled open my curtains and stared at the glass. After a couple of minutes, I did notice the reflection start to slowly waver, and the landscape change!

I wasn't staring at the darkened mountains or lake anymore, but some kind of grassy plain with a little stream of water instead. I couldn't make it out properly, because it did seem kind of blurry. So I tried to concentrate harder, thinking harder of England or something else 18th Century. But my eyes started to feel sore and dry for not blinking for so long, so I stopped.

Bugger. I wonder if I was nearly there? I wonder what would have happened if I had of concentrated properly?

==

20/ 05/ 01

Diary,

Had a chat to Dad on the phone in Nell's office this evening. He's fit and well, but unfortunately Gran isn't. Apparently time has caught up with her, and Dad and Aunt Gabby have decided to put poor Gran in 24 hour care. She hasn't got Alzheimer's, but full-on dementia, so much so she can't take care of herself anymore.

I remember when Granddad went, how lonely Gran was at first. I remembered she stayed with us for a month after the funeral, nearly driving us all batty, telling us what to do. We didn't have to wait on her or anything, but she re-organized the kitchen, then the linen cupboard, and constantly made 'suggestions' on how things should be done. She kept saying, "now of course you don't have to do this, but..." I remember how well Mum took it on the chin. Face to face, she was patient with Gran, but then to Dad she grumbled when they were in the privacy of their bedroom and Gran had gone to bed on the other side of the house.

Mum and Dad both worked, which I wondered if Gran approved of when she stayed with us. Mark and I didn't have to go to after school care, we got to go straight home which was nice. And she did bake a lot, so there was always something yummy to eat for afternoon tea or dessert at night. And she did crochet a beautiful bed spread for me, which I have on my bed even now (one of the nice things Dad remembered to pack for me when I was first sent here). Now I hear that she can't cook for herself anymore and she hasn't crocheted anything in the last two years because of her arthritis.

When I saw her last Christmas, I did notice she was a lot quieter. Then when Aunt Gabby and Dad were preparing Christmas Dinner, it was the first time I didn't see Gran in there as well, bossing everyone about. Gran always insisted on having fresh peas as well as other fresh vegies with our meals - frozen stuff was a definite no-no. But this Christmas Aunt Gabby used frozen peas and carrots with our roasted vegetables and Gran didn't say a thing. I guess that was one of the signs. Also she called Mark, Edward (Dad's name) a couple of times too, I guess that was another sign. She did call me Grace (Mum's name) once, but I didn't mind. A few of our rellies have told me I'm almost the spitting image of my Mum, which I've always taken as a compliment.

Now poor Gran, after driving us batty at one point in time or another, is going batty herself. Thanks to the degeneration of brain cells. Thanks to fatigue. Thanks to the aging process. Thanks to time itself.

This has kind of been like a wake-up call for me. I mean, sure, I'm not a stranger to death. My grandparents on my Mum's side passed away when I was 2 and then 4, Granddad died when I was 8, Mum when I was 13, and now Gran is severely weakened... but now I know I have these strange powers. Well, I guess they're not powers, because it's just one ability. I now know I will have to become accustomed to seeing all my family die around me.

Great, they're all going to drop like flies while I keep buzzing along. While I can slow time around me and me alone, my father, brother and relatives will all wilt and die. This ability I have is an isolated thing, when not even my family can join in.

Now I understand what Dr. Kell was telling us. How 'ours can be a lonely gift'. How the Circulate can offer companionship and support. I had started thinking that this Circulate idea, of always being monitored, was a claustrophobic idea. Now I wonder if maybe it's not.

I surprised Zack at dinner tonight when he caught me staring at him and everyone else at our table in the Caf tonight. There were the usual five of us, Peter, Zack and Nelson talking away, with Pat reading a book beside his plate, studying while he ate dinner. I was quietly observing them, and thinking about our situation, especially in contrast with Gran and the rest of my family.

"What?" Zack gave me an uncomfortable look. "Have I got ketchup on my face?" Self-consciously he wiped the back of his hand around his mouth as a just-in-case-of.

But Nelson half guessed my thoughts already. "Is it something to do with your conversation with your Dad?"

"My Gran's gone into 24 hour care." I announced to everyone.

"Oh, I'm sorry." Zack instantly stopped what he was doing and took my hand sympathetically.

"And it made me realize, that as the years go by, pretty soon all of our families are going to go into care, and then die, and we five will still be sitting here, having dinner together." I stated.

Nelson nearly choked on her food with laughter as soon as I said that, even Peter shared the chuckle himself.

"Speak for yourself! I'm hoping to get a life before that happens!" Nelson stated back.

"But what life? What Elisha is saying, is that when we do try to get lives of our own, we will out live the people in them. All we have is a series of moments in time, as our time stretches out, and everyone else's time is shrunk to the size of keyholes." Pat looked up from his book.

"Thank you Patrick." I nodded.

"That was very profound mate. Did you get it from that book you're reading?" Peter started laughing at him next.

Pat lifted up the book so we could see the cover. It was a book on Calculus. So he showed him no, he didn't.

"Have you ever thought about looking up your relatives in this time?" I asked Pat.

He looked at me for a moment or two, before answering. "Yes. Of course. But do you think I can? Can you imagine the response?"

I could see his point. "But that's also what I mean. This is just so surreal. I mean, one minute we're in an ordinary boarding school, the next minute it's haunted, then in another our teachers can travel through time and will teach us to do it too. Now, we're studying with somebody who has traveled through time. Plus, we learn, we can internally slow down time as well as move through it externally. My Gran will be the last of my grandparents to die, and she's halfway there. Then it will be my parents and Aunts and Uncles, then my brother and my cousins, and then it will be down to me, who may or may not still be young, and still meeting up with you guys for dinner."

"I know what you mean. Using the dinner table metaphor, let's say everyone was seated at once. Then only we would get up and leave afterwards, while everyone else have turned to skeletons and the food has gone all mouldy." Peter suddenly agreed.

"Yeah." I nodded to him.

"I think I saw that on TV once..." Peter thought out loud.

"You did. In a 'Dr. Who' episode, when they were stuck in E space." Pat said, not looking up from his book.

"Back to 'Dr. Who' again." Nelson rolled her eyes.

"Well it could be worse. It could be Batty Potter." Peter said.

"Hey, I like those books." I gave him a dirty look when he said that.

"You also still read 'Narnia' books. What's next? 'Where's Spot'?" Peter raised his eyebrows at me.

"Fuck off Peter." I glared at him. "At least I don't go through life just looking for chances to drug myself out of it."

"No, you'd rather hide from it." He glared back at me. "Or should we say, end it?"

"Hey! Guys! Chill out!" Nelson waved her hands in front of our faces as if to wake us up. "Where did that come from?"

We didn't answer her, but we just sat there glaring at each other. Zack looked at us both in surprise, also surprised by what just took place. I was tempted to stand up and walk out, but I knew if I did that it would be a sign of weakness. So I stayed just to give it back as good as I got.

==

22/ 05/ 01

Diary,

This evening after dinner when I met up with Dr. Knight in her room, she had a surprise waiting for me. She had a dress and matching undergarments for me to try on. I know this sounds dorky, but I couldn't wait to try on the corset and everything! She even had shoes and stockings to go with them. And get this, the stockings were held up by ribbons in those days, and only went half way up the thigh.

In the background she had a CD playing of the kind of music that was being played by musicians in the era we'll be traveling to. And as I tried on the dress, or rather, stood still with my arms sticking out like a scarecrow and she dressed me, Dr. Knight quizzed me on 18th Century trivia. I'm glad to say that I answered everything with nearly a 99% success rate.

"Very good." Dr. Knight nodded with approval, taking a step back to look at her work when she had finished. "What do you think?"

I turned around and looked in her full-length mirror. The dress was a dark sea green silk with gold and silver embroidery, and white and silver ruffles on the sleeve. The neckline was square, and the shoes on my feet were also gold embroidered material with a large silver buckle on top.

"Cool! This is so cool! I love it!" I gleamed, and turned around in a circle to see the back of it too.

"That's good. For the rest of our lessons you will be wearing 18ᵗʰ Century dresses so you can become accustomed to them." Dr. Knight announced. "And tonight's tutorial will teach you how to dance in them."

"Really?" I asked in surprise and suddenly felt self-conscious and a little silly. "But it's really heavy." I tried lifting up the skirt, petticoat and hoop above my ankles, but there was so much material to grab hold of, it kept slipping from my grip.

"That's why you need to get used to them." She said simply, coming to stand beside me and she scooped up my hair in her hands, and tried to sit it in a puffy look on top of my head. But my hair is only just past my shoulders, so it didn't stay up properly. "Hmmm. We'll need a wig I think."

Then there was a knock on her door, which she answered immediately. I felt even more self-conscious just standing around, looking like this. I hoped it wasn't Peter or Nelson at the door, as I'd hate them to see me like this. I could just imagine Peter crack up laughing or Nelson shaking her head at me.

Thankfully it was neither of them, but it wasn't much better. It was Brett! He came inside Dr. Knight's room at being invited by her to do so, and his eyes immediately went wide when he saw me! How embarrassing! I flinched, waiting to hear a glib remark or something worse.

"Woah," was all he said. "Cool dress. Is this for your trip?"

"Correct." Dr. Knight answered. "Now, I asked Brett here so he can be your dance partner. I can show you some of the steps myself, but I'll also need to instruct. So to start with, I'll show Brett the first of the steps so he can take the lead, and then Elisha, I'll show you what to do next."

I sat on her bed, while in the center of her room (which is fairly big, like the size of four dorm rooms put together) I watched Dr. Knight show Brett the basics of one of the dances. She had to show him a couple of times for him to get the hang of it. I tried not to laugh at him, and I wondered if he never had to get dancing lessons when he was at school? I remember when I was primary school and we had a few school dances, and we used to have lessons before them to show us the Australian 'Bush' dances. I remembered the 'Heel and Toe' and 'Bush Waltz' and 'Strip the Corn' and even one square dance where the theme for 'Bonanza' played. But watching poor Brett try to get the knack, made me think he never had to do any of these.

Next it was my turn and I stood up and was shown by Dr. Knight what my movements would be. It didn't take me that long to remember the steps. But when she put the two of us together, mayhem let loose!

At first I trod on the bottom of my dress and fell sideways into Brett, then he trod on my dress and I nearly fell backwards! Then we accidentally head-butted each other when I was supposed to do a turn under his raised arm!

"Oooww!" we both yelped and backed away.

Dr. Knight had a good laugh at our expense, but she wouldn't let us quit. For two hours we had to practice. Brett had to do these special steps where he had to go on tippy toes a few times, as well bend his legs and hold out his arms in a special way as we held hands and I followed his suit. I could tell he was starting to feel really uncomfortable. I knew what was going through his mind tonight, 'lucky no-one else can see us at this moment'. I knew because this was exactly my thought.

"All right. You can stop now." Dr. Knight announced after giving us a little applause for our efforts. We had only mastered one dance tonight, I guess she thought it would be too much to try and teach us another one as well.

Brett was shown out the door and then Dr. Knight helped me out of the clothes. Man, it felt good getting back into my regular clothes. I thought I had been wearing too many clothes back in winter with the thermal underwear, but that was nothing when compared to the costume I just had on.

Going back up the stairs in my jeans, sneakers and jumper to my room was almost a luxury after what happened tonight! But I learned another piece of history, and I have to learn at least six more dances to master before my trip to the Ball back in time. Poor Brett. Apparently he's going to be my dance partner for the rest of the time before I go!

Speaking of which, when I reached my floor I found Brett sitting on the floor outside my door, waiting for me. He instantly stood up when he saw me coming, and I think I flinched again, at imagining him saying something like 'you were crap, I don't want to do that again'. But then I saw his cheeks looked a little pinkish, and I wondered if he felt pretty shy about it all too.

"Hey." He greeted.

"Hey." I said back.

"Sorry about treading on your toes."

"You didn't." I tried to reassure him. "I think the dress was the only victim in that catastrophe."

"I think Dr. Knight needs to ask somebody else. As you can see, I can't dance to save my life." He shrugged boyishly.

"Well, have you done it before?"

"What, dance? Yeah, but not like that before." He answered.

"Then why don't you stick around and learn. To be honest, I think I'd rather have as few people as possible in this school see me in dresses like that. So if you stick at it, then Dr. Knight doesn't have to go and ask somebody else." I tried to make a joke of it.

"Yeah, sure." He chuckled and started to walk away, back down the hall to his room. Then he stopped and turned and looked at me again. "Hey." He said again. "You don't look half bad in those dresses."

I didn't know what to say to that, so I just smiled back and rolled my eyes, trying to make a joke of it before taking my key out to unlock my door.

===

TO: s_parson@snailmail.com
FROM: ebaker_hamiltons@evers.com
SUBJECT: First school excursion
DATE: 27/ 05/ 01

Hi Sally,

How are you? I guess you thought I wouldn't email you again. But I thought you'd like to know my first excursion is coming up soon. So soon it's the 31st May. Dr. Knight will be taking me to a Ball in London in 1755 AD, Zack will be taken by Dr. Myles to a Zero-G Football match in 2083 AD, Peter's going to Woodstock with Professor Hamilton, Jordon got Egypt in 1200 BC with Dr. Kell and then Professor Hamilton again will be taking and Numu to the Babylonian Empire in 590 BC. Then Dr. Kell will take Wong back to the Ming Dynasty in 1370 AD.

I guess the teachers will be taking us each to their specific areas of expertise. Dr. Knight knows Aristocratic London in the 1700's, so she's the one who's taking me there. Both Professor Hamilton and Dr. Kell know their Ancient Histories, so they're taking Numu, Jordon and Wong to their chosen sites. Dr. Myles is all for the future and is all into sports and computers, so he's taking Zack. And Peter? Well you know Peter, they probably think only Professor Hamilton can keep an eye on him with him running rampant at Woodstock… especially with the last time Peter nearly tried to experiment with drugs.

So far I've been having one-on-one tutorials after class with Dr. Knight to prepare me for my first journey through time. We all have with the teachers who will be taking us. I've been brushing up with English history of the 1700's, from Walpole to Selwyn, the 7 years war, social etiquette and even dancing lessons in the gown I'm going to wear. I've also been told by Dr. Knight that I'll have to wear a wig coz my hair isn't long enough to be put in the hair styles that were the fashion of the day. But, I've learned, this won't be weird coz even in the 1700's, up until 1770, a lot of people dressed to the hilt, with powdered wigs and jewels and everything.

I just thought you might want to know all this coz you always seemed interested in this kind of era that I'm going to. And I'm sure you would want to know what everyone else is doing. So if you wanted to write back or whatever, I can keep you updated, if you want.

==

TO: jeni_B@goggleyes.com

FROM: ebaker_hamiltons@evers.com

SUBJECT: A hallo from a stranger

DATE: 28/ 05/ 01

Hey cuz,

Sorry it's been long time no write. But we have been studying a lot and our whole year has been restructured. I was even given extra classes outside of the usual classes! Needless to say the ole social life has suffered and I can't even remember the last time I participated in a 'Brown Day' and went into town and saw a movie or anything like that. Actually, I can't even remember the last time I did anything a normal teenager might do.

It's like since all the weird stuff that went on in January all the teachers here treat us like proper young adults instead of children anymore. And we're expected to act like young adults and they've heaped all this responsibility on us. It's like there's this humungus weight on our shoulders now, and we're trudging up this path, and with all the weight we're carrying now, we don't have the strength or the inclination to go off the beaten track, because we know it will just make this burden (or gift, or whatever you wanna call it) harder.

We have the scholarship to go to this private school, that acts as a gateway to the best colleges and universities in the world, that acts as a door to limitless possibilities and privileges, but it also closes us in. It's like the remote location of the school from the rest of our families and even the world is just training us for the days ahead when our alienation cuts us off even further. I sometimes wish I was still at home, that I never did that thing with my wrists, and that I could still see you on holidays. Then I could at least still be in the same country let alone the same state so I could see Gran in her final days.

Sorry if I sound a bit like a drama-queen. It's late and I've just finished a very long day. There's a big school excursion coming up that we have to have meetings for, and that's on top of the usual class assignments that we still have to do. You could say that this excursion is very important for our futures, so there's heaps of preparations and responsibility involved. But before I go ahead, I just wanted to let you know I miss you heaps, and I know this sounds kind-of sucky, but please give your parents a hug and kiss for me. And even Gran too when you next see her in the nursing home, I hear Aunt Gabby visits her nearly every day.

===

TO: mbaker@hotmail.com

FROM: ebaker_hamiltons@evers.com

SUBJECT: Sorry I haven't written much lately…

DATE: 29/ 05/ 01

Hey bro,

It's your little sis here writing to say sorry about the long time, no write. But the work load around here has been unbelievable, and if I did tell you what's been happening around here, you really wouldn't believe me. But I'm OK, I have my friends here, and I just wanted to drop a line or two your way to let you know.

I hear Gran is in 24 hour care now. Have you visited her lately? Have you seen Dad lately? What have you and Patrice been up to? Lets hear all the news.

School holidays are coming up soon, at the end of June we have a three month break. I think it's compensation that we only get two weeks off for Christmas and a week off over Easter. But it will be summer here in the Northern

Hemisphere. And the school will be running summer classes for students who will be staying on.

Don't say anything to Dad, coz I'll tell him myself when I call him next Sunday… but I'm thinking of staying on at school for two months and only coming home for a month. There are a lot of classes that I don't want to miss in the summer program and a few excursions that really interest me… like a week in Paris! So one of the subjects will be French with a trip to Paris at the end of the program! And another program I want to pick up will be music, and the other will be self-defense. Dad doesn't have to pay for Paris, it's covered by the school under the scholarship program. I just found out all of this today when they posted the summer program list on the board outside the Caf today.

I think they're also trying to compensate for overloading us with the gargantuan workload of the end of semester so they're offering to treat us. But what I haven't told you Mark, is that I'm already going on an excursion very soon, in a couple of days in fact, for 12 hours. It's a historical journey, you could say. And to prepare for it I've had to have tutorials after my usual days classes, which severely cuts into my homework time I can tell you. I've nearly had to hand in assignments late with the rate they're piling work on top of us! So a trip to Paris in the summer instead of back to the Blue Mtns in winter sounds like welcome relief to me! I've had enough of winter, I can tell you!

I better go now. I hope this email is enough to compensate for my oddly quiet behavior the last couple of months. Say hi to Patrice for me and I'll text you again when I have the dates of when I'll be home again for the hols. Also maybe look in on Gran for me, OK? I know it's a hassle to drive down to Wollongong, but think of all the toffee she used to make for us when we were little.

===

30/ 05/ 01

Diary,

I can tell I'm not the only one nervous about our upcoming trips backwards or forwards in time... I even caught Peter talking to his parents on the phone in the Dorms today! He NEVER talks to his parents! He bitches about his parents, but doesn't talk to them. I think even Professor Hamilton has had to act as a mediator in talks between Peter and his parents, as he's had to relay messages between the two. Such as, "Peter doesn't want to go home this summer, but rather stay and participate in our summer program". Then it's, "yes Peter, your parents are allowing you to stay on at school for the summer".

Speaking of which, there are signs and stuff on the notice board outside of the Caf advertising that the College will remain open throughout the three month summer break, offering extra-curricular classes and programs for students who want to stay on. It's offering more of the usual Math's and Science subjects, but also French, Italian, Spanish and Latin languages, Self-Defense classes, Music, Drama, and Art subjects. The bonus to the French program is that at the end it takes you to Paris for a week! In this time-frame, but still, a trip to Paris! I'm going to call Dad and let him know about the program and ask to only go home for a month instead of three. When I go home, it will be to see Dad and my family only. It won't be to see Angela or any of my old school 'friends'.

Zack and Nelson suggested at dinner tonight that I only go home for two weeks, or even not go home at all. Zack got all mushy and took my hand and told me he'd miss me too much when I'm gone, which made Peter and Nelson act like they were nauseous. But to be honest I'm looking forward to getting away from Hamilton's for a little while. This place, with preparing for the trip to a Ball in 1755, and everything, has been feeling a little claustrophobic lately, especially this week. I'm feeling pretty stressed out. When I emailed Jen a couple of days ago, I realized how much everything here is about what we are now. We are Circulators and Calculators. We are different from the rest of the human race. Everyone else will die around us. We are apart of the Circulate.

I would like a little break from the Circulate.

I'm even starting to feel a little claustrophobic hanging around the same people all of the time. So after dinner tonight I told Zack I had another meeting to prepare for my trip (which I didn't) and I grabbed my homework and went to study in Brett's room with him, Maya and Raj instead of in the library with Zack, Peter, Nelson and Pat. Even though our homework is different now, when I got stuck on a problem, Brett was still able to help me with the calculations. He didn't complain and let Maya burn one of her incense sticks in his room while we studied and played some music softly in the background. He even let me choose the music!

It's just so weird seeing how all this Circulate has affected everyone now. Enemies have become friends, best friends turned into enemies. Relatives are dying around us, and we have private tutorials on how to travel in time.

==

TO: ebaker_hamiltons@evers.com

FROM: s_parson@snailmail.com

SUBJECT: Bon Voyage

DATE: 31/ 05/ 01

Hey Elisha,

I just got your message, sorry it took a little while to get back to you. My stupid lap-top crashed! I hope it's not too late to wish you all luck.

Of course I care what happens to you all. I still think about all of you all the time. And you-know-who. But don't tell him this.

Say good-luck to everyone for me. And if you did want to email me afterwards and tell me everything, I will reply I promise.

Take care of yourselves, all right?

==

TO: s_parson@snailmail.com
FROM: ebaker_hamiltons@evers.com
SUBJECT: I did it!
DATE: 01/ 06/ 01

I'm back…I'm back…And I went…I can't believe I went! Been there and back again!

I can't believe it really happened! And that it happened to me! With the assistance of Dr. Knight of course… but I went and danced and drank and ate and flirted at an Aristocratic Ball in London in August, 1755 AD!

Now I'm back to 21st Century boarding school life, back as an ordinary post-modern teenager when only just 24 hours ago I was a young Lady experiencing her first London Season with perspective husbands in the nobility, summing me up as a prospective bride!

Even though the experience was a good one, I just wish it had a better ending.

Firstly, I didn't have to go to any of my classes so I could do some last minute preparations with my studies of the era. That was up until about 4 PM. Until then though, I was holding the ipod, doing some last minute reading, and dancing at the same time. It felt weird dancing alone, and in jeans and not in one of those long dresses, but I wanted to make sure I remembered all the steps.

I had to go straight to Dr. Knight's room in the dormitories. There she helped me dress again, only this time she dressed me up to the hilt! Perfume, make-up, jewelry and a wig! The wig wasn't white as I expected, and Dr. Knight told me that white wigs (or powdered coiffeurs) were only for very formal occasions, such as for visiting court and so forth. The wig she put on me was brown hair that looked almost exactly like my own natural hair color. She told me that the poor women used to sell their long hair to be made into wigs for the wealthier classes. So the wig I'm wearing, is real hair! And it was an object of beauty in itself, it was tied up elaborately with little rings of curls hanging down. And Dr. Knight put some kind of hair clips in my hair, that I learned weren't just everyday sparkling ones that I wear, but were real diamonds! The jewels she put on my neck and ears were all real diamonds too!

"How much exactly am I wearing?" I asked her.

"Well, in my day, it would probably be about two thousand pounds… these days they'd be worth a hundred thousand." Dr. Knight laughed at my shock. "A sizable sum in both times. Both amounts in both times could shelter and feed a family for at least a year or more."

"I'll try to be really careful." I gulped.

Dr. Knight was mostly already dressed herself, but she got me to help her pull and tie up her corset, then lace up the back of her gown that had a train from the shoulders to the floor to hide the join. I was wearing the dark green silk, she was wearing a Navy blue colored silk dress. We both sparkled with diamonds. I'm sure if we got mugged together, the thieves could purchase two first class tickets for a cruise around the world.

Then I don't know why, if it was the girlie mood of the two of us getting ready for a party together or something, I found myself with this undeniable urge to ask her this personal question.

"Dr. Knight?"

"Yes Elisha?" she answered, looking into the mirror and dabbing a tiny bit more red color onto her lips.

"Were you ever tempted to marry and settle down in the era you were born in? I mean, you would have had a comfortable life and everything." I asked her.

Dr. Knight finished with what she was doing and grabbed a tissue to wipe the color off her finger with. Then she turned and looked at me. I thought she was about to go into the big, long spiel or whatever, but she didn't. She just smiled at me.

"If you were offered the chance to marry a millionaire with one hitch, that you couldn't continue your education, you had to stay at home with no career, only children, that your only entertainment were social events with other millionaires and their wives who were in the same predicament as you… and your only option and even duty was to breed sons… what would you do?"

I thought about her question.

"Could you still go shopping?"

She let out a loud, but still dignified laugh, then went and stood beside me.

"Are you ready Lady Durrant?" she addressed me.

"Quite, Lady Dunmore." I answered in my fake English accent back.

"Then look into the mirror." She faced the both of us to look into her full-length mirror again with her hands on my shoulders.

And so it began…we stared.

At first our reflections changed from the images of the two of us standing together in all our full regalia, then even the reflection of her room faded away.

The walls, floors and ceiling all dissipated and melted away in a blurry wave, to be replaced by a pure white light.

Then the white light made way for a vision of a completely different room with antiquated furniture and an overall grander appearance.

I felt myself being pushed forward… and I realized it was Dr. Knight guiding me. We were walking into the newly materialized image. Only I almost felt drunk, like I wasn't walking, I was giddily gliding into the image of where we wanted to be. Where the mirrors edge used to be, was just the borders of the bright white light that seemed to engulf us, and the white light was so bright that it made me want to squint. But I was too afraid to, too afraid of what might happen if I broke my concentration.

Suddenly I realized Dr. Knight had let go of my shoulders, and that I felt my feet were standing on a hard wooden floor, and that the room temperature was different.

I ended up blinking madly as if a whole dust storm had just flown itself directly into my eyes, and I couldn't get my eyesight to adjust properly. Actually, no it wasn't like dust… it's like when you get up in the middle of the night and go to the bathroom and turn on the light and it hurts your eyes. That's how my eyes felt at that moment.

"How are you feeling?" Dr. Knight asked me.

"Dazed and confused." I tried to back away for a moment, and nearly fell sideways from a momentary dizzy spell.

"I'm not surprised." She grabbed hold of my shoulders again to steady me.

"Why? Everyone gets like this on their first phase?" I asked her, still blindly.

"Not at all. On a Circulator's first phase, normally it is the guide who phases the student. Only a small percentage of students actually phase with the teacher."

"Oh, OK." I said, not getting it, still concentrating on my returning vision.

"Elisha, you just phased with me." Dr. Knight stated.

"Huh? What?" I finally could focus on her.

"You just turned your body into light waves with out my assistance."

"No way…" I gaped at her. "No way!"

Dr. Knight's silence was my confirmation.

"So was that the bright light I saw?"

"That, and from the machine that transported our light waves to this place." She answered.

"Where is this place?" I asked baffled. It looked like a drawing room, and it was so quiet, it made me wonder if we were the only two people in the house.

"We are in my family's London town house. From here we will leave for the Ball." Dr. Knight informed me. Then she walked over to a wall with a sideboard and some silver wear sitting on top of it, and that had a small silver bell. She picked up the little bell and rang it.

A minute later a middle-aged man wearing livery and a wig answered her summons. "Ma'am." He bowed his greeting.

"Smith, I have just arrived here from the country for the Fox's Ball this evening. Don't worry about our luggage for the moment, but please have the town carriage sent round front." Dr. Knight ordered in her most proper English accent possible.

"Yes Ma'am." He bowed again, and left us again.

"What, he believes you already?" I said in wonder. Man, that was an easy scam!

"The servants are used to my sudden comings and goings… only the exact nature of the mode of travel is kept from them. When you establish set points for visitation places, you will have accommodation to always go to as well. In the Circulate, we have many 'safe houses' where our comings and goings can be hidden from the larger community." Dr. Knight explained to me.

"Have you ever accidentally phased into a crowded room before?" I asked her.

"No. We can see the destination we want, so we phase when we can see the coast is clear." She answered me. "It has been proven time and time again that letting the public know of our ability to transmigrate in time is indeed unwise and extremely foolish."

Just then the door to her drawing room opened again with the entrance of Smith, who announced our carriage was being brought around the front now. And Dr. Knight, or should I say, Lady Dunmore flounced out of the room like a true Aristocrat. But, not before leaving, did we have these kind of capes put over our dresses. Not the kind of cape Dracula had, but another silken material with frilly hoods and ribbons. I guess these were the instead for coats that noble women in this era, to go over the huge, expensive dresses.

With the help of a footman, I was helped into the two-horse drawn carriage, that had two wide leather seats facing each other. It wasn't top-less, like the kind of carriages you see people take a ride in in a park somewhere, but it was boxed in. The walls and even the ceiling were lined with blue padded leather, like an old leather couch, with Navy silk curtains framing the glass windows.

The carriage ride was only fifteen minutes long, as we were taken to the Ball at Holland House. The Ball was being held by a Lady Caroline Fox and the Mr. Fox, a member of Parliament in those days (their young son is destined to become prime minister!). But even driving through 18th Century London was a sight to behold! I stared at all the other carriages going by, the people walking past, and even the people selling things on the side of the streets! It was sunset, and there were still heaps of people, hard at work, trying to sell their wares. I even saw a little flower girl, trying to sell the flowers in her basket. I remember reading about those poor children, trying to help their families with any income possible, and it was surreal now seeing them.

"Wow. I'd hate to be poor in this century." I thought out loud.

"In every century I've visited where there's human civilization, there is also human cruelty. It is apart of the human condition. Of course, if the so-called ruling classes suddenly turned around and worked on large-scale equality we might be able to completely abolish hunger and poverty. But there are a lot of selfish and corrupt people who would even sacrifice human lives to prevent that from ever happening." Dr. Knight told me.

"Why? To keep themselves in power?" I guessed.

"Correct." She said simply.

When we arrived at our destination, we were driven through these gates, then along a gravel drive way that was lined with torches (sticks that were lit up with fire at the top of them) and driven towards a large house. The house had a large balcony on its side, also lit by lanterns and torches. I could see there were couples mingling on the balcony and just by the front entranceway.

Our carriage paused a few times, before coming to a complete stop and new footmen arrived promptly to open our carriage doors and help us out.

I suddenly felt really nervous and self-conscious and my hands went all shaky and sweaty. As we went up a few steps and through the large front door, I felt like an intruder, like somebody who shouldn't be there. I felt like everybody was looking at me and probably thinking so.

Another footman took our capes from us and we proceeded forwards through a grand entranceway and in the general direction of a drawing room with all the other guests. I tried to walk as regally as possible while not tripping over my long skirt. Tripping over at the moment was at the top of my not-to-do list, I mean, I'm the girl who can trip over flat surfaces!

"Ah, Lady Dunmore." A man wearing a dark green velvet and embroidered coat with long dark hair gave a slight bow. He looked middle-aged and overweight, but he did have a friendly smile.

"Mr. Fox. Allow me to introduce to you to my niece, Lady Durrant." Dr. Knight gave a curtsey and then a wave in my direction, which I followed suit and curtsied as well.

"Lady Caroline." Dr. Knight greeted. "This is my niece of whom I wrote to you about, Lady Durrant."

Lady Caroline Fox was a much younger woman than her husband, which gave me a bit of a surprise. She had blue eyes and red hair and wore a dark pink gown. She seemed as curious about me as I was about her though.

"You are welcome here, Lady Elisha." Lady Caroline kissed my cheek.

"I thank you." I smiled back at her.

"When will you be presented at court? I do not believe I have ever seen you there." Lady Caroline examined me for a moment or two.

"She has not been presented yet." Dr. Knight/Lady Dunmore answered for me. "In fact, this is Lady Elisha's first ball."

"Really? Extra-ordinary. And did you enjoy your childhood in Scotland and then the Colonies, Lady Durrant?" Lady Caroline asked me.

"Ah yes. Immensely." I lied. I didn't know what else to say. Well, in a way you could say that Australia was just another English 'colony'.

"And will you stay in London for the entire season?" she asked me next.

I looked at Dr. Knight to answer for me again.

"Lady Elisha's entire stay with her family has not been confirmed as yet." Dr. Knight said.

"Then I shall hope to look forward to seeing you in society again." Lady Caroline smiled at me again.

Then I guess it was time for us to move on as Lady Caroline and Mr. Fox greeted their other guests. Dr. Knight/Lady Dunmore and I moved into this beautiful gilt drawing room where a small orchestra was playing some music. But no-one was dancing, but they were standing around mingling and obviously checking out everyone else's dresses. I remembered dancing came later, after supper was served, and usually the option to play cards through out the evening as well.

Servants wearing white wigs and livery moved among the guests with trays of red wine called burgundy and also with champagne. Dr. Knight even let me have a glass of the champagne! But she told me that I'd have to drink it very slowly and make it last, so it would be more of a social look to be holding the glass than getting drunk.

We chatted to some Ladies and Gentlemen, as I was introduced to a Duke and a few Lords, and I noticed I received a lot of curious looks. But I tried to talk less and listen more, or let Dr. Knight do most of the talking for me. Her being my chaperone, it wasn't strange for her, the older woman, talking and taking charge of me, her 'niece'. So I guess you could say I just stood around, fanning myself, trying to look alluring to the young men in the room. And even in this day you had to be careful on how you used your fan, because it could have several different meanings, from the angle you hold it, to how high you hold it!

When I took a good long look around the room at one stage, I saw a small group of men, all wearing military uniforms. They all looked to be in their twenties and thirties, and at that moment, they all turned and looked at me at the same time! When they noticed I noticed them, they all looked away and carried on their conversation. But one of them even nodded to me, and gave a slight bow.

I didn't know what to do back, I didn't want Dr. Knight to notice… so I gave him a small smile and raised my fan higher to hide my lips from her momentarily.

Eventually we went into supper and were seated at one of the many long tables that could seat 10 a piece. But we were seated boy-girl-boy, so Dr. Knight and I were separated. The gentleman seated to my right, between Dr. Knight and myself was the elderly Lord Burrough, and a gentleman in his thirties was seated to my left. His name was Captain Greyson. He was the guy who gave me the nod and bow!

I got his name from the place card on the table, and when we were sitting down, he even held my chair for me.

"If you will forgive me Lady Durrant, I must ask you a favor." Captain Greyson smiled at me.

I thought this was strange behavior for this day and age, so I said warily, "a favor?"

"For your humble forgiveness at my impertinence." He bowed his head to me again.

"Why?" I asked him.

"For I exchanged place cards with my friend over there so I could be privileged with your pleasant company." He pointed to the table next to us.

"Really?" I laughed, almost not believing him. "Surely there were other ways of making my acquaintance. You could have asked me to dance after our supper."

He gave me a funny look, before saying, "Surely a beautiful young Lady such as yourself would know it would be extremely impertinent of me to introduce myself without a mutual acquaintance playing the role of the introducer."

"So Lady Caroline, in deciding where to put the place cards, is playing the mutual acquaintance in her role as hostess?" I asked him.

"This is correct."

"And you were impertinent enough to exchange those place cards, and in doing so, making yourself the mutual acquaintance." I continued.

"Guilty as charged my Lady." He smiled cheekily.

"Then your sins can be forgiven sir."

"Indeed?"

"Yes, but on a provision, of course."

"And what provisional basis would that be, my Lady?"

"To be a gentlemen and wave down that footman and fetch me another champagne." I smiled cheekily back at him.

"Your wish is my command." He gave another small little bow and followed through on my request.

Captain Greyson was very handsome, even for a man in his mid-thirties. He had dark brown eyes and hair. Over supper I learned that his father is an Earl, but being the younger of two brothers he won't inherit the estate. So his commission in the army was bought for him. He's very interested in the 'colonies' (the U.S.) where he thinks I've come from, and kept asking me heaps of questions. I remembered what I could about the States in this era, and made up a story that on my 'plantation' in Virginia, we had slaves and such. I was almost tempted to pull his leg and tell him that the slaves were white people who were zombified as retribution by the witch doctors of the people of Africa who were kidnapped. But since the War of Independence, let alone the War between the Northern and Southern States of the 'colonies' hasn't been won yet, I didn't think he would get the humor.

What they call a 'supper' and what we would call a formal dinner, was amazing! There was lobster, crayfish, game pies, roasted quails, baked fish, oysters, vegetables and salads, lamb ragout, bantam eggs with herbs, and I even got to try sweet meat pies! And I actually liked them! So much so, I ate two! I completely stuffed myself over dinner, and Captain Greyson got me two more glasses of champagne (which Dr. Knight gave me a warning look over). I was quite happy and comfortable by that stage. My surroundings and the congenial company was starting to make me feel quite at home.

I could tell Greyson thought I was an intriguing, different kind of Lady he hadn't met up until now. I tried to engage him in a philosophical discussion over the current English judicial system and its habit of either hanging or transporting its criminals, but he had a laugh at me and asked me if I'd like to dance instead. Dr. Knight nodded her permission to me so I allowed myself to be shown back into the gilt drawing room where the dancing was being held.

After the first dance, I wondered where Dr. Knight was as I couldn't see her in the room, and Captain Greyson suggested that she might be in another room, playing cards.

I wanted to go in and see for myself, not wanting to be too far away from my guide and my 'get-home-ticket', when another Gentlemen suddenly joined us. He and Greyson obviously knew each other, and he looked at me expectantly, waiting for his introduction. Just like a couple of other men here, he was wearing a uniform. I don't think it was an Army uniform though.

"Lady Elisha Durrant, would you allow me the pleasure of introducing to you Sir Guy Robertson." Captain Greyson did as his friend wished, and his friend gave me a small bow as I mirrored it with a slight curtsey.

"A good evening to you, my Lady. I do hope that supper with this stranger here was not too disarming for you. But I thought I had better apologize to you if any inconvenience was caused." Sir Robertson gave me another small bow.

"Oh, you're the one who he switched place cards with." I realized. "No harm done, sir."

"I thank you for your immediate forgiveness. Now, since my friend here has had the delight of your company all through supper, and then the first dance, may I seek solace in asking for your hand in the next dance?" Sir Robertson asked me now.

He also had dark hair and eyes, and looked to be in his mid-twenties. I thought he was attractive, so I said yes. And while we waited for the current dance to finish and the next one to begin, we began to chit-chat.

"Sir Robertson, are you also in the army, or what kind of man of leisure, are you?" I asked him. In 20th Century talk, I think I just asked him what he did for a living, but in 18th Century talk where men didn't have to have 'livings', I probably sounded stupid.

"Why yes, I also am in service to the King, but am proud to call myself an officer in the Royal Navy." Sir Robertson said.

"No, Robertson here won his commission and his title based on bravery and honor, unlike us 'layabouts' here, my Lady." Greyson joked.

"Really?" I asked, suddenly a lot more interested.

"Indeed, my Lady." Robertson answered, slightly embarrassed. I wasn't sure whether he was embarrassed by his friend advertising this fact from modesty, or for another reason. I soon found out why when he continued, "yes, this is my first Ball in this kind of society. If it wasn't here for Captain Greyson introducing me to Mr. Fox or Lady Caroline Fox, I doubt I would have received this invitation tonight."

"Really?" I asked again, fascinated. I was trying to work him out. He has an upper class accent, so what's the deal?

"Yes my Lady. I grew up in Cheapside, my father is an attorney and his father before him, was one of the King's tailors." Mr. Robertson said, suddenly a little defensively. I think he thought I would be ashamed to dance with him now, with connections so low. He even then said so. "I would like to discharge you of any promises you have made to dance, my Lady. I'm sure a more fitting partner can be found for you."

Then he suddenly bowed again and turned to leave.

"Come now man, any offense taken should be my responsibility." Greyson tried to tell him, but Robertson had already walked off.

Greyson now looked embarrassed, probably for this indiscretion taking place in front of me, a Lady, and for probably being the one of embarrassing him by bringing up his 'lowly' background.

"If you would please excuse that outburst… Robertson isn't usually like that. In fact, he's one of the bravest souls I have ever met, and if you could only know the man's integrity…" the Captain now turned to me.

"Captain Greyson, it's all right. Really. Now lets find your friend and tell him so ourselves." I smiled reassuringly to him.

He looked impressed by this, then he offered out his arm to me, and away we went.

I would have gone after him by myself, but a Lady running after a man at a Ball in this society… it simply was not done.

Anyway, it didn't take long to find him. Robertson was standing out on the balcony, looking down moodily onto the lit up manicured lawns that surrounded Holland House. He was standing alone, with a few of the other guests eyeing him up and down, as if surmising that this was a guest that they didn't really want to socialize or associate themselves with anyway.

This annoyed me, and we walked right up to him, with my head held high.

"Sir Robertson, would you please forgive any indiscretion I have made. I certainly did not mean to offend you. As this is also my first Ball, and I was passed on this invitation through my Aunt, I certainly feel an empathy to your situation." I chose my words carefully. What I really wanted to say was, 'please don't confuse me as one of these snobs'.

He seemed touched that I apologized and he gave a small smile and nod in acknowledgment.

"Friend, if my outburst at your achievements caused you pain in any way… would you please accept my apologies also." Greyson asked.

"Of course. Otherwise, who would be my partner in Pharaoh?" Robertson smiled good humouredly to his friend.

While the two men shared a chuckle in male bonding, it took me a few seconds to realize they were talking about a card game and not a dead Egyptian king.

Just then I noticed the music change, and I spoke up. "Sir, did you not promise me the next dance?"

"Of course." Robertson said, then he took a step backwards, bowed deeply, and offered his hand. "My Lady?"

"Thank you, kind sir." I took it.

We left Greyson on the balcony for the moment, and went inside, back into the gilt drawing room.

As we danced, I realized Sir Robertson was studying me carefully. As was the custom in this time period, there was some conversation while you dance. And Robertson used this opportunity.

"Lady Durrant, your father is an Earl in Scotland, is that not so?" he asked me.

"Quite."

"And you also own a large plantation in South Virginia, in the Colonies?"

"Correct again."

"Is your accent Scottish, or Colonial?"

Whoops. I think it's been slipping. I'd better be more careful.

"Colonial." I lied. It would be another few decades before Australia, or New South Wales as they called it first, would be invaded and colonized as well. So I can't call it that.

"Do you have slaves on your property in the Colony?" he asked me.

"Yes." I lied uncomfortably.

"And do you think it is a natural state of being, believing one human being is in a higher state of evolution than another, and use it as justification to put down another?"

I nearly stopped what I was doing when he said that, and I glared at him. What is his deal exactly? Is he trying to suss me out? One minute flirtatious, the next a moody bastard?

"Do you mean as a natural state as having First and Second classes? Or the British Royal Navy looking for more land to conquer for King and country? Or owning a dress and jewelry that could feed and shelter a poor family for years to come? What an interesting question, Sir Robertson. Perhaps you can tell me where your accent comes from?"

"My grandfather was the Kings tailor. He used this favoritism to give his son the highest education he could afford. My father is a successful solicitor. He also hired the best tutors he could afford to teach his children. He believed his two sons should make their own way in this world. I joined the King's Navy to do just so." Robertson answered.

"How did you and Captain Greyson meet?" I asked him.

"In battle in India." He said simply, not going into further detail, probably from modesty.

"Is that where you won your commission and elevation into the Knighthood?"

"You assume correctly, my Lady."

"So, are you finished with battles, Sir Robertson? And are now looking for a rich catch?" I arched my eyebrow. I was through with pleasantries by now.

"I am still in active service, I can assure you. I am here only to receive my Knighthood and commission, and I return the following month." He said stiffly.

"Back into immediate battle?" I swallowed, suddenly feeling a little sorry for him. From my studies, I knew that battles in this time period was messy and unorganized. I remembered the image of one of the battle scenes from the movie 'The Patriot' where the two forces just stood in front of each other, shooting, with no protection between either of them and neither side taking any cover.

"If circumstances are unfavorable." He looked away.

We danced the rest of the dance in silence now, and when the music ended, we walked back to the balcony where Captain Greyson was waiting for us, with another gentlemen he was in conversation with.

Before reaching them, I stopped us and faced him.

"Sir Robertson, I just want you to know, that there are many things in this time that I do not approve of… class systems, the slavery issue, and even war. But I do wish you every success and I hope you stay safe."

He looked surprised a third time that night since I'd met him, and he squeezed my hand as his resolve softened.

"I thank you for your concern Lady Elisha."

Just then something interrupted our little moment, as it caught my eye.

Down in the garden, near a dark, clump of tall trees, far away but I could still make out a figure, was an old lady. What made her so unusual, was that she wasn't wearing the costume of this period, but a knee-length dress and cardigan, and her tied back differently. I think she was looking up at me, as if watching me.

Then she faded away. She dissolved into the night. She had been a specter. She had been an omen.

She had been my Gran.

I must have let out a gasp or something, because Sir Robertson held firmly onto my hand and asked me repeatedly if I was all right. He even looked into the garden to see what I was looking at, but he mustn't have seen anything, because he looked back at me. I think he thought I must have been feeling faint or something, because he asked me if I wanted to sit down or something.

"No, I thank you. But I must find my Aunt immediately." I turned and almost ran back inside, when Sir Robertson caught my arm.

"Then let me escort you, my Lady." He gently reminded me of the protocol and then took me inside.

We found Dr. Knight playing cards at one of the tables inside a room I hadn't seen yet, but instead of admiring the decor, straight away I went over to her seat and leant down so I could whisper in her ear.

Then she stood up, smiled to her fellow partners, and excused herself.

Together, with still Sir Robertson in tow, we found Lady Caroline and Mr. Fox and curtsied and thanked them for the wonderful evening and asked for our carriage to be called.

As we waited on the front landing, Sir Robertson was still 'escorting' me. He even offered to see us home. But my 'Aunt' thanked him, and told him it wasn't necessary. And when our carriage did arrive, she hopped in first and let me have a moment to say my good-bye.

"Will I have the pleasure of your company at the Marlborough Ball next Saturday night?" Sir Robertson asked me.

"Pleasure? When all we did was quarrel?" I smiled playfully at him.

"That was indeed the pleasure, my Lady. Your conversation and wit was one of the most refreshing I've had since I've arrived in London." He bowed and kissed my hand.

"I cannot guarantee, as a family emergency has just arisen. But please know that you will be in my thoughts and prayers, Sir Robertson." I gave another curtsey, then I turned and still holding onto his hand, he assisted me into the carriage.

As it started off, I looked out the window to see if he was still there, watching. He was. Wow. It looks like I have a romantic suitor in this era.

"Can you tell me what you saw?" Dr. Knight asked me now.

"My dead grandmother." I told her.

"Where? In a reflection in a mirror or glass?" she asked me surprised.

"Standing in the Fox's garden."

"Is she English? Maybe she's visited here before in your era. You could have seen an echo in time." Dr. Knight suggested.

"She's never even left New South Wales, let alone Australia. And the last time I knew, she was still alive."

As soon as we arrived back at the Dunmore town house, we didn't waste any time returning back to our era at Hamilton's College.

I stumbled back into Dr. Knight's room, blind as a bat again, as Dr. Knight guided me to sit on her bed to wait till the dizziness stopped and my vision return to normal. Once it had, I tried to change clothes as quickly as possible with Dr. Knight's assistance. Then I left her room and ran up the stairs to my own bedroom. I still had some 18th Century style make-up on, but at that moment, I didn't care.

The dormitory seemed almost deserted, with everyone asleep with their doors shut and no sound was heard. Even Pat's door was closed. I looked at my watch, it was 2 AM.

As soon as I had unlocked and opened my door, my mobile that was sitting on my desk started beeping. I picked it up and read what was on the screen. I had two messages waiting for me, one was a message left from Dad, and then one from Mark.

They both said the same thing... Gran had passed away an hour ago.

===

02/ 06/ 01

Diary,

I'm writing this on the plane on the way home. Technically, we're not due to go home until another week, but Professor Hamilton is letting me go home early due to 'a tragedy in the family'. What the tragedy is, you ask? Well, on my first excursion through time, I found out Gran is dead.

I've done all the major assignments for class, there was only going to be an exam for History and Biology, but they're letting me do those when I come back.

I'm going home early for Gran's funeral. I'll be home for two weeks, then Dad is letting me come back early for the summer program. I thought that was pretty nice of him actually. I was worried he'd demand that I stay home for the whole three months off for summer break (which is winter in Australia), but maybe he's impressed that I want to stay on and do the extra curricular classes. I told him that I was looking forward to the trip to Paris, and I guess he's letting me do that too.

While the teachers were discussing me in their staff meeting whether to let me go home early or not, I sent a long email to Sally and told her all about my trip through time. I told her how I was dressed to the hilt, arriving by horse and carriage to the Ball, meeting all those Aristocrats, dancing with two handsome Gentlemen, the huge supper of lobsters and champagne... I thought she might enjoy it. She's always been interested in that kinda stuff, like I am.

I met a Captain Greyson in the Army and a Captain Guy Robertson in the Navy. They'd both been in battles in India. Captain Greyson is the youngest son of an English Earl (even though he's in his thirties) and Robertson is in his twenties, with dark brown eyes and hair and very handsome. You could call him intense too, and not snobby at all. He even thought I could have been a snob! I hope he doesn't think that now. We even argued about society's conditioning in that era, and even though I was agreeing with him, he kept sort of accusing me. And then when I thought he didn't like me, he acted really chivalrous when I saw Gran's apparition in the garden. He helped me find Dr. Knight and saw us to our carriage when we left. He even said he was hoping to see me at another ball next week. But I guess that's not going to happen now.

Speaking of which... Gran's apparition... I think the teachers are a little surprised by me at the moment. First of all, I phased with Dr. Knight rather than letting her phase me. I don't know how I did it, but apparently I managed to, all by myself, turn myself into light waves and pass through the mirror. I don't remember much about it... it did make me dizzy, and I never knew it actually blinds a person for like, five minutes afterwards. It's like staring into a really bright light, and then when it gets switched off, you have to adjust your eyes back to the dark again. Then seeing Gran in the garden... Professor Hamilton wanted to talk to me in his office about it with Nell present before I left.

Professor Hamilton told me how he and the teachers decided that I could go home and catch up on the exams afterwards, and he talked to my father on the phone about it. And then he and Nell started asking me questions on the phasing, then how I saw Gran. I didn't know what to tell them, that it was... well, I don't know what it was.

"When you phased, what did you feel?" Professor Hamilton asked me.

"Well..." I tried to think. "It felt warm. The light felt warm and tingly. Almost like I had a few drinks or something."

"Can you tell us what you mean?" Nell leaned forward.

"Like, you know when you're drunk or something, and you don't feel yourself walking, but you just glide over to where you want to go." I answered.

Hamilton and Nell exchanged glances.

"How did you feel when you saw the apparition of your Gran?" Hamilton asked me next.

"Scared."

"Was that because you knew it was an apparition that you were seeing?" Nell asked me.

"Yeah. She didn't look like a normal person. She looked faint, like not all there." I nodded.

"When you were looking at the apparition, did you feel the same displacement as you did that night when you followed Peter, Brett and Sophie into Alpha Building the night of the Halloween party?" Hamilton asked me. His eyes looked really intense again, as if trying to see into me. It was like the first time I met him in the hospital wing, when I first arrived at the college.

I tried to remember. "Kind of. I don't know. I just saw her."

"Have you ever seen something like this before?" Hamilton asked me next.

"You mean dead people? No."

They left at that for the moment, after exchanging another glance, and then Hamilton started to give me this long spiel about how not to use my ability outside of the college. He said it's because I'm still largely untrained and I might not be able to control it properly. He lectured me on the dangers of phasing into the wrong place or wrong time, rah rah rah, walking into windows and glass breaking, rah rah rah, and then, most importantly coz he stressed this point, that someone might see me.

Afterwards I went back to the dorms and started packing. I was leaving first thing the next morning (this morning). I flew by a small aircraft to the airport at Thunder Bay, and from there another plane to Vancouver. Now I'm on the long hall back to Sydney. Most of the people around me are asleep and the plane is darkened. But I can't sleep. Too much has happened.

I keep thinking about Captain Robertson. He said he was only in London to accept his Knighthood and rise in commission for bravery in battle. Then he'll go back to India, probably back into battle. I wonder if he's somewhere in the history books? I'd like to know what happened to him.

I hope this isn't cheating on Zack. Isn't cheating on someone if you kiss or have sex? Well, I didn't do these things, but I don't want Zack to know. Maybe Sally might be able to help me find out these things, like what happened to Robertson. She's in the UK, there might be some kind of war museum, or some other historical records somewhere that she can look through. I'm gonna ask her in my next email.

Zack came into my room last night as I was packing. He was still buzzing with the excitement of our first trip and wanted to tell me again about his goal scoring during the game of zero-g football, and what a really cool place the future looks like. He also wanted to have sex again before I left for two weeks, as kind of good-bye sex. He started to kiss me and tell me how much he's gonna miss me, but I didn't want to. I pulled away and said I was sorry, but I'm just not in the mood with my Gran dying and everything. He said he understood, but I could tell he was disappointed.

It may have been low using my Gran as an excuse, when really it was Captain Robertson. But I can't stop thinking about him! I even wish he had never swapped place cards with Greyson so it would have been him that I dined with and got to know better. I keep fantasizing about still being at the Ball with him, dancing and flirting...

I know about Peter's trip, he was boasting about it at the Caf at dinner last night. But I was looking forward to my next class with Dr. Kell to hear about Numu's and Woong's and Jordon's adventures. I guess it'll have to wait until I get back.

===

TO: ebaker_hamiltons@evers.com
FROM: s_parson@snailmail.com
SUBJECT: Sorry about your Gran
DATE: 03/ 06/ 01

Hey Elisha,

Sorry to hear about your Gran. But I'm sure she's gone to a better place, and she's with your Grandpa and your Mum now. I'm sure they all still love you very much.

Thanks for the fantastic email about your trip! I'm glad you included the details… it's just what I thought a Ball in the 1700's would be like. Captain Greyson and Sir Robertson certainly sound hunky! Do you think you'll ever see them again?

Hey, I need to ask you a question. If I had stayed at Hamilton's College, would I have gone on an excursion too? Would I have been able to come with you? Why was it that only you, Zack, Peter, Numu, Jordon and Woong went?

Write back and tell me more if you want.

==

03/ 06/ 01

Diary,

The plane touched down at 6 AM and Dad was there to meet me with Patrice and Mark. We immediately drove home to change clothes and then we drove down to Wollongong for Gran's funeral that was at 2 PM. Afterwards we were all at Aunt Gabby's place for the wake, up until 7 PM when Dad then drove us back home to Glenbrook. So as you can imagine, today has just been a total rush job, nearly always on the go.

I cried my eyes out at the funeral. But Dad didn't shed a single tear. He stood there, all alone. I mean, Mark and I were there, so was Aunt Gabby and Uncle Pete and Jenny and Tina, but he still seemed alone with out Mum. I stood close to him and held his hand to let him know I was there for him, and I think he understood coz he squeezed my hand back.

The poor guy has now lost both his parents and his wife. All he has left is his sister, Aunt Gabby. And of course he still has Mark and me, but I wonder if he feels more alone now? He must. He lives in an empty house all alone, with no wife and his kids have left home. He still has his work friends and the neighbours next door to socialize with, but essentially, I think he feels lonely.

Dad let us get 'Hungry Jacks' on the way home for dinner. I nearly laughed at the irony. After going to an Aristocratic Ball and dining on lobster and champagne, to be given one of my old favorite junk foods to eat as a 'special treat'.

When we got home Mark and Patrice stayed the night at our place instead of driving all the way back into the city after the long day. I thought it was nice that we were all together after today anyway. Like it was a nice family moment.

While we all sat at the dining table eating our dinner, Dad made an announcement.

"I'm going to sell the house and move to Wollongong."

I didn't know what to say. It kind of surprised me, but it kind of didn't. Mark didn't look surprised at all.

"Well, the market is good right now. And Glenbrook is a popular area. You should get a good price." Mark said casually.

"With you kids now living your own lives, it's time to move on. And in Wollongong we have your Aunt Gabby and her family down there. I think now is the right time to move." Dad continued. "So whenever you come and see me, you'll be seeing your Aunt Gabby and your cousins too."

I guess he has a point. I'm not going to school here anymore, and I haven't talked to Angela in months. I guess there's nothing tying me to this place anymore except Dad, and soon, when he leaves, there won't be anything left at all.

Except the bush behind us, and how Mark and I had played hide and seek in the caves and valleys. And the two graves in the backyard of the dog and cat we had while growing up. And the family picnics we had by the swimming hole in the National Park. And Mum's beloved camellia bushes planted all around the front fence line. And the water fights Mark and I had with the neighborhood kids, also all grown up. And riding our bikes up and down those steep hills to the local swimming pool in summer. And...and...

...I started crying again.

===

06/06/01

Diary,

Nothing much to say. Haven't had a fight with Dad yet, which is kind of surprising. He's taken time off work, and we've been doing some packing.

He asked me to pack up my room, and go through my stuff and decide what I want to keep, and what I want to chuck. So I'm giving all my old toys a careful examination, trying to remember which ones were the most important in my childhood. I definitely can't chuck out my talking 'Bugs Bunny' and 'Big Bird' doll, or my two 'Cabbage Patch Kids'. The eyes are chipped on the animals and the hair is looking a little mangy on the kids, but they mean too much to go. I remember Mark used to torment me when I was little by chucking the dolls down stairs, into drains, and even over a cliff once. That was until, after watching some movie on TV and getting an idea in my head, that I kicked him in the balls! LoL!

I've found two of my old diary's... and man, what a laugh it was reading them! The dribblings of a 12 year old me... nearly every entry was a prayer to God to make Mark drop dead. Ramblings about fights with girls at school... and the entry I made when we did that school excursion to Government House and I saw the dinner party through the window, back in time. Then I read the entry when Mum was diagnosed with cancer. I got goose bumps reading that entry, especially when I remembered the previous entry I made about the night I saw my dead Mum in the mirror when I had the chicken pox. I've decided to bring these diaries back with me to Hamilton's.

I also found some of the old tapes I was given before I started High School and developed any taste at all... I completely forgot I had a New Kids On The Block, 'Hangin' Tough' album! And a Michael Jackson tape here as well! John Farnham, 'Age of Reason'? When did I ever listen to that? And even a couple of tapes, with the top 10 recorded off the radio from like, years ago! What a laugh!

Dad was doing the same with his possessions, and he came into my room and asked me to come with him because he wanted to show me something.

Lying on the bed was some jewelry, which I immediately recognized as Mum's.

"Your mother asked me to keep this for you, until you're old enough. Now, with this piece, she asked me to give you on your 21st Birthday... but this ring here, do you remember it?" Dad held out a gold ring.

"Mum's signet ring." I answered correctly.

"I took it to the jewelers and had it readjusted so it will fit you. Your mother wanted you to have this." He put it on my finger.

"Oh, wow. Thanks Dad." I smiled at him, turning it on my finger and staring at it. I remember this ring very well. Along with her wedding ring, she never took this ring off. And neither will I.

"And this necklace, she wanted you to have this necklace as well. She was given this necklace when she was confirmed. Now it's yours." Dad came and stood behind me and put it around my neck.

It was Mum's small gold crucifix. She never took this off either, well, except for special occasions when she wore her other jewelry. Now I'll do the same.

I looked down at the bed at Mum's other jewelry collection.

"When do I get the rest?" I asked him, half jokingly.

"On your 18th and 21st Birthdays." He said seriously. "Until then, I'll hold them for you."

I guess the rest of the jewelry was nothing compared to the huge ostrich egg sized diamonds I wore only a couple of days ago to the Fox's Ball, but that jewelry held no emotional comparison to this.

"Thanks Dad. It means a lot to me." I smiled tearfully at him, and he smiled back at me. But we didn't hug, I guess that would be too awkward. So I turned around and left back to my room, admiring my new keepsakes.

==

TO: s_parson@snailmail.com
FROM: ebaker_hamiltons@evers.com
SUBJECT: To answer your questions…
DATE: 07/ 06/ 01

Hey Sal,

Thanks for the well wishes. Yeah, I know she's gone to a better place. I just wish I could have seen her before she went. I have some nice memories of Gran. She really helped us out when Mum first died, she stayed with us for a month and cooked and cleaned and looked after us all. And now she's with Mum… I have no grandparents left. And Mum was an only child, so besides Dad and Mark, my Aunt Gabby and her family are all we really have left. So Dad's made the announcement that he's moving from the Blue Mtns to Wollongong to live closer to them.

Sorry it's taken so long to reply to your email. I was allowed to go home early from college so I could go to Gran's funeral. I'm only going to be home for two weeks though, then Dad is letting me go back to Hamilton's for the summer program where I'll do my last two exams for the term and then I'll study French and Art and Drama for the summer classes. And guess what, at the end of French, we get to go to Paris for a week! Isn't that cool? I'll practically be only a Channel crossing away from you.

About your question… why it was only Zack, Peter, Numu, Woong, Jordon and I who journeyed through time… well, lets see. In the Circulate, we are made up of two groups of people, those who can see and calculate using time, and those who can see and move through it. The two groups are called Calculators and Circulators. Zack, Peter, Numu, Jordon, Wong and I are the Circulators in our year. We can move through time, by phasing and it's like turning yourselves into light waves and passing through glass. Everyone else in our year are Calculators, they can see through time and calculate what can happen, like events in time and space. Eventually they'll join the other Calculators in the Circulate and there is a special device that can move a Circulator to different areas on the planet when we're phasing through time. So like Dr. Knight and I did, we were able to phase from 2001 to 1755, then a Calculator was able to distribute our light waves from Ontario to London.

Circulators are learning to travel through time before a Calculator is, because when Calculators travel, they will be taken with a Circulator, kind of like being piggy-backed. I think you will be, or are meant to be, a Calculator. When you want to travel through time, it will be me or another Circulator who will take you. And it will be another Calculator using a special machine to transport our light waves to a different location as I would be transporting you to a different time… does that make sense? They explained it much better back at college.

Actually, Calculators can also travel through time without Circulators occasionally. You do this when you pick up holes in time, like time warps. You know how I told you about those time warps where you might accidentally walk into a room in either the past or the future? Calculators can also pick this up when it is about to happen. In class we've learned how different Calculators were able to travel through time with out Circulators taking them, by entering and staying in that temporary hole in time.

You know, if you came back to Hamilton's College you could learn how to do all of this too…

```
=============================================
```

TO: ebaker@yowser.com.au

FROM: zreece_hamiltons@evers.com

SUBJECT: Are you OK?

DATE: 08/ 06/ 01

Hi Elisha,

Are you OK? How was your grandmother's funeral? Everything OK with your Dad? I miss you a lot.

Hamilton's is pretty lame with out you. We had our last day of classes today and to celebrate the teachers put on 'fun night' early. Peter's been eating chocolate bars non stop! He's also started up smoking with Pat and Nelson. He says he's so bored he's tempted to try and get some other illegal substance again. Don't worry, I won't let him.

Before summer classes start in a week's time, the teachers have posted on the notice board that they'll do a weekend in Thunder Bay so the kids who are staying on can get away from the school for a little while and get away and can like, do movies and shopping and stuff. Will you be back in time? Just in case you are, I put your name down as well on the sign up sheet. Nelson says you'd be interested, to get away from that pathetic little store in Brownsville and get some real clothes. That's what Nelson says anyway. I think you look good with or with out clothes anyway ;-)

I miss you so much. I hope you can come back early. I hate it when you go away.

Love from your boyfriend Zack.


```
=============================================
```

10/ 06/ 01

Diary,

Bugger. Got an email from Zack practically professing his undiminished love for me. I wish I could say I felt the same. But right now I'm starting to feel trapped, even when we're on opposite sides of the planet from each other.

As to the shopping part... since it's my birthday next week, Dad is going to take me shopping anyway for new clothes as my birthday present. I want to go to Jay Jay's and get some more jeans and jackets and stuff. Then I won't have to worry about missing the shopping spree in Thunder Bay.

I still can't stop thinking about Sir Captain Guy Robertson. I don't know what to call him, Sir or Captain, since he's both. He's pretty young to be a Captain of his own ship. Didn't they have to fight off scurvy in those days too? I worry about him. If it's not war, it's disease that he has to contend with. I've been reading up more on the Navy in that era. Dad has a book about it. I've asked him if I can take it back with me to Hamilton's, and used the excuse it was for an assignment or whatever. He bought it and let me keep it. I had to grab it quick coz he's packing up all the other books.

I didn't ask Sally to look him up for me in my last email. I will in my next. I'm just waiting for her reply. I wonder if I've scared her off again? I told her that she's meant to be a Calculator, that's what Dr. Knight told me. Maybe I wasn't supposed to tell her, and let her figure it out in her own time. Oops. I hope I haven't done the wrong thing.

I don't know what to do about Zack though. Should I break up with him? I mean it's not like I can have a relationship with Robertson. We exist in different time frames for fucks sake! We're in different centuries let alone countries! I may never see him again. Or maybe I can... maybe I can try to see through time, like the mirror exercise, and try to see him that way? But we can only seeing through time of the same location, not with different points in geography. I guess you need this whatever it's called machine that the Calculators use in the Circulate Headquarters, wherever that is, to see different points in space as well.

Bugger.

===

TO: s_parson@snailmail.com
FROM: ebaker_hamiltons@evers.com
SUBJECT: I need to ask you a favor…
DATE: 10/ 06/ 01

Hi Sally,

I'm sorry, I can't wait for your reply. I didn't mean to freak you out in my last email, if I did. Do whatever you want. If you don't come to Hamilton's, I understand. But it would be good to learn all this stuff with you anyway.

I need to ask you a favor. Can you try to find out any information you can about Sir Guy Robertson? Or it might be under Captain Guy Robertson? He received his Knighthood and rise in commission in 1755 for honor and or bravery in battle in India or something.

Whatever you can find, I'd reeeally appreciate it. I'd owe you one big time. So please help!

===

16/ 06/ 01

Diary,

I'm on the plane again, this time flying back to Canada. I've got my Biology and History books in my hand luggage so I can do some more studying for my exams, that are waiting for me back at Hamilton's. It's not a nice feeling, knowing you have exams waiting for you as soon as you get back. It's also not a nice feeling that you're going back to a boyfriend your contemplating breaking up with.

I still haven't heard back from Sally. I asked her in an email to find out that stuff about Sir Guy Robertson. I wonder if she will? Or is she freaked out and not emailing me again for a while? I wish I knew what was going on. I feel so... anxious right now. I think this will be another 20 hour flight with little or no sleep.

As to my stay at home... it was actually a really nice one. Well, except for the part where I saw Angela and a couple of other girls I used to go to school with in Penrith Plaza the other day. Dad was really nice to me and he took me clothes shopping for my birthday (I'm 17 now, can you believe it? One more year and I can legally start drinking!) and he took me to the shops I wanted to go to and didn't say a thing about prices. But Jay Jays' is usually pretty cheap so I didn't completely abuse his kindness, LoL! And anyway, we bumped into Angela and the others in the food court where we were eating our lunch. I saw them sitting five tables away.

I was tempted to get up and say hallo to the other girls, but I guess I was worried what Angela would say and do. Angela looked over and saw me. She didn't smile or anything, and then she leaned over and said something to the old gang, and they all then turned and looked at me. One of them smiled my way, but the rest of them quickly turned away and I think they were talking about me.

How fucking immature! I was tempted to go over and tip the rest of my lunch over them! It really spoilt the rest of my day.

After Dad had finished eating I asked him if we could go home. He was surprised and asked if I'd changed my mind or something, coz he thought I wanted to look at a few more shops. But I said I just wanted to go home, and made up an excuse I felt head-achey or something. So we left.

So yeah, that was my trip home. I'm still amazed Dad and I didn't fight at all. I guess we were both pretty quiet after the funeral, and we did work together well with packing up most of the house in boxes. He even let me listen to one of my CD's in the stereo in the lounge room while we worked.

Maybe he's a lot lonelier than I thought. Maybe that's why he really liked me being home for a little while. And when I did some studying for my exams after dinner two nights ago, he even complimented me on it, and made me a cup of tea. Usually it's HE who makes ME make the tea.

==

19/ 06/ 01

Diary,

When I arrived at the airport at Thunder Bay, I had a nice surprise. I already knew Nell was going to meet me off the plane and that I'd return back to college with all the other students going back after their weekend away. But there stood Zack, with a bunch of flowers, beaming when he saw me. I thought that was so nice of him, being there, to welcome me back with flowers.

I guess it was also a reality check. I mean, here I was, fantasizing about another man whom I had no hope at having a relationship with, and here was this man, who I am in a relationship with, totally in love with me. I gave him a big kiss and hug and it felt good when he squeezed me back tightly.

The college had hired a bus to take us back since there were so many students. So it was an all-day bus trip, catching up on the gossip and telling them my own. Nelson and Pat and Peter were also on the bus, along with Brett, Maya and Raj. Nell let us crank the music up pretty loud on the bus ride home and the eight of us hogged the back corner of the bus and played card games on the way.

Maya, Raj and I learned how to play poker and I already knew the rules for Black Jack. Peter kept trying to make us play 'for real money', but none of us wanted to make the bets any higher than a dollar. He kept calling us 'whimps' and 'pussies' but stopped after Nelson turned around and made the classic insult, "you wouldn't know what a fucking pussy is, would you? Except for what you would see in a veterinarian!"

We arrived back at the college pretty late, like at 10 PM or something. When they were unloading our luggage, Zack carried in my suitcase with his, which I thought was sweet of him again. Peter started laughing at him and joked that maybe he could carry his as well.

He just dropped off his travel bag in his room, locked his door again, and then carried my suitcase to my room and closed my door behind us.

As soon as my suitcase had hit the floor, he practically pounced on me! He was trying to kiss me at the same time as he tore off his jumper and started on mine next. Man, he was hungry for it.

I was still a little uncertain about my feelings, but I guess his passion was infectious. I didn't object, and I ended up really enjoying it. So much so, I wondered why it was so different? Zack ended up trying new things he hadn't done before. It actually made me nervous that maybe he'd been speaking to Peter or somebody else about us and getting tips or something?

When I was lying naked on the bed, he started to go down on me! I immediately sat up in surprise! Or was it shock? I guess I was embarrassed too.

"What are you doing?!" I grabbed his head.

"I - I'm going down on you." he said, also in surprise, by my reaction.

"Why?" I asked, still in shock.

"Why not?" he asked back.

"Don't."

"Why?"

I think I started blushing. "Just don't."

"Why?" he pulled my hands off him.

"Because... it's my... private area."

He had this goofy smile on his face now. "You're not embarrassed, are you?"

"Yes." I sat up away from him now. "Zack, what's changed? Why are you doing this now? You haven't been talking to Peter about us, have you?"

"No!" he gave me a funny look. "It's just…"

"What?"

"Well, you've been kind of distant lately… like before you left. I thought you might have been… I don't know… getting bored… or something." He confessed.

"Bored of the sex?" I asked him.

"Yeah. Have you?"

I didn't know what to tell him. So I lied. "No. I just wanted some space, that's all."

"I just thought that if we tried some new things…" he started.

"Yes?"

"I don't know… it might… spice up our love life." He recited as if reading off a card. But I saw the imaginary card, and what he was leaving out was, 'to make Elisha love you again.'

This made me feel sorry for him, and guilty at my own naughty thoughts I'd been having about another man.

"We're still together, aren't we?" I reached out and caressed his face. "And we'll probably be together for another while."

I guess this was enough to placate him, and he grabbed my hand that was caressing him, and he kissed it, and pulled me down to him.

"Then come here." His boyish grin returned and he pushed apart my legs again and returned to what he was doing.

Wow. My Gran dies. I turn 17. I get snubbed by old school friends. My father and I don't fight. Now I get my first head job.

===

24/ 06/ 01

Diary,

I got my marks back for the two exams. I aced both of them! Both of my scores were higher than 90%!! I'm sure that will make Dad happy. Maybe I can hope for a slight increase in my pocket money? It will help me save for France at the end of August.

Today was the last day of 'layabout' week. Tomorrow summer classes start. I'm doing French, Art, Drama and Music. I already know how to play bits and pieces on the piano from when Mum taught me when I was little, but now I want to learn the flute.

I'm going to be in French with Nelson, Pat, Peter, Zack, Brett, Maya and Raj. Actually, the whole year has signed up for French, I guess everyone wants to go to Paris. So they've broken up the subject into two classes, but at least I'm in the same class with the rest of my friends.

Yesterday was 'Brown Day'. Yep, they're still running us into town so we can do movies, shopping, whatever... As usual, Peter, Nelson, Zack and I went to the diner for lunch, and where Nelson and I can buy our cigarettes from Lee-Anne's brother.

When we were there, I noticed Lee-Anne kept looking at us. I wonder if it's because we haven't been in there for a while. I hadn't been in that diner in like nearly three months. Maybe she had given us up for ghosts.

When she came over to take our order, she asked us how our investigations were going.

"Investigations?" Peter gave her a funny look.

"Oh yeah, the ghost business." I suddenly remembered. That was the last time we had spoken to her.

"Fine, thanks." Peter said dismissively and held up his menu extra high so he wouldn't have to look at her.

I thought that was really rude of him, and I guess so did Nelson, coz she kicked him under the table.

"Oow! What is your problem, you psycho bitch!" Peter shouted back at Nelson.

"Sorry about him. We're looking into the possibility that he might have a mental illness." I apologized to Lee-Anne. "No, our school is haunted. But we haven't been able to attach the ghost to any one person. We're thinking it was from somebody who lived in one of the buildings before it became a school." I ended up lying.

Lee-Anne suddenly gave us all a dirty look.

"The buildings have always been a school."

Then she took our menus from us and turned on her heel and flounced off.

I guess she saw right through that one.

==

25/ 06/ 01

Diary,

Today after summer classes Dr. Kell called our Circulators' class together for a meeting so we could all discuss our first excursions.

I found out I wasn't the only one who went to a formal occasion. Both Jordon and Numu when they visited Egypt and Babylon also attended formal banquets, as well as got to wander through the magnificent cities of old. Peter boasted of his good time at Woodstock, and Zack (this time with a little modesty) told of his achievements, playing in a zero-G football training match in the future.

Everyone listened intently as I told them about the Ball at Holland House. I spoke about the sumptuous dinner, the gilt room, the dresses, the snobbery, and meeting two officers, one in the Army and the other in the Navy. I also told the about the social protocols of how a Lady had to behave and how it affected who I could meet and how. Of course, I left out the actual flirtation with Sir Guy Robertson. But bringing this up, it made me want to ask Dr. Kell another question.

"When do we start planning our next excursion?" I asked him.

Everyone wanted to know the answer to this one.

"Well, the schedule for Circulators going on a second excursion in time isn't due until next October." Dr. Kell announced.

"Can't we do it any sooner?" I asked, dismayed. I think I've still been kind of hoping I'd still make it somehow to the Marlborough Ball.

"You've experienced the taste of the fruit being offered to you, eh, Elisha? And now you want more." Dr. Kell sighed. But by the way he looked at me for a moment then, I wondered if he knew something.

"Well..." I tried to choose my next words carefully. "There was another Ball I was hoping to go to."

"On a Circulators second excursion we would usually transport you to a different location and time." Dr. Kell told me.

"Why?" I asked, dismayed again.

"If we continually sent a Circulator in training to the same location and time, how would the trainee learn new things?" he arched his eyebrows.

"But can't we start Circulating for fun now? Can't we go on monitored excursions for our own... enjoyment?" I pressed.

"You mean like a trip into town for the day? No. You may have the ability to phase by yourself Elisha, but there are other students who haven't reached that stage yet. We should all progress together, and stay on the learning schedule." Kell stated.

"You phased by yourself?" Zack asked me in surprise. "You never told me that."

"I didn't really know I did it. Dr. Knight told me afterwards." I told him, then I turned back to Dr. Kell. "But we've already started these classes ahead of schedule. If I knew what I was doing, and I was really careful..."

"No!" Kell said a little more forcefully. "If you have any further complaints, then I suggest you take this up with Professor Hamilton and then perhaps, the Circulate Council."

I leaned back in my chair in a huff, and crossed my arms angrily. I felt like I was being patted on the head like a child again. I thought we were past this. I may be temporarily defeated, but I decided right then and there that I would try to get past this.

"What was it like? Phasing by yourself?" Numu leaned forward to ask me.

==

TO: ebaker_hamiltons@evers.com

FROM: s_parson@snailmail.com

SUBJECT: Sorry it took so long to reply…

DATE: 03/ 07/ 01

Hey,

Sorry it's taken so long. But I've got the information you wanted. I couldn't really find it in Glasgow, but I have a friend attending a boarding school outside of London and I got her to go to the National Army Museum and look this up.

So, here we go. Captain Guy Robertson, borne 4th April, 1729 AD, died 12th June, 1757 AD, in the Battle of Plassey (which took place in India somewhere). He was fighting with the future Clive of India of all people. That makes him 26 years old when he met you, and then 28 years old when he died. So I guess he died two years after meeting you. Kind of freaky, ay?

I couldn't get anything else on him, except that he won his commission and Knighthood for bravery in battle, which I guess you already told me that. I hope this helps. I'm sorry it's bad news though. But I guess it's not totally unexpected, I mean, they were crappy times back then.

How is the summer program going? How is everyone? How is Peter?

==

03/07/01

I got a reply from Sally. My worst fears have come true. Robertson dies.

I mean, I already know he's dead... it is more than two hundred years later.

But he died in battle. In India. Fighting with fucking Clive of India of all people. In some war called the Battle of Plassey. I have to find out where it is, and what happens.

I have to.

It's midnight at the moment. The library is closed so I can't look up the battle. Since I got Sally's email I haven't been able to stop pacing around. I can't go to sleep tonight. How can I? Even the thought of Guy getting shot, or even one of those canons... no, I can't. I can't let myself try to imagine it, or I'll throw up.

If I could send him a letter somehow... warn him or something. I wonder if I can? I wonder if the teachers would try and stop me.

Two years later... two years after I meet him, he dies.

This can't be right. Fuck not being allowed to screw with the time line. I have to do something!

==

04/ 07/ 01

Diary,

I skipped breakfast this morning and went straight to the library. I even missed my classes today. I've been researching as much as I can, trying to find out more.

Battle of Plassey was a victory for Clive of India, 12th June, 1757 AD. It was a battle of dethroning Suraja Dowlah and his infantry of 35,000 arson with 15,000 cavalry and a small detachment of French soldiers. Then Clive with only 1,100 men and 2,000 sepoys (whatever that is) and 10 light field guns somehow won. It broke the French hold in Bengal and Clive put a Mir Jafar into power.

That's all well and good for Clive of India, but what about Captain Guy Robertson?

I think my best bet to get a letter to Guy is to send it to Fort George on the Coromandel coast. I bet his ship would be there, taking supplies and weapons to Clive. Then when the Battle of Plassey starts, I guess he will leave his ship and go from there. So when should I try to send the letter? 10th of June? 11th of June?

What I really need is an experienced seer. A Calculator could help me with this. But who to ask? None of the teachers would help me, I know it. They'd probably even stop me. I'll have to ask one of the students. It might have to be a Senior coz I doubt Pat or Nelson would be that far advanced in their education yet.

===

05/ 07/ 01

Diary,

I skipped dinner last night as well. I was holed up in my room, with my door locked, trying to compose a letter to Guy. When Zack knocked on my door I opened it a little bit, but just to tell him I was working on something and needed my privacy. I can tell the poor guy was a little hurt about all of the secrecy, but he respected it enough to leave me alone.

Around 11 PM there was another knock on my door. This time it was Nelson. I told her the same thing as I told Zack, only this time she either didn't care, or didn't buy it, and she pushed past me and sat on my bed. But not before snatching the letter off the desk I was trying to write.

"Hey!" I tried to snatch it back but she was too quick for me.

"'Dear Guy. Your life is in danger…'" she read out loud. Then she glanced at my door still being open and said next, "are you going to close that or what?"

I closed my door for the privacy (and Pat with his door open, gave us a funny look from sitting in front of his computer as usual) and I sat down defeated, next to Nelson, as she continued the letter.

"'You cannot fight in the Battle of Plassey or you will die'. Well, you don't mince words, do you?"

"What else am I supposed to say?" I sighed. "I've been working on this for three hours now and I don't know how to explain it."

"Well how the fuck would he know what the Battle of Plassey is? Maybe he'll be in the middle of it, and suddenly remember your letter, and then it will be too late." Nelson pointed out.

"Then what else am I supposed to do?" I whined. "I'm trying not to put too many details in there that might disrupt the time line. I can't tell him the details, like, 'you will be in battle alongside Clive of India against an evil Raj called Suraja whatever-his-name-is.' And I can't tell him who'll win. All I can tell him is not to go into battle."

"Then how will he know which battle not to go into? And even if he doesn't die in this battle, what if he dies in another? Are you going to send another letter then? What is your next letter gonna say, 'duck'?" Nelson practically laughed at me.

"Don't laugh! This is no laughing matter! A man is going to die!"

"He already is dead! You met him over two hundred years ago!"

"You think I don't know that?! Look, we met, we danced, we conversed. He was handsome. I wouldn't say charming... we even fought. But he was interested in me..."

"And you're interested in him?" Nelson arched an eyebrow at me.

"...yes..." I squirmed. "That's not cheating on Zack, is it? I mean, we didn't do anything but dance..."

"A couple of dances and you try to save his life? This guy must be some dancer." Nelson smirked.

"So will you help me write the bloody letter or what?" I glared at her.

"Sure." She shrugged.

"And what about sending it. I'll need your help to send it." I told her.

"Me? How? You're the one who can phase." Nelson gave me a funny look.

"I need to know where to send it. Can you see a safe location, or where he will be? Can you Calculate the destination for me?" I asked her.

"Hey, all we can do is see backwards and forwards in time from the location we're in, not in different countries on the other side of the planet! The machine at this so-called Circulate Headquarters is the only thing that can help us do that!"

"Bugger." I fell backwards onto the bed and laid down and stared at the ceiling. "Then how do I do this?"

"If we could get the letter to India…" Nelson thought out loud.

"We know Maya… she's Indian!" I sat up excitedly.

"But she's here right now. Hey, what about Sally in Scotland? Your boy's English, maybe she could leave the letter somewhere in England that he could find somehow." Nelson continued.

"Nup. Sally's a Calculator, not a Circulator. She wouldn't be able to send the letter back through time." I moaned again, falling back onto the bed.

"How do you know this?" Nelson asked me.

"Dr. Knight told me."

Then Nelson went quiet for a moment. "Maybe we should just ask Dr. Knight to do this for us."

I sat up right again in surprise. "But she wouldn't. She's a teacher. She'd try and stop us."

"Well then, I'm out of ideas." Nelson shrugged.

"I had been thinking of even asking one of the Seniors…"

"But the teachers monitor their adventures with time too." Nelson stated.

"Yeah." I sighed. "It's almost like I have no options left. It's almost down to the point that I'd have to fly to England or India and then phase through time, and take the letter to him myself."

Nelson was quiet for another moment, before she said, "but that would be a really stupid thing for you to do. You'd be risking expulsion from the school, and you'd be putting yourself in danger by going back in time with out a guide."

Then she got up from the bed and headed towards the door.

"What would you do if it was someone you thought you were in love with?" I asked her one last time.

I thought she wouldn't reply when she opened the door and exited, but before closing the door behind herself again, she did say, "I wouldn't let myself be so stupid in the first place."

==

08/07/01

Diary,

I've written the letter to Sir Guy Robertson. Now all I have to do is send it somehow. I tried the two options before I had no other choice but to do 'something stupid', as Nelson put it so eloquently.

First I asked two Seniors that I had become acquainted with. One is a Calculator, and the other is also a Circulator. The Calculator basically told me the same thing as Nelson did, that they'd need the device in Circulate Head Quarters to see into India. And the Circulator basically told me the same thing, that they'd need the machine to send the letter to the location if they did indeed send it through time for me. Either way, I'm stuffed.

So I decided to bite the bullet and go and see Dr. Knight. I was thinking that since she met Sir Guy Robertson that maybe she'd like to save the life of someone she had become acquainted with. I mean, he's not just some nobody to us.

I knocked on her door in the Dorms and asked if I could speak to her. She said "of course" and let me in. She sat at her desk as I sat on her bed and told her everything. I told her how and when he was going to die and how I'd written a letter for him.

"Oh Elisha..." Dr. Knight sighed and rested her forehead in the palm of her hand tiredly. "We told you that we need permission from Circulate

Headquarters before we change the timeline. I'm afraid I won't be able to help you with this request."

"But you've met him! Are you just going to sit by and let somebody you know die?" I asked incredulously.

"Elisha," she said my name again as she leaned forward. "I know this is going to be hard for you to accept, but what I've learned in the Circulate and monitoring human history, is that there are some people that are meant to die. Some lives are meant to end, or it can affect other influences in another way, like a reverberation in space-time. How do we know that if Sir Robertson lives, that Clive of India won't win the Battle of Plassey? How do we know what would have happened if the French retained possession of India? What will happen to the Indian people either way?"

"Then can I go the Marlborough Ball then, and see him one last time?" I pleaded with her. "He was expecting me to come."

"And you were also hoping to go?" Dr. Knight raised her eyebrows with concern. "Elisha, establishing a relationship with a man in his twenties that's destined to die, with a 200 year gap between you, is not the wisest course of action."

"Fine! Don't help then! I'll do this on my own! You can't stop me!" I stood up and marched out her door.

===

TO: mbaker@hotmail.com

FROM: ebaker_hamiltons@evers.com

SUBJECT: I need to ask you a huge favor…

DATE: 08/ 07/ 01

Hi Mark,

I really need to ask you a huge favor. It's really important, otherwise I wouldn't be asking. I need some money for an airfare.

We have to pay in advance for the trip to France at the end of the holidays and Dad's money is tied up in the move and buying the new house at the moment and I don't want to miss out. Dad will reimburse you as soon as all the transactions have gone through. I think he's got a buyer for the house now. I talked to him on the phone last night about it.

The reason why Dad hasn't asked you himself for this is, well, you know how stubborn and proud he can be. And I really don't want to miss out on this opportunity coz Dad is unsure if it will be a couple of weeks till all the paper work is done. I need to have the money in my account in a couple of days.

Dad will pay you back and I'll owe you one big time.

==

(TEXT MESSAGE SENT BY MARK TO ELISHA DATED 09/ 07/ 01)

Hey, have put $1000 in your account. Tell Dad everything is OK and pay me back in own time. Be sure to send Patrice & I a few postcards of your trip!

==

10/ 07/ 01

Diary,

I went to classes today and I tried to act like normal, like nothing was wrong. But secretly I'm biding my time. Tomorrow I'm going to run away, and fly to India. I'll go to the location where Fort George used to be, and send the letter through time to Sir Guy Robertson.

I know this is a really low thing to do, but I lied to Mark about needing money for the Paris trip when the school is already paying for it. I lied to him that Dad will pay him back. But all I have in my savings account is $400, which won't exactly pay for a ticket, even if it is only one way.

I don't care if I get expelled. I don't want to join the Circulate anymore. I don't want to join a group of people who don't care and sit idly by while others die. It all sounds so corrupt anyway. They can go to Balls and formal dinners in any era they want, wear huge diamonds, dine on the best of foods, and then look the other way when someone they know dies.

I can't do that.

I'm going to tell Zack tomorrow just before I leave. I don't know whether I should include the part about my feelings for Captain Robertson, or would that be too cruel? But then what if he says he'll come with me... maybe I should just be honest with him.

My plan is that tomorrow night after dinner I'm going to tell Zack, then sneak off campus, and walk into Brownsville. From there I'll hitch a ride to Thunder Bay, and then at the airport I'll buy a one way ticket to Bengal. From Bengal, I'll make my way to the coast, to find the old Fort.

==

11/07/01

It's 9.45 PM. Have just told Zack I want to break up with him. Did not go well. I think he's going to hate me for the rest of his life. I hope I haven't screwed him up even more than his parents have.

Oh God, what was I thinking? I feel so bad! I'm running away from a man who worships the ground I walk on... to warn another man that has probably forgotten all about me.

I'm breaking a million rules, and usually I'm the good child. I'm mostly a good student at school who doesn't do drugs, and even at home when Mark was still living with us, I was considered the good child out of the two of us! Now I'm lying to get money and I'm running away? What am I, nuts?

No, no, I can't chicken out now. I just feel badly about Zack, that's all. I didn't tell him I was running away, I just said I wanted to break up with him.

When I told him he cried and tried to hug me and kiss me and pleaded with me not to do this... but I'm too far-gone now. I keep telling myself that there's a life at stake. I keep telling myself that I have to do this, that I have to save somebody's life.

I'm going to leave behind this laptop. It's probably still school property anyway. I doubt that it was ever really mine. Anyway, I probably won't need it where I'm going. I'm only taking a backpack with two changes of clothes in it, and some toiletries. Also my notes on the Battle of Plassey, and a note book and pen and my mobile. Plus my passport, better not forget that.

I better go now. I'll email Sally and let her know what I'm doing. If something went wrong... I'm sure she could tell someone for me.

==

TO: s_parson@snailmail.com
FROM: ebaker_hamiltons@evers.com
SUBJECT: Call me a lemming, and give me a cliff.
DATE: 11/ 07/ 01

Yep, I mean just what the subject title says. I know you're going to think this is stupid. Nelson does. But I'm running away to India to try to warn Sir Guy Robertson.

You won't be able to stop me coz this will be my last time I use email for a while. I won't be taking my laptop with me. I'm only taking my bare essentials in one backpack with me.

Please don't think this is your fault. If you hadn't told me about Sir Guy's fate, I would have found out another way. I guess you could just say I'm destined to jump off this cliff.

If I don't contact you again in like, say, two weeks... assume the worst.

Good bye for now, Sal xoxo

==

(THE FOLLOWING ENTRIES WERE WRITTEN DOWN IN ELISHA BAKER'S NOTEBOOK AS SHE CHRONICLED HER JOURNEY. THE TIMES IN OUR ERA FOR THE FOLLOWING EVENTS TOOK PLACE BETWEEN THE 12/ 07/ 01 AND THE 17/ 07/ 01)

12/ 07/ 01

Have made it to the airport in Thunder Bay. Feels weird being back here again, under such circumstances. Last time I was here, I was being met off the plane by a loving boyfriend with a bunch of flowers and I thought I could put all of this behind me. I guess not. Now look at me.

Got here OK. Walked into Brownsville. It was pretty freaky walking in the dark with no streetlights, only by the light of the moon. Luckily I saw no cars so I didn't have to dart into the woods and hide. Arrived into town and found out Lee-Anne's brother, who's name is Todd, our cigarette contact, was driving towards Thunder Bay. I offered him $100 to take me with him. He charged me $300 the bastard. It was the only safest option, as hitch hiking with one of the truckers didn't sound appealing. Plus his Mum and sister know me so I didn't think he was going to try anything.

We left Brownsville at midnight and got into Thunder Bay at 12 PM today. Have bought my one-way ticket to India and have to wait 6 hours for my flight. The tickets cost me $750, so that leaves me with $350 left in my account. I thought I should try to conserve as much money as I can, so I didn't buy any books or magazines to read while I wait. I just spent the last three hours standing in the aisle reading a travel book on India in one of the shops on the concourse. I have a better idea of where I'm going now.

13/ 07/ 01

Am writing this on the bus, leaving the airport and heading towards the coast in Bengal. Had to change planes at New Delhi to get to Bangladesh. Now am on an old rickety bus that I'm sharing with the locals.

I had two meals on the plane over, and was served curry on the second flight within India. At airport I exchanged $100 into local currency and am going to try to make it last as long as possible. The exchange rate was favorable in my way, which was a relief. The bus ticket seemed really cheap compared to what I was expecting.

I don't know what I'm going to do about accommodation. I hope I can find a backpackers hotel where I'm going. I don't think I've got enough for a real hotel.

13/07/01 - later on...

Found a YHA. When I checked in I showed them my passport and paid by eftpos for a week's accommodation. They were surprised that I didn't have a credit card and looked at me closely, and asked, "how old are you?" I told them 17, and the English lady who worked at the desk said, "you're a bit young, aren't you?" For what? Traveling around the world? Lady, if you only knew where else and how I've traveled before, you would know getting here was inconsequential.

14/07/01

Am bloody hot. I wanted to sleep in my underwear last night, but when you're sleeping in a dorm where you don't have your own room, but only rows of bunk beds... you don't have much of a choice. I was told usually the hostel has air-conditioning, but right now it's broken. Of course, it would be, bloody typical knowing my luck.

I'm starting to regret that I've only brought jeans. The change of clothes that I did bring were underwear, three T-shirts and two jackets. It was bloody cold walking to Brownsville at night, now two days later I'm on the other side of the world, melting.

Met some nice people though. Two Pommy tourists, Jack and Kelly, who were kind enough to share their breakfast of eggs on toast with me this morning. I told them I wanted to find the old Fort, and they said they were actually going to be doing the same thing today. We've arranged to meet in half an hour where we'll catch another bus together.

I wonder if today is the day… whether I should attempt to send the letter or not. Or how will I actually manage to do it? What if there's no glass to do it? What if there are too many people around? I'm getting pretty nervous. But I keep telling myself, hey I've made it this far. It would be pretty lame to stop now.

(RIPPED PAGE)

09/ 06/ 1757

Holy shit, I've phased through! The letter didn't just make it, so did I!

(THE REST OF THE ENTRIES ARE INELIGIBLE TO READ DUE TO NOTEBOOK IS RIPPED AND SMEARED WITH BLOOD - WITH ONE ENTRY REMAINING…)

Oh god, he's been shot. I was too late! Damn him! Why did he still go through with it?!

==

17/ 07/ 01

Diary,

I'm back in my room, at Hamilton's College.

How, you ask? What happened? Did I make it? Did the letter make it?

The letter not only made it, but I accidentally sent myself back in time as well. I sent myself to the 10th June, 1757, a day before the battle. Now for the 'how' part.

When I was in India I met some other really nice tourists, who were backpackers. They traveled to Fort George with me, that's on the coast, and left over from old English Colonial times. I knew, like it was a feeling, that Robertson's ship would be docked there if he was going to participate in any battles. So I was going to send the letter I had written of warning him to stay away from the Battle of Plassey at the Fort.

The Fort was pretty wrecked, with half of it missing from time and war through the ages. But it was still pretty interesting to see. I walked around it at first, trying to get 'a feel for the place'. I guess I was trying to sense if there were any 'hot spots' or time displacement holes there already. But there weren't. And I was glad to see that there weren't that many people around either, so when I phased, there wouldn't be any witnesses.

Then for the glass problem.

Most of the windows were smashed or missing, but there was one part of the building that was small and being used as an office, probably to run and organize the tours around the old Fort. But there were people inside of there. I decided I'd have to wait until the end of the day when everyone would leave to go home.

I told my tourist companions that I'd meet them back at the hostel, and I got my letter out of my backpack, and I sat on the wall and watched the sunset and waited for my chance.

My chance came, and I saw the two people in the office leave, and lock the door behind them. Then I quickly ducked down and hid behind the wall I had just been sitting on so they wouldn't see me or try to make me leave as well. When they were gone, and all of the lights were turned off, I stood up and examined the place again.

The Fort looked pretty creepy. It was empty, quiet, and very, very dark. So I definitely shouldn't have any disruptions.

There wasn't much moonlight, with only a quarter moon in the sky. But I made my way back to the office with its glass windows and after finding what I considered to be the biggest window, I stopped and stared at it for a good while.

But nothing happened.

I think I wasn't concentrating properly. The reflection in the glass wasn't changing. I think my nerves were probably stopping the transformation. And somehow the silence of the walls around me was deafening. It was a hot, muggy night, but even the tiny sea breeze gave me goosebumps.

"C'mon Elisha, snap out of it." I closed my eyes and shook my head. When I opened my eyes again I concentrated on the tiny reflection of the quarter moon in the glass.

I stared and stared and stared. I tried not to blink. I tried to concentrate very hard. I even repeatedly murmured the date I wanted through half open lips. "10th June, 1757... 10th June, 1757... 10th June, 1757..."

Gradually the little moon in the window started to grow bigger and blur and go into a pattern of light waves streaming out towards me...

Suddenly I saw more than one light in the window, suddenly the reflection of the walls behind me weren't dark, but lit up with torches and lanterns, and an English soldier in the old red uniform walked past...

Soon the light was engulfing me in a familiar dizzying wave. I recognized what was happening from my first journey with Dr. Knight, and holding the letter, I raised my hand which went through the glass. I wanted to release the paper from my hand. I knew it was now and then.

Right then I broke my concentration. I thought I heard a voice, a noise, just beside me! With the dizziness I stumbled forward when I turned my head to see... Oh oh...

I don't think I should have done that.

"Oy, wot are you doin' down there?"

I couldn't see! I blinked as the blindness that I experienced the first time returned. Then I wondered why my hands and knees were pressing down on something cold and hard. Finally I realized I had fallen to the floor.

"Please help me... can you tell me where I am?" I asked the voice.

"Where you are?" the gruff, male voice replied incredulously.

"What date is it today?" I asked worriedly.

"Who are you and where did you come from?" a hand reached down and pulled me up, not caring that it pulled on a few hairs on me head either.

"Oow! My hair!" I slapped his hand away. I still couldn't see anything, and my eyes were hurting. But by his rough English accent, I'm assuming I accidentally posted myself and not the document I intended.

"Tell me! Are you a spy? Huh? Wot you doin' here then?" his hand grabbed the front of my T-shirt and shook me.

"Let fucking go of me you low life!" I tried to push him away. "My name is Lady Elisha Durrant, and if you would be so good to show me to the quarters of Captain Guy Robertson, he can tell you so himself!"

"What would a Captain of the Royal Navy know of a blind whore like yourself!" he spat in my face.

"More than an ill-educated toad like yourself!"

Suddenly there was loud laughter all around us, and I realized that it was directed toward us. I also realized the Fort would be swarming with men. I realized I was making for some entertainment. I realized I had to get out of there very quickly.

I released myself from his grasp and straightened my T-shirt. I knew I had to play this right. I tried to do a quick revision of my notes I took before my first excursion to England.

"If you would be so kind to take me to a commanding officer, then he can tell Captain Robertson that a Lady Elisha Durrant is here to see him. But believe me, if you refuse me this courtesy, and continue in your disrespectful discourse, a flogging will be the least of your troubles." I crossed my arms and held my head up high in the snobbiest manner possible.

I heard all of the men break out into laughter again, and the man, whoever he is, standing beside me, grumble.

"All right... this way."

He grabbed my arm and half pulled, half dragged me along.

My eyes started to see blurry images, and I slowly made out shapes of the men we passed, and of the staircase in front of us which I was soon dragged up that as well.

In it's hey-day, the Fort was starting to look a lot different than the ruins that I had been exploring a couple of hours ago.

"Excuse me sir." The man suddenly came to an abrupt stop and I made out some different kind of blue uniforms in front of us. "This girl here says she knows Captain Robertson."

"She'll have to wait, he's in a very important meeting with Governor Clive and Captain Greyson." The man in blue replied haughtily in an upper class accent.

"Excuse me sir. This is an urgent matter that cannot wait. I am Lady Elisha Durrant, and have been traveling in disguise. I have some very important information for Captain Robertson." I spoke up in my very best upper class accent possible too.

"Really?" the man sounded impressed. "Then perhaps you can tell me, and I can tell the Captain for you."

"No, I cannot sir. I have been given the strictest orders not to divulge this, even under pain of death, unless it is to Captain Robertson directly." I flat out lied.

"Even under pain of death? How interesting." He sounded like he had an evil grin on his face. Unfortunately I couldn't see properly. "Put her in my office. I'll deal with her later."

Oh fuck. That's not what I wanted to hear. Shit! Now what do I do?

I was led inside a small dark room with only a single candle burning on top of a desk. The burly officer who had first caught me dumped me on a stool in the corner and then turned around and left me there. I thought it wise to stay put until my vision returned properly, and I prayed that it would quickly.

After a couple of minutes, it eventually did. I looked at my watch, it read 7.59 PM. I felt like I was running out of time. I had to move fast, and to think fast.

I stood up, about to leave, when the man in the blue uniform and upper class accent came into the room.

"Where are you going, my Lady?" he asked, but I didn't like the way he asked it. I didn't like the way he was looking at me right then either.

"Do you know who my family are? My father is the Earl Durrant. My relatives are the Dunmore family. Do not let this costume disguise the fact that I am higher than you in society, and should be treated as such." I held my head up high.

"And what, pray tell, would an English Lady be doing in India, scurrying around like a little mouse, dispatching important information? And where, especially, would this Lady be getting her information from?" he teased, sitting on top of his desk, folding his arms too.

"Do not be deliberately obtuse with me. Also in my listing of acquaintances are Captain Guy Robertson and Captain Greyson. I met them at Lady Caroline Fox's Ball. Now, if you do not take me to them, this instant, I will tell them when I see them that you deliberately delayed my visit with malicious intent!" I hissed at him, trying to think of as many big and long words in a short as space as possible to get my act across.

"Malicious intent, my Lady? Those are grave accusations indeed." He uncrossed his arms and walked towards me. "I will take you to Captain Robertson, or indeed Captain Greyson, if you desire it." Here he paused and gave me a good look and up and down. "But I must know what kind of information you have, to know if it is important enough to interrupt their meeting."

That's it. I rolled my eyes. I was getting really sick of this.

"Take me to them right now, or pay a heavy penalty for this act of treason!" I tried to drill my eyes in to them as my cheeks puffed out in anger.

"Is your information in this letter?" he arched his eyebrow.

Oh oh, I'd almost forgotten it was still in my hand.

"Don't you dare!" I tried to shove the letter in my pocket, but the man was too quick and he grabbed it from me. He even started to open it! Shit! Now what do I do?

I panicked. Then I lost it. I launched myself at him. At first he thought he was easily defending himself against a weak, flailing woman, and then when he was exposed, I kicked him in the groin, kneed him in the stomach, and when he was hunched over in pain... I punched him in the back of the head!

He crumpled to the floor, half unconscious, when I grabbed the letter and ran for it!

I ran past the two soldiers who were probably guarding the door to his office, which gave them a big surprise. Then they were after me, so I ran down the steps I assumed had been the ones I had been taken up before, and I ran towards the direction of the water. I'll have to find Robertson's ship, maybe I can seek some shelter there.

"Oy! Stop her! Stop her! Oy!" one of the soldiers behind me cried.

Shit. I knew I wasn't going to make it to the waters edge. I'd have to hide here and now.

I saw a door, I had no idea where it went to, but I opened it anyway. I slammed it behind me and tried locking it... but there was no lock. So I grabbed a heavy trunk that was sitting against the wall next to me and slid it across the floor instead. It made a pretty good doorstop actually.

"Oy! You! In there! I know you're in there! There's no way out!" the burly soldiers banged loudly.

I suddenly realized something else. That maybe I wasn't alone in the room. I could feel it behind me.

"May we help you?" another male voice, also with an upper class English accent, asked.

I turned around… to be met with the sight of Sir Guy Robertson.

He was standing with two older male officers, also with Captain Greyson. They were all standing around a table with a map and a lamp on it, probably doing their battle plans. The two slightly older officers looked highly unamused to see me.

"As I said, may we help you?" one of the older officers repeated himself.

"Ah, yeah. I came to see Sir Guy Robertson." I said, suddenly feeling even more shaky and sweaty and nervous than ever.

Guy and Greyson looked completely stunned to see me.

"Captain, are you in acquaintance with this young lady?" the older officer who spoke before, asked.

"Ah, yes, indeed I am." Robertson replied. But I guess he was too flabbergasted to say anything else, all he could do was stare.

"A pleasure to meet you Gentlemen. I am Lady Elisha Durrant. Please excuse the costume, but I have had a little adventure of late." I walked over and offered my hand to the older army officer, who took it.

Suddenly, four soldiers barged through the door, breaking the wood and knocking over the trunk. And then the sleazy officer also came in, and when he saw who I was with, his eyes widened. He gave a salute.

"Please excuse this interruption, sir. I was trying to catch this woman here…" sleazy guy inferred me.

"This was part of the adventure." I rolled my eyes to the older officer. "Excuse me sir, but are you aware that you have officers under your command that stop messengers from getting in your camp, even if they carry important news that can affect the outcome of the next battle in days to come?"

"Indeed?" the older officer asked, raising his eyebrows.

"Forgive me sir, but we are a little skeptical of strangers coming into our camp, are we not? Particularly when there are spies about, and even assassins." Sleazy guy inferred me again.

"An assassin? Really? How interesting. And whereabouts on this costume, sir, do you suppose is a Muscat hiding? Or a knife or sword?" I raised my arms and did a little turn.

"Your bag, madam." Sleazy guy was giving me daggers now.

"OK then. Let's see." I put my backpack on the table on top of the map and opened it. "Hmm. T-shirt, T-shirt, T-shirt, ooh, women's underwear. Shall I continue? How about we go through my toiletries bag next? I'm sure my father will enjoy hearing the story of how his precious, only daughter, heir to his fortune, member of the King's court, was treated when visiting a camp full of his soldiers, and supposed trusted members of his officers." I glared back at sleazy guy.

"I've seen and heard enough, thank you Commander." The older officer now frowned at sleazy guy as I quickly repacked my things, trying to hide my folder with my notes in it.

"Sir." Sleazy gave a bow, shot one last dirty look in my direction, and then was gone.

"And what important message do you have for us, my Lady?" the older officer asked me now.

"And who might you be, Sir? We have not been properly introduced." I said warily.

"I am Richard Clive, a Lieutenant-Governor of Fort St. David. I am also in charge of this offense." He said, half amused at my ignorance and arrogance, and probably half annoyed.

Shit. He's Clive of India. Have I arrived too late?

"What's the date?" I turned to Guy.

"The date? Why, it's the 10th June." He said in surprise at my lack of knowledge.

"I need to talk to you privately." I grabbed his arm.

"Excuse me, my Lady." Clive said annoyed. "Did you bring an urgent message, or not?"

Bugger. I'll have to make something up. Quick. I tried to remember my notes of the Battle of Plassey.

"I've come with information about the enemy. Suraja whatsisname…"

"Suraja Dowlah?" Clive raised his eyebrows unimpressed.

"Yeah, him." I swallowed nervously. Captain Greyson looked like he was trying not to laugh at my expense. I guess he found all of this quite amusing. "Dowlah's got 35,000 infantry, 15,000 cavalry, 53 heavy guns and a small detachment of French soldiers."

Captain Greyson no longer looked like he was trying to laugh, and neither did any of the men in the room at that moment.

"Damn it all!" Greyson banged his fist on the table.

"That's almost as twice as many as we had been informed!" the other older army officer said to Clive.

"How do you know this?" Guy asked me. I still had my hand on his arm, and he raised it so he could examine the watch on my wrist. I quickly took my hand back and folded my arms again to cover the watch. It wasn't digital, but it was glow-in-the-dark. So it was sure to raise some questions to my background.

"Somebody told me to tell you. When they found out I knew Captain Robertson and Captain Greyson, they passed on this knowledge. I think you guys have a sympathizer in the other camp." I blatantly lied again.

"And why are you in India?" Guy asked me again.

"Visiting." I shrugged.

"Where are your parents? Who is your chaperone?" Guy asked me next.

"My parents are back in Scotland. I lost my chaperone." I continued to lie. "I think she's back in Bangladesh, or somewhere."

"Then if you would permit us to take care of your safety, Lady Elisha. It would be our privilege." Clive now smiled kindly to me.

"I thank you, sir. It would be my honor." I smiled and nodded back to him.

"Now, you must be very weary after your trying day. Perhaps Captain Robertson, if you would be so kind to show our Ladyship to one of our guest rooms, I'm sure she would like to rest." Clive nodded to Guy.

Guy nodded back and walked over to the door, and held it (what's left of it) open for me and then when we were outside again, offered me his arm and I took it.

We walked along the battlement, away from the barracks and towards another large stone house.

From here the view of the ships could be seen. They looked splendidly elegant, bobbing slightly in the waves as the tide was rushing up the beach towards the fort. The night I left there was just a quarter moon in the sky, now this vision before me had a full moon. I wanted to keep this moment of us together with this view etched in my memory.

"It is quite miraculous, that you have had this amazing adventure, and were able to make it safely to our Headquarters and tell us this news." Guy suddenly said coldly.

I stopped us in our tracks.

"You don't believe me?" I asked him, feeling hurt. Not because I did lie, but because he doesn't trust me, even still.

"How exactly, did you come across this news, my Lady?" he demanded.

"I read it in a book exactly." I crossed my arms again, partly from the return of anger, but mostly because I started to feel cold in the sea breeze.

"You read it in a book?"

"Yeah, along the date of your death, 12th June, 1757. I came to deliver this letter to you. But I accidentally posted myself instead." I slapped the envelope into his hand.

I stood staring out at the sea, while Guy ripped open the letter and read it impatiently.

I think he read it all. When he had finished, he slowly lowered it and looked at me intently. I don't know if he believed me or not.

"Are you some sort of witch or lunatic? How do you come to the conclusion that I will die? And how do you know so much about the enemy camp?"

"Well, you could call me crazy I guess. I ran away from school so I could try to warn you! Even if I make it back, I don't know if there's anything to go back to. I did act crazy, because I wanted to warn you! You can't go into this battle. Don't. Sail away. Say you have a sick relative or something. Say your grandmother died." I walked right up to him and yelled in his face.

"My grandmother has already died." He still frowned at me. "But tell me how you know so much."

"Isn't it obvious?" I moaned. "Look at what I'm wearing. You saw my watch, see it now!" I pressed one of the side buttons on my blue plastic, glow-in-the-dark watch and now the panel lit up for a moment with a pulsing blue light, and then it stopped. "Listen to my speech! I have an accent from a country that hasn't even been discovered yet! Look at my passport!" I pulled it out from my bag and let him look at it.

"It says your name is Baker and not Durrant." He frowned at me.

"Is that all you can say? My name isn't right? Here I am, telling you that you have somebody from the future who is trying to save your life, and you're worried about a fucking surname?" I was shouting at him.

He just stood there, looking at me. It made me angry. It made me frustrated and worried. It made me act even more impulsively.

"You met me when I was 16. Now I'm 17 for Christ's' sake. Don't you think that's a bit strange, only aging a couple of weeks' when to you it would have been two years? Look at my birth date in the passport. It says I'm not even born yet! I'm not lying! Your life is in danger. I came to warn you. Please don't fight in the battle, please... please..." I started crying.

He still just stood there, looking at me.

"Since that first night at the Ball I couldn't stop thinking of you! But I thought I wouldn't see you again... ever. Then when I learned of your fate, I felt I had to do something! I love you Guy." I said lamely, and then I turned around so I wouldn't have to face him and stared out to sea again.

If this had been on a daytime soap opera, I probably would have changed channels by now. But it was happening to me. This was real.

He came and stood beside me now and held out my letter and my passport for me to take back. So I did. I put the two of them in my backpack.

"I wrote to you too." he said, also staring out to sea.

"Really?" I sniffled and shivered.

"Three letters, to be exact. One to an address in Scotland, which was supposed to be your fathers property. Another, to an estate in the Colonies. And thirdly... well, I even tried to write to you at the address of your Aunt, Lady Dunmore in London. That was two years ago and I never received a reply. I assumed your family were aware of my 'low' connections, and presumed to keep us separated." He said stiffly, his arms behind his back.

"I tried to go to the Marlborough Ball. But we were told there wouldn't be any more time traveling excursions for another couple of months. And then I was told I wouldn't be allowed to visit the same era again. So I ran away from school and I lied to my brother, got some money, and flew here." I confessed.

"You... flew here?" he looked at me strangely.

"On a machine called an airplane." I told him.

"You ran away from school?" he started chuckling, his stubborn resolve melting.

"Women in my century are educated the same as a man. As a man reaches a certain point in his education before being accepted into University, so does a woman. I'm studying so I can go to University one day." I told him.

"And then what? You will hold down a profession, the same as a man as well?" he smiled in amusement at me.

"Yes. I just don't know what to do with my life yet." I said.

"But you put all of this in jeopardy, so you could warn me of the upcoming battle?" he took hold of my hands, his whole demeanor changed now.

"Yeah, a little." I tried to say modestly, getting a little shaky and nervous again from our close contact.

"Then I guess our social protocols are still a little foreign to you, perhaps?" he leaned in closer.

"You mean with kissing a strange girl, on a beach, with no chaperone or proper company in sight?" I smiled now, and let out a laugh.

He raised his hand and wiped my cheek dry.

"That is exactly what I mean." He smiled again, softly this time.

And then we kissed. And it wasn't just a peck either. And I think I still surprised him, when I opened my mouth and easily let his tongue through. And also probably when I rubbed myself against him. But I wouldn't let him pull away that easily. I wanted this to last as long as I could have him.

"So do you believe me?" I asked him when we did pull away.

"It is quite a story you've just told me. But fact or fiction, your actions seem genuine."

"It's true Guy. Everything I told you. Even about the upcoming battle." My eyes met his and held them. "Your life is in danger."

At these words he pulled away slightly, and returned my hand to his arm and began walking us along again. I tried to see his expression but he looked in the opposite direction, out to sea, probably in the vicinity of his ship. I wished at that moment I could know what was on his mind. Did he still doubt me?

When we reached our destination, and Guy walked me to the door of the Governor's House, the Housekeeper met us at the front door. She was about to show me inside and up to one of the guest bedrooms, but I didn't want to leave Guys' side. I pulled on his hand, expecting him to come with me (which the Housekeeper thought very strange, she gave us a funny look) but he laughed and said no. He had to return to the meeting at hand.

"But you won't go into battle, will you?" I pleaded with him.

"I'm afraid that that is out of my control." He sighed.

"No it's not. I'm sure you could be doing something else, somewhere else." I pointed out.

"And be called a turn coat or a deserter?" he raised his eyebrows at me.

"Come on Guy. Don't let this trip for me be a waste of time." I held his hands and tried locking onto his eyes with mine. "I want you to live. I want to see you again."

"And you shall." He bowed and kissed my hands. "But for now, a good night and sweet dreams do I bestow on you."

*****

The Housekeeper had been given the heads up of my arrival, apparently. Clive had also sent a little messenger boy on ahead of us. I thought that was nice of him, kind of like, good ole formal English hospitality.

The Housekeeper showed me up the staircase and to one of the guest bedrooms as promised. Candles were lit, a basin of water had been prepared, and even a nightgown had been provided. This was all such a welcome relief, that I wasted no time in quickly washing myself down, changing, and crawling into bed. I was utterly exhausted.

When I woke up the next morning, I quickly discovered how late I had slept in, and how late I was in another area.

It was 11.30 AM by the time I finally opened my eyes. When I sat up in bed, I found the Housekeeper in my room again, preparing some clothes for me. It was a dress and some undergarments the Governor's wife was lending me. I thought that was really nice of her. But I can't believe how late I slept in! It must have been from a combination of jet lag and physical fatigue from the phasing.

As the Housekeeper, Mrs. Benson I found out her name was, dressed me, I asked her about the men.

"Is Governor Clive and the Army and Navy officers still in a meeting about Suraja Dowlah?" I asked her as she tightened my corset.

"No Ma'am. They've left the barracks. They'd be on their way to the battle, by now." Mrs. Benson informed me.

"What?!" I turned on her. "But the battle isn't until the 12th of June!"

Mrs. Benson gave me a funny look.

"Of course, a battle in one day? I guess those things just don't really happen like that, do they? They'd be battling over a couple of days, and then be announced the victors on a certain day." I realized, crestfallen. "Oh shit, I am too late!"

I walked away from her while she was still in the middle of dressing me and went to go look out the window. Now what do I do? Maybe I should get out of this dress. Maybe I should go and try to find Guy out on the battlefield? Would that work? But then, what would a woman be doing out on the battlefield?

What if I caught him when he was down? And tried to phase him back into the future with me? A hospital in my day should be able to save him. Would that work? But then again, all those news reports on TV about shootings and people dying were still prevalent in my day as well.

Oh god… I was still too late!

I didn't care for breakfast, and as soon as the dress was on me properly, I walked back over to the barracks, unescorted. I knew from there I should receive regular updates. I was past worrying about being perceived as a Lady right then, I had to just focus on the status of battle.

I found the barracks virtually empty, with nearly all of the men gone into battle. Unfortunately there was only one hiccup. I couldn't believe who had been left in charge. It was Commander Sleazy.

"Ah, Lady Elisha Durrant. Your new dress becomes you so." he greeted, now standing in the same room the officers had been in last night, where I first saw Guy. Now he was seated at that table where the map is, examining it himself.

I ignored the remark and came over for a look at the map myself.

"Any news?" I asked him coldly.

"They left at the crack of dawn this morning. They've taken their positions, and by now they would have engaged the enemy. Would you care for some tea... my Lady?" he picked up his porcelain tea cup and sipped from it slowly, looking me up and down again.

"No." I glared at him.

Just then what sounded like the low rumble of thunder from a storm that was still far away, could be heard.

"Ah. See, I was right. That would be the enemies arsenal right there. They have, as you did say, 53 of the heavy guns, wasn't it?" he arched his eyebrows at me.

I ignored that remark too and turned to leave to wait it out somewhere else when sleazy guy stopped me again.

"Lady Elisha..." he stood up and came around from the table.

"You may call me Lady Durrant."

"I will call you whatever I choose, do you understand me?" he grabbed my arm. "You may have been able to fool everyone else in this insipid hellhole they call a military Fort, but you have not fooled me!" he pulled me closer to him and hissed in my ear. "You are no more aristocratic than I am! Mark my words, you whore, that the odds are not favorable for your lover right now. Soon I will be in charge of this Fort, when the battle leaves no survivors. Then who will be your protector? No-one!"

"Threatening me and insulting me? What exactly is your name, sir?" I stood my ground.

"Commander Wilson. I suggest you remember it well. For when the men chase you next, you will be crying out my name!" he grabbed my breast!

"But until then..." I stamped on his foot.

He grunted in pain and released me for a few seconds, which I used as my opportunity to quickly get away from him.

I hurriedly walked away from the barracks now and towards the beach again. Tears, this time of fear and not just sorrow were watering my eyes again. But I kept trying to fight them back and hold them inside of me. I couldn't let this creep think he's winning.

I stayed on the beach until sundown. I sat on the sand, watching the ships, almost like life-sized toys, rock gently in the water. I looked at them, wondering which one it was that Guy was Captain of.

This Commander Wilson guy didn't really frighten me. He just gave me the creeps. I really wanted to hurt him badly for acting so disgusting towards me. I fantasized of every horrific way to die that I'd ever seen in a movie, with this Wilson guy in the place of the victim.

I could hear the heavy guns, which I guess were the canons, firing constantly. I tried not to replay the battle scenes from the movie 'The Patriot' in my head. I prayed that Guy would return safe. I even closed my eyes and tried to relive last night in my head. I know it sounds wet and mushy, but being in his arms, and kissing him... it was definitely worth any punishment that might come my way when I return to the future.

That night I returned to the Governor's House to sleep in the guest bedroom again. And then the next morning, I woke up and dressed at 8 AM this time, again with the help of Mrs. Benson. And then again I returned to the beach, next to the barracks in the Fort, and waited for news.

Around 4 PM the sound of canon fire ceased. I found myself clenching my dress. I tried to hope for the best. Then around 8 PM I heard shouting, lots of it. I stood up and turned and ran back to the Fort. I ran as fast as I could. I ran barefoot, carrying my stockings and shoes I had taken off on the beach in my right hand. I didn't even bother with putting them back on again.

There was cheering going on, along with some singing. The men were marching back victoriously. I guess the time line was uninterrupted so far, but I was shaking. I had to see Guy.

I stood to the side of the road coming into the Fort, and watched the horses and carts bring back the wounded and dead. They came last, behind the victorious ones that made it back alive and untouched. And then finally, I saw Captain Greyson riding behind, with a grave look on his face, next to a one-horse cart, that was being pulled along slowly.

I immediately knew what this meant.

"Is he alive? Is he alive?" I screeched, running towards them hysterically.

Greyson got off his horse, which he handed the reigns over to another soldier riding near him, and put up his hands to stop me.

"He breathes my Lady, but barely." He said sadly. He had blood and dirt on his hands and face, with a huge tear in his uniform coat. But I knew it wasn't his blood.

Shaking now, I went around to the back of the cart, and saw Guy.

He was stretched out on his back, unconscious, with a gaping hole in his stomach.

"Oh god..." I uttered...

There was a cut on his forehead as well, and half his face was smeared with blood.

"Oh no..." I climbed up onto the cart and knelt beside him. My skirt ended up being smothered in the pool of blood that was emanating around him. "Oh no. Please no. Guy... Guy can you hear me?"

I cradled his head in my hands so our faces were only inches apart.

"Guy, can you hear me? It's Elisha."

He opened his eyes. Oh thank you! He opened his eyes!

He looked up into my face and tried to smile.

Then he closed his eyes again.

And that was it.

I could hear the air leave his chest for a last time.

"GET A DOCTOR!" I screamed at Greyson.

"My Lady, the surgeon has already looked at him…" Greyson shook his head tearfully. "There is nothing more that can be done…"

God no! No! This isn't how it's supposed to end! NO!!

My fear and heavy sorrow was suddenly replaced with steel-like determination.

An idea ran into my mind, and new hope sprung up with it.

"Help me get him up." I tried to sit Guy up by pulling him up by the shoulders.

"My Lady?" Greyson gave me a funny look.

"Help me get him off this cart." I ordered him, now sitting behind Guy's back and trying to push him towards the back edge.

"My Lady please, let the man go peacefully!" Greyson got up on the cart as well and grabbed my shoulders. "He died admirably. He died in battle. Let him go with honor."

"Greyson, listen to me. I can take him to a place where he will be healed." I said desperately.

"My Lady! Listen to me! The man is dead!" Greyson yelled, shaking me now.

"No he isn't! We can bring him back! But I need your help!" I pushed his hands off me, then I spoke quickly, pleadingly. "Captain Greyson, when I first met you both at Lady Caroline Fox's Ball in London, you told me that there wasn't a fellow better in the world than Guy. You told me of his integrity and honor. Now help me repay him with his life for all the good deeds that he has done! I can bring him back! But I need your help to do it! Please don't turn your back on your friend now. We can beat death! I have a secret that can save him! Please help me! Please!"

Greyson studied me for a minute. Then he looked down on his friend, before returning his gaze to me. I think my face said it all.

"What is required of me, Lady Elisha?" he said gravely.

"Help me get him down. Help me carry him to a large glass window."

"I beg your pardon?"

"Don't question me now. I'll tell you everything later. Please, we have to hurry!"

The two of us hauled poor Guy's body off the cart, and Greyson then heaved the blood sodden carcass of his friend over his right shoulder, and then waited for my next request.

"Follow me." I quickly walked ahead of him into the barracks.

I found an empty room as fast as I could, and once Greyson and Guy were inside, I closed the door and tried to barricade it with putting a table and chair against it. I couldn't have any interruptions. I had to do this right.

Greyson looked like he was about to unload his friend to the floor when I stopped him.

"No, keep holding him. Please, come and stand beside me, and face the window." I told him.

"What is this?" Greyson looked like he was either losing patience, or losing faith, or probably both.

"You will see why." I waved him over.

Thankfully he did what he was told. I put my hand on his shoulder and my other hand Guy's back and stood partially behind them, and faced the window as well. I could see the light of a lantern outside, which made it possible for me to focus on.

"Now please, don't talk, and in a couple of minutes, you'll see why." I said. And then I concentrated. And I concentrated harder than I had ever done before in my life.

I envisioned help for Guy. I envisioned a future with superior advances in medicine. I envisioned a hospital environment. I stared at the light of the lantern filtering through the dirty glass. I envisioned that the light was growing around us, encompassing all of us.

Suddenly there was a knock on the door.

"Captain Greyson, are you in there? Is the 'Lady' Elisha in there with you? Governor Clive needs to speak to you immediately, sir." Commander 'sleazy' Wilson's voice sounded on the other side of the door.

I couldn't let him break my concentration, and when Greyson looked like he was about to move, I held onto him more tightly.

"Don't move!" I said with clenched teeth.

I stared harder and harder into the light of the lantern.

"Captain? I'm very sorry to bother you, Captain, but I have been given orders by Governor Clive to retrieve you sir, for a meeting." Wilson started banging on the door.

"See here, My Lady... " Greyson tried to turn to me, and I was about to lose my control.

But then finally the light of the lantern started to waver, and come towards us in waves. The view outside of the glass started to change. No longer did we see a lantern hanging on a stone wall at night, inside an English Fort in India. Instead, it was daytime, and there were rolling green hills, and a pale green sky.

The light waves grew brighter and brighter, and I knew it was working. I felt the cool change of air around us, caused by the static electricity being generated, resulting in the tingling sensation of our hairs standing up. As the bright light engulfed us in a brilliant flash, I suddenly pushed all three of us through the wall with the glass window.

*****

I was blind again.

Suddenly I felt all of these hands helping us up and all of these voices, asking us questions, barking out orders. I guessed we were in a medical facility, because I recognized some of the medical terminology being used. And the place had the slight disinfectant smell of a hospital, only not as strong, but more sterile.

"Please, he needs help! He stopped breathing 5 minutes ago! Please revive him! He'll probably need CPR! He needs his heart jump started again! He's lost a lot of blood! It was a gun shot wound!" I cried out.

I could hear Greyson swearing as he was temporarily blinded too. I could hear him try to put a fight when they tried to take Guy's body away. But I reached over and grabbed him, to stop him.

"Where the buggery are we? Why can't I see anything?" Greyson cursed.

"I don't know. But they're helping Guy." I said.

"Elisha Baker, you are safe now." A strange male voice spoke suddenly.

"Where am I?" I asked desperately.

"Circulate Headquarters."

I was stunned.

"How? Why? When I was phasing, did you pick up our light waves and bring us here?" I asked, moving my head around, trying to pin the source of the voice.

"No. No we did not. You brought you three here all on your lonesome." The voice said, slightly mockingly.

"But that's impossible! A Circulator can travel through time, not space, on their own! We can phase through the layers of time..."

"But not the same with geography?" he finished my sentence.

"Yeah." I started to see blurry images again. I rubbed my eyes, trying to speed up the process of my sight returning.

"The same could be said for seeing. Circulators can see through time, but not through space. But you've managed it, again, all on your own."

"What do you mean?" I spat accusatorily, getting sick of the tone of his voice.

"Then let me show you." a hand gently took my arm and led me a short distance away. "Your eyesight should return at any moment."

And it did.

And I found myself looking out of a wall of glass, at one of the most beautiful sights I had ever seen...

Rolling green hills, a clump of impossibly tall trees of a kind I've never seen before... a small stream with a little cascade of water over some red rocks... The ground was covered in lush-looking, long, green grass. And the sky had this curious green and orange hue over the horizon.

There was something familiar about the rolling green hills… and I realized that I had seen them before. It was the night in my dorm room, where after my mirror exercise in Dr. Kell's class, that I tried to see through time myself. I saw these rolling green hills, but I had seen them at night time, when this was all darkened.

"Where is this? When is this?" I turned to the man now. He looked to be in his fifties, and was wearing a white, futurist, simplistic suit with white pants and white shirt and jacket with no buttons or holes.

"Near Mare Acidalium, in the Northern Hemisphere of Mars. When is the date, you ask? Well, by Earth's calendar, you could say this is a few hundred thousand years in Earth's past."

"The past? But I wanted the future!" I said in further surprise.

The older, futuristic man smiled at me. "From your date, this is the future."

"How?" I asked him, confused.

"Because in your future, when mankind is on the brink of extinction, we decided to extricate ourselves from the destruction and to build a colony here. We decided the safest option would be to build a sort of, hmm, what might you call it… base camp? Headquarters? Here on Mars, where in this time, the planet is safe and habitable." He answered.

"But this planet isn't safe. In our century it's uninhabitable with an unstable atmosphere, weak gravity, and atmosphere 100 times thinner than on Earth." I accused him.

"Yes, it is, in YOUR time. And that won't happen for a few hundred thousand years yet. We know of the planet's fate. Of course we do, which is why we've settled here in the past. But even our habitation here isn't finite, it is merely a stepping stone. A safe haven, call it if you will. We are also constructing another colony on another planet, on the other side of this galaxy. But here, on Mars and so close to Earth, can we continue to visit the different time periods of our mother planet." The man explained.

I guessed something else. "Do I come to know you in my future?"

"No, you come to know me in your present. I am Lucas Hodge, and I am pleased to formally make your acquaintance, Miss Baker." He offered his hand.

I shook it, still feeling a little wary of the situation.

"Am I going to be punished?" I asked him. "Kicked out of the Circulate? Expelled from school?"

"Certainly not. Whatever gave you that idea?" Lucas chuckled.

"Well, I ran away from school and Circulated against the permission of the teachers."

"In the future, Miss Baker, I know you will do certainly worse than that." He smiled softly to me.

"And you don't kick me out even then?" I asked, in further surprise.

"Of course not."

"Why not?"

He clasped his hands behind his back and stared back out at the lovely view again. I wonder if he's contemplating on whether he would or should tell me something else. So I tried his reasoning for a moment.

"I suppose you can tell me now, coz I'm only going to find out later." I smiled to him knowingly.

"Indeed you are." He sighed. "Hamilton's College isn't going to remain a school for the Circulate much longer."

"Really?" I asked, worried. "Why?"

"Because there will be no-one else to teach."

"What do you mean?" I pressed him.

"After 1985 AD, no other human beings with the ability to calculate time or to circulate through time are borne." Lucas stated. "The total count of members of the Circulate remain at 696." Then he turned to face me again and gently put his hands on my shoulders. "That is why every single member of the Circulate is precious to us. That is why you are important to us Elisha. With your ability, you become the strongest one of all."

Captain Greyson had remained silent and listened to all of this take place in front of him. He found out my secrets as I did. He was looking at me very strangely now, when he wasn't looking out the window at the green and orange colors of the sky.

*****

It only took the medical team with their advanced medical instruments an hour to revive Guy and then heal over fifty percent of his injuries.

He was awake and able to have visitors almost immediately after the procedure they performed on him.

I was still wearing the blood soaked olden day dress, along with Captain Greyson in his blood splattered army uniform. We walked solemnly into his room, still half expecting the worst to come. But my pent up fears and anxieties that had been building up over the past week or so completely melted away when I saw Guy's smile.

"You lucky devil! Good to see you man! With luck like this on your side, any fool would think you'd never lose a game of Pharaoh again!" Greyson beamed and hugged and clapped Guy on the back.

"Well, with you at my side in battle, I might believe it too." Guy joked, then he turned serious. "Thank you for bringing me back. Thank you for not just leaving me there, on that field..."

"Nonsense! Tish-tosh! You would have done the same for me." Greyson tried to shrug it off.

"And you... my Lady..." Guy smiled at me next. "Am I correct in assuming that a few more rules were broken in rescuing me?"

"Yeah, but who's keeping count?" I joked, coming to stand by his bed.

"Thank you my Lady." Guy took hold of my hand. "Your grace and yet your willfulness knows no bounds." He joked back.

"I am a modern independent woman, Sir Robertson. We often make up our own rules as we go along." I said haughtily, and then we both laughed. Then I looked at Captain Greyson. "But you really do have to thank your friend. He trusted me enough to help me. And I hope I haven't abused this trust."

Greyson gave me one of his typical good-humored grins. "Now, if I could get you in a game of Pharaoh, could you tell me what I need to win?"

"Yes, another woman with ESP, because unfortunately my ability doesn't run like that!" I laughed again, and so did they.

Guy turned serious again. "What happens now? Will you return with us to our time?" he stroked my hand with his finger.

"I don't know. I'll certainly take you back. Oh yeah, I forgot my backpack. I'll have to get that." I mentally kicked myself for forgetting about it and leaving it behind.

"And then will you return to your own time?" Guy asked me sadly.

"I don't know. Probably." I sighed. "But it doesn't mean it's good bye, I promise you. No matter what happens, even if I have to keep running away from school and disobeying my teachers, I'll keep seeing you again."

Captain Greyson looked thoughtful for a moment. "If you are not Lady Elisha Durrant, who are you?"

"Elisha Baker. I'm Australian, which is a country that hasn't been colonized by you lot yet." I said in my thickest Aussie accent possible. "G'day mate, how's it goin'?"

"This large inheritance that you were entitled to..." he started to ask.

"Doesn't exist. But in a way, if I wanted to be, I could be rich." I thought out loud and remembered what Professor Hamilton said. "Money is just a means to achieve our goals... so they have the money and use it when they need to."

"Of course it exists. If you were to return to Captain Greyson's time, and Captain Robertson's, you would still be Lady Elisha Durrant, entitled to the fortune of the Earl of Durrant." Lucas walked into the room and joined us. "Also do not forget what Dr. Knight told you... that there are numerous safe houses scattered through the different countries and ages on Earth that we visit. Wealth, when we need it, is no obstacle."

"There you go Robertson. You couldn't make a better catch! The woman you love still has a large fortune that can enable the two of you to live happily ever after." Greyson half joked, nudging his friend.

Lucas ignored that remark and he turned to me. "You had better return your friends to the correct time frame. We cannot heal your Captain Robertson any further on fear that it will alert the suspicions of his peers, if he returned completely well."

I nodded, but then asked in concern, "what of his injuries? They won't become infected or anything in his time frame, will they?"

"We have given Captain Robertson a high spectrum anti-biotic which will last in his system for the next six months. I doubt he could even contract scurvy on his long voyage home." Lucas half joked, and smiled and nodded to the two gentlemen. "And what of your decision? Will you return to Hamilton's College when this adventure has ended?"

"Um, I guess so." I shrugged, still unsure myself.

"I'm sure your teachers hope so." Lucas put his hand on my back in a supportive manner. "I know I do."

"Well then. There's no time like the present. I'm sure our absence is missed." Guy swung his legs over the bed to leave. He looked at Lucas. "Thank you for saving my life."

"Your welcome Captain Robertson. I wish you a safe journey home." Lucas nodded, and then he turned back to me. "I can escort you to our gate."

"Gate?" I asked.

"Yes. While you phase forward through time, our device will transport your light waves to south India. We call the device the Gate." Lucas explained once more.

"Oh, well, at least it has a name now." I said.

Guy grunted as he stepped onto the floor, and both Captain Greyson and I put one arm each of his about our shoulders to support him while he walked.

"Are you OK?" I asked him, worried if he was in any pain.

"I'm a lot better than I was, thank you." he smiled reassuringly to me.

Lucas escorted us himself to the Gate, which was in a large glass room that was in the center of the large building we were in. I was kind of disappointed we weren't seeing more of the place. It all looked so metallic, white, gray, black, rounded, smooth and clean. It kind of reminded me of the sci-fi movies, 'Lost in Space' and 'Gattaca'. The inside walls were of glazed glass, with the outside walls all transparent, letting in the light and colors of the outside world easily inside. We passed people also wearing simple suited clothing, only in different colors than Lucas's white suit.

The people we passed smiled and nodded in politeness as we walked by. But I was surprised that they weren't surprised to see strangers here, walking around in the clothes that we had on. I wondered, if to them, this kind of thing was commonplace?

What I gathered from what I saw of Circulate Headquarters, was this place was inside a giant, clear dome. The floors and furniture were all smooth and metallic in the white, gray and black color theme. The doors were all automatic, and slid open to let us pass. There didn't even seem to be any security codes or anything either, as we didn't have to put in any codes or swipe any passes. I guess they wouldn't have to worry about those sorts of things, coz anyone who does visit this place would be either in the Circulate or a guest of the Circulate.

When we arrived at the Gate, we found it inside a completely glassed in room. We stood on top of an elevated platform which was one huge circular mirror, also with another huge circular mirror on the ceiling. Behind another wall of glass, stood Lucas, and another man at an ultra-modern control panel that looked to be made of both steel and glass. He must be one of the Calculator's who operated the Gate.

"Do you feel strong enough to phase the three of you again?" Lucas wanted to double check.

"Yes. I'm pretty sure I can." I answered, still with my arm about Guy, supporting him on one side as Greyson did the same on the other.

"Then look up." Lucas instructed. And I understood why.

The picture in the mirror above us changed from being one of our reflection, to showing a completely different view. The view changed in waves, as if there was water behind the glass. Like the water on a beach, the site of ourselves was washed away to show Fort George looking like it did in 1757 AD.

The tiny sparkles of light in the glass was soon replaced by the sparkling lights dancing on water. The water was next to a beach. The beach was next to Fort George. The Fort looked just as it did in it's hey-day, with lanterns and torches all casting reflections into the waves of the sea.

"June 12th, 1757, 10 PM!" I suddenly mentally commanded myself.

Suddenly the view in the mirror changed again, and a lot faster than before. It zoomed into the Fort, as if bringing us closer. I felt like the machine was targeting a specific location to drop us in.

I couldn't let myself blink. I concentrated as hard as I could. And then it happened, and it was a lot faster than before. Instead of the light growing in luminosity, and coming towards us like those waves of water, a brilliant light was cast over us... to leave us blinking and standing in the dark again.

Silence.

There were no other people about, and the sounds of the sea and movements around us were muffled.

"Where are we?" Greyson asked.

"I would say the Fort." Guy guessed. "I can hear the sea close by."

"In a room somewhere. The clever Calculator transported us to an empty room. Good on him!" I cried out in relief and laughed.

When our eyesight started to return to normal, Greyson released Guy for a few moments and went over and looked out the window. "We're in the barracks. We had better get a move on. We must look a little suspicious."

Greyson opened the door, and with Guy hobbling along, his arm around my shoulders still, he closed the door again behind us.

We were indeed inside the Fort again. And with Greyson's help, we next hobbled over towards officers quarters. I think we were on our way to see Governor Clive.

"There they are! Seize the girl!" an annoyingly familiar voice called out.

A band of six soldiers rushed up to us and ripped me from Guy's and Greyson's grasp.

"What is going on here? Let go of her at once!" Greyson roared.

"What is the meaning of this?" Guy asked bewildered.

"I'm afraid you cannot help in this matter, sir." Commander Wilson walked up to us. "She is charged with treason and for being a spy for the enemy."

"Treason? A spy? This is ridiculous!" Guy protested.

"Our orders are to arrest her on sight and take her directly to Governor Clive." Wilson said snidely to Guy and Greyson.

"We are heading in the same direction. We'll take her there ourselves!" Greyson tried to grab me back again but Wilson stepped in front of him.

"I'm very sorry sir..." Wilson said, almost gloatingly. "But our orders came directly from the Governor himself."

Greyson and Guy looked like they were about to draw their swords... so I quickly spoke up.

"If we're already ALL going to the Governor, lets all go there together."

I tried to lock eyes with my two wannabe saviors, and shook my head slightly.

They sheathed their swords again and glared menacingly at Wilson.

Then we all left the barracks and headed towards the Governor's office.

When we all entered the room, we found Governor Clive seated at his desk, with my backpack on the table. All of the contents had been poured out of it, and the Governor was reading my notebook. I immediately froze when I saw my passport was open on the table as well, displaying my photo clearly on the inside cover.

"You are not Lady Elisha Durrant at all, are you, Miss Baker?" Clive looked up at me.

"Sir, I can explain all this..." Guy hobbled up to the front, with his hand resting on his sore stomach.

"So can I sir!" Greyson followed suit.

"Captain Robertson, I am glad to see that you are greatly improved. But you should be resting sir." Clive ordered Robertson.

"I thank you Governor, but I am feeling much better. And it is thanks to this woman here..." he inferred me.

"Then I am sorry to do this in front of you. But I am arresting this woman for being a spy." Clive stated.

"But why? The information she brought to us was correct! She warned us! She did us no harm." Guy argued.

"Impersonating a member of the Aristocracy is a serious offense, Captain Robertson. And since she may not even be English, and we have no way of knowing where she got all of this information..." he waved my note book in the air. "How are we supposed to assume that anything else this girl here tells us is the truth?"

Oh shit. Now I was really worried. I glared at Wilson, knowing it was probably he who somehow managed to get my pack to Clive. The slimy, sleazy, evil bastard!

"Let me guess, you came across this information in my bag from Commander Wilson here?" I asked.

"Commander Wilson did hand this in, yes." Clive said stiffly.

"Not exactly gentlemanly behavior, to go through a girl's bag like that." I shot Wilson a filthy look. "But then, his behavior towards me since I've arrived has been anything but gentlemanly."

"Please, sir." Wilson rolled his eyes. "Will you let the ravings of this woman here deter you from the case at hand?"

"I think we should hear her out. Let her defend herself!" Guy glared back at Wilson.

"Very well then, Captain. For your benefit, I will hear her out." Clive acknowledged Guy, then he said to me angrily. "Keep it brief, madam, as my patience for your lies wears thin these days."

Bugger. What do I say now? In my panic, I was all out of ideas. I looked helplessly at Guy and Greyson, hoping they might telepathically put the answer into my head. But they couldn't.

"Take her away." Clive sung dismissively, and I was started to be dragged backwards, when Guy spoke up again.

"Wait! This is a mistake! This woman came here to help us!"

Just then the door opened again and a younger officer poked his head in and addressed the Governor.

"Sir, the HMS Beaufort just docked in! And Earl Durrant and Lord Dunmore are coming! They say they're here on urgent business!"

Everyone's eyes widened at the exchange of this news. Wilson looked temporarily worried and Clive looked even more angry. I looked back at Guy and Greyson and shrugged, telling them I knew nothing of this. But I had a good feeling though. It was perfectly timed. Like the timing of a certain return home my real father made home from work all those months ago.

Two well-dressed gentlemen, one elderly and the other middle-aged, along with Dr. Knight also dressed to show she was reprising her role as Lady Dunmore, my Aunt, now entered the room regally.

"Elisha! My beloved daughter!" the well-dressed, middle-aged gentleman beamed and held out his arms to me.

I took it that this was Earl Durrant.

"Father!" I pulled myself from the soldier's grasp and ran happily into his waiting his arms.

It was a relief to play this role. I had no-idea who this man really was though. But Dr. Knight is one smart chicken, I'll give her that.

"Grand-daughter!" the other older man cried, and I hugged him next.

"Grandfather!" I played up to him next.

"Who is responsible for keeping my niece safe?" Lord Dunmore asked the group of men.

"They are!" I pointed out Guy and Greyson. "He was about to arrest me." I pointed out Clive. "But it's not his fault, because HE..." I pointed at Wilson, "sexually assaulted me and made up lies about me!"

"What?!" both Earl Durrant and Lord Dunmore exclaimed.

"What?!" Guy and Greyson uttered angrily.

"When I arrived here with the important news for the Governor, at first he wouldn't let me through, and I had to even fight him off! Then when the Governor and Captain Robertson and Captain Greyson were off, heroically winning the war and getting injured for their troubles, the predator accosted me! He called me a whore... and... and tried to..." I dramatically started to cry.

"What is the meaning of all this?!" Lord Dunmore roared at Governor Clive. "I expected to come here and offer the Kings congratulations to one of history's greatest battle scenes..."

"But he was nice. He let me sleep in a guest room and treated me with warm hospitality, before he believed this monster's lies!" I half defended the Governor.

"It would seem that nothing is as it appears to be here, Lord Dunmore." Clive fumed. "Everyone out of this office at once! Except Commander Wilson, you can stay."

Basically it was only the soldiers that left.

Lady Dunmore/Dr. Knight now put her arms about my shoulders in a comforting way as I stood back and watched it all unfold. I looked up at her and smiled, showing her how impressed I was with her for managing this, and she winked back at me. When I was about to speak again, she shooshed me, and whispered to "let the men have it out".

"But who are these men?" I leaned in and whispered back.

"My father and my brother." Dr. Knight answered.

Wow! They were for real? They were really real! And Dr. Knight wasn't lying! But I always thought her family didn't know about her ability?

Lord Dunmore told Clive how the King knew of a plan to seek out a new and experimental way to have important information get through in crisis situations. They were using me and my travels to get the information across, since the enemy, would not have thought a white woman, and an Aristocrat no less, on vacation, would be a threat to them. As a once off, to serve my King and Country, I left for India with the expressed purpose of relaying information between the Forts. But in case anything did go wrong, I would have a change of clothes and false passport to assume a new identity.

"Where is... Australia, exactly?" Clive asked the gentlemen.

"It's an island in the pacific ocean, Governor. I own an estate there. To the French, they see Australia as half under the English, and half as something else." Lord Dunmore half lied comfortably.

"And this is Lady Elisha's chaperone whom she became separated from?" Clive inferred Dr. Knight.

"Indeed. She is my daughter, Lady Vivian Dunmore. Lady Elisha is her niece." Lord Dunmore concurred.

"Well, my Lady. I must commend you on a very affecting disguise. Please accept my most humblest apologies, as your ruse worked a little too well." Clive gave me a short bow.

"Apologies accepted, Governor." I curtsied back.

"And as for you..." Clive now turned on Wilson.

"Please Governor... I was only doing my job..." Wilson swallowed nervously.

"Your job?!" Clive repeated incredulously.

"To defend the Fort against any spies or assassins..." sleazy Wilson tried to convince him.

"By sexually assaulting them?!" Clive yelled.

"Governor, if I may. This is a matter of honor. Since Lady Elisha and I are engaged..." Sir Guy hobbled forward, unsheathing his sword again. "It is my honor that has also been affected by this blaggard."

Engaged? Dr. Knight looked at me in surprise and I shrugged, I was just as surprised as she was! But I couldn't wipe the smile off my face though.

"No, it is my duty, sir." Greyson now stepped up, also unsheathing his sword too. "My friend is injured and is in no fit state for a duel. It would be my pleasure to see that this incident be put right."

"Fine. Take him outside and do what you will with him. But if he's still alive afterwards, throw him in the brig." Clive waved his hand dismissively.

Greyson grabbed Wilson's arm, and was about to do just that, when I stopped them. Even though he was a disgusting pig, I didn't want him dead. I didn't want to be responsible for a man's death.

"No. Don't kill him." I spoke up, and then I left Dr. Knight's side and crossed over to stand beside Guy once more. I took hold of his hand and met his eyes with mine again, before looking back at everyone else. "You also must realize, that when I was assigned to this mission, that I was slightly prepared for it. The King was not so unwise to send a completely useless woman out into the wilds and wars of India. I had some skill in self-defense. I said that Commander Wilson ATTEMPTED to attack me. I was able to fight him off. Let him live with this dishonor. Let him live with the fact that a weak little woman was able to beat him."

Governor Clive and Earl Durrant exchanged glances, and then both men nodded.

"If that is what you desire." Guy squeezed my hand.

Greyson saw to that Wilson was lead away and imprisoned.

"So, you are the young man my daughter has chosen above all others." Earl Durrant crossed over to us. "Congratulations. I look forward to introducing you into our society upon your return to England." He offered Guy his hand to shake.

Guy looked at me puzzled, before back at Earl Durrant and giving his other hand to shake in return.

"My dear, we must leave to sail back tomorrow. Your family are worried about you. You are due in court to tell the King in person what happened here tonight." Earl Durrant said to me gravely.

"Very well, father." I said a little disappointedly.

"We will wait for you back on the ship." Lord Dunmore spoke up, and then he offered his daughter his arm and they left, with Earl Durrant walking behind them.

"Sir Guy, would you be so kind to escort me to the ship?" I asked him.

"Of course." He offered his arm and I took it. "If I may be excused, Governor?"

"Away with the two of you." Clive smiled back to us.

*****

Guy and I slowly hobbled down to the wooden pier the ships were moored to.

"Who was that man, pretending to be your father?" Guy asked me after a while.

"Earl Durrant."

"No, really."

"Yes, really." I nodded.

"And he's pretending to be your father?" Guy asked surprised.

"His daughter is my teacher at the school." I told him.

"A teacher? Her? Why would she teach? Doesn't she attend court?" Guy asked confused.

"Only when she has to. She'd much rather teach. She can also travel through time. Did you know that in my era, she's also a doctor?"

"No!" Guy laughed.

"Truly. That's how far a woman can go in my society. Technically, she can have the same freedoms a man has."

"Technically?" Guy questioned.

"Yes. But in actuality, some of the time it's a man who still gets paid more money though. Like a man and a woman could hold the same job in a company, and do the same thing as each other, but it's the man who has a higher pay packet." I said annoyed.

"If you and I did marry and live together in this era..." Guy thought out loud.

"Yes, you'd still get a large dowry paid your way from the Earl of Durrant." I answered. "Because I would assume the role of his daughter. And it probably wouldn't really be his money you'd be getting, but we would just call it that anyway."

"But you wouldn't be happy, would you?" Guy stopped us and turned me around to face him. "How could you? A sailors wife, tied to the sailors life. My comings and goings would be sporadic..."

"Lets not talk about marriage." I said uncomfortably. "If it happens, it happens. Right now, lets just concentrate on us, and the moment we have left, together."

"I suppose honor is not such an important thing in your time." He said a little hurt.

"You mean you want to do the honorable thing before you have me?" I smiled at his moral outlook.

"You are offering yourself before marriage?" he asked in surprise.

"Only to the men I run away from school for." I tried to make him feel better. "But I don't want to return to school, with out having done this..."

I grabbed him by the coat and kissed him long and hard again.

Just then there were a couple of cheers and wolf-whistles around us from a few sailors that happened to see us on three of the ships that were docked.

We pulled apart and shared a chuckle together.

"Which one is your ship?" I asked him, looking around.

"Here, the HMS Harbinger." Guy pointed out.

"I've always wanted to see what the Captain's quarters look like. I hear they can be quite small." I said playfully.

"I believe you've been misinformed, my Lady. My quarters are quite comfortable, I assure you." Guy reached out and caressed my neck, running his finger around my collarbone.

"Why don't you show me these quarters, then, kind sir. I would like to witness this mistake myself."

Guy looked around to see how many witnesses we might have, before helping me up the plank and then onto the deck.

"Sir!" two crewmen who were on guard, instantly stood to attention at his arrival.

"At ease. I am giving the Lady Elisha here a tour of the ship. Let us just hope that you kept her in good condition in my absence." Guy said to his men.

"We have sir." One of the crewmen assured him.

Needless to say the first point of our 'tour' was the Captains quarters.

Now Diary, this is where the really memorable moment of this whole escapade started...

As soon as the door shut, Guy came up behind me, untying the back of the dress and kissing my neck at the same time. As soon as the blood sodden garment touched the floor, he started on my corset next. It actually took us a few minutes to get the damn thing off! I thought it was kind of ironic, having two first times and both of them involved struggling to get so many layers of clothing off! But we had a laugh, which was good. But what felt really good was to finally be naked, standing next to him.

He guided me over to the bed, and slowly laid me down. Then he also laid himself next to me, and kissed me and slowly ran his hands up and down my body. He was being very gentle, I guess partly from his sore stomach, and partly because he may have thought he was dealing with a virgin. I kind of wished I had still been a virgin, because this night was turning out to be a good deal more romantic than with Zack. Then I felt bad, when I remembered how tender Zack had tried to be with me. Then I felt even worse for even thinking about Zack at this moment with Guy.

It felt wonderful being touched by this grown man. I'm assuming he's not some sex expert or the type of sailor who had visited too many brothels in every port during his career. But he did seem to know what he was doing, or how to touch me to make me feel both excited and like I was melting. He guided me, and took control, and I didn't have to intimate anything that I wanted, because he seemed to already sense it. This night was passionate and sensuous, both the things that Guy was to me. There was no clumsy fooling around, he didn't rush through the foreplay and he seemed to enjoy it just as much as he made sure I enjoyed it. I felt like every part of my body had been explored and worshipped. I felt tingly all over.

When he was inside me he never lost any of his control or attentiveness to my needs. His lips caressed my neck, my shoulders, my breasts... I felt like I was some beautiful goddess that this mortal man wanted to please and pleasure. He caught me smiling like a Cheshire cat at one point, which made him smile back at me before a passionate kiss took them away. Many times our eyes met and held, like our lips did. I wasn't just having sex with this man, but I was completely sharing this moment with another wonderful human being. I felt like I had won the lottery for these moments of beautiful bliss. I thought everything I had gone through for Guy had been worth it and this night paid for it well.

*****

As we were getting dressed again, I examined his wound more closely. It was virtually completely healed, with reddened scar tissue in the place where the hole used to be. I gently ran my fingers across it and looked into his face.

"Is it sore?" I asked him.

"The stomach muscles around it are sore." He answered.

"Of course. When you had a hole blown through you, it would have torn them." I ran my hand across his abdomen now.

"There is no need for concern now. You healed me." he caught my hand and held it in his.

"I didn't heal you. I just took you to some people who could heal you." I said lamely.

"You healed me." he repeated, and kissed my hand.

I sighed and looked at the door to go back out on deck. "I don't wanna go back. Not yet. I wish I could stay a little longer with you."

"When will I see you again?" he asked a little hesitantly. "Please don't say in another two years." he pulled me to him and kissed me on the lips this time.

"Definitely not. Even if I have to run away again, and keep running away, I'll always try and find you. Where will you sail to now?" I asked him.

"Back to England." He replied.

"Then how about I meet you there?" I leaned in and kissed him back.

"At another Ball?" he asked playfully. "I do not know if it will be wise to meet in public, for I might want to ravage you again!" he nibbled on my neck.

"I'm sure wherever we meet, we'll be able to arrange something." I caressed his cheek. Then I turned serious. "I love you, Guy."

"I know. And if I didn't know how much of a sacrifice it was for you to stay with me, in this century, I'd ask you to be my wife, so I could spend the rest of my life proving my affections for you too." He caressed my lips with his finger tip.

We hugged very tightly one last time, before returning to the outside world.

Guy helped me down the gangplank of his ship, and then up the gangplank of another. There, we met up again with Earl Durrant, Lord Dunmore and Dr. Knight. The three of them were talking, out on deck, and looked at me expectantly when we joined them.

"Elisha, after much consideration, I think it would be best if we left tonight." Dr. Knight told me.

"I thought as much." I said. Then I turned to Guy, whose hand I was still holding. I squeezed it as I said my good bye. "I guess this is farewell for now. But please remember everything I told you."

"Aye, my Lady. And take my fondest wishes and desires with you." he bowed and kissed my hand once more.

Dr. Knight studied Guy carefully before she gave her nod to him, then she escorted me into the Captain's quarters.

"Back to Hamilton's?" I asked her.

"Yes, back to the college." She answered.

"Then I'll pack up the rest of my stuff, if you like, and leave." I said warily.

Dr. Knight gave me a funny look. "I thought Lucas told you that wouldn't be necessary."

I still flinched though. "But I'm sure there's going to be some kind of ramifications for my actions."

"That will be discussed with Professor Hamilton." Dr. Knight said elusively.

Then I turned on her. "But before we go back, know this. I'm going to want to see Guy again. And I might want to see him on a regular basis."

"Elisha, I think we've all figured that out by now." Dr. Knight said dryly, and then smiled at me.

I just looked at her, confused. I couldn't make this out. Why was she being so nice to me? "So are you going to let me see Guy regularly?"

"That is a possibility." She said elusively again. "And it will also come under discussion."

I decided to leave it at that for the moment. I think so did she. For then we both turned and faced the huge glass window that was on the stern of the ship. And we both started to concentrate...

*****

To the three men still standing on deck, they saw a growing bright light, which culminated into a brilliant flash, and then it was over. They felt a slight chill and tingling sensation as the hairs on the back of their necks prickled. But neither three were concerned over these symptoms.

"That is one unusual young Lady you have decided to give your heart to, young man." The older man, Lord Dunmore, spoke to Guy.

"Unusual, yes. But beautiful, nonetheless." Guy said plainly.

"We would like to reiterate our congratulations on your victory, today, sir. And also to offer our hospitality to you whenever you should need it in London, sir." Earl Durrant told Guy.

"I thank you for your kindness." Guy said a little modestly, not knowing what he had done or how he deserved such acknowledgment from the aristocratic class.

===

TO: s_parson@snailmail.com
FROM: ebaker_hamiltons@evers.com
SUBJECT: Back at Hamilton's
DATE: 18/ 07/ 01

Hi Sal,

Yep. Am back at school. And yes, I did make it. Not only did the letter reach Guy, but so did I! It was wonderful seeing him again. For me it was just a couple of weeks later, but to him, it was two years!

He still went into battle though, the silly man. And he still got shot and died. But he's alive again... thank god. Long story, which I will tell you one day, but not today.

When I got back to school I was sent to Hamilton's office for 'the talk'. I wasn't yelled at, which surprised me. But I was given a stern telling off. I was told we have rules for a reason, rah rah rah. You know, the usual shit. They're also going to give me the money to pay my brother back that I scammed from him to pay for the airfare to India. There is one catch though, of course, since nothing in this life is for free. I'm on one month's cleaning duties in the Caf. So after dinner every night for the next four weeks, I'm sanitizing dishes. Oh yippee. You can almost see this as detention for running away!

But saving Guy's life would be worth a lifetime of sanitizing duty.

==

18/07/01

Diary,

Last night Dr. Knight and I arrived back at Hamilton's via the window on the second floor in Alpha building. The very same window we first saw her disappear into, and then the window we first saw Dr. Kell in his Centurion's uniform. And now it is me who is crossing from the other side... kind of spooky, hey?

I was immediately taken up to Professor Hamilton's office for 'the talk'. I wasn't yelled at, but I was given a stern talking to. I had to listen to the usual rigmarole on why we have rules, rah rah rah. Basically, you know, the usual crap teachers go on about. But the good side to all this, is I'll be allowed to visit Guy on a regular basis from now on! Usually once a fortnight! Yay!

The bad side to all this is, I kind of do have a detention from all this. Professor Hamilton said he will give me the money to pay back Mark for the airfare to India, but to pay back the 'loan' the school is giving me, I'll have to wash dishes for a month! So after dinner in the Caf for the next four weeks, I'm on sanitizing duty. Bugger. He also said that we wouldn't have to get my father involved in this or tell him how I'd run away (in case Dad gets so angry with me he tries to pull me out of school) and also so Dad won't find out that his daughter can travel through time like a ghost.

It felt weird hearing a teacher talk like this. Most teachers that I'd known up until now, always thought telling the parent of their child's misbehavior was the first thing to do on the list. Now this teacher was telling the child that it's better idea not to tell the parent! I thought this was kind of amusing, actually.

Dr. Knight handed me back my backpack which she'd been minding since I got it back in Governor Clive's office. And me still in my blood-soaked dress walked back from Alpha building to Beta building. It felt weird to still be in the dress now, back in my own era. And it was still Governor's wife's dress! Maybe I could wash it and return it to her somehow?

I walked up the stairs to my floor and sort of 'whooshed' down the corridor in the long skirt and petticoat layers, to my room.

"Cool dress." Nelson stuck her head out the door when she heard me putting my key in the lock.

"Thanks." I said, not looking at her.

"So, was the mission a success?" she left her room and followed me inside mine.

"Completely." I said.

"Well?" she sat on my bed, hungry for details.

I looked at my clock. I was tired. The time here only read 9 PM. But considering all I'd been through last night, surely back in the era I'd just left it would have been 4 AM or something.

"Nelson, I'm tired. Can I tell you about it tomorrow?" I yawned.

"Fine." She shrugged and bounced off my bed and headed out again.

I was about to shut my door to change and get some sleep, when Pat from his room, sitting at his computer as usual, spoke up.

"Who's blood is that?" he asked me, inferring my dress.

"Not mine. I'll tell you tomorrow. Goodnight." I closed my door, now more determined.

Then this morning in the Caf for breakfast, a lot of people crowded around, wanting to know the details of my adventure. Brett, Raj, Maya, Nelson, Pat, Jordon, Numu and Wong. But not Peter or Zack. They sat at another table, not talking to me.

I told them of the sleazy Commander Wilson, meeting Clive of India, Guy still going off to war and then coming back injured. And then they all wanted to know the details of my trip to Circulate Headquarters. They were shocked to learn when and where it is.

"Mars?" Nelson asked incredulously.

"Back in time, before it loses it's atmosphere." I nodded.

"And you phased yourself there?" Numu asked shocked.

"Apparently. I mean, all I wanted was the future, but I got that instead." I shrugged.

"They must have transferred you there. There is no way you could have phased yourself that far with out help." Nelson shook her head.

"Why not?" Brett asked her.

"Flying through time, yeah, sure, fine. But through space as well? Come on!" Nelson rolled her eyes.

"But she could have. It could be a sort of fail-safe mechanism in all of us. That when something goes wrong, and we need help urgently, that we all get pulled back to Circulate Headquarters." Brett reasoned.

"That makes sense." Pat agreed.

I looked over to Peter and Zack. Zack was looked like he was trying to concentrate on eating his breakfast, which he hadn't touched, and Peter was talking to him. I felt guilty again. I could see the pain written all over Zack's face. I was kind of hoping that time would have started healing him by now.

"How is Zack?" I asked Nelson.

"As much as you'd expect, broken hearted." She said.

"Still?" I asked, feeling really guilty now.

"You were the love of his life, and you walked out on him for another man." Pat said, as if to say, 'what did you expect you idiot'?

"Should I try and talk to him?" I nearly got up but Brett stopped me.

"I wouldn't." he cautioned.

"I think he just needs some time." Maya tried to offer some advice.

"He needs a fucking miracle." Pat got up from the table, after hearing all he needed to hear of my story.

When we went to French class that morning, I noticed that Zack wasn't there. Brett whispered to me that he had changed to the other French class, and so had Peter. Oh great. That made me feel REALLY rotten.

In class I quickly realized I had missed out on a lot and now I was pretty behind. Brett and Maya offered to help me catch up, which I appreciated. So after lunch when we took some drinks and sandwiches outside to eat on the oval in the sun, we had our French textbooks open and going over what I had missed.

Catching up with class work won't be a problem. But catching up with other things, now that will be tricky. I saw Peter, Zack and Pat leave the Caf as well, after lunch, and head back inside Alpha building for their next class. I could tell, even from a distance, that Zack was trying not to look at me.

===

21/07/01

Diary,

I finally have some strength to write again.

I've found out the down side to phasing too much, too often, too 'early in my development' as Dr. Knight and Nell put it two days ago.

I woke up on Thursday morning feeling really weak and ill. I felt like I had the flu and I couldn't get out of bed. I could barely even get up to turn off my alarm clock, it was that bad! I just felt like all the energy had drained out of me and I felt nauseous and dizzy.

When I didn't show up for breakfast, Nelson came back to the dorms to look for me. She knocked on my door, and lucky I hadn't locked it, so I didn't have to get out of bed and she could come right in.

"What's wrong? Are you depressed again?" she asked in her typical, Nelson like, gentle way of putting it.

"No. I feel sick. Really sick. I think I have to see Nell." I moaned back.

"All right. I'll get her for you." with that, which is another typical Nelson way of showing her concern, she left it at that and left my room.

Nell must have come immediately after Nelson alerted her. She brought a small medical kit with her and she used it to check my temperature, heart beat and blood pressure. She looked pretty concerned.

"Is it Bali belly? Could it be food poisoning?" I asked her weakly. I remembered the stories I'd hear of tourists catching some kind of bug after eating overseas food.

"No, I don't think so. I'd better get Dr. Knight to have a look at you." she frowned. "Do you want me to get you a sandwich or something from the Cafeteria?"

I shook my head, and probably by the face I pulled at even the very thought of food right then, nearly made her laugh.

"OK then. But I'm going to bring you back a bottle of water. I'll get a bucket to put beside your bed, just in case. But you need to keep up your fluids." She then gave me one of her usual comforting grins, ruffled my hair slightly and stood up and left as well.

She came back 20 minutes later with the water and bucket as promised, and with Dr. Knight in tow.

Dr. Knight took some blood from me to do a test and then checked me out for a couple more things. But by the way she and Nell looked at each other a couple of times, like in silent communication, it made me wonder if they knew what was going on? Did they know something about me that I didn't?

"What is it?" I asked the two.

"I'm pretty sure of the diagnosis, but I took a blood test just to make sure." Dr. Knight informed me. "You see Elisha, whenever a person phases, it is a huge expenditure of energy on the body. That explains why Circulators report of loss of eyesight and severe dizziness on their first attempts after phasing. I believe you do have a slight infection, but on top of that, you have low blood pressure and a low immunity level, as well as a low electrolyte level."

"So before we give you an antibiotic, we also want to concentrate on getting you red and white cell count back up, as well as your energy levels back to normal. For the next couple of days you'll need complete bed rest. I can bring you sandwiches and juice." Nell told me.

"Do all Circulators get sick like this?" I asked surprised. If this is going to happen all the time, I don't know if this ability is worth it!

"Not all. But you seem to be first in your class, remember?" Dr. Knight almost teased me. "You may well be the first to phase on your own, and the first Circulator of your age to even phase others with you, and then with the phasing to Circulate Headquarters? You really pushed yourself hard the last couple of days."

"Oh." Whoops. But seeing Guy lying like that in the back of that cart, all blood spattered and nearly dead... it was worth it, I decided.

Nell helped me sit up for a couple of moments as she had to feed me the water from the bottle. I was so weak, and my hands were shaking, I couldn't even drink water by myself! It was pretty embarrassing.

With the water, Dr. Knight gave me some tablets that she said would help me, (I can't remember what they were meant to do though) and as soon as they left, I fell back asleep, exhausted.

The next time I woke up, my clock said 3.23 PM, and Brett and Maya were knocking on my door.

They brought in a bottle of juice and a sandwich, which Nell asked them to do, and they also brought their French textbooks.

"Hey." Brett sat on my chair and Maya at the end of my bed. "How ya feelin'?"

"Not good." I couldn't even sit up to talk to them properly.

"We thought we'd tell you what we learned in class today, so when you're able to come back, you won't be so behind." Brett waved the textbook at me.

"I'm sorry guys, I don't think I can concentrate properly on French let alone English right now." I said sleepily.

"Here, have some juice." Maya tried to pass the bottle to me, but I couldn't even sit up to grab it. So she came over to the side of the bed and helped me sit up a little and drink it.

"Hang on, we might as well sit her up properly." Brett now came over and heaved me up into an upright position, leaning me against the wall as Maya propped up my pillow behind me.

"Thanks guys." I blushed, even more embarrassed now, for being so useless.

Maya left the juice bottle in my hands and went back to the end of my bed, as Brett did the same with my desk chair. They took out their notepad and pens and opened their French text books and did their homework out loud so I could just sit back and listen to them. I thought this was really nice of them. Even though I wasn't quite there, they still tried to include me.

"Je Voudrais une chambre avec salle de balcon." Maya said to Brett.

"I would like a room with a bathroom?" Brett guessed.

"Not quite. A balcony." Maya laughed at him. "Bain is bathroom."

"I knew that. Try another one." Brett urged.

"Quel est le prix pour une nuit?" Maya asked next.

"What is the charge for... une...hmm, one... nuit ...night?" he asked back.

"Yes. Or, oui!" Maya congratulated him.

Suddenly Nelson came into my room and sat on my floor of my doorway, with a phrase of her own. "Pouvez-vous me rembourser?"

That made both Brett and Maya start flicking through the pages of the books.

"You want a refund?" Brett said before Maya could.

"Yeah, I want a new French teacher!" she moaned and started kicking my doorframe.

"Madame Coultard isn't that bad." Brett shrugged.

"I like her." Maya agreed.

Oh yeah diary, I guess I forgot to tell you. We have a few new teachers here at Hamilton's to teach us French and English and Art and Music and Drama. Partly because our current teachers have asked them to come, and partly because Miss Inez who usually teaches some of these subjects, has gone away during the summer break. At the moment we are with out a Den mother. Which means... (drum role) not having to wait until midnight until we can light up a cigarette in our rooms! And I'm assuming that these teachers are also apart of the Circulate.

"Why don't you like her?" I asked Nelson.

"It's supposed to be summer break, but with the amount of homework the old ball and chain has heaped on us... it makes you wonder." Nelson complained.

"Well, we only have three months of this. And she's probably trying to prepare us fully for the trip to Paris at the end of the holidays." Maya pointed out.

"Oh yeah, have you guys heard? Our self-defense classes are finally about to start soon. It will be on after lunch on Mondays, Wednesdays and Fridays." Nelson said to us.

"Self defense? I'd be in for that." I nodded.

"Me too." Brett agreed.

We all looked at Maya.

"I don't think my parents would approve." Maya looked down, then she changed the subject. "Je voudrais juse manger un snack."

"I only want a snack." Brett and Nelson said at the same time.

"Come on Maya, your parents aren't here, are they? How would they even know?" Nelson needled her.

Maya looked really uncomfortable, so she tried to change the subject once more. "Rien pour moi, merci."

"Nothing for me, thanks." Brett answered for her, as Nelson just sat back and looked at her.

"Well, you haven't told them what's going on here at this school now, and all this time travel business, have you? So why would it be any different if you learned self-defense as well?" Nelson tried to push her point.

"Allez-vouz-en!" Maya glared at Nelson.

"Go away." Brett said duly.

"Whatever." Nelson shook her head at her and got up and left again.

===

22/ 07/ 01

Diary,

I'm feeling a hell of a lot better now. Partly coz of the antibiotics Dr. Knight has me on, but mostly coz I received a letter from Guy! Yeah! A real live letter, sent from the 18th Century!

He wrote it on board ship, on route to England! Well, he had to make a slight detour to Spain on the way... so when he bumped into another English Navy ship that was sailing straight to England, he asked them to take the letter back to London and messenger it to the Dunmore home! So then Dr. Knight got the letter from her father! For me! Yay! I received an 18th Century love letter!

I love his handwriting! I love the feel of the parchment! I love the crest of the stamp imprinted in the wax!

Here is what he wrote...

To My Dearest, Most Darling Elisha,

It is the custom of our century to declare ones feelings diplomatically and announce ones intentions of courtship. This letter is to do this emphatically, since many of the instructions so far have not yet been so regarded respectfully... of which I am also to blame for. May you produce these intentions to your 'family', the Dunmores, so that I may call on you in London next August, when my ship is next in port.

Until then, my love, may you also know of my fondest thoughts in your regard. As a sea man for many a year, and then Captain for the last two, I had always believed the ocean laid first in my affections. That was until I met you. Your dark beauty and your evervesence are now what burns in my heart. As the waves curl and churn and toss our ship about in rage or in shine, it only reminds me of you. Your features, your curves, can outdo the statue of Venus, and your sparkle outshine many of the goddesses, Michaelangelo, or even Raphael ever sought to create in paint or marble.

As my ship is called away temporarily on a short detour, please be assured of my undying affections. My ardor is genuine, my heart ache at our parting is infinite. Be rest assured you are first in my thoughts when I wake in the morning, and are the last, when I return to my bed at night. And when the sea rocks me to sleep in her cold, watery bosom, I murmur your name, and dream of a warmer, softer one that inside rests the heart of the woman I love.

Your Guy.

Oooohhhhh.... Wow... my first love letter! And it came from the man I love! I'm so excited, I'm giggling like a schoolgirl... well I suppose that sounds stupid coz I am a schoolgirl. But a schoolgirl with an amore in the 18th Century? I guess not many people can say that!

Dr. Knight told me the messenger who dropped the letter off at the Dunmore London Town House was a messenger from the Navy. He was from the ship, the HMS Salute, which had rendezvous with the Harbinger in Spain. As Guy's ship had to do something in Spain, he gave the letter to the Captain of the Salute since it would reach London a couple of weeks before the Harbinger.

To Guy, we've already been separated for a couple of weeks, when to me, it's only been a couple of days! So I guess that's why he's missing me more. I've already asked when I can see him again, and they've promised me Dr. Knight will take me to London in 1757 AD for a whole weekend!

I'm to be presented at court, as the King would like to meet and congratulate me for getting the news to Governor Clive in India about the enemies forces. Also it's a protocol thing that all Aristocrats have to be presented at court, and it will look too suspicious if I don't. Also we will attend another Ball, which Guy will go to. But I'm going to try and spend more time with Guy outside of these events. I have to. I miss him like crazy.

I asked Dr. Knight if I could send a letter back to him, but she said I may as well wait to see him and give it to him myself, since it's only a week away. Also, she warned, it's hard to keep up correspondence with a Naval officer, as the ships are often away from home so often and isolated from any other ships in those days.

So, the weekend of the 28th July, Dr. Knight and I will return to London and reprise our roles of Lady Durrant and Lady Dunmore, when in Guy's time it will be the first weekend in August.

Oh yeah, I found out what was wrong with me and why I was so sick. I was weak and tired because of the phasing draining all my body's energy. So when my immune system was so low, I picked up a virus in India. That's why I was nauseous. To be honest, I was very relieved when Dr. Knight gave me these results from the blood test, I was worried I could have had morning sickness! I couldn't exactly keep up with regular doses of the pill with all my travels and incognito!

==

24/07/01

I just had something pretty freaky happen to me! It was Zack, he scared the shit out of me! He came into the kitchen when I was alone and doing the sanitizing after dinner.

The cook and other cleaner had gone out for a break and I was rinsing all the dishes in the sink before putting them in the sanitizer. I was off in my own little world, listening to my Walkman, day dreaming about Guy. I was thinking how strange it is, me doing all this cleaning when in a couple of days time I'll resume the role of Lady Dunmore and be presented to King George the 2nd. Then when I turned around, I nearly dropped a whole pile of bowls to the floor when I saw Zack.

He was standing there, watching me. He was looking at me with such hate and hurt in his eyes... They started getting tearful again and he didn't say anything.

He just stood there, angrily staring at me. I didn't know what to do or say. What could I say? What did he want me to say?

So I started to continue what I was doing, when he yelled at me!

"I trusted you! I loved you! Why, Elisha? Why did you do this to me?!"

I was stunned. I struggled with what to answer him with... What did he want me to say to him? Did he expect me to somehow take it all back? I'm not in love with him, I don't think I ever was. Not as in love with him as he was with me, that was for sure. I just looked back at him, and shrugged helplessly. I didn't know what else to do.

"Say something! Why?" he rushed forward at me. His hands grabbed at me! I thought they were going to grab the front of my jumper when they grabbed me about my throat! "Why, Elisha? Why?"

Zack was half strangling me, and half shaking me! I was so scared! I didn't know what to do! He was hurting me! I tried to push him away, but he was too strong! I was getting really frightened now.

"Is he better than me? Huh? In bed? What does he do to you, that I don't?" Zack yelled at me tearfully. Then he put one of his hands on my crotch and hissed at me, "I'll do it! Whatever he does... I can do it too!"

That was it. That was the moment my fear response of either fight or flight kicked in. I did both.

I raised one of my knees, and using it and both of my arms, I pushed him off me as hard as I could! But he was still trying to grab hold of me! He knocked my Walkman off my jeans pocket and I nearly fell backwards, which I accidentally then knocked over the pile of bowls I had been about to wash. As both my Walkman and the bowls smashed on the floor... I ran for it!

I ran out of the building and straight for Beta building, as fast as I could.

I didn't even look behind me to see if he was chasing after me.

I ran up the staircase and down the hall and barged through Nelson's door and slammed it shut and locked it behind me.

Nelson had been reading a book on her bed, and instantly sat up in surprise at my entrance.

I burst into tears and slumped to the floor, still leaning against the door.

"What is it? What happened? Elisha? What's wrong?" Nelson got up from the bed and knelt down beside me.

"Zack... he ... he..." I couldn't say it, I was crying too hard. I was too upset, still too frightened. Also I was trying to catch my breath.

"What did he do? Elisha, tell me, what did Zack do to you?" Nelson put her arm about me, concerned.

"He didn't do that..." I guessed what was on her mind. "But I think he might have tried to..." I gulped for air, petrified at the very thought of what I had just escaped from. "I fought him off..."

Oh god, what have I done? Have I driven Zack insane, that he might have taken me by force? Out of jealousy? Have I driven him insane with jealousy?

"What have I done to the poor guy?" I bawled.

"Oh please, not that old story! It's never the girl's fault! You didn't hold a gun to the guy's head and make him try to force himself on you, did you?" Nelson rolled her eyes. "The guy is the guilty one, not you."

"Maybe he wasn't going to... I just got scared..." I shook my head in denial.

"Don't do this! It sounds like you got away just in time! Don't talk yourself out of this! We should find a teacher..."

"No!" grabbed her arm before she could stand up. "No, I don't want to."

"Elisha, we should tell someone!" Nelson glared at me.

"No." I vehemently shook my head. I had done this to Zack. I wasn't going to make things worse for him. "No. It's not his fault. It's mine, it's my fault."

Nelson shook her head at me disapprovingly. "Then can you tell me what those red marks are, on your neck?"

I didn't say, and I pulled my jumper up higher to try and cover them.

"You are so weak." Nelson said with disdain.

==

26/ 07/ 01

Professor Hamilton came and saw me the next day after the incident with Zack. He wanted to know why I just piked like that, and left behind a pile of broken dishes and my broken Walkman. I didn't tell him, I lied and said I got an urgent text message from Mark about something. He looked at me sternly, like he didn't believe me, and said not to leave a job half done again. My detentions of sanitizing had to be completely finished until all the dishes were done.

I've been wearing turtleneck jumpers again, to cover the red marks on my neck. It's annoying, but it's easier than answering any questions about the marks. I just hope they go away by the weekend, when I see Guy. I certainly don't want to get him riled up and pulling out his sword again and swearing vengeance and honor.

I think Pat is a bit suspicious, but he hasn't said anything. He asked me if I was hot wearing my turtleneck jumper when we were sitting outside on the grass at lunch time. I lied and said no, when it was obvious I was sweating. He's been pretty nice to me too, actually. He's taken my Walkman off me and he thinks he can try and fix it. The plastic lid that holds the tape has broken in half, and I don't know if we can sticky-tape it back together or what. But inside the motor must be damaged too, coz the little wheel-things aren't turning anymore either.

Bugger, I depend on my Walkman so much!

Nelson may think I'm being weak about all this. But she's being incredibly nice and protective of me. The last two nights after dinner, she's remained behind in the Caf, doing her homework there, as I'm doing the sanitizing in the kitchen. Then last night, Pat joined her, and the two of them called out all these French phrases out to me, and I had to guess what they were in English.

Anyway, with all the sanitizing I'm doing, it's paid off so far. I've transferred the $1000 back into Mark's account and in my email I sent to him I lied again and said I had made a mistake and that the school will be paying for everything anyway. He bought it, and I don't know if he's said anything to Dad about it, which I hope not. Dad already knew that the school's paying for the trip. I'm worried Dad will see right through my lie and try to ban me from doing the trip.

06/ 08/ 01

Diary,

Before I went to Dr. Knight's room to phase with her to London, in August 1757, I got changed in my room with Nelson's help. I put on a simple 18th Century dress. We weren't putting too much effort into it, as I was only going to get out of it again as soon as I arrived.

The weekend schedule was this; arrive Saturday morning and be presented at court in the afternoon. Then in the evening go to another Ball at the Fox's house, and the next day before phasing back to Hamilton's College, I would spend most of the day with Guy. Unfortunately with the social customs of the day, I couldn't spend time with Guy in the way that I wanted to. But the good side to all this is he will be presented at court with me for his commendation and heroic deeds in India. And he will be going to the Ball with me. So I'll be seeing him at least three times over the two days that I'm away.

"Stay still!" Nelson growled at me as she was trying to tie up my corset.

I was standing in the middle of my room, in my 18th Century underwear that consisted of a long white pantaloon that covered me from my shoulders to my knees, and then a petticoat over the top of that. Then there was another petticoat with rigid hoops that made the dress stick out at my hips, and then the corset which Nelson was now tying up from behind me. But to be honest, I was starting to regret asking Nelson to help me dress, coz she was being bloody ruthless in lacing me up!

"Nelson! What are you trying to fucking do? Cut off my breathing!" I snapped back.

"You're supposed to have these things this way!" Nelson retorted.

"Look, Dr. Knight didn't tie the damn thing this tight when she put it on me!"

"Then next time get her to do it for you." Nelson shook her head at me.

Just then there was a knock on my door. I looked down at myself and decided I was wearing enough layers to make me decent, even if it was all underwear. So I yelled, "come in!"

Pat opened my door and then stood in the doorway. He leaned against the door frame so he could get a good look at me. "You're not going in just that, are you?" he asked.

"No!" I rolled my eyes at him and pointed at the light pink silk dress that was lying on top of my bed.

"Oh." He nodded, then he looked back at us. "Enjoying yourselves?"

Both Nelson and I gave him a dirty look for our reply.

"I've got something for you." he pulled a CD from his jacket pocket and went over and put in my stereo. "This should lighten the mood a bit." He turned the volume up high, and soon new Dance music was blaring out.

"Much better!" I smiled appreciatively for my new CD and I pulled away from Nelson, jumped up on my bed, and started dancing.

Pat and Nelson started laughing at me, coz as I was swaying my hips, the hoops were swinging out widely.

"You look like one of those little vibrating Hawaiian girls that sit on people's dash boards!" Nelson pointed at me, laughing really loudly.

"Have you got anymore of those things? So I can try one on?" Pat jumped up on my bed too and tried swinging his hips really widely. He also lifted up his T-shirt and jacket, exposing his belly to try to authenticate the affect.

"You're both a pair of rejects!" Nelson was laughing so hard, she had tears rolling down her cheeks. But in the midst of this she still had enough sense to quickly rescue the pink silk dress from the bed so it wouldn't get stomped on.

Quarter of an hour later, with me properly dressed now, I made my down to Dr. Knight's room with Nelson and Pat in tow.

I knocked on her door, and when I heard the 'come in', I entered, still with Pat and Nelson behind me.

I was met by the sight of a Senior girl, Mesina, tying up Dr. Knight's dress from behind for her.

"Do you always need to travel with an audience?" Mesina teased, inferring Nelson and Pat.

"We wanted to see how it happens." Nelson told her.

Mesina looked at Dr. Knight, probably wondering if her role as assistant dresser was over and now if she was to become a bouncer instead.

"Thank you Mesina." Dr. Knight nodded to her, letting her know it was all right. "Elisha, aren't you forgetting something?"

"No...?" I wondered what she was talking about.

"Here." She handed me a hair clip.

"Oh!" I remembered my hair was still down. So I pulled it up into a French knot and used the clip to keep it into place.

"We'll take this with us." Dr. Knight handed me a box next.

"What's inside here?" I opened it and saw the wig I wore to the last Ball. "Oh yeah, this might be handy." I'd have to wear it to the Ball at Holland House tonight.

Nelson came over for a closer look, and from the gasp she made, I gathered she was impressed. She took the wig out of the box and examined the intricate bee-hive style with the curls hanging down. "You wear this?"

"I have to. My hair is too short for the style of the day." I told her. "And when I'm in a ball dress, we put little diamond jewelry clips in the hair. It looks really nice."

"I wish I could see this." Nelson sighed. "When is it my turn? When can I go back in time?" she turned to Dr. Knight.

"Your first excursion through time does happen this year." Dr. Knight promised both Pat and Nelson.

This reminded me of something, which happened the last time I traveled through time.

"Dr. Knight..." I began. "How come your brother and your father now know about your ability to cross through time? I thought they didn't know, and that's why when we first saw you all ghostly and that, you were wearing period costume."

"My brother, Earl Durrant, has always known. He has always been my alibi. When I'm traveling and return to London, I have always said my absence has been due to my retirement to his estate in Scotland, or on his property in Virginia. And then to claim you as my niece, and his daughter, we had to eventually confess this secret to my father, so he can publicly claim you as his granddaughter." Dr. Knight told me.

"How did he take it?" I asked her. I could just imagine my Dad's reaction if I ever tried to tell him something like this... instant dismissal attributed to mental illness and being accused of being deranged.

"My brother and I told my father when I had to convince them both to sail to India to be your alibi. At first he behaved as you would expect of one being given such news as this, he didn't believe us. So I phased the two of them to 21st Century London so they could see for themselves of the place I dwell in. My father was still reluctant at first to portray your grandfather, but once he heard of Clive of India's win against Suraja Dowlah, and of your involvement, he changed his mind." Dr. Knight continued.

"Really? Why?" I asked hesitantly.

"It was very foolish what you did, but some also might see it as heroic." Dr. Knight smiled at me.

"Really?" I blushed a little.

"I see it as just plain dumb." Nelson gave us her opinion, which made Pat chuckle.

And on that note, Dr. Knight decided it was time for us to leave.

Dr. Knight and I stood in front of her full-length mirror, and began to concentrate, as Pat and Nelson stood back and watched.

I held the box with the wig inside of it in front of me, and I stared at the bright reflection of the sunlight coming through the window of her room. I stared and stared and stared. I concentrated on the date of August, 1757. I stared as hard as I could. My eyes started to sting, and go a little blurry, but I refused to blink.

Gradually, the light grew bigger and brighter, and the familiar waves seemed to stream out of the mirror toward us.

The reflection of the room in the mirror was no longer Dr. Knight's room, but a different bedroom, also lit up by the morning sun, with a four poster bed and antique tall boy and dressing table.

We stepped forward...

*****

Nelson told me afterwards that from her perspective, what she saw still gave her goose-bumps. She and Pat felt the room drop in temperature and the electrostatic charge made their hairs on their necks and arms stand on end. And when she saw the bright light come out of the mirror and Dr. Knight and I go all see-through, she really did think we were turning into ghosts. And then, when we were absorbed by the light and we crossed over... she was actually worried for a few moments that maybe she'd never see us again.

*****

"Are we there yet?" I blinked, blind as a bat, stumbling forward.

"Yes." I felt her hand grab hold of my shoulder to steady me.

"How come I'm always bloody blinded, but you're not?" I asked annoyed.

"Experience. You won't always have this side effect." She promised.

I think she must be right, because my vision started to come back a lot faster this time.

I looked about the bedroom, with the four-poster bed and antique furniture.

"Where are we?" I asked her, baffled.

"My bedroom." She answered and went to look in the dressing table mirror to adjust her hair.

"In the London town house?" I asked her.

"Yes. Now, lets go downstairs. I believe we're expected." She walked over to the door.

"Expected?" I asked surprised.

I followed Dr. Knight down the staircase and into the foyer where a footman immediately opened the door for us to the drawing room.

We certainly weren't alone in the house this time. It looked like it was a family gathering I was being thrown into. Two Gentlemen immediately stood up upon our arrival, while another Lady remained seated, sipping her cup of tea. She looked to be Dr. Knight's age.

I recognized the two men to be Lord Dunmore and Earl Durrant.

They bowed to me, and I remembered protocol and gave them a polite curtsey in return.

"Father." Dr. Knight walked over and kissed his cheek. "Charles." She kissed her brother's cheek next. "Doreen, how are you?" she now addressed the dour looking woman, who was still seated, sipping her tea.

"Well." was all the woman replied with, now eyeing me up and down next.

"Doreen, this is Elisha Baker, our new adoptive daughter." Earl Durrant said jovially, probably thinking this farce was an interesting and funny joke.

"How do you do." Doreen said coldly.

"Well, thank you." I said.

"How old are you, girl?" she asked me distastefully.

"I'm 17, woman." I retorted, this woman's snobby attitude was already getting on my nerves.

"Don't worry Doreen, Elisha does come from the 'proper' family." Dr. Knight rolled her eyes.

"She does not speak 'proper' English. Is that because of her life in the colonies?" Lady Doreen arched her eyebrow.

"Haven't you ever been to the States?" I asked in surprise, realizing this. "Don't you own land there?"

"My husband attends to those matters." She rolled her eyes at my ignorance.

"I'm actually from a country that hasn't been colonized by the English yet, called Australia. That's where my accent is from. But be rest assured, Lady Durrant, I will put on my best snobby accent possible when in your society today."

Earl Durrant looked like he was trying to stop himself from snickering, and Lord Dunmore looked a little surprised at this chilly exchange. Now I understand how Earl Durrant kept his sister's secret, because he was much more open minded than his wife. He probably married the cow, not out of love, but for the dowry and family connections.

"Lady Elisha, would you like to take some tea with us before changing for court?" Lord Dunmore waved his hand welcomingly to the available chairs in the room.

"Thank you for your kind hospitality Lord Dunmore. Tea would be most refreshing." I started my 18th Century speak.

A butler handed me my tea with cream and sugar, and then presented on a silver tray some cucumber sandwiches and small slices of cake.

"Lady Elisha, to portray your father successfully, I must assume to know some facts about yourself. Would you be so kind to tell me some things about where your interests lie?" Earl Durrant asked congenially.

I chewed on my sandwich and tried to think of how to word it carefully.

Dr. Knight jumped in for me. "Elisha is an accomplished student. She can play the piano and flute, and is a competent actress."

"Indeed?" Lord Dunmore nodded in approval.

"I like to write." I also added.

"Write?" Earl Durrant asked.

"Stories." I told them.

"I'm sure this situation would warrant a good yarn." Earl Durrant chuckled to his father.

"Elisha is one of the top students in her class for her writing." Dr. Knight told the room, and almost looked sideways at Doreen to make sure she heard it.

Doreen still looked dour and unimpressed.

"Well, if I have a daughter who is a doctor, what is a grand daughter who is a celebrated woman of letters?" Lord Dunmore sighed. "If she marries neither, then that's another less dowry to be paid."

"And what of the engagement to this... Captain Robertson?" Doreen inquired of her father-in-law.

"Yes, what of this engagement to this Naval officer?" Lord Dunmore looked at Dr. Knight and not me for the answer.

"An engagement for convenience." Dr. Knight told her family. "The feelings of the couple are genuine, but in our time, Elisha would be thought of too young for such a serious commitment at this time of her life."

"I was married at 18." Doreen stated, as if this would justify it.

I almost retorted with, 'is that why you're such a miserable old bitch?'... but instead I kept my mouth shut and exchanged a glance with Dr. Knight instead.

"Do you have children?" I asked Earl Durrant and Lady Durrant.

"Aside from yourself?" Earl Durrant let out a chuckle again at his own joke.

"We have a son and a daughter." Lady Durrant answered.

"Where are they?" I asked.

"In our house in Scotland." Lady Durrant said.

"Why?" I asked, thinking this was odd.

"We never take our children with us when we come to London." Lady Durrant gave me a look as if I should know this.

"Which is convenient in this part we will play, in claiming you as our daughter. We have very few guests in Scotland, which is where we will say you have spent most of your life." Earl Durrant told me.

"I thought country houses played host to Balls, and hunting parties..." I remembered my notes of the era.

"Most of that entertaining takes place at my country house." Lord Dunmore stated. "Many guests feel more comfortable visiting an English manor than a Scottish one."

"Than why do you have a house in Scotland that you don't visit much?" I asked them, puzzled.

"It was my family home." Lady Doreen Durrant stated coldly. She sounded annoyed, as if she was pissed off to have to give it away to the males of another family, since she, being female, was not granted the right to have it in her name. Now I could understand why she might be so dour.

"Ah yes… real estate rights. In my time a woman can own property as well as a career." I said, looking at Lady Doreen.

She looked back at me in surprise.

"Why would a Lady need to work or own any property when her husband can look after her and this as well?" Lord Dunmore gave me a look as if I were mad.

I opened my mouth to reply, but Dr. Knight gave me a warning look and shook her head for me not to.

"No, do not silence her. We would like to know the answer." Earl Durrant told his sister.

"In my time, a woman has the choice to stay at home or work. She can virtually work in any field of employment she chooses. She can earn the same amount of money than a man. She can vote. There are some areas in the Defense Forces that a woman can fill." I told them.

"Yes, our daughter has already told us this news." Lord Dunmore said dismissively.

"If your time is so perfect, then why are you so fascinated with ours?" Lady Doreen challenged me.

The two Gentlemen waited to hear this one.

"I love the dresses." I shrugged.

And on this note, Lord Dunmore announced it would be a good time to change dresses and prepare for court.

I followed Dr. Knight upstairs to her bedroom again where the maids had been busy preparing our garments, headdress and jewelry.

Our current dresses were taken off and the court dresses were put on over our layers of petticoats and hoops.

I couldn't believe how beautiful the dresses were!

The ball gowns I'd seen before were nothing compared to these! The embroidery, the silk, the brocade... It was breath taking! The whole design of the dresses were so elaborate, so delicate, so ornate!

My court dress was an ivory silk with tiny pearls and gold embroidery over the entire garment! And at the front going down the bodice was more gold embroidery and crystal sequins that ended where the skirt began. There were huge white lace ruffles at the end of the sleeves that went just past my elbows.

Dr. Knight's dress was different, it was a leafy-patterned sky-blue silk that had a white triangle of silver embroidered lace with silver and diamond clasps going down her bodice. She also had large lace ruffles where her sleeve ended but also more blue silk material ruffle over the white lace. She looked quite regal.

Both our faces were puffed over with a light, white powder, and red coloring was applied to our lips. We also both had powdered white wigs put on our heads, and to top it off, three huge white ostrich feathers with gold sequins placed in a standing position on top our wigs! I burst out laughing when I caught a glimpse of us in the mirror.

I looked like 'Big Bird' in drag!

"But a rich bird. One that could possibly buy the whole of "Sesame Street"." Dr. Knight added, after she inquired to what I thought was so funny.

And then it was time for the jewels. A huge, thick, diamond necklace was tied behind Dr. Knight's neck that sat on her trumped up cleavage. Huge diamond drop earrings were next put on her ears. Last but not least, was the tiara. More diamonds in the silver shape of three large flowers were placed on top her head, in front of the feathers.

Then it was my turn.

A smaller diamond necklace that had a flowery pattern as well was put on my neck, along with smaller diamond drop earrings. My tiara was not just a diamond tiara, but was made of gold and was in the shape like an elegantly looped curved V with the pointy-bit sticking up in the air. There were pearls in between the smaller diamonds, which I think looked quite elegant, and certainly went with the pearls on the dress.

At that moment I wished I had a camera. I would have loved to have taken a photo of us. I wish Nelson and Sally could see me like this. I would have loved Mum to have seen me like this.

"Penny for them." Dr. Knight asked, coming to stand beside me as I was looking in the mirror, staring at my reflection.

"I wish my friends could see this." I sighed.

Dr. Knight smiled and put her arm about my shoulders. "When you all graduate from college, you will be able to visit where and when you like, as often as you like. One day this will be you and Nelson, and maybe even Sally."

"Where did this dress come from? Did your father order it? Did he know about me being allowed to see Guy?" I asked her.

"My father received the orders from the King that he would like to meet his granddaughter, the one who assisted Governor Clive in his war with Suraja Dowlah. It is improper, in our time, that a member of the aristocracy would be allowed to move in society without yet being presented at court. That's why this court presentation is going ahead. If you would like to keep visiting this time period, this protocol will have to be met. As to this gown... when I was first presented at court, I wore this dress." Dr. Knight inferred my gown.

"Really?"

Dr. Knight nodded.

When we came back down the stairs again, I had to make sure I walked very slowly. The dress may have been breath taking to look at, but it was also breath taking in the fact it was so heavy! I practically had to heave it where I wanted to go!

There in the foyer we found the rest of the family in full regalia as well. Lady Doreen wore an embroidered pink silk dress with huge jewels and ostrich feathers as well. The men also had their hair powdered white and wore elaborately embroidered velvet knee-length coats and silk vests.

"Lady Elisha, your carriage awaits." Earl Durrant gave me a small bow to show how impressed he was at my transformation.

"Thank you, kind sir." I gave a small curtsey before almost having to step sideways, to get out the front door.

We drove to the palace in two coaches, one with Earl and Lady Durrant, the second with Dr. Knight, Lord Dunmore and myself.

We passed through the gates with relative ease. The palace guards had a quick look inside to see who was being admitted, but we didn't have to show any identification. I guess our appearance said it all.

Our coaches slowed down, and we had to sit inside and wait as the other coaches in front of us alighted their nobility first, and then we were driven up to the front door, and we were let out.

The footmen at the palace were also dressed regally, even if it was just a uniform. They all wore white wigs. They all even had a snobby air about them. They opened our coach door for us, helped us alight, then bowed as we walked past them and inside the palace.

I tried not to stare too obviously or show my amazement at the ornate richness of the rooms of the palace. I didn't want to seem out of place. I had to keep reminding myself of the charade I had to play.

We entered the throne room where the King sat at the far end, on his huge gold and red velvet throne, on a small dais. Beside him stood some Lords or Dukes or whatever nobility they were, talking with him. And all around the walls stood the English aristocracy, wearing their jewels and decorative dresses. All with their white feathers and tiaras for the ladies, the men also with their powdered hair.

We turned a few heads with our entrance. People looked at me with curiosity in their eyes, some with even jealous indifference, and others were obviously giving me a good stare up and down. They didn't even bother to hide their examination of me.

Lady Durrant entered on the arm of her husband, Earl Durrant. Both Dr. Knight and I entered on the arm of Lord Dunmore, standing on either side of him. I felt so nervous and so judged right then and there, I clung to Lord Dunmore's arm so tightly it was almost like I was deep in the ocean and he was my only life raft.

Then, standing in the back corner, I noticed a familiar sight. It was the back of a Naval coat, next to another familiar sight, a red coat. Both coats had lots of gold trim on them, showing they were the formal uniform the men were donning. Attached to the red coat was the smiling face of Captain Greyson, with his dark hair that wasn't powdered white, talking to another dark head that also wasn't powdered white, that was attached to the blue Naval uniform.

Captain Greyson smiled and nodded at me, and when he did, the owner of the Naval coat turned around, and my heart skipped a beat. I couldn't wipe the smile off my face. He was a sight for hungry eyes, he was my Guy.

Guy and Greyson left their corner and walked over to us, instantly following protocol by giving us a bow upon reaching us.

"Lord Dunmore, Lady Dunmore, Lady Elisha." Guy smiled.

"Sir Guy." I curtsied, beaming back at him.

"Sir Robertson. I hope you are well." Lord Dunmore nodded back in recognition.

"Very well, thank you sir." Guy nodded back.

"Ah, my dear." Earl Durrant caught the attention of Doreen. "This is Elisha's fiancee, Sir Guy Robertson."

"Sir Robertson." Lady Doreen said dryly, now giving Guy a disapproving look up and down.

I could have slapped her! The bitch! Sure, snob me, but don't you dare snob Guy!

"Sir Guy has been called to court to be congratulated by the King himself for his heroic deeds in India." Captain Greyson spoke up to Lady Doreen, trying to ingratiate his friend to his cold, perspective mother-in-law.

"Captain Greyson, I believe you've met my father and my grandfather. Allow me to introduce to you, my mother..." here I glared at her, "Lady Doreen Durrant."

I bet dour Doreen loved being called my mother in public, I think I even saw her flinch!

"Greyson? Is that any relation to Earl Greyson?" Doreen asked Greyson.

"He is my father, my Lady." Greyson answered.

"And will you inherit Usher Park in time to come?" Lady Doreen asked him.

"I will not my Lady, as my brother born before me stands to inherit." Greyson said prickly, giving up on being polite to this snob.

"But as such, you are accustomed to court, are you not?" she asked him, as a sideways insult to Guy.

Man, if I could only get this woman alone in a room somewhere! I'll bitch slap her from here to kingdom come! I looked at Dr. Knight for help. Her family which was supposedly covering for me in this era, was doing more damage than anything.

"Sir Guy Robertson has been to court before, my dear." Earl Durrant spoke up, seeing my look on my face directed towards his wife. "When he was Knighted."

"Yes. Of course." Lady Doreen said. I thought this had shut her up, when next she addressed Guy, "And Sir, where does your family reside?"

"In Cheapside. My father has a practice there. He is a solicitor."

"Quite. And you made your way in the world in the King's Service." Lady Doreen said coolly.

"You're awfully good at re-stating the facts, mother." I said through gritted teeth. "Sir Robertson is making his way through the world quite successfully with honor and dignity. Would you like to re-state this fact as well? Or will you just step back and curtsey and watch as the King does it for you? When His Royal Highness gives his commendations to my fiancé in front of the entire court?"

Lord Dunmore looked at his daughter, Dr. Knight a little miffish. So Dr. Knight started giving me another warning look to tone it down. Both Earl Durrant and Captain Greyson were trying not to snicker.

Guy was smiling at me. I thought this was all that mattered. He was proud of me (so he told me later).

Then the presenting and the paying of respects started, thank goodness.

"Sir Robertson, if you would like to escort the Lady Elisha?" Lord Dunmore offered Guy my hand.

"Why thank you Lord Dunmore." Guy took my hand and placed it on his arm. "I would be honored."

This was a big thing, I later learned, that I would be presented to the King on the arm of my fiancé. It meant the family approved of our match, no matter how many scowls Lady Doreen threw in our direction. And Guy put his hand over my hand, and squeezed it as he looked upon me.

As we lined up and waited for our introduction behind Lord Dunmore and Dr. Knight, and then Earl Durrant and Lady Doreen, I used this opportunity to talk to Guy.

"Do you like my dress?" I asked him.

"You look beautiful." He smiled. "But you would look even more beautiful with out it."

I tried not to laugh.

"Not like that..." he stammered, in shock at how it came out. "When I saw you that night, for the first time in two years, wearing those pants... you looked beautiful then too."

"When I told you I crossed over time for you?" I asked him softly.

"Especially then. On the beach, under the stars... when we kissed." He squeezed my hand again. "I wish I could kiss you now."

"Well you could you know... I wouldn't object." I smiled cheekily at him.

"I certainly can't kiss you now! And prove your 'mother' correct? In a gathering such as this?" he chuckled back.

Then we heard Lord Dumore and Dr. Knight's introduction and realized how close in front of the line up we were now.

"Lord Dunmore, and his daughter, Lady Vivian Dunmore." The speaker called out.

We watched them walk up to the dais, and Lord Dunmore bow and Lady Vivian Dunmore walk up and offer her hand to the King and curtsey.

"Thank you, good fortune." The King said back.

"Earl William Durrant, and his wife, Lady Doreen Durrant." the speaker called out next.

Guy and I watched my 'parents' now walk off from in front of us and bow and curtsey next. But the King wasn't really looking at them now, he was studying Guy and myself. He said, half heartedly, "thank you, good fortune..."

"Sir Guy Robertson, Captain of the Royal Navy, and his fiancee Lady Elisha Durrant." the speaker called us out now.

My heart started pounding! I guess Guy was just as nervous, as he squeezed my hand back just as tightly. We both walked up with our heads bowed, and as he bent his upper body I released his hand, curtsied, and offered my hand to the King.

"Are you the Captain Robertson of whom I am supposed to commend for bravery in battle?" the King asked Guy boisterously.

"I am that man, sir." Guy stood up from his bow, but kept his head lowered.

"And your Ladyship, are you the brave heroine who made her way around the French to deliver the information to Governor Clive?" the King asked me as I stood up from my curtsey.

"I am, your Highness." I said, taking back my hand.

"What a clever little mouse you were, using your feminine charms to get through the enemy and to the Fort. A pretty one at that too, aren't you?" the King leaned forward to get a better look at my lowered face.

The room burst out laughing, not because it was funny, but to pander to the King.

"Tell me Lady Elisha, just how did you do that?" the King asked me.

I was so nervous, my hands were shaking! So I clasped them in front of me to hide it and I looked up at the King now. I had to show no fear and remember my charade.

"I was traveling with my chaperone, my Aunt, Lady Vivian Dunmore. When Lady Dunmore became detained by the French, I slipped through and made it by foot to the Fort. There I was able to tell Governor Clive of the enforcement's the French and Suraja Dowlah had at their disposal. When Lady Dunmore was released, we met up again at the Fort, after the battle, Your Majesty."

"I hear you were even clever enough to bring a disguise!" the King let out a chuckle, and the whole room burst into laughter again.

"I was fortunate enough to buy the disguise while in India, your Highness."

"And now you're marrying one of the war heroes." The King looked at Guy. "So your traveling days with your unmarried Aunt will soon be at an end." He inferred Dr. Knight.

"Perhaps not, your Highness. My husband may travel, he may even be posted abroad. I'm sure I will see the rest of the world with him some day." I smiled at the King. "I enjoy traveling."

"Oh, do you?" the King asked back. "Then tell me, Lady Elisha, how does the rest of the world compare to England?"

I knew what the old man wanted to hear, sitting there on his throne, with his white wig and jeweled brooches on his silk vest.

"Nothing compares to England, your Majesty." I gave a curtsey again.

The King let out a hearty laugh once again, followed by the rest of the room.

"Well said, Lady Elisha. May I wish you good fortune on your forthcoming union with your chosen husband. As to the man himself..." he waved over one of his lackeys, who came over, carrying a cushion. He took up a medal from the cushion, and waved Guy over closer. "To the hero of the day, Sir Guy Robertson." He stood up and pinned the medal to Guy's chest. "I wish you good fortune on your union to this young pretty thing." He patted Guy on the chest.

"I thank you, your Majesty." Guy smiled and bowed again, so I followed suit and curtsied again, and then taking Guy's hand once more, we moved away.

We re-joined Lord Dunmore, Dr. Knight, Earl Durrant and Lady Doreen who were standing to the side of the room.

"Congratulations sir." Lord Dunmore offered his hand to Guy.

"Thank you." Guy shook it.

"If you have no other plans, I hope you will join us for dinner tomorrow, Sir Guy." Earl Durrant offered his perspective and honored son-in-law.

"Why thank you, yes, I would be pleased to accept." Guy nodded to Earl Durrant.

I guess since the King's accepted us, everyone else seemed to accept us. Since the King showed us favor, everyone else did too. Suddenly we had people coming up and congratulating us. And among these strangers, I recognized a couple.

"Mr. Fox. Lady Caroline." I gave a curtsey as they joined us.

"Lady Elisha." Lady Caroline kissed my cheek. "You look well."

"I am well, thank you." I answered.

"Congratulations on your medal, Sir Guy." Henry Fox nodded to Guy.

"Thank you Mr. Fox." Guy smiled back.

"Do we have the honor of your company to our Ball tonight?" Lady Caroline asked us.

"You do indeed. We would be honored to attend." Guy said back.

"Then we look forward to hearing about your heroic deeds tonight at the supper table." Mr. Fox smiled at us, before he and Lady Caroline moved away again to talk to some other people.

I looked at Dr. Knight, a little overwhelmed by all this attention on us.

Damn it... I guess I won't be getting any alone time with Guy out of this visit.

*****

After another hour at court where we met the other Aristocratic snobs who deigned to introduce themselves to us and congratulate the Kings temporary 'favorites', I was relieved when we could finally leave.

Guy and I were separated again, and I was driven back to the Dunmore town house (or town mansion coz it was so big!) to prepare for the Fox's Ball.

I suddenly didn't feel so excited at the prospect of spending another evening with the elegance and snobbery of the ruling class of England of this time period. All I wanted was to be alone with Guy again. I was trying to think of a way to do this.

When it was time to leave, I learned Lord Dunmore would not be attending the Ball with us this evening. Instead it would just be Dr. Knight and her brother and sister-in-law. So we four were bundled into the carriage again and taken to Holland House.

I was wearing a red silk dress this evening, with the same diamond jewelry I wore the first time I went to the Fox's Ball all those months ago, and met Guy. But in this time, it would be like, all those years ago. I was also wearing the wig I brought, with the diamond clips in my hair again. My face was cleaned from the white powder, but I kept some of the red coloring on my lips.

As soon as we were out of the carriage and inside the Fox's Holland House, my eyes were immediately searching for Guy again.

I spotted Captain Greyson first, again, and then Guy standing beside him as usual, with his back turned. I waved to him, and then got nudged by Dr. Knight for accidentally breaking protocol by my obvious gesture. But who cares? Everyone knows that we're 'engaged' anyway, so aren't I allowed to be a little obvious?

Greyson smiled at me again, which made Guy turn around and see me. He instantly smiled my way as well, and both men began to make their way toward us. They were wearing their formal dress uniforms still. I guess they had to, regimentals seem to come in only one style for dress uniforms.

I wanted to let go of Dr. Knights arm and run up to Guy, but I think she guessed this, and grabbed hold of my arm when I let go, anticipating me.

"Elisha..." she sung softly. "Remember where you are."

Bugger this. I tried not to give her a dirty look. But all this formal behavior was starting to drive me batty.

"Lady Dunmore. Lady Elisha." Guy greeted and gave us a slight bow, with Greyson following his suit. We curtsied back to them.

Guy offered his arm to me and I took it with relief, and Greyson offered his arm to Dr. Knight and we were both escorted into the gilt drawing room, with Earl Durrant and Lady Doreen walking behind us.

"You look beautiful this evening." Guy smiled at me.

"You don't look half bad yourself." I smiled back at him and he squeezed my hand and chuckled.

"I have been looking forward to this evening, dancing with you, holding you in my arms, all these weeks past." He took me to stand to the side of the room and held my hand in both of his.

"Well, I've actually been looking forward to doing more than that, somewhere more private." I leaned in closer and said quietly in his ear.

Guy let out a surprised laugh and I actually made him blush!

"You truly have no fear, do you, of uttering such things in company as this." He shook his head smilingly at me.

"Don't act all squeamish with me, Sir Guy Robertson. You weren't that squeamish in your quarters on your ship in India." I smiled teasingly.

"Yes, well, that was a mistake I can ill afford to make again, here, in England. And then it was because I was afraid I would never see you again." He told me.

"Huh? What do you mean by, that you can 'ill afford to make again'?" I raised my eyebrows.

"Elisha, I meant what I said in my letter to you. I would like to formally announce my intentions to court you." he turned serious.

"But we are 'courting'." I said confused.

"Yes, we are now. And I would like, that one day, for our 'engagement' to turn serious, and not be just a charade to hold up in front of people to hide our true feelings for each other." Guy told me.

"Oh." I took back my hand in complete surprise. Oh shit. Not him too. Now what do I do? "Don't people just go 'out' for a while here?"

"Go 'out'?" he asked me.

"Yeah, you know, they like each other, and so they date. Marriage may come at the end, or maybe it doesn't. But in my time people don't marry until they're like... I don't know... 30 or something."

Guy stiffened at my words. I saw the hurt in his eyes and the offense taken on his face. I felt my stomach drop with fear that I may have just dug myself into a hole, instead of out of one.

Right then I thought we should get out of this room.

"Look, I'm going to go tell my 'Aunt' that I have a head ache, to which you graciously and heroically offer to escort me home. Then we can talk about this, OK?" I put my hand back in his, then I began to pull him along behind me.

Dr. Knight and Captain Greyson were talking with Earl Durrant and Lady Doreen, on the other side of the room. They all looked at us in surprise to see me escorting the gentleman behind me, and not the other way around, across the floor. They also looked surprised by the expression on Guy's face.

"Excuse me father and mother. Excuse me, Aunt Vivian. But I have a slight head ache. I would like to be taken home." I addressed them in my fake accent.

I waited for Guy's cue, which came and went. So I nudged him. He still said nothing.

"A head ache? But we have only just arrived." Earl Durrant said in surprise.

"We have yet to greet our hosts, Lady Caroline and Mr. Fox." Dour Doreen said stiffly.

"I will take you home." Dr. Knight stated. She was looking at me closely, I think she could see right through my ruse.

"I thank you, Aunt, but Sir Robertson offered earlier." I nudged Guy again to say something. He still kept silent.

Captain Greyson picked up something was amiss. Then he spoke up. "Come Robertson, this will not do. Let us together escort the Lady Elisha home."

Both gentlemen then bade their farewells to my 'parents' and 'Aunt', then on Guy's arm we left Holland House.

Once inside the carriage, on our way back to the Dunmore town house I let out a huge sigh of relief and flopped back into the rocking seat.

"Aren't you glad to get away from all of those snobs?" I asked the two.

Captain Greyson let out a hearty laugh. "Rescuing us again, my Lady? That's twice in a row we are now in your debt."

"Really? Careful now Greyson, one day I might come to claim the debt!" I laughed with him.

"Then where shall we head towards now? I know of another party on the other side of London. Now there will be some entertainment!" Greyson let out this evil laugh.

"Greyson, really!" Guy snapped at his friend. "I would say there are Ladies present, but even now I even doubt it myself." Guy now rolled his eyes at me.

Woah! That was a bit mean. But I figured he was still pretty upset, so I let it slide. But Greyson's remark about another party gave me an idea.

"I've got an even better idea…" I said to them. "I know of a party that will rock your socks off!"

"I do not think that is a wise idea Elisha. We promised to escort you home, now escort you home we shall do so." Guy said forcefully.

Greyson looked in surprise at how 'serious' his friend was acting, but I winked at Greyson to let him know that I had a plan. He winked back at me to show that he would play along. My plan could involve returning to the Dunmore home first, in fact, it might even be the best idea to start the night from…

*****

When the carriage dropped us off at the front door, Guy seemed ready to leave me there for the night. But Greyson and I grabbed an arm each and pulled him inside, on the idea that we would just have a 'nightcap'. I was a little hurt that he was trying to get away from me just because I thought I was too young for such a serious relationship, but I thought to myself, with the plan that was brewing inside my head, I would make it all the better for him. I would show him the benefits of having a girlfriend that could travel across time, and now and again, take him too.

I think Greyson suspected what I was thinking of doing, and he was playing along to what ever I suggested.

So as we stood in the Drawing room, sipping our small glasses of port, I eyed to Greyson that we should stand particularly close to the window.

"I say, isn't that Dobbs and Sims walking along the foot path?" Greyson suddenly looked out the window.

"What?" Guy came to stand beside him to look as well. "Those two men? They aren't even in uniform! You're seeing things Greyson. Are you sure you have only had two glasses of wine at Lady Caroline's house?"

I came to stand behind the two men, and I concentrated on the reflected candlelight that danced in the windowpane.

Greyson tried to keep Guy engaged in conversation on how or why those two men could still be Dobbs and Sims, whoever those two men were, as I tried to engage my ability to phase.

"Wait a minute... Greyson, do you see this? The glass, it's starting to look... wobbly..." Guy said alarmed, when suddenly I pushed the two of them from behind. "What the...!"

The three of us fell flat on our faces onto the outside pavement. We had phased not just through the 18th Century window, but through the wall and floor and onto a 21st Century street. We were still on the street where the Dunmore town house was situated, but instead of horse drawn coaches passing by, there were models of Nissan or Ford KA's or the latest Toyotas parked on the narrow cobbled street.

"Elisha! What have you done?" Guy demanded of me.

"I'm taking you to a party." I told him. "My kind of party. Come on." I grabbed his hand and started to pull him down the street.

"Take us back right now!" Guy refused to move.

"Don't fret, man! Aren't you at all curious to see where your great love comes from?" Greyson tried to point out to Guy.

"He's right. I've brought you both to my era. It's the year 2001. And I have a friend who's told me of a great rave near here, so come on!" I tried pulling on his hand again.

"A rave? You're both raving mad! Does your 'Aunt' know that you've brought me here?" Guy demanded of me.

"Guy, relax! Come on! You'll love it here!" I pleaded.

Just then in the corner of my eye I noticed one of the black cabs driving down the road towards us. I released my hold of Guy and ran out and hailed it to stop. When it did, I waved Guy and Greyson over, and Greyson pulled his friend over.

"Come on, get in!" I told the two.

"I don't think we should be doing this..." Guy tried to reason with his friend, but Greyson wouldn't hear a bar of it. He was too busy enjoying the new surroundings. He pushed Guy onto the back seat, next to me, and then hopped in last.

"The Monkey Bar." I told the driver.

"Great costumes." The driver had a chuckle at us.

"Thanks." I laughed, and so did Greyson.

"Costumes?" Guy objected, but we shooshed him.

The taxi-cab started driving, and I told Guy and Greyson to get out their wallets and see how much cash they were carrying.

The good thing was they had about 20 pounds between them... but the bad thing was the notes looked so old fashion I doubt they would be accepted. But I thought it would be good to try. I mean, with some of the coins they had, they would be considered antique, and probably worth a small sum of money.

The cab reached the nightclub and we all got out. I went to the window of the driver and started to haggle with him over the coins and notes I got from Guy and Greyson. I was fortunate to discover, that this driver was actually a coin collector! Now what are the odds of this happening?

Bargain! Not only did I pay for our trip with some of the old coins, but I even sold the rest of the coins for 50 pounds!

I suspected that I could have got even more for them, but for the moment I was happy with the 50. It would pay for a few drinks, as well as even pay for another cab fare back to the street where the Dunmore house used to be... in this era, to get us back to the old era. Gees that sounds weird... I wonder if it's still in the Dunmore family in this age as well? I wonder what would happen if I knocked on the door and asked the residents now?

We three then walked up to the front door and the bouncers took one look at us, me in my dress, the men in their short trousers and stockings and military coats... and burst out laughing!

"Go girl!" one of the bouncers gave me a high '5' and let us in straight away! Excellent! I must look older in this dress! I didn't get sprung for being underage!

The dance music was pumping, and I walked hand-in-hand in between the two men. The room was dark, with strobe lights flashing around. The music was deafening... with half-dressed people dancing madly away. There were those glow-in-the-dark plastic long sticks either tied in a ring around people's necks or on top of their heads, or even around a few of the girls waists.

I looked at Greyson, who was busy looking at the girls dancing, and I saw the big grin stretch out on his face. I looked at Guy next, who looked back at me, not so happily. So I steered us to the bar first. I'm sure a few drinks would loosen him up.

"Three orgasms." I told the bar person, a pretty blonde girl so skinny and wearing such tight black jeans, she could make a stick insect turn bulimic.

The three small plastic shot cups were placed before us and I handed one to each of us after paying for them.

Guy and Greyson examined the fluro yellow plastic that held the liquid, Greyson with curiosity, Guy with trepidation.

"You drink it in one gulp." I told the men. "On the count of three... one, two, three!"

Down the hatch it went. It was sweet and delicious. Greyson was quite surprised by it. I guess he's used to drinking harder, harsher liquors.

"What was it?" Greyson yelled in my ear above the music.

"An orgasm." I told him. "How about we try a Sex on the Beach next?"

"What?!" Guy exclaimed.

So we had another round of shots, and for the next round, I introduced them to the traditional Cocksucking Cowboy. After these drinks we went out onto the dance floor and I tried teaching them some moves.

Greyson looked like he was having the time of his life! He was laughing, and getting into the music. When he accidentally bumped into the girl dancing next to him, he bowed and apologized, which the girl totally went for. Then the next thing we knew, he was dirty dancing with her!

I tried dancing really closely with Guy, but he kept backing off from me.

I noticed a couple of gay guys dancing together, and to illustrate to Guy on how you're supposed to dance in this place, I pointed them out.

But then Guy acted like a stunned mullet when he saw the men kiss. I couldn't resist teasing him... He was acting like such a fuddy-duddy! I next pointed out the two girls on a platform, dancing and kissing too.

Guy looked really disgusted. He looked from the two guys, to the two girls, and then looked at his friend Greyson dancing very closely with a girl he had only just met, who was moving very sexily next to him. He looked like he was getting fed up with this place.

I told Guy and Greyson I was going to go to the ladies room, and Guy offered to 'escort' me. This made me laugh at him. I said that here, if a guy escorted a girl to a cubicle, then it wouldn't be for nature calling... it would be for doing the wild thing! That made him stand even more stiffly.

So I left my 18th Century boyfriend standing like a frozen fish on the dance floor and went to the bathroom.

This wasn't going as well as I had hoped or planned.

On my way into the cubicle, I noticed these two transvestites fixing up their make-up in the mirror. I thought this was weird, as wouldn't they have to go use the men's room, and not the ladies? I wasn't going to say anything, I was just curious... but then, they gave me an idea...

From Guy's perspective, he stood on the dance floor, not moving, but scowling, waiting for his amore to come out of the bathroom. His best-friend was having a swinging good time. He was disturbed and disgusted by all the half-clothed debauchery happening all around him, amongst this deafening god-awful noise they presumed to call music. He wanted to go home.

Finally after what seemed longer than usual, he finally saw a woman in a tall wig and a long, wide, ruffled red silk dress. But she was moving in the wrong direction... away from him. Maybe she didn't see him? He didn't want to get separated from her in this place... he would have to go after her.

He had to push, weave, dodge and barge his way through the moving throng of people.

When he thought he had caught up with her, he grabbed her shoulder.

She turned around in surprise... and he stepped backwards in horror.

A man wearing make-up stared back at Guy underneath huge false eyelashes, the wig and the red silk dress.

"You want a piece of this muffin?" the man drawled in a camp voice and reached out his hand towards Guy.

"Pardon me... I ...thought..." Guy uttered in complete shock, then turned around and barged his way through the crowds again to get away.

I watched all of this happen and was laughing so hard with Greyson, from the podium where the two girls were dancing earlier.

Guy looked up and saw us laughing, with me just wearing all my undergarments and jewelry.

He got angry.

He got really angry.

He turned around and now started for the EXIT sign.

"Oh shit, where's he going now?" I pointed to Greyson.

We quickly jumped down and followed.

I found ourselves back out on the street with a jovial army captain and a furious navy captain.

"What the hell were you doing, back in there? What the hell were you thinking, bringing us here?" Guy shouted at me.

I was taken aback. I was shocked into silence. I just stood there and took it.

"First, you break every rule by traveling back in time to save me. Second, we're presented to the King as future Man and Wife. Third, you tell me you may not marry me until you're 30 years old. Then you tell me you may not marry me at all and that I'm a bit of fun. And then you compound your point by bringing me to this place, full of deviation and rank with sin and telling me this is where you come from?" Guy yelled at me.

All I could do was stand there while Guy ranted and raved at me. He wouldn't rave inside, but he would rave outside, and at me? Great. But what do I say?

"Come now man, be reasonable..." Greyson started, but Guy turned on him next.

"Don't start, William! I am being reasonable! I am the only one here being reasonable! You both should be ashamed of yourselves! I will not be made a fool of any further on this night! Now madam, take me home this instant!" Guy demanded.

"Madam? I'm a madam, now am I?" I put my hands on my hips. "Look, I said I'm from this era, I wasn't born and brought up in a fucking night club, OK? I've been to one or two, that's all. I brought you all here because I thought you would enjoy yourselves! And do you really think that everyone here in this era all behaves like that what you saw inside, all of the time? Well that's a pretty stupid thing to think! Everyone in there was just out for a good time, which is what I thought we were out for too!"

But Guy didn't hear me. His back was turned and he had already started walking down the street. He didn't even seem to bother to wait for me.

I wanted to go back inside and get my dress back from the tranie, but I guess I wouldn't have time. It was a lucky thing I still kept my jewelry on. I looked at Greyson for help, to try to reason with the man. But all he could do was shrug, then offer his arm for me to take.

I thought this was a kind gesture after getting blasted by his bestfriend, so I took it.

We hailed down another cab and got dropped off outside the town house we wanted.

I phased us back through the window into the 18th Century drawing room of the Dunmore family.

"What is the meaning of this?!" an astonished upper class accent sounded.

When our eyesight returned to normal, we found ourselves in the company of Lord Dunmore, Earl Durrant, Lady Doreen, and Dr. Knight.

Lord Dunmore looked mortified that I was standing only in my undergarments.

"I wanted to show these two gentlemen a little of the era I come from. Unfortunately my dress was stolen." I half lied.

"How is your head ache, my dear?" Lady Doreen asked coldly.

Actually, ironically, I was starting to get one now.

"Worse." I moaned, grimacing.

I don't think alcohol and phasing through time mix well... I felt really dizzy!

"Just how was your dress stolen?" Dr. Knight raised her eyebrows, unamused.

"A transvestite took it." I told her.

"A what?!" Lord Dunmore spluttered as Lady Doreen looked like she was trying not to snicker.

"Gentlemen, I must ask you to leave now." Earl Durrant excused Guy and Greyson. He was unimpressed with this situation as well. "Captain Robertson, I'm afraid our dinner tomorrow will have to be postponed."

Guy nodded, not meeting his gaze, and then he and Greyson did a small bow and then both men started to leave.

"It's not their fault! It was my idea!" I quickly told Dr. Knight. "And Guy kept telling me it was a bad idea, but I kept insisting. I wanted to show them 21st Century London."

"I'm glad to hear that Captain Robertson thought it was a bad idea. It shows some good judgment on his part. I would be quite worried if a Captain in His Majesty's Royal Navy did not put up some resistance to a bad plan if he were in the middle of it." Lord Dunmore said dryly.

"I apologize for the unfit state Lady Elisha was returned home in. With your permission, I will take my leave." Guy bowed his head, still silently fuming, I could see, and then he and Greyson departed.

Just as the two men walked out the front door, I followed after them. I was desperate that Guy shouldn't leave angry with me. I didn't want us to part with bad blood between us.

"Elisha!" Dr. Knight called after me. "Be mindful of what you're NOT wearing!"

"Guy please!" I grabbed his arm to stop him. "Please don't be angry with me. I wanted to show you a good time tonight."

Guy didn't say anything, and he turned to leave again but I wouldn't let go of his arm.

"Guy, please say something!" I nearly started to cry, scared of what was happening between us.

"Lady Elisha, I release you from our engagement." Guy said flatly.

"No! Please! Don't say that! I just want to be with you!" I clung desperately to his arm, now tearful.

"But not enough to marry me." he said.

"Why can't it be enough for you that we have some time together?" I tried to hold him back as he tried to walk away. "Why does it have to be such a fight to be with you? Why does everything have to be so black and white with you? Why are you always fighting me?"

Suddenly he turned on me, ripping my hand off his jacket and forcefully putting my hands to my side. Then, just as quickly, he released me, and said, looking directly into my eyes, "Goodnight and goodbye, Elisha." Then he walked off down the street, with a surprised Greyson in tow.

No!

"I love you Guy!" I yelled after him, sobbing.

Please no! I didn't lose him to death, I lost him to pride! I lost him from his temper! Did I really stuff up that badly? Why is he so angry with me?

I probably made it worse, by my public outburst... my public outpouring, it probably embarrassed him even more. I can't stand all this upright and uptight social code system in this place. I had had enough of this era!

I wiped my face dry, held my head up high, then picked up my heavy skirts and bounded back up the stairs and through the door inside.

"Lets go home!" I said in a huff to Dr. Knight. "I never want to visit this place again!"

*****

And now I'm back in my dorm room, typing all of his out.

And I'm grounded, so to speak.

My 'phasing privileges' have been annulled.

Yesterday morning I was sent to Professor Hamilton's office, where Dr. Knight was present, and I was given another telling off.

"Elisha, you can't just go off on your own like that. You told Dr. Knight that you would be at her family's home in London, and that is where she expected you to be. In that time frame, mind you. By your impulsive actions you jeopardized not only your own safety, but also the safety of two other lives." Professor Hamilton said sternly.

"How? How did I 'jeopardize' anybody's life?" I retorted.

"You are 17 years old. You are still only learning only just the beginning of this gift of yours. What if something happened that you were unable to deal with? You placed yourself and two other people in a situation that was risky, to say the least, and where no-one else knew you to be in." Hamilton continued.

"But I thought the Calculators would be able to send help if anything ever went wrong. That's what you told us." I reminded them.

"That's true. Calculators can see the ramifications. But when Circulators travel it is usually after notice has been given when and where their destinations will be. And not to mention your underage entry into the nightclub, and then your drinking… do you know how dangerous it is for a Circulator to try to phase under the influence?" Hamilton gave me one of his long, hard looks on this point.

"I only had three drinks." I said lamely. "And it wasn't like they were tequila shots or anything."

"The Circulate has actually lost a life of one of its Circulators from phasing under the influence of either alcohol or drugs. If you don't concentrate properly… or even come out of the phase too early, you could be half buried in a wall or something worse." Hamilton warned.

"Really?" I asked surprised.

"Death is almost instantaneous and very painful. Half of your body would be comprised of bedrock." Dr. Knight added.

"And how and when and where you phased, Elisha... onto a street in London in the early evening. Do you know how risky that was, and did you think of what would happen if anyone did see you?" Hamilton pressed on.

"But no-one did see us." I said.

"Dr. Knights family saw you. Now can you explain how you managed to phase into an occupied room? Why didn't you see them before you phased?" Hamilton asked me next.

Actually, that was a good question. "I don't think I was looking properly."

"A Circulator should always phase to an unoccupied room. There are not always guarantees that the person who sees you phase through time are in the know. What if you should have accidentally phased and complete strangers who are not in the know of the Circulate, saw you?"

"Wouldn't they just assume I'm a ghost?" I shrugged. That's what I did when I saw Dr. Knight phase for my first time.

"A ghost they can catch? Once your transition is complete, they could accost you." Hamilton said.

I wasn't completely sure what 'accost' meant, but I assumed it was a bad thing.

"Elisha, after this incident, it has proven to us that you are not yet ready for the responsibility of phasing on a regular basis, and that you need more supervision. I'm afraid we are going to have to disallow any further excursions to the 18th Century or any other Circulating unless it is for a class exercise." Professor Hamilton pronounced.

This didn't really bother me that much, and I think this surprised them.

"That's OK. I don't think Guy and I will be seeing each other anymore anyway." I slumped back into the chair.

==

11/08/01

Diary,

Nothing much to say really... life here at school continues like it always does. I just felt like talking to someone. Someone other than Nelson.

I really miss Guy.

Every time I even mention his name, Nelson tells me to shut up. She tells me to 'get over it'. She says she's sick of my whining.

I just still think it's so unfair... the way he just dumped me like that!

Why can't he understand that I'm only 17? That marriage is a really big deal here, in my time period. I know that 17 is of marriageable age in 19th Century England, but it's not where I come from. I was just a tourist there! I don't want to spend the rest of my life there, in those times, in that place. It's too constricting, too many rules, I know I'd suffocate in under a month!

I don't even have a photo of him. All I have is his letter. His one letter, confessing his undying love for me. Well, if it was so undying, I guess somebody found either a wooden stake or holy water to pierce his immortal affections and now everything we had is dust.

I've read the letter probably 100 times now. I haven't told Nelson this, or she would just think me pathetic, but I sleep with the letter under my pillow. I guess it's an old childhood habit I haven't broken yet. When I went through my Dean Cain phase (pardon the pun!) growing up, I used to sleep with his autographed photo under my pillow, that I was sent from his fan club.

I guess you could blame Mum for this slight addiction. When I was little, we put our teeth that fell out, in a little felt bag that Gran made for us, under our pillows. Then when we woke up the next morning, we found a few dollars the Tooth Fairy left for us. For Christmas, we didn't have stockings at the end of our beds stuffed with presents from Santa Clause, we had pillowcases. So I guess all this pillow talk has ingrained itself in my psyche that if I go to sleep with something under my pillow or in a pillowcase, I'll find a surprise the next morning.

It didn't work.

Dean Cain never materialized, nor now has Guy's return of affections.

Bugger.

I wish this ability to phase through the layers of time was linked to some magical powers, like witch craft. I wish I was a witch. I wish I could brew up a love potion that would bring the suitor I choose to come and announce his unswerving devotion (I read that quote in a Jane Austen book - I think).

I feel so depressed.

It's like I have this gaping hole inside my chest, and it's growing bigger and bigger. It's so heavy... sometimes I think I can't breathe. It's like a black hole inside of me, sucking in all of my energy, and whatever is going on in my life is pulled in by its gravity, and that nothing can escape from it. The only release I have is when I finally get some alone time in my room, and I shut my door, and I start to cry.

Last night I lied and told Pat and Nelson I was really tired, and I went to bed early. And I cried into my pillow for like, two hours. I had to cry into my pillow, coz I didn't want anyone to hear me. I sobbed into my pillow... and it got all wet not just from the tears, but my nose was running as well. So then I had to get out of bed and change pillowcases so I wouldn't sleep in my own snot and dribble. Sorry, that sounds disgusting, doesn't it?

Maybe it doesn't. Maybe it symbolizes my life right now. My life has turned into snot and dribble. Life with out Guy... is snot and dribble, and sobbing.

Maybe I am as pathetic as Nelson likes to remind me daily.

Angela thought so.

I still am tempted now and then to email Angela to see how she is and what she's up to. If only she could know that all my paranoia ended up being justified. I wish I could prove to her that I was right, all along. I really miss her. We had so much fun together growing up. I'll never forget when her parents first put the pool in their backyard the fun Angela and I had writing up a guest list for our first pool party and planning everything. Even writing out a list of food we wanted to buy and what music to play was exciting. We wanted to be like Edina and Patsy from "Ab Fab", and organize the most fabulous event ever!

I sometimes wonder what my life would have been like if I had never slit my wrists that afternoon. Would I still be going to the same high school? Would Professor Stephen Hamilton still have contacted my father on sending me here, to his college? Would I be learning about all this Circulating stuff? Would I want to live, in my mediocrity, with not knowing I had the ability to phase through the layers of time? To have never stepped on Mars? To have never seen Mars with plant life and an atmosphere? To not knowing that not only was the world my oyster, but perhaps time and space as well?

I confess to you Diary, but I couldn't say this to Nell... I don't know what she would do if she knew this... but sometimes I stare at my scars on my wrists, and wish that wounds were still open.

I'll never forget that afternoon, for as long as I live, of staring down at the blood trickling down my skin and dripping onto the bathroom floor. I'll never forget that feeling of complete release and freedom that I experienced, at knowing of what I had done and what it could mean. I felt justified. I felt happy. I felt at peace. I was letting all of the badness, and the sadness that had been building up inside me for months and months, out onto the floor. I was ESCAPING.

Nell says from our sessions together, that she thinks I'm suffering from Post-Traumatic Stress Disorder and Survivors Guilt, after the death of my mother. She thinks that that's the reason why I wanted to kill myself. She thinks I was trying to punish myself. Now I admit, Dad could really make me feel guilty sometimes, and if I did one little thing wrong he would overreact and come down on me like a ton of bricks, and maybe in some way she was right. That was some of the badness I wanted to let out of me. But ultimately, I think it was because I wanted to escape, to get away, and end everything.

I was sick and tired of everything. Everything seemed so cliché and so... done before. Nothing was new or exciting. It was like being seated at a game of Monopoly, and three hours into the game, where everything is bought and mortgaged, and you were bored and didn't want to play anymore, and you wanted to leave the game but no-one would let you. People kept telling me this was fun, but I kept telling them this wasn't fun to me anymore.

Coming to Hamilton's has helped me. It has been new and exciting. It has been a temporary escape. But the effects are starting to wear thin. I'm starting to get bored again. And I'm scared of this. I know what it means. When the boredom sets in, and I feel like I don't feel or touch or taste anymore (Nell calls this disassociating myself - the feeling of not being real), then the depression sets in.

I can't stop thinking about Guy. His dark eyes, looking at me. His stubborn look, when his jaw was set, made him look so handsome. I know it sounds cliché, but you know the saying "you're beautiful when you're angry"? Well, that's what Guy was. He was his most handsome when he was angry, I admit. But then when he smiled at me, in the throne room when we were presented at court... that made me feel so warm and gave me such a natural high. And he doesn't have a toothy smile either, whenever he smiles it's just with his lips. I like that kind of smile... it's like a kind of soft sort of smile.

I'll try to think stop thinking such dark thoughts, and I'll just concentrate on my memory of Guy. The memory of that night in India, on his ship... when we were in bed together. I'll remember him like that. Or when we kissed under the stars, the first night we saw each other, when I first arrived at the Fort. I'll remember his words in his letter;

My ardor is genuine, my heart ache at our parting is infinite. Be rest assured you are first in my thoughts when I wake in the morning, and are the last, when I return to my bed at night. And when the sea rocks me to sleep at night in her cold, watery bosom, I murmur your name, and dream of a warmer, softer one that inside rests the heart of the woman I love.

I'll be strong for Guy. I can't imagine what he would think of me if I ever did something like slitting my wrists again. I don't want him to think of me as pathetic. I can be strong for him. I will be strong for him. I will behave myself from now on. I'll study hard, learn all I need to know, and when the time is right, maybe I'll return to him. I want to see him one last time.

===

TO: jeni_B@goggleyes.com
FROM: ebaker_hamiltons@evers.com
SUBJECT: Four days to France and counting!
DATE: 14/ 08/ 01

Hey Cuz!

How's life treating you? I'm OK. Just really looking forward to our trip to Paris at the end of the week! I can't believe that summer holidays are nearly over so fast. But the good side is, it means Paris is only a couple of days away!

We've all been studying hard for our trip. Yesterday in French class we were handed out itineraries for our trip:

FRIDAY 17TH: Catch the bus to Thunder Bay and overnight in hotel.

SATURDAY 18TH: Fly to Paris.

SUNDAY 19TH: Arrive in Paris, and check into hotel. In the evening, do the Paris Illuminations tour and the Eiffel Tower.

MONDAY 20TH: Do a tour of the city, Notre Dame Cathedral, Place de la Concorde, Louvre (outside only), Hotel de Ville, Latin Quarter, Arc de Triomphe, Champs-Elysees, Les Invalides, Opera and Montmarte. Then in the evening have dinner on a Seine cruise.

TUESDAY 21ST: Visit inside the Louvre and Musee d'Orsay.

WEDNESDAY 22ND: Visit Giverny - Monet's home and then to Versailles for a tour inside and outside of the palace.

THURSDAY 23RD: Free day and then at night Moulin Rouge Dinner and Show.

FRIDAY 24TH: Leave Paris and drive down to Lyon, on the way visit and tour Fontainebleau Chateaux.

SATURDAY 25TH: Tour the Palace of the Popes, before driving on to Nice.

SUNDAY 26TH: Tour of Nice to see Castle Hill, the Chagall and Matisse Museums, Queen Victoria's winter palace, the Franciscan Monastery and Roman ruins, Promenade des Anglais and the Old Town.

MONDAY 27TH: Free day with an evening a tour of Monaco and dinner in a Monte Carlo restaurant.

TUESDAY 28TH: Fly back to Paris, then back to Canada.

WEDNESDAY 29TH: Arrive back in Thunder Bay, stay overnight in hotel.

THURSDAY 30TH: Drive back to College.

So how about that? It's nearly two weeks we get to get out of this place, and just a little over a week we're in France! Man, I can't wait!

We were told by our French teacher that the hotel rooms would be twin share, and Nelson and I instantly looked at each other and nodded. I guess we didn't even have to say it. We'll be bunk buddies, so to speak. Then Pat asked Brett if he wanted to share, and he said yeah. But poor Maya looked a little lost. Soong and Wong were already set up, and so was Numu and Jordon. But then Rosa who usually hangs out with the French student Giselle spoke up and told Maya that she could probably triple share with her and Darianne. Giselle wouldn't be going on the trip, in fact, she's already in France coz she's been home for the holidays.

This made me feel bad that they were offering this, when Maya usually hangs around us more now. So now I thanked Rosa for the idea, and asked that if triple sharing was allowed, that maybe Maya could also share with Nelson and I. Maya looked happy about this, but Nelson kicked me under the table!

I promise to send you heaps of postcards and stuff. I promised Dad and Mark too. Hey, would you like any little souvenirs or anything? Maybe I could get you a couple too. I've saved some of my allowance up. I mean, all our breakfasts and dinners are already being paid by the school along with the trip, hopefully buying lunch over there won't be that expensive.

===

TO: s_parson@snailmail.com
FROM: ebaker_hamiltons@evers.com
SUBJECT: Watch out Paris, here I come!
DATE: 16/ 08/ 01

Guess what! I can afford Paris! I know the school was already paying for it and everything… but I was getting worried I would hardly have any spending money! And in your last email warning me how expensive everything is over there… it got me really worried.

Dad put an extra $200 in my account this month for the trip! So altogether from him I got $400! And Mark also put $300 into my account, though he joked it was on the condition I use some of it to buy his girlfriend Patrice a bottle of French perfume. And I've saved around $300 over the holidays by not spending all of my allowance money, so altogether I've got $1000 spending money!

Then in French class today, which wasn't really a proper class, but it was more of planning for our trip, they handed out these museum passes. So the school has paid for our entry into the Louvre, Musee de Orsay, Fontainebleau Castle and Versailles. So I won't have to pay for those! And we were told all the other entrance fees of the places we visit will also be covered. What a relief!

Then Professor Hamilton stopped in, and gave us an even bigger surprise.

He handed out these envelopes with our names on them, and inside them were travelers cheques! He told us that the school would also be sponsoring our spending money for lunch and small incidentals... but when I took a look at how much he was giving out... I accidentally swore out loud in surprise! Nelson's eyebrows were raised, and Maya instantly packed the envelope into her bag for safe keeping.

There was 250 pounds worth of travelers cheques in my envelope!

"Now the amount that is in each envelope is different to each person. The reason being is that some people may have some money of their own accord. We would like to make this trip as enjoyable as possible for all of our students. I have had it on good advice from Madame Coultard that all of you have worked very hard these past three months, and all of you deserve this reward." Professor Hamilton stated.

When he left the room and everyone started talking at once. I think we were all in shock of what had just happened! Wow, this Circulate business really do like to take care of their own!

Over dinner in the Caf tonight, Brett asked us how much money we got.

"Do we have to talk about this?" Pat stared down into his dinner and started stabbing at his steak.

"How much did you get Maya?" Brett asked her.

"Enough." Was all Maya would say.

"I got 250 pounds." I ventured, not minding the topic of conversation.

"Then your dear Daddy must have given you a lot for the school to give you less." Nelson sneered my way.

"Well how much did you get then?" I demanded, not liking the tone of her voice. It annoyed me. I did work hard for that money!

"750 pounds. So as you can see, Pat and I don't have the luxury of having parents who still try to take care of us." Nelson full on glared at me.

"Look, I worked hard for that money! Don't forget my month of washing dishes! And I saved up my allowance money! The only thing I've bought from our Brown Day trips has been cigarettes!" I retorted.

"Allowance money? Pat and I don't get allowance money that our Daddies put in our accounts each month! The fucking school gives us our allowance money! My mother hasn't even sent me one fucking letter since I came here! My father could be dead for all I know, since he left when I was four! Fuck off Elisha, I'm tired of hearing your problems all the time!"

Nelson slammed down her cutlery and stood up and stomped off.

"Whoops." Brett raised his eyebrows. "Touchy subject."

"I'll go after her." Pat stood up and left as well.

I was so angry at her! Why did she just go off like that? I felt the tears well up in my eyes, but with everyone in the Caf now looking at me, I didn't want them to show. I was so angry, that when I tried to lift up my knife, my hand was shaking!

"It's not your fault." Maya put her hand over mine.

"No, it's mine. I'm sorry Elisha." Brett put his hand on my arm too.

I couldn't eat any more dinner and I got up to leave too.

Peter and Zack, who were sitting at another table, were watching us. Peter leaned over and said something in Zack's ear, and chuckled at his own joke, which was probably about me. I gave him my most evil stare before leaving the room.

I went back to my dorm room.

As I walked down the hall, I had to pass Nelson's room. The door was shut, but I could hear her and Pat inside. Nelson was yelling, and it sounded like she was slamming things around. It also sounded like Pat was trying to console her.

I sat on my bed and fumed.

I don't want to share a hotel room with HER. I'm tired of her criticism. I'm tired of her always being a moody and sarcastic bitch! I think you were right about her Sally. I'm not going to make excuses for her anymore.

But I won't let her ruin my trip. So I'm going to get up from the bed, put some music on really loudly to spite her so she can hear me, and then I'll do more packing. I've already done most of it, and I'll have to do the last of it tomorrow morning after I've brushed my teeth and then I can pack away my toothbrush.

I wish you were here, so Maya and I could triple share with you instead.

==

19/08/01

Diary,

I'm writing this on the plane to Paris! There is only three hours to go, and then we land... in Paris! Me! In Paris!

The last two days feels like it's gone by so slowly. On Thursday night, I had a major fight with Nelson. She went ape-shit over the subject of spending money. She yelled at me and told me to fuck off in the Caf at dinner! So Maya and I assumed that we wouldn't be sharing a hotel room with her anymore.

We didn't speak to each other yesterday morning, when we all got on the bus for Thunder Bay. I sat next to Maya, with Brett sitting in front of us. He was basically sitting sideways so he could talk to Maya and me, and the three of us tried to play games to keep us amused. We started off with Eye-Spy, then Hangman, then the 'If' game. You know, the one where we ask questions like, "if you won a million dollars, what would be the first three things you would buy?" or "if you could sleep with any celebrity, who would it be?" Pat and Nelson sat a few rows down from us, with Nelson deliberately not looking at us.

I started to wonder if I had somehow managed to piss Patrick off as well, because he seemed to be trying to not look at me either. This made me kind of uneasy... I mean, it's bad enough going on an exciting holiday with two people who wish me dead (Zack and Peter), but to add two more people...? I started to consider if I was contagious with an anti-Elisha antibody or something. First Zack, then Peter, then Guy, and now Nelson and Pat?

When the bus stopped and we all got out for lunch, I received a nice surprise though.

Brett, Maya and I were sitting in a booth of the diner at the truck stop we were at, looking at our menus, when Pat and Nelson came over and sat with us.

"I've got something for you." Pat handed a small wrapped up package to me. "You might need it on the plane."

I opened it, to find my repaired Walkman!

"You're a genius!" I squealed and hugged him! "How did you manage to fix it?"

"You'd be surprised at how well we're stocked in parts in our science laboratories, and in tools." Pat smiled at me.

"Thank you!" I smiled back at him, so grateful. Then I looked at Nelson, to see if there was peace between us too. But she looked away and picked up a menu and pretended to read that instead.

"Look, we're not angry at you because you get an allowance from your father. That would just be stupid." Pat gave Nelson a hard long look. "We're just angry of the circumstances we're in because we're not."

"Well, if you did start getting cheques now from your mother or father, I suppose then you'd really have to be worried." I tried to joke with him.

"Yeah well, if I did start getting them now, it probably wouldn't be very much anyway. Not with the huge difference in the cost of living in those days to today. They'd probably only send me something like 10 pounds a month or something." Pat had a chuckle.

"Look on the bright side. With the slump in the Australian dollar compared to the pound, your 10 pounds would probably amount to $200." I continued.

"I feel richer already. So, is the first lunch in Paris on me?" Pat asked the table.

"Yeah, we'll pick the most expensive café on the Champs Elysees." Brett chimed in and we all laughed, well, everyone except Nelson.

We got into Thunder Bay at 7 PM where the bus took us straight to the hotel.

Madam Coultard and Monsieur Philippe, our French teachers at the college, are our teachers and baby-sitters for the trip. After we got our suitcases unpacked from the bus, and we were all assembled in hotel foyer, we were given our room keys. They told us we weren't allowed to go out or leave the hotel. Our dinner would be in one hour in the hotel's restaurant.

Maya, Nelson and I, with Nelson in charge of being key-holder, all made our way up to our room.

"Are you going to shower and change for dinner?" Maya asked us as we put down our suitcases and flopped onto our beds.

"Nah, I'll shower before I go to bed." I told her.

Maya looked at Nelson next, who shook her head as well, so then Maya used this opportunity to have the bathroom all to herself.

Nelson also used this quiet, alone time of just the two of us to have a word with me.

"I'm sorry about last night, OK?" She said abruptly.

I didn't say anything back. I was still annoyed about her yelling at me in front of practically the whole school. I was also still hurt that she said that I keep dumping my problems on her, when actually there is a lot I hold back from Nelson. But then what she said back to me, that she hasn't talked to either of her parents and is cut off from them also made me sympathetic.

"Why didn't you mention your thing with your parents earlier?" I finally asked back.

"I don't like to talk about my problems." She said coolly.

"So I've noticed. But we can't really call each other friends if we can't talk honestly and openly to each other." I tried to point out.

"Well it hasn't stopped you in the past." She said snidely.

That hurt. I was through with trying to be nice to her. I got up from the bed and started for the door. I wouldn't put up with this.

"I didn't mean it like that." Nelson called out after me as I opened the door to leave. She got up from the bed too and came over to me. "Look Elisha, there is a lot about me that you don't know. I don't want anyone to know about some of the things that went on in my past. That's why I don't exactly... open up to people."

"Fine. I can respect that. But you're a bitch! You say hurtful things to people who try to be your friend. I'm not asking for a full on interview where you divulge your deepest secrets. But if you don't want to talk about them, then you shouldn't let these dark secrets affect your life now. Because you bit my head off last night with out warning! You've never told me about your problems with your parents, so how do I know when to keep my mouth shut about my own?" I glared at her.

"Hasn't it been obvious...? My trouble with my parents? They never call, they never write! I never call anyone outside of the school! Sometimes it's like all you see is your own problems! Do you know what that's like, having nothing but this fucked up college? Then to hear you boasting, 'ooh, my Daddy gave me some more money today..' it hurts like hell!" Nelson yelled back at me, suddenly tearful.

I closed the door to our room again, and I tried to hug her but she walked away.

"OK, here's the dossier on what I know about you. You are an only child. Your mother raised you. You started seeing things that happened in the past from a very early age, like that incident in the bank. I'm not sure when, but you ran away from home and spent some time on the streets. I'm guessing this was when you broke into that store and you were arrested. That's when you came to college, when Professor Hamilton made a deal with the D.A. Is that all correct? Oh yeah, hang on, your father left your mother and you when you were four years old. Did I get all of it?" I asked her angrily, putting my hands on my hips.

"Who told you I lived on the streets?" she mumbled sadly, sitting on the end of her bed again.

"I think it came up very briefly during the week that I thought the teachers were going to put drugs in the food, remember?" I sat next to her. We both laughed at that memory. "And I also remember how you tipped your fries on Peter when he was paying me out about it all."

"So I'm not a complete bitch then?" Nelson asked me half-joking.

"I don't know. I'm still wondering about it." I said. "You can act wonderfully protective over me sometimes, but you still are my harshest critic."

"I thought true friends were meant to be honest with each other." Nelson stated.

"Well in that case, Sally must have been your bestest friend." I joked.

"Oh man... did I drive her away?" Nelson put her head in her hands.

"No. This whole Circulate business did that." I put my arm about her shoulders. "But I am in email contact with her. She is mildly interested in all this time traveling business. She certainly was when I told her all about meeting Guy."

"She probably thinks the two of you are a great romance novel." Nelson scoffed.

"Yeah, she probably does." I sighed. "I haven't told her that he dumped me."

"You haven't? Why?" Nelson gave me a funny look.

"I don't want to break her heart." I said, then we both burst out laughing. I turned serious again. "Oh yeah, and to add to your dossier... I think there was a guy involved in your life too."

"What do you mean by that?" Nelson straightened up, suddenly uncomfortable.

"I'm guessing that when you ran away from home, it was over a guy. Probably your mother didn't approve. But then things didn't work out with this guy, and you were left with no home, and no boyfriend. I think that's why you tell yourself you won't fall in love again, and you hate all that mushy kind of stuff now." I told her.

"I never told you any of this." Nelson gave me another funny look.

"No, but I can tell by your personality. You've told yourself you're not going to get burned again. It's probably why you keep yourself distanced from a lot of people." I said.

"You make me sound like such a cliché." She moaned.

"Patrick likes you." I told her.

"Yeah, as a friend." She tried to dismiss it.

"You know it's more than friendship. You've known it all along. Remember that night in your room when we were waiting till midnight so we could smoke? You said you knew he liked someone. And I've seen the way he's always tried to be with you, and to help you, and the way he humors your indifference towards him and everyone else. But he's madly in love with you." I told her.

"We just have a lot in common, that's all." Nelson stood up and went over to open her suitcase and pretend to be occupied with something inside.

"Yeah, the no parents situation has given you both something to talk about. And he's had it tough too. But it still doesn't mean that he cares for you only as a friend." I sat back and watched her.

"I think Maya has the right idea. I think I will have a shower before we go down for dinner." Nelson changed the subject and went over to bang on the bathroom door.

So Diary, I guess you could say the air has been cleared between Nelson and I. But I have a feeling I'm never going to know what's really going on in her brain. There are still too many walls up around her.

Yesterday we arrived at the airport two hours before our flight was due to take off.

After checking our luggage in, Madam Coultard said we could separate and look around the airport.

Maya, Nelson, Brett, Pat and I all went to look inside the Duty Free shop. Nelson and I didn't have a camera. My camera, which is a cheap, kiddy camera, was sitting at home in Wollongong, packed in a box somewhere. And I couldn't go through France with out a single photo taken. So as I was looking for the cheapest camera possible (the cameras they had were all over $100 and that was with out tax!) with Nelson, Brett and Pat and Maya were checking out the digital cameras in another case.

"Why don't you get one of these?" Pat asked me, pointing at a $700 digital camera. "Then you can put your photos on your computer, or on the Net, and print them out on your printer."

"Yeah, like I'm really going to get a camera that would take up nearly all my spending money, even before I get on the plane for my holiday." I shook my head at him.

"Go halves with Nelson." He shrugged casually.

Nelson and I looked at each other, and immediately shook our heads in unison.

We both ended up buying the same camera though, ironically, because it was the cheapest they had in the store and would take up less of our spending money.

Then we five went into the bookshop that also sold some lollies, film and magazines, which we all bought one of each of these things. So I had a roll of film on me, to start me off as soon as the plane would land in gay

Paree. And I had lollies and magazines to keep me entertained on the way, along with my newly repaired Walkman.

But being in the bookstore again, kind of made me nostalgic. It reminded me of the time when I last stood inside the shop, reading in the travel section, when I ran away from school and flew to India with the money I lied to Mark to get. When I felt I had to save Guy's life, at all costs. Then I succeeded, and I won Guy's heart... only to lose it again because of my refusal to marry him and then showing off my time frame...

"Earth to Elisha, come in, Elisha." Nelson nudged me when she caught me staring off into space. "Where were you just then?"

"Nothing, nowhere." I said quickly.

"If you say the 'G' word again, I'll start lecturing you on life and love next." She teased.

So far the plane trip is going OK. I'm sitting between Maya and Nelson on the window side, with Brett and Pat across the aisle from us in the center section. We've eaten our meals, watched the movie, and now all the lights have gone out and people have started to sleep. But I can't sleep, so I've put on my Walkman and started typing on you.

I can never sleep on planes. I can't sleep on buses either, or in cars. I don't know why. When we used to go on holidays growing up and Dad would drive us either down to Wollongong or up to Queensland, Mum would be out like a light, so would Mark. So it was just Dad and I awake, with him driving, and me playing Eye-Spy with him.

Nelson and Maya are sound asleep, so is Brett. Only Pat and I seem to be awake at the moment. I've lent him the magazine I bought to read. It looks so funny, seeing Pat read the "OK" magazine with all the celebrity gossip. Pat couldn't care less about which actress had plastic surgery or which couple have recently divorced. He must be really bored! I even took a photo of him reading it, when he wasn't looking! I doubt we'll ever see him do it again.

==

20/ 08/ 01

Diary,

Wow! What a day! We've just got back to our hotel room now after the cruise. But man, what a day! It was so wonderful!

I suppose I should start from the moment we touched down in France.

Another bus picked us up from the airport and took us to our hotel. There we had two hours to wait before we had dinner in the hotel's restaurant and then begin our Paris Illuminations tour. Nelson and I didn't stay long in our room, we went and visited Pat and Brett in their room. Raj came and visited Maya in our room though, holding a map and a tourist brochure, as he wanted to discuss with Maya what should they do and see on our free day. I think Raj really likes Maya, but I also think she's playing hard to get, coz she's not sure of her own feelings for him.

Anyway, they were of the first of the couples to start forming.

So we're in Pat and Brett's room, and Pat asks us what we want to do on our free day.

I answered that I wanted to check out Rue St. Honore for the shopping. I would like to see what it's like for the 'other half' to live, to be able to afford the expensive clothes and things. Also I had to buy Patrice a bottle of Chanel No. 5, remember? To my surprise Nelson even seemed to like this idea, so Pat and Brett reluctantly agreed, on the provision that it's not a whole day trip.

We hung out in Pat and Brett's room until dinner. And then when we had to go down to eat, we found it was pretty ordinary. Salad and ham, nothing special. But I swallowed it all down, I was so excited about what would come after dinner, the tour of the city at night.

And my excitement was worth it! We drove around the center of the city, and saw the Champs Elysee all lit up! Our bus went around the Arc de Triomphe three times! It was mad, because there are no actual lanes for cars to stay in when they're on the round about! Then we drove along the Seine and saw the Notre Dame Cathedral, as well as the Musee de Orsay, and the Louvre all lit up and reflected in the river.

At the end the bus let us off at the Eiffel Tower. We had tickets to go to the top of the Eiffel Tower at night to see the view. I couldn't wait!

We had to line up for the elevator to take us up to the first level. Even there it was pretty high to give us a wonderful view over the city! I could even see Euro-Disney from there! Then we had to line up again for the next lift to take us to the top.

Nelson and I took turns at taking each other's photo, and then we got Rosa to take a group photo of all of us together, with Maya, Raj, Brett, Pat, Nelson and I.

I used my new camera to take some panoramic shots of the city. I guess it's a good thing that I had to buy a new camera. With my old camera back home in Australia I doubt I could have taken as many good pictures or that they would come out as clear. And then Nelson and I started arguing on how to use the cameras. She was using the flash as she took her panoramic shots of the city, and I was trying to tell her that she didn't need it on. It's not like the flash of the tiny light bulb was actually going to reach that far! I ended up getting Pat to agree with me and tell her himself because she wouldn't believe me!

Then Pat and Nelson kind of went off on their own a little, kind of on the premise that Pat was going to help her get some good shots of the city laid out beneath us. Then I noticed how close they were standing at one stage. I wondered if Pat was going to use this trip as his chance to make his move on Nelson? By the way they stood closely together then, with Nelson not moving away from him... he just might have his opportunity.

I started to feel a little cold, so I told Brett, Maya and Raj that I was going back to the ground now. I also wanted to check out the souvenirs that were being sold by the hawkers. I wanted to start buying some postcards, so I could post them on my free day. I thought it would be nice for Dad and Mark and my cousin Jenny to receive some Parisian post cards with a Paris post mark on them.

Brett offered to come with me, but I could tell he would much prefer to stay and keep looking out at the view, so I said that I'd be OK.

I went back down and wandered around underneath the Tower. It's actually quite pretty at the base. On one side you've got these beautiful parks, and the other, there's streets with lots of old, lit up buildings. There were plenty of other tourists milling around, and the hawkers wondering around them, trying to sell their wares. I bought a bunch of post cards and three Eiffel Tower key chains.

There were also artists, trying to sell you portraits of yourself. They were sitting on these small fold-away stools, with either charcoal or colored crayon type things. Some tourists sat, eagerly awaiting a personal masterpiece, while other artists approached you and tried to haggle with you. I was one of the tourists an artist approached.

"Madame moiselle, portrait of you?" he asked me. He looked to be either Chinese or some Asian descent. He asked me in an Asian accent, and not a French one.

"No, but thank you." I tried to politely decline and smile and walk away.

"Madame moiselle, portrait, under Eiffel Tower?" he started to follow me.

"No thank you." I shook my head.

"5000 francs? Portrait with Eiffel Tower?" he kept walking behind me.

"NO thank you!"

"MADAME! MADAME!" he started shouting at me!

"Allez-vous-en!!!" I freaked out and ran away!

I ran across the road, and a car screeched to a stop and honked at me!

I just got nearly hit by a car, trying to run away from an artist trying to hock a painting of me!

I ended up sitting on a seat in the park area by the Eiffel Tower, in the meeting place where we were to be picked up at the end of the evening. When everyone came back down from the Tower, and joined me, I didn't tell them what just happened. I thought it was kind of funny in a bizarre, and inconsequential way.

This morning we had to get up at 7 AM to dress and breakfast before catching the bus at 8 AM. All this room sharing with both Nelson and Maya has actually opened our eyes to each other's little idiosyncrasies. Maya and I had trouble sleeping last night because of Nelson's snoring. She snored really loudly! Maya and I ended up turning the light back on, and discussed if we should try rolling Nelson onto her side, to see if it would shut her up. So we did, and Nelson is such a deep sleeper, she didn't even wake up when we moved her! But then 15 minutes later she rolled back and started snoring again! Maya put her pillow over her head and I put my Walkman on to try and drown out the bloody noise. Now with this morning, Maya was in the bathroom for a full half hour! She had already showered in the evening, but then she wanted another shower. And then she took forever doing her hair and make-up. I woke up, busting to go to the toilet, and nearly having to wait half an hour to go! So I gave up and ran to Pat and Brett's room instead to use their bathroom.

Our tour began at Notre Dame Cathedral, where we got out to take photos and hear a little of the history. Nelson was absolutely fascinated by the three doorways of one end of the Cathedral, and the carvings of demons around one of the doors. I guess this goes with some of the Goth-ness about her. She took heaps of photos of the building's architecture and gargoyles sitting around the corners of the roof. I was interested to learn that they no longer have weddings inside the Cathedral, but still do funerals. And then we went around to the other end of the building, and took heaps more photos of the pretty gardens and took turns posing with each other.

We drove past the Louvre, where the bus dropped us off again. From here Madame Coultard and Monsieur Phillipe told us we would do a walking tour. So from the Louvre, we walked through these gardens to the Place de la Concorde, and then up along the Champs Elysees in the direction towards the Arc de Triomphe. On the Champs Elysees, we stopped for lunch at a café. We all had to greet the waiters in French and order in French.

"Est-ce que je pourrais avoir saumon fume et salade verte?" I asked the waiter, half from the top of my head, half reading from the menu.

"Oui, madame-moiselle." The waiter nodded, writing it down.

"What did you just order?" Nelson asked me.

"The smoked salmon and green salad, I hope." I said worriedly.

Luckily when our orders were brought out to us, I found I had ordered correctly.

After looking at the Arc de Triomphe and taking more photos, the bus picked us up again to show us the rest of the afternoon sights. We saw the Hotel de Ville, Latin Quarter, Les Invalides, Sacre Coeur and Montmarte.

The bus left us in Montemarte for two hours to give us time to look around and have afternoon tea in one of the many cafes. Here we split up from the rest of our class, and Maya, Raj, Nelson, Pat, Brett and I went and had a café au lait in an outside café. Well, most of us had a latte to enjoy, but Maya who doesn't like coffee, sipped on a cup of tea instead.

I was starting to feel a little relieved that we had split up again, so I could get away from Zack who had been giving me death stares all day. I mean, here I was, seeing one of the most romantic cities in the world, smiling into the camera like I was having the time of my life and posing with my friends. Then there was my ex-boyfriend in the background, looking like he was waiting for a huge boulder to fall on my head like in those 'Road Runner' cartoons. I'm glad he wasn't there last night when I was running away from that artist and I nearly got hit by that car... if he had been the one driving it I doubt he would have put on the brakes.

And yet, sitting there at our outside table, and looking around me at the beautiful trees and joie de vie atmosphere about us, it also made me miss Guy.

I wished it was just me and Guy sitting at the table, the two of us stirring our coffees and our feet touching together under the table. We could just stare dreamily into each other's eyes. I wished it was with he that I strolled down the Champs Elysees with, and we could have done it hand in hand. I wished it could have been with him that I was on top of the Eiffel Tower with last night.

Oh Guy... I miss you so much.

I don't know what happened here, or even if it could have been my imagination. But as I was staring off into the distance, the scenery about me started to change! All the other tables and chairs and customers started to fade away in a blurry fog.

The whole cafe environment suddenly vanished, and even the outside of the buildings around us changed and looked different!

Then there were people walking around in olden day clothes, in dresses and costumes from the 1700's!

As this blurry image started to refocus itself, I started to make out the faces of the people and not just the clothing they were wearing.

I suddenly picked out one face in the crowd.

Guy was walking in his Captain's uniform, looking older than when I last saw him, talking with another Naval officer.

He walked down the cobbled lane way, deep in discussion with the other man in uniform.

I watched him walk right past me, he was only just a meter away...I

He didn't see me! I wanted to call after him, to get his attention! But I felt like I was stunned. It wasn't just from the surprise of this new vision before me, but it was like I was in some kind of trance...

"Earth to Elisha, come in Elisha."

Suddenly a kick under the table jolted me out of my reverie. I realized it came from Nelson's foot. She started waving her hands in front of my face, and my vision through time quickly dissipated away.

"Wake up woman! Pat just asked you a question!" Nelson said curtly.

"You were far away then." Brett commented. "What were you just thinking about?"

"What?" I asked them all, snapping back to reality. I looked around at all the other tables, before looking back at my friends. Everything seemed back to normal again, well, except me.

"I said, do you want to go back to the Eiffel Tower on our free day, after we've gone to rue St. Honore, so we can look out at the view when it's day time?" Pat repeated his question.

"Huh? You guys didn't just see that?" I asked them in surprise.

"See what?" Brett asked me.

"I just saw this place as it looked two hundred years ago! I just saw Guy!" I told them excitedly.

"Yeah right." Nelson rolled her eyes.

"No, I'm serious! Suddenly there were no more cafes or tourists, and everyone was walking around in olden day clothes! And I saw Guy, looking older, walk past us!" I said. "You see that building there? That was painted yellow, and not blue!" I pointed, trying to prove it to them.

"Were you just thinking about him?" Pat asked me.

"Yeah. I was thinking about him, and then I saw him." I nodded.

"That's a pretty cool trick. You must have been concentrating on him pretty hard, so that your ability to see through time kicked in and focused on the time Guy was here." Pat agreed.

"But we can only see time as a reflection. There are no mirrors! Did you see all this in the reflection of a window?" Maya asked me.

"No, we can also see through the layers of time with out mirrors or windows." Nelson corrected her.

"What, you can too?" Maya asked her surprised.

"Sometimes." Nelson shrugged.

"But I didn't know that Guy would be here." I told everyone. "It was a fluke that I accidentally saw him."

"Oh great. Here we go, through another week of non-stop talking about Guy again." Nelson moaned, shaking her head at me.

"Well if it's anything like your snoring last night, you deserve it!" I retorted, and Maya snickered.

"I don't snore!" Nelson said indignantly.

"You snored so fucking loudly we tried to role you over!And then I had to sleep with my bloody Walkman on all night!" I bitched to her.

"It's true." Maya confirmed when Nelson looked at her next.

"Hey, let's go and ask the shop owner if the building has ever been yellow, or if they only just recently painted it blue. Then we'll know if Elisha really did see through time." Brett changed the subject to avoid the upcoming bloodshed.

When we had finished our drinks, we got up from the table and went inside the building that was now a shop to ask the owner our question. Luckily he understood English. So we asked him if the building was ever indeed painted yellow, and he pointed at a painting he had hanging behind the counter.

It was of Montmarte as it looked a hundred years ago. And the building that we were standing in, was indeed, yellow. He looked quite impressed at our knowledge of the past, and asked us how we knew.

"Lucky guess." Pat told him.

I gave Nelson a smug look, and she pulled a face back at me.

Later on in the afternoon, about 5 PM, the bus picked us all up again. We were driven back to our hotel. This evening we had our dinner on the Seine cruise so we all had to change into evening dress.

Again Maya took up the bathroom for half an hour for another shower and to wash her hair and do her make-up. I put on my jeans and my best top I had. I started to regret that I didn't own a nice evening dress. I hadn't bothered buying one to be honest since Mum died. Before she was diagnosed with cancer she would always take me shopping, and always insisted that I had a nice dress for special occasions. Well, being in Paris was a special occasion. I bet Mum would have been proud that I was here.

The cruise was wonderfully romantic. I noticed Maya let Raj sit close to her at the table and allowed him to pay her compliments on how she looked tonight. I even noticed Pat and Nelson sit kind of closely and Pat seemed to talk to Nelson quietly. But then it just left Brett and I to sit a little uncomfortably, since we didn't have a romantic partner that night.

I looked over to another table where Zack and Peter were sitting. They chatted away with Jordon, Numu, Soong, Wong and Yuichi. Well, Peter seemed to do most of the talking, and laughing at his own jokes. I accidentally caught Zack looking over at me and this time he didn't look at me with hatred, which surprised me. So as I was looking back at him in surprise, our eyes met and held.

Then he got up from the table and started to walk towards me! I quickly looked away from him and out the window at the sites we were cruising by, but then I accidentally knocked my fork off the table from my sudden turn. And then, when I had to reach down and pick it up from the floor, I raised my head too fast and I bumped my head on the bottom of the bloody table!

"Oow!" I yelped.

"Are you OK down there?" Brett asked me, trying not to laugh.

"Elisha, can I talk to you for a minute?" Zack asked, coming to stand closely behind me.

Suddenly our whole table stopped talking and everyone looked from me to Zack, and I realized Zack's table had done the same.

"Elisha, you don't have to if you don't want to." Brett now put his hand on my arm in a protective gesture.

"Stay out of this. This is between me and Elisha." Zack glared at Brett.

I saw Brett was going to say something else, but I didn't want this scene to get any bigger than it was turning out to be.

"It's OK." I told Brett, and then I stood up and followed Zack out of the dining area and out onto the open part of the back of the boat.

We stood awkwardly, and quietly for a few moments. Zack looked like he was trying to find the words to say, and I waited, feeling nervous, at what they might be. I was kind of hoping on hearing 'can we still be friends'. I didn't like being so alienated from him, especially in a school as small as ours.

"I heard you and this Navy Captain have broken up." He started with.

Now why wasn't I surprised that word of this had reached him? But I didn't like the fact that Zack brought it up. I certainly didn't want to talk about it with him.

"Yes." I said stiffly.

"Are you and Brett together now?" he practically accused me.

"What? No!" I retorted. "What kind of person do you think I am? I just move from guy to guy?" excuse the pun.

"So you're not dating anyone at the moment?" he asked me.

"No."

"Then do you want to get back together?" he asked me.

"What?!" I exclaimed. "I'm not just going to go running back to you because I was dumped! It would be wrong!"

"It would be wrong if you came running back." He agreed in a softer tone of voice. "But I'm asking you to come back."

"What?" I asked in complete surprise.

"It would be wrong if you asked me back out. So I'm asking you back out instead." He tried to take my hand.

"But - but..." I spluttered, instantly pulling my hand back. "I treated you like crap! You don't want me back! I'm a bitch!"

"Elisha, I love you. I don't care if it makes me look weak! I just want you back!" he tried to put his arms around me but I backed off from him.

"But think of what people will say..." I tried to reason with him.

"I just told you I don't care what people will think! I love you Elisha!" he repeated, as if this was the most important thing in the world.

Oh god, what do I do? I'm still seeing visions of Guy over café au lait in Montmarte, and here is my ex-boyfriend propositioning me? The irony of it all is, here I am daydreaming of the miraculous reunion between Guy and myself, the same way as Zack is still fantasizing about me.

"I'm sorry, Zack. But I'm still in love with Guy." I told him the truth.

"In love? You've only seen him three times!" he scoffed.

Actually, I had never thought of our time together in such a small dose. But whatever time we spent together was potent. Especially in India, when I was there for those couple of days.

"No Zack, I'm sorry. I don't want to hurt you, but I'm not in love with you." I shook my head.

He turned away angrily so I couldn't see his face. I suppose now I should probably go inside and make my escape. But I felt too guilty to just leave him out here. So I sat down on the side of the boat and waited.

"Go away." He said in a choked voice after a little while.

"No." I replied.

"FUCK OFF ELISHA!" he yelled at me.

Everyone turned and looked at us. Even the people sitting inside looked at us. But I stayed put. I clenched my hands into fists and decided that tonight we had to resolve this. I almost expected him to push me overboard next. But I knew in my heart I had to stay put.

"Please just go away." He said again.

"No."

"Why?!" he turned on me again.

"Because I think you need me just as I need you, as a friend." I told him. "And I want to apologize to you for deserting you. I didn't mean to. I wanted to end our romance, not our company. I miss hanging around you. I now know that I hurt you. I want to try to make it up to you."

"Do you really think we can be friends after what you did to me?" he spat at me, but I saw he was tearful.

"I don't know. But I want to try. Before we did get together romantically, we were friends before that. I know you've always wanted more than friendship, but remember what it was like when we hung out together with Sally? And we had some funny times studying together in the library, too, didn't we?" I smiled at him.

"I can't just turn off my feelings Elisha, like you seem to be able to switch them to another man." He sneered at me.

"You think I'm not hurting about Guy? Get this, I was missing him so much today, that over coffee I saw him walking through Montmarte! I am absolutely fucking miserable that the man I love and risked expulsion from school, running away from home, and even my own life, dumps me after I tell him I'm too young to marry!" I retorted.

"I don't want to hear about this Guy!" Zack snapped at me.

"I'm sorry. I won't bring him up again." I sighed. "Look, aside from the two of us getting back together again, what can I do to prove to you how sorry I am?" I asked, then quickly added, "Aside from me dropping dead?"

Zack glared at me for a few moments, probably thinking of other painful alternatives, when he finally said, "if you're really sorry, then jump into the river right now."

"OK." I started to untie my Doc Martins' boots.

"No, I really mean it." he said defiantly.

"OK, I believe you." I handed him my boots.

"And don't just put your feet in the water, but you have to completely jump in and get soaked." He continued.

"I know. That's kind of obvious when one does jump off a boat into a river." I said sarcastically and then I went and climbed over the small railing.

"Wait! What are you doing?" Suddenly Zack changed his mind and dropped my boots.

He rushed forward to grab me, when I beat him to the punch and fell backwards into the Seine!

Shit! Gees the water was cold and dark! I quickly resurfaced and waved at Zack as the cruise boat kept continuing down the river.

"ELISHA! ELISHA!" Zack yelled frantically, starting to take off his jacket and getting ready to jump in after me.

I watched the commotion on the boat as everyone suddenly left their tables and ran out onto the open area and pointed and yelled at me.

Fuck this water was cold! I didn't know what to do now... I hadn't exactly expected that I would be this stupid. I didn't think the boat would stop and turn back for me, so I started to swim for the riverbank.

Then to my surprise, Zack jumped in as well and swam towards me! I stayed in the one spot, treading water so he could catch up to me. And everyone started shouting and yelling about him too!

I started laughing... I couldn't help myself!

"Are you OK? Are you all right?" Zack asked me worriedly when he caught up with me in the water.

"Yeah! Of course I am! It's only water!" I laughed at him, but my teeth started chattering from the cold.

"Lets get out of here!" Zack stated and we both started to swim for the side.

"Zachary Reece! Elisha Baker! Where do you think you're going?!" Madame Coultard screeched at us from the boat.

"We'll meet you back at the hotel!" I called back to her, and waved good-bye to Nelson, Pat and Brett who stood outside, watching us.

"You pair of rejects!" Nelson called out after us, as she and Pat were laughing at us, while Brett looked worried.

Zack and I made it to the bank of the river and we clambered up the cement incline and onto the gravel footpath.

Once we were standing on solid ground again, we looked at each other... With our wet clothes sticking to us and the pools of water growing about our feet... We burst out laughing!

"Well at least this will be a night we'll never forget!" I chuckled.

"Yeah." He smiled back at me.

Then I sneezed and hugged myself from the cold.

"C'mon, lets get back to the hotel." He put his arm about me to warm me and we walked up to the main road to hail a taxi.

I realized it was a good thing that Zack came in after me, because I left my purse on the boat! And Zack had his wallet on him, so he could pay the taxi driver. But then I realized I didn't have my room key on me, so we went up to Zack's room instead.

He let me have first shower and leant me some clothes to temporarily wear, boxers and a T-shirt. Then he showered and put on the same thing. Then I laid under the covers in Peter's bed, as he laid under the covers of his bed. And we talked.

We talked and talked and talked for the next two hours, till everyone came back from the cruise.

It was almost like the old days again. We used to have some pretty good D & M's (deep and meaningful talks) in those days, and we had another one tonight. He told me how lost and hurt he was when I left him, and how depressed he got and had to have extra sessions with Nell. And then he even asked me about India, and I told him about my adventure... fighting off Commander Sleazy, meeting Clive of India, and then Circulate Headquarters. Of course I left out the romantic bits I had with Guy.

When everyone came back from the cruise, I went back to my room with Nelson and Maya. I may have cut my cruise and dinner short, but in my opinion, I kind of feel that I had an even better time than everyone else now. Maya was nice enough to return my Doc boots and purse to me, even though Nelson threatened she threw them in the river after me.

Right now Nelson is sound asleep, snoring even louder than she did last night. So I'm up, typing on you, as Maya is tossing and turning in bed, unable to sleep either. Even though Maya is a strict Hindu and probably believes in Karma or Reincarnation or in some kind of penance in the next life, I think she's probably very tempted right now to put her pillow over Nelson's head instead of her own tonight... LoL!

===

TO: s_parson@snailmail.com
FROM: ebaker_hamiltons@evers.com
SUBJECT: C'est la vie!
DATE: 21/ 08/ 01

Hey Sal,

I am writing this in gay Paree, just across the channel from you!

So far we've done the Eiffel Tower, and the outside tour of the city and even a Dinner cruise down the Seine. Also today we did a tour of the inside of the Louvre and the Musee d'Orsay. You know, taken around and shown the paintings and sculptures and stuff and told the history of the artists and the kinds of art, like impressionism… rah rah rah. I found it kind of interesting first, but by the end of the day I couldn't wait to get outside and away from the place.

I mean, it was nice to see all those expensive paintings to see what all the fuss was about. But while Madame Coultard kept going on and on about the time it was painted, and about the painter, I was ready to move onto the next picture. I did like the part of the Louvre with all the sculptures though. I liked the Venus de Milo, and the sculptures of the Greek gods. I found that part much more interesting. I've always been more into Greek mythology. And I love looking at the curves of the bodies and the power behind the carving. Like, almost lightening could have hit the rock and carved the beasts by the hand of God himself. I dunno, I guess I'm just dribbling shit. But I love pottery, and I love when we get to do clay sculpting in art class, which those sculptures reminded me of. There seems to be more of the artist in the sculpture, well that's my opinion anyway.

Sally, I've got to tell you something. Guy and I broke up. I guess it wasn't much of a relationship anyway, with the huge gap of time between us, with how we live in different time frames and even the difference between our ages. And I guess because of this is why he ended it. But I still love him, and I still think of him.

Yesterday I was sitting in Montmarte, in a café with Nelson, Pat, Brett and Maya. We were drinking lattes and relaxing after all the touring had finished. And I just seemed to drift off into space for a moment, and I saw him. I saw Guy, back in time.

It wasn't anything special, I just saw the way Montmarte looked in the 1700's, and I saw Guy walk past me, wearing his Naval uniform. He didn't see me. I wasn't, I don't think, officially back in time, I just had a vision back in time. He looked older than when I last saw him though.

I need to ask you another favor please Sally. I don't mind if I have to pay you somehow to make this happen. But I need you to please find out more information for me about Guy. I want to know what happens to him. I don't care what little insignificant points you find out, but anything you can scrape up would be greatly appreciated. Maybe your friend in London can check out any records in the Births, Deaths & Marriages? Please… anything you can find out for me… I need to know.

Would you like an Eiffel Tower paper weight? Or even a bottle of French perfume? Am willing to do anything (well – almost!) for what information you can find.

===

22/ 08/ 01

Diary,

Today we visited Giverny, Monet's home, and then we went on to Versailles for the tour inside and outside of the palace. I really enjoyed the trip to both places, but probably more so with Versailles. It was so unbelievably beautiful, it truly has to be seen to be believed… as well as seeing something, or someone, who is also beautiful to me, that my friends couldn't believe.

Giverny was OK. It was good to see where the artist did some of his work after seeing the actual work yesterday in the Musee d'Orsay. It was very pretty, especially with all of the flowers in the garden outside in bloom. I guess you could say it put it into perspective, and made the artist seem more real. Especially when you can see maybe where some of his inspiration came from. I wonder if his house and gardens looked like this when he was alive? If it didn't, then where did he get his inspiration? Maybe I should add this to my things-to-do list, of when I leave college with my phasing ability completely worked out, I'll visit this place again and maybe meet the painter himself?

But then after lunch when we did Versailles... it just blew all of these thoughts away! We saw the State Apartments with the Hall of Mirrors. And I thought Lady Caroline's gilt drawing room was impressive... but it was nothing compared to this! I wonder if she got her idea from the Hall of Mirrors?

This time I paid attention to Madame Coultard's history lecture as we walked through the rooms. There are so many Louis... I, V, XIV's and XVI's – it made me wonder why the French never bothered with any other different names than Louis to name their Kings? Like King Frank, perhaps? Or what about King Bob or King Tom, King Harry, or even King Dick? LoL!

"So you think perhaps that maybe Louis XVI's head wouldn't have been chopped off he had a name like Rufus or something?" Pat asked back, after I whispered to him and Nelson my idea on our tour.

"Maybe." I shrugged.

"It doesn't exactly sound French though." Maya gave me a funny look, over hearing our conversation and not getting the joke.

Nelson burst out laughing at Maya, which earned a dirty look from our teacher.

I instantly stopped talking after Madame Coultard gave us the look. I'm already on her bad side over jumping in the river. I guess I haven't mentioned yet that yesterday morning before we went on the Louvre and Musee d'Orsay tours Zack and I got a stern telling off over our shenanigans on the dinner cruise. So even when I got bored on part of the tours yesterday, I tried to look like a dutiful student who was paying attention. I even pretended to write down some notes, but what Madame Coultard didn't know, was that I were passing them to my friends.

It's good that Zack and I are friends again. He and Peter walked some part of the way of the tours with us. So when I was passing the notes around, Zack also had his pen and pad out, and passed some back to me. But what I couldn't figure out was why Brett seemed a bit distant or annoyed about something. I guess he doesn't like Zack and Peter that much, though I'm not sure why. So when we were sitting down at lunch, Zack and Peter still sat at different tables to us, which showed that the feelings were mutual. I wish I knew what was going on.

After the internal tour inside the former French court, we were allowed to split up and look around the gardens.

Brett and Maya went in one direction, Pat and Nelson went in the other direction, and I didn't see where Zack or Peter went. But it gave me some alone time, and it was a lovely warm day. So I found a quiet place to sit and admire the scenery around me.

It was nice to get a few moments alone since I've been around people constantly. If it's not Maya hogging the bathroom, or Nelson's cynicism and snoring, or Zack and I fighting or making up... I've hardly had any time to myself, except in the shower. And even then I can't shower for a long time without someone banging on the door to let me know my time is up.

I know it sounds pathetic, but I started thinking about Guy again. I hope Sally can help me find out more stuff about him. I want to know what happens to him. I just want to know that he's OK. I also started to wonder if I went back to Montmarte tomorrow on my free day whether I could see him again.

I started to stare off into space again.

As I was pre-occupied with Guy thoughts, my eyes had just rested upon one of the doors to the palace. I wasn't really looking at it, I was almost staring through it. And my vision became unfocussed and blurry as I thought about Guy.

Then it happened again.

Like what happens when I phase, when you stare into the reflection and what you see changes and goes all wavy and blurry, the gardens around me started doing the same thing! And when I focus on a bright light in the mirror or reflection, I noticed that the sunlight all around me seemed to go a little brighter and hotter. I felt like my eyes were starting to dry out and I fought against blinking, not wanting to break my concentration.

It happened a lot faster than it did in Montmarte. Almost instantly the tourists walking the gardens around me vanished to be replaced with new people. The jeans and T-shirts were replaced with long dresses and bonnets and long coats and powdered wigs. And the doors to the palace I had been staring into, now opened.

Guy in his Naval uniform walked through the doorway and instantly squinted from the bright sunlight. He was with the other Naval officer I saw him with from the last time. They both paused in their steps, heavy in serious discussion, before moving on again as a uniformed guard closed the doors behind them.

They were walking towards me now. I could hear the sound of their shoes crunching on the gravel path, winding in between the many rose bushes. I could start to hear their voices, and snatches of their conversation. I could see his face clearly, and even see that some of his hair was gray. He had some new lines around his eyes and mouth. But his dark eyes still held the intensity I remembered well.

Like in Montmarte, I felt like I was in a trance. I wanted to stand up, or shout, but I felt like I was super-glued to the spot. I could open my lips, but it was like my voice box had turned itself off.

He couldn't see me. I noticed no-one in the gardens notice me. Everybody carried on with no regard to me or the bench I was sitting on.

He was about to walk past, and I felt I had to do something.

I clenched my fists, and with all of my might, I struggled to stand up.

My legs wobbled, and I nearly fell forwards flat on my face! But I opened my mouth as wide, and I strained my voice box to yell as loudly as I could. I had to try three times before anything came out!

"GUY!"

Suddenly things changed.

He turned around in surprise and looked around.

"Guy!" I yelled a fifth time, waving my arms at him madly.

He still didn't see me, but he heard me. He heard me! Yes! He heard me!

"It's me, Elisha! I'm behind you!"

He looked behind himself, to the spot I was standing in, but he still didn't see me! He was looking right through me. He looked like he was in shock. I think my voice startled him.

But why is only my voice able to come across, and not me?

My eyes started to water, and everything became blurred, this time for good.

Instantly Guy and his companion vanished, the sunlight lost its brightness and returned to normal, and I fell crashing forward onto the gravel path.

The trance like state stayed on, and I felt like gravity had turned on me. I couldn't pick myself up, and I couldn't even move. I felt like I couldn't even breathe properly! I felt like this enormous pressure was pushing me to the ground. I felt so out of it, I wondered if I had even fainted?

"Elisha? Elisha? Can you hear me? Elisha?"

I wondered why I could hear Zack calling to me then.

I moaned my response, it was all I could do.

"Elisha, what have you done now, you stupid idiot?" I heard Nelson say crossly.

I was pulled off the ground as I felt four pairs of hands tried to stand me to my feet, but my legs gave way again.

"We're going to have to carry her." I heard Pat say. "I'll take her feet, if you want to carry her under the shoulders."

I suddenly felt really embarrassed. I didn't want to be seen carried out of Versailles! Shame!

"No..." I managed out. "I just need to sit down."

So Zack helped me sit back on the bench and they passed me a water bottle to take a drink from.

After 5 minutes my sight and some of my strength started to return to me.

"You tried to see him again, didn't you?" Nelson shook her head at me. "You're fucking hopeless."

"See who?" Zack asked her.

"Who else? Guy Robertson." Pat stated.

"You just tried to phase back in time?" Zack asked me in surprise.

"Nah mate, just see through time. She did that the other day." Pat told him.

"It looks like she tried to do more than that." Nelson guessed.

"I spoke to him... I tried to stand up, and he heard me, but he didn't see me." I uttered out. "It was almost like I could have phased. It was like I half-phased." I looked at Zack now. "Everything went bright and wavy, like when we phase."

Zack looked shocked. I think this news covered over the hurt he was probably feeling about me trying to see the other man in my life. He didn't know what to say, so Pat tried to explain it.

"But isn't that what you did in Montmarte?" Pat asked me.

"No, that was just staring off into space and then accidentally seeing through time. This was like when we phase, and things go bright and wavy, like the rippling of time. When things go wavy, it's time's ripples as we phase through time, like jumping into a pond." I told Pat and Nelson.

"Well it's a pretty stupid thing to do, trying to phase with out a mirror or window." Pat said.

"I didn't do it intentionally! It was an accident, just like Montmarte was an accident!" I snapped back at him.

"Maybe this place has displaced time pockets floating around. Remember a couple of years back there were these tourists here who claimed to have seen how this place looked hundred of years ago? They were walking around these gardens and suddenly they saw women in long dresses walking around too." Nelson offered an opinion.

"I remember reading that. It was in 1901 this happened, so it was more than a couple of years ago. And it happened in the Petit Trianon section of gardens." I nodded.

"Hang on, where did you guys find this out?" Peter now spoke up.

"It was when we were researching ghosts and hauntings in the library, funnily enough, the day of the fight. Remember when you didn't believe us and made fun of us and Nelson kicked the crap out of you?" I reminded him. "Then so did Zack."

"Nelson couldn't kick the crap out of anyone, even if she tried to." Peter said indignantly, still the sore loser.

Nelson was about to turn around and probably have another go when Pat suddenly stepped in between the two and tried to keep the conversation going to diffuse the situation.

"Do you realize that's exactly a hundred years ago this happened, to the time you mentioned? 1901 and 2001? We should probably go and check out Petit Trianon and see what happens."

"That sounds like a good idea." Zack agreed with him. "Can you walk now?" he asked me.

"Yeah." I sighed, not wanting to leave my seat. Also I knew we wouldn't find anything. I knew that what had just happened to me wouldn't be repeated. "Anyway, what's it going to prove? What's my nearly phasing got to do with a time pocket? I can already see through time with out a time warp to help me."

"It will explain how you felt like you could have crossed over. Don't you pay any attention in class? Instead of just using mirrors and windows all the time, we can use naturally occurring time warps." Peter said in a condescending manner.

Zack and I gave him a dirty look, and now I felt like hitting him! If it's anyone who doesn't pay attention in class, it's him! I think I liked it better when he stayed away when Zack and I were fighting.

When we got there, we didn't see anything out of the usual.

I was right.

At least we got to see the Petit Trianon gardens though. It was a miniature model town. It looked so cute and adorable! I almost wanted to jump over the perimeter and look inside and play with everything! I guess I still haven't gotten over my childish dolls house phase. I'll give it to Marie Antoinette... before she had her head chopped off, she had some good ideas inside of it occasionally.

==

TO: jeni_B@goggleyes.com
FROM: ebaker_hamiltons@evers.com
SUBJECT: Bonjour from France!
DATE: 24/ 08/ 01

Hey Cuz!

I'm writing this in Lyon, city of the popes. We've left

Paris and tomorrow we'll arrive in Nice. France is excellent! I posted all your postcards yesterday on my free day, along with a few souvenirs and stuff.

Paris has been wonderful. You know how you hear stories how the people are rude and everything…? Don't believe it. They've always been polite and helpful to me. I guess it's probably because I've always tried to use the language as much as possible. I mean, if a Japanese tourist walked up to you and asked you for directions in Japanese, you wouldn't have a clue what they were talking about, huh? So I think the French people appreciate it that you are learning their language.

We did all the sight seeing around Paris, including the sight seeing on top of the Eiffel Tower. The day before yesterday we went and saw Giverny, Monet's home, and after lunch it was Versailles (I took heaps of photos, you have to see how beautiful it is!). Then yesterday was our free day where we could get away from the teachers and do what we   wanted.

A group of friends and I went and checked out Rue St. Honore, an expensive shopping district. It had lots of labels and couture houses. I bought Patrice, Mark's girlfriend, a bottle of Chanel No. 5, and I bought one for you and Tina and Aunt Gabby to share too. I also bought a bottle for me. And one shop was having a sale to get rid of last season stock, so I bought this really nice little black dress. I don't have any nice evening dresses, so it was kind of necessary. And I even bought a bikini! It's brown and cut in this classic kind of style and I love it! It will be perfect to wear on the beach at Nice on our next free day. I guess you'll see it when I wear it on the beach next Christmas when I come home for a week.

Then last night we all went to the Moulin Rouge for a dinner and show. And the Moulin Rouge had the windmill sitting on top, just like in the movie with Nicole Kidman and Ewan McGreggor! And the dancers did the Can Can for us. It was so cool! I had the Can Can tune from the movie in my head though, and I could almost hear Harry Ziggler shout out, "Because you can can can!" We weren't allowed any wine or champagne though with our meal, but our teachers had a glass or two! I thought that was a bit unfair. I bet the boys in our class probably enjoyed the experience more than the girls! LoL!

This morning when we left Paris and started the drive down to Lyon, we visited Fontainebleau Chateaux. It's a castle which was apparently the favorite residence of the Kings of France, including the Emperor Napoleon. So we looked around the outside at the gardens and inside of the castle. I saw Napoleon's apartments, which were quite luxurious looking. I'm surprised the fat little Italian wasn't just happy to live there, but instead kept invading other countries and warring with England. I bet Josephine would have been comfortable there before he kicked her out for the Austrian princess.

Anyway, I have to go. It's time for dinner in the hotel's restaurant. Hopefully it won't take too long for you to get the postcards and package I sent to you. If you see my Dad, let him know that his postcards and package are on their way too, OK?

==

26/ 08/ 01

Diary,

Yesterday we did the tour of the Palace of the Popes, before driving on to Nice. It was OK, though to me it was nothing special. Maybe because I'm not Catholic, but a Protestant. I learned something new about Zack though, he is Catholic. He seemed really interested in learning the history. It's weird how I only just learned this now, and how it never came up before. I guess in this day and age religion isn't such an issue as it was before. Well, excluding the Middle East anyway.

Zack and Peter are hanging out with us more now, which is good. Well, good to hang around Zack again, but not Peter. He is such an dickhead! Before we got on the bus yesterday morning and Zack wanted to sit with us for the ride down, he started arguing with Zack that he shouldn't be talking to me let alone hanging out with me again. It's funny, he hates his bestfriend's 'ex' more than the actual bestfriend does. I guess Peter hasn't forgiven me for the way I treated Zack. Personally, I don't blame him. But when we stopped for lunch, he even made snide comments about how Pat and Nelson have been hanging together a lot.

I think Peter is jealous of Pat, and it reminded me that Peter might like Nelson more than he lets on. The reason why this reminded me, was because Sally was jealous of Nelson because she likes Peter. And what I don't get, was with the fight in the library last year, Peter actually hit Nelson back when she went ape-shit over him teasing us about the ghost business. I'm glad Nelson and Pat are slowly getting together, I think Pat will be a lot better for her than Peter would ever be.

Zack and Brett, as well as Peter and Brett still aren't talking. I wish I knew what was going on there. I know Peter and Brett stopped talking after that whole drugs episode, but I don't know what the deal is with Zack and Brett. What happened yesterday, was if I was talking to Zack, Brett would go off and talk to Maya and Raj, who are another couple forming. Then if Brett and I were talking about something, then Zack wouldn't come over until he saw that Brett had moved away. Then Brett would then stay away because Zack had come over! It's getting ridiculous!

What is this, fucking 'Melrose Place'??

Today wasn't any better. We did our tour of Nice and saw Castle Hill, the Chagall and Matisse Museums, Queen Victoria's winter palace, the Franciscan Monastery and Roman ruins, Promenade des Anglais and the Old Town. I was trying to balance spending time with both Zack and Brett. I felt like I was stuck in the middle coz the newly formed couples of Pat and Nelson went off together, and so did Maya and Raj, which left Brett and I flying solo and single, along with Peter and Zack. And to make matters worse, Peter then walked off to hang with Yuichi, Soong and Wong, abandoning Zack to just hang with Brett and me.

As we were exploring the Roman ruins after lunch, all I wanted to do was enjoy the lovely sunny day, and admire the view of the beautiful turquoise Mediterranean sea. At first both guys were quiet. I tried to lighten the mood with a few jokes, which didn't work. You know how when you're in an awkward situation, you end up dribbling shit because you don't know what to say? Well, this was one of those horrible moments.

"I can't wait until we're on the beach tomorrow. Won't it be nice to sunbake and swim in that sea?" I commented.

Silence.

"I wonder what makes the water so blue. I wonder if that's kind of blue around Greece too?"

Silence.

"It's pretty warm here. I wonder how cold it gets in winter?"

Silence.

I gave up, and said in exasperation, "well, say SOMETHING! It doesn't have to be much! You can even tell me to shut up if you want to!"

"You mean you were asking us a question? I thought you were just making an observation." Brett shrugged.

"It was both." I said annoyed.

"I don't know what color the water is around Greece." Zack said moodily.

I'd had enough. I turned around and confronted both of them. "Look, I don't know what it is between the two of you. But we're on a holiday. H-O-L-I-D-A-Y. It's supposed to be fun! Would you please relax and enjoy yourselves and just ... I don't know... move on?"

The two just looked from me to each other, and back to me again.

"I am having fun." Brett shrugged dismissively.

"No you're not." I glared at him, putting my hands on my hips.

"You're telling us to move on?" Zack asked me incredulously. "You could give yourself the same advice."

"What?"

"We've been here for a week, and it's already been twice that you've seen your ex-boyfriend. You nearly knocked yourself unconscious just to fucking see him! Why don't you follow your own advice you hypocrite!" Zack said angrily at me and started to walk off.

"Don't call her the hypocrite you wanker! Why the fuck are you hanging around then? Why the fuck did you ask her back out?" Brett shouted back at Zack.

Zack instantly whirled back around and charged at Brett.

"Wait! Wait! This is my fault!" I instantly jumped between the two of them and held up my hands in a surrender gesture. "I'm sorry I brought this up, OK? I'm sorry."

"You don't have to apologize for anything. He's the one who should apologize!" Brett accused Zack.

"What fucking for?" Zack shouted back at him.

"We all know what you did. We all know what happened that night in the Cafeteria." Brett glared at him.

This took both Zack and I by surprise.

"What? How?" I asked lamely. "I mean, what do you think happened that night in the cafeteria?"

"He attacked you! You had bruises on your neck for a week!" he said angrily. "We were all trying to decide if we should report him in. I said we should have, but Nelson said that you didn't want to."

Damn. I really didn't want anybody to know. I suddenly felt really angry at Nelson. "Did Nelson say something to you?" I demanded.

"Don't be stupid! Why the fuck would anyone wear a woolen turtleneck jumper in the middle of summer? And it was pretty obvious when Nelson and Pat started studying in the Caf at night while you were sanitizing dishes." Brett said to me. "They were guarding you from HIM!"

Suddenly I didn't know what to say. Neither did Zack. Brett looked like he could have said a few more words, but decided to keep his mouth shut.

Zack then turned around and started to walk off again.

I didn't know what to say to Brett now. I ended up walking away in another direction. I was feeling pretty upset. I think I was feeling a mixture of embarrassment, shame, guilt and anger. I needed some time to myself.

I went and sat on the grass in the shade away from all the tourists. I could feel my eyes start to sting and get watery, but I didn't want to cry. I didn't want anyone to see me upset.

Brett came and sat next to me, but right at that moment, I wished he would go away.

He didn't say anything. He just sat down and started to pick at the grass around his feet. It was one of those heavy silences where the other person wants to say something, but doesn't know how.

After five minutes, I blurted out, "look, I know I seem like this weak, selfish person. But I just felt really bad at how I treated Zack. I know I was being selfish, but I just completely fell for this other guy, and I broke Zack's heart. And I know it seems weak that I let Zack get away with what he did in the Cafeteria... but you don't know what Zack went through in his childhood. I know, and yet I still hurt him. He's been hurt very badly, possibly in one of the worst ways a child can be hurt... he's still only coming to terms with it."

"I didn't come and sit here to talk about Zack." Brett now smiled at me, and to try to lighten the mood he threw some grass at me.

"Then why are you here? I'm sure there are less fucked up people out there you could be hanging with instead." I tried to joke back to him.

"Hey, compared to Sophie, you're doing pretty good." Brett smiled at me again.

"What was wrong with Sophie?" I asked him. Remember Sophie? She was Brett's friend who left the college after that infamous night we all learned about our gift, along with two other students, which included Sally.

"Sophie had schizophrenia." Brett said matter-of-factly. "Her ability to see through time as well as her delusional paranoia were closely linked together. She didn't just leave Hamilton's College to go back home, but right now her parents have thrown her into a mental institution."

"What? No way! How do you know this? Why hasn't Hamilton or Dr. Knight done anything about this?" I asked, suddenly angry in empathy of poor Sophie's situation.

"Well, when they invited her to come to this college, she came straight out of a mental institution. Dr. Knight and the school counselor Nell Kennard were treating her schizophrenia. They knew that not all of Sophie's delusions only existed in her mind. But unfortunately, when they tried to tell her this, it only made her condition worse." Brett sighed.

"Are you still in contact with Sophie?" I asked him.

"Yeah, we write. She's not allowed access to the Internet or the phone. And even then I think her letters are opened and read before she can get them. So I have to be very careful what I write. We've practically made up a secret language so who ever reads the letters, only Sophie and I know what it really says." He laughed.

"Really? Like, give me an example." I asked, fascinated.

"Well, when I tell her about some of the classes we have on time manipulation, I tell her that today Barney the Purple Dinosaur did his happy dance in an anti-clockwise circle today."

We both burst out laughing.

"Yeah. I'm still in contact with Sally. I email her very descriptive explanations of my classes to her. I guess I'm trying to woo her back." I sighed. "Do you think Sophie could come back?"

"I don't know." He sighed and leaned back on his hands. "But she's got an amazing ability. I bet if she had stayed she probably would have been a Circulator."

"Yeah, I know. And Sally would have been a Calculator." I nodded.

"Did one of the teachers tell you this?" he asked me.

"Yes."

"Did you know that Sophie can even 'see' what she's going to do the next day, or events that will happen? Like ESP, in a way. She has prophetic dreams too. That night when we got sprung for nearly doing drugs the night of the Halloween party, Sophie had a dream of seeing the ghost of Dr. Kell. So when we started to hear the odd noises, she knew what was coming. That's why we left before Peter did."

"Peter said you left in a hurry." I said to him. "But what are her delusions? Why is she schizophrenic?"

"Whenever she sees a vision in time, she thinks it's out to get her." Peter told me.

"Yeah, well, what we see can be pretty scary. I mean, we only just learned that we weren't seeing ghosts, but people manipulating time." I pointed out.

"Yeah, but when she had the dream that Dr. Kell would be arriving in his Roman Centurion uniform, and then we later learned he would be one of our teachers... Sophie saw him as a demon coming to attack her. That's what scared her out of her wits and made her run as soon as she heard the first noise. Everything Sophie sees, are demons or monsters coming to get her. Dr. Knight and Counselor Kennard and even Professor Hamilton tried to reason with her for hours on end. They tried to tell her that what she saw were harmless visions through time. But it was like telling a brick wall that it is a brick wall and not a tree."

"And she's still having these visions?" I asked him.

"Yeah. In her letters she tells me about them. If it's a harmless vision, she writes that she had a dream about Mickey Mouse. If she has a scary one, which she frequently does, she tells me in her dream she's being chased by Snow White's evil Stepmother. If she dreams that something will happen to me, then she says 'Pluto was chased last night by the Stepmother'."

"So you're a Disney cartoon incarnation of a dog, huh?" I joked. "Has any of her dreams about you come true?"

"Yeah, a couple. When I left for home at Christmas time last year, my brother and I nearly had a car accident. I remembered her telling me about the dream a month earlier, so I knew to grab the wheel and turn left instead of right." Brett tried to shrug it off.

"No way!" I said in disbelief and impressed at the same time. But all this talk about Sophie helped me piece a few more pieces of the puzzle together. "You know how I went through that week where I thought the teachers were going to put drugs in the food? Well, now I realize they could have been talking about putting Sophie on medication, because they said the counseling wasn't working. And when Peter was nailed on the drugs scandal, Hamilton did say that Sophie was on medication and the drugs you guys were about to do would have made her overdose. I'm surprised Sophie didn't foresee that."

"Well, Sophie was already on medication before you thought the teachers were going to drug us. They were talking about upping the dosage. And when Sophie thought that Roman Centurion was going to attack her, and she was going to die, she dreamed she wasn't going to be impaled on his sword or anything, but he was going to poison her." Brett raised one of his eyebrows and gave me this knowing look.

"So, she did dream that she was going to overdose, and it had something to do with the Roman Centurion. Only instead of it was Dr. Kell's interruption making you run away and it saved her life, but her schizophrenia made out he was the bad guy." I smiled, getting the idea.

"That's it." Brett said.

"Were you guys just friends, or were you going out?" I asked, already half-guessing the answer.

"We still are going out." He said simply.

"Did you know each other before College?" I asked him next, suddenly feeling very curious about this Romeo and his Juliet.

"No, but I don't live too far from the Institution she's in. So whenever I go home now, I try to see her." He shrugged.

Wow. Brett has surprised me yet again. Here I was, thinking he was a complete arsehole a few months ago... and here he is, the champion of beaten women and the insane. I never expected I'd have a conversation with him like this back in January.

29/08/01

Diary,

I'm back on the plane, with three hours to go before we touch down in Thunder Bay.

France was wonderful. I had the most amazing time, with sights that you just had to see to believe, with even the unbelievable happening. I never expected to see Guy again so soon... even if it was just me seeing him and him not seeing me. I emailed Sally a couple of days ago and asked her to try to find out more stuff on Guy for me, for I'd like to know what happens to him. I still haven't heard from her. I hope she's not getting pissed off at me for always asking her to do these things. I hope I can return the favor for her one day, maybe when I'm a Circulator and she needs to be taken to a certain place or time.

My last day in France was excellent! It was our free day in Nice with an evening meal in Monaco. So I got to try out my new bikini on the beach, as well as my new little black dress that I bought in Paris. It was nice hanging out on the beach and sunbaking and swimming, and it was fun to dress up for the dinner in Monaco. Even Nelson, who's usually my worst critic said I looked nice! Maya and I were so shocked at the compliment coming from her, I joked, "Oh quick Maya! Run for the hills! Hell just froze over!"

Since that blow up at the Roman ruins, Zack has been staying away from me again. This must make Peter happy, surely. But what makes me happy which also makes Peter unhappy, is that Nelson and Pat are officially together now! I'm really happy for Nelson, even though I feel a little sorry for Pat. Today on the beach, I noticed Pat and Nelson go for a walk together and Pat tried to hold her hand, but she still pulled away from him. I guess she's going to take a while to thaw and let the mushy stuff come back into her life. But Maya and Raj look like the cute couple. They've been hanging out together incessantly and always holding hands. Raj pulls her seat out for her and opens the door for her... which I think is really romantic. But from the way Maya acts is if she expects this – and even yesterday afternoon when Raj bought drinks for them both when we were on the beach – I have a feeling that Maya is going to be a 'high maintenance' kind of woman and keep Raj busy!

All this separation and joining of people have kind of pushed Brett and I together... but only as friends! We hung out yesterday on the beach with the other singles left in our class, Soong, Jordon, Numu and Darianne. It's kind of weird how everyone else has just coupled together... but I guess in a school as small as ours, and even a year that's tinier with only 18 students, it doesn't give us much room to be choosy. And then at the dinner in Monaco, Jordon and Numu sat at a table with Peter and Zack. Peter did the same thing in Monaco as he did on the dinner cruise in Paris, laughing at his own dirty jokes and was a loud-mouthed idiot. Does he really think this behavior impresses girls? I don't know what Sally sees in him.

===

30/ 08/ 01

Diary,

I just learned something really strange from Brett, and even about Brett. It's kind of disturbed me. It came up in a conversation on the bus ride back to school today. At first it was about Sophie, then it became about Brett.

Brett and I were sitting together on the bus and we were playing cards with Nelson and Pat. I made mention that I never expected in January that I would be hanging out with Brett so much, and that he would turn out to be a really cool guy. Brett asked me why did I say that, and Nelson in her usual tactful manner stated he had been such an arsehole for the first half of semester.

Brett didn't take offense, and he even laughed! He asked if he had really been that bad. Pat said yeah, he had been sometimes. So I asked him next why he and Sophie hardly hung out with many of the other students, besides Pat sometimes.

"Well, she was scared of a few of them." Brett confessed.

"Scared?" Pat chuckled. "Of who? Of Nelson when she's in one of her moods?" he immediately flinched expecting his girlfriend to hit his arm, which she did in true Nelson style.

"Sophie had schizophrenia." I blurted out, then I realized what I had just said. "Sorry Brett!" I wasn't sure if it was meant to be kept a secret or not, bad luck if it had.

Pat and Nelson looked from me, to Brett in surprise.

"Yeah she did." Brett sighed. "And still does."

"They were talking about upping her medication because the counseling wasn't working, that was when I thought they were going to put drugs in the food." I said to them, as if to say, 'see, I didn't make the whole thing up'. "And that's why Hamilton said to Peter that night, that if Sophie was already on drugs and if they took the other drugs they were going to do, she could have overdosed."

"Ooohhh…" they both said in a unison of understanding.

"Well who was she afraid of then?" Nelson asked.

"Oh, just a couple of people." Brett said dismissively. "Is it my turn to deal?"

"No way! You have to tell us the rest of this now!" Nelson immediately snatched the cards from him and we all looked at him in anticipation.

"No, I don't think you should know." He looked out the window at the passing forest.

"C'mon mate. We've started this tale, we might as well finish it." Pat pressed him.

"Well actually, she was afraid of Nelson." Brett said at first.

"Ah ha! Thought so! Nelson, you could scare a mugger away in dark alleyway!" I burst out laughing at her, and Pat joined in as Nelson rolled her eyes at us.

"But she was more terrified of you." Brett looked at me next.

Now it was Nelson's turn to laugh and wave her finger at me. "What were you saying, Freddy Krueger? How is Elm Street looking tonight?"

"Me?" I asked incredulously. "Why me?"

"Why Nelson?" Pat asked him next.

Brett went quiet again and looked back out the window. He really didn't want to talk about this, I could tell. But when somebody tells you that a gifted person who has amazing premonitions, even if she is a little on the nutty side, is afraid of you... I think you should find out why.

"Fine." Nelson gave up on waiting for Brett's answers. "I'll deal."

She started shuffling the cards and was about to deal them out, when I asked him next, "did she have a dream or a vision about us?"

"Dream? Vision? You mean she saw something ahead in time?" Nelson tried to correct me.

"Sophie didn't need windows or mirrors to see through time, like you and I don't always need them. And geography doesn't seem to be an issue either. She has visions and dreams of people no matter where they are. And they always come true." I said seriously now.

"Then why is she schizophrenic if her hallucinations are real?" Nelson asked us next.

"Because she interprets what she sees as demons and monsters coming to get her." I told her.

"Well in that case, I'm not worried if she's afraid of me." Nelson shrugged and then started to deal the next game.

Nelson may have been able to diss this, but I couldn't.

"Brett, please tell me." I asked him worriedly, but he ignored my request and picked up his cards to study them. "In the dream, is it a Snow White's Evil Stepmother kind of dream? Am I Minnie Mouse, getting chased by the Evil Stepmother? Does it involve Barney the Purple Dinosaur dancing in an anti-clockwise motion?"

"What the fuck?!" Nelson looked at me as if I had gone crazy.

"All of the above." Brett said flatly, still not looking at me.

As I was contemplating his words, I then had a realization of my own.

"That's why as soon as Sophie left the school you came over to us in the Library and asked to hang out. You could of gone and hung out with Yuichi or Wong or Jordon or Raj or anybody else... but you came over to our table in the library, sat down, and asked us to hang out from now on. It was because of what Sophie has told you, isn't it? And then when Zack, Peter and Nelson were complete arseholes to you, you then offered to help me with my homework and we became friends that way! And when I broke up with Zack and ran away from school and went back in time in India, and came back to school... you were the only one who acted like it was OK, and you were even supportive of me, because you knew this was going to happen!" I grew louder as I grew angrier, as all of this came to me.

Pat and Nelson exchanged funny looks before giving me the same expression, probably wondering what I was dribbling on about now.

"And when I started having my dance lessons for my first excursion in time, you volunteered to help me! You knew I would meet and fall in love with Guy! And you knew we would break up! And you know something else but you're not telling me! Did Sophie tell you all of this? What are you not telling me?!"

The whole bus had turned silent and everyone was watching us, intrigued by the show.

"And when I saw Guy in Montmarte, you weren't surprised! You believed me! You even suggested that we find out if the building was yellow to prove that I was right! But you weren't there with me in Versailles when I saw Guy a second time, when I almost phased myself there by accident! You were off with Maya and Raj! You didn't see that happening, did you? Or hasn't Sophie told you about that yet?" I demanded.

"She did actually. Which is why I knew I had to leave you alone so you could almost phase yourself back in time with out the aid of any mirrors, windows or water." Brett casually put down his cards and looked me square in the eyes. "Yes, I know your past, present and future Elisha. I know it well. You are important to us Elisha Baker. With your ability, you become the strongest one of all."

The way that he said that... the way he looked at me then... I had seen this expression on his face before ...the same way I had heard these words before... only then I thought it was a different person.

The whole class watched us, fascinated, waiting for my response now. But I couldn't look away from his eyes. His familiar blue eyes, now young and wrinkle free. I knew I should have connected the two together by the voice, but even that was slightly different, and with a different accent. How could I have not known until now??

"Lucas Hodge...?" I managed out in shock.

He didn't reply. He didn't need to. He just sat there calmly, looking back at me.

"Who?" Nelson asked me, then she looked at Pat. "Who did she just call him?"

"Lucas Hodge is Lead Counselor of the Circulate Council." Pat said in a deadpan voice, sitting in awe of what just took place.

"So why did Elisha just bring his name up?" Nelson said confused and irritated. "And how the fuck do you know who's head of this Council?"

"Because I met him when I was first brought to Hamilton's College." Pat said uncomfortably. "And he's sitting in front of us now."

"Where?" Nelson looked behind Brett/Lucas and myself.

"Right in fucking front of you! He's Lucas Hodge!" Pat lost his patience and stabbed his finger in the air at Brett's/Lucas's head.

"Oh... fuck me." Nelson said in shock.

"But... but... you said you went home this Christmas and you and your brother..." I remembered the story told to me back at the Roman ruins.

"I didn't tell you what time frame that happened in, now did I?" Lucas now smiled at me.

"Wait a minute..." I said, still baffled. "Are you the old Lucas who I met? Or are you a young Brett who later turns into Lucas? And if you know so much, why are you still in school?"

"I've come through Hamilton's College several times. In fact, this is my third time. And I know what you're going to ask me next, so let me just give the answer to you. I come to befriend students to offer my help and guidance as much as I can. I tried to help Sophie, but now I realize that any assistance I try to offer to her now in this stage of development is useless. So I then turned my help to you. You're a strong young woman Elisha, even if you don't think so. You just needed a little nudge now and again." He gave me an even bigger grin and patted my hand.

Another realization swept over me now, and all my anger and confusion and surprise were now replaced with just one emotion... sadness.

"You're leaving now, aren't you?"

"Can you see any point of me staying on? My ruse is over. And if I did stay on at the college, don't you think it might look a little peculiar, a man in my position, openly attending Junior year classes?" he joked. "My period of time here has been drawing to a close, which is why I told you about Sophie back at the Roman ruins in Nice and gave you those clues just now. I had faith in your abilities to work this out for yourself."

"So when will I see you again? Will you be the old Lucas, or the young Brett? Will it be when I graduate from College and can freely travel to Circulate Headquarters?" I asked him.

"Elisha, do you really think that you'll behave so well that it will be after College?" he winked at me. "Now seriously, please take this last piece of advice that is offered from a friend. Listen to your teachers, and let them guide you. We in the council didn't appoint idiots or zealots to guide our next and last generation of the Circulate. Trust in this, and in yourself."

Just as Brett/Lucas said these last words, the young image of Brett slowly started to turn see-through and then disappear, with out having the need to pass through the glass of the window beside him. But in the last second before he was gone for good, I saw his shape change, back into the form of when I first saw him... as the older Council Leader Lucas Hodge. And then with out any bright flash of light, but still our skin tingled from either the creepiness of seeing somebody fade away or an electrical charge in the air, he was gone.

Huh? What just happened then? I can't believe all of that just happened then!

The whole bus was silent, with everybody either kneeling on their seats or standing up in the aisle for a closer look to see where Brett might had vanished to.

Our whole class... Peter, Zack, Maya, Raj, Jordon, Numu, Yuichi, Wong, Soong, Darianne, Rosa, Paulo, Jose... and everyone else, all looked about us, at each other. We could see the shock of what just happened written on all of our faces. We were all too dazed and in awe of what just happened. To discover one of our own was one of them? And to discover that even you will eventually become one of them?

I guess in the past few months, when we learned about the Circulate and these gifts that were supposedly inside of us, it still seemed far-fetched somehow. But what everyone just witnessed on the bus just then, made it seem very much more real. And learning that you had classes with the Lead Counselor in the Circulate Council? It made having icy water thrown in your face look like jumping under a warm shower.

"This trip home will probably be more memorable than the actual trip itself." Pat said after a while, breaking the stunned silence.

"Well he was a dirty old man then." Nelson suddenly said, surprising us all again.

"What? Why?" Pat nearly half choked, and half chuckled at the same time with some of the things Nelson comes up with.

"He was 50 year old bonking a 16 year old girl!" she said indignantly, inferring Sophie.

"Somehow I don't think it was quite that way." Pat tried not to laugh at his girlfriend.

Ah yes, Sophie. Poor Sophie who everyone tried to help, but no-one was able to. Schizophrenic, highly talented Sophie, who was scared of me for more reasons than one. And they involved Disney characters and commercialistic childhood icons.

Then I just realized something else. "Hey, he left with out telling us about Sophie! He left with out telling us the reasons why Sophie is so afraid of us!"

"Don't worry Elisha. If you're so special and I'm so scary, maybe we can join forces. While I mug people in dark alleyways, you can then kill them and hang the bodies out in Elm Street." Nelson sighed and picked up the cards again.

===

31/08/01

Diary,

We got back to school yesterday at around 8 PM. Even though the Caf had stayed open late to serve us dinner, I wasn't hungry. After all that had happened, I wanted to have some alone time. I wanted to write everything down immediately as it was fresh in my mind. So my last entry is a true and accurate account of all that happened on the bus ride home yesterday.

Now that I think back on it all, and remember everybody's responses... two people's reactions now come to mind the most.

Madame Coultard and Monsieur Phillipe didn't even bat an eye-lid to Brett's revelation and ruse. No blinking, no flinching, not even a raised eyebrow. In fact, they even exchanged a knowing look once it was all over and Brett/Lucas had disappeared. And then when the driver was unloading the bus of all the luggage... they simply grabbed Brett's bag and carried it over to Alpha building.

Then this morning, I noticed Brett's door to his room was open. When I looked inside, I found it was empty. After I went inside for a closer examination, I found it was completely empty, with just a bare mattress sitting on the bed frame and a desk chair sitting at an empty desk. I even opened the cupboard for a look... and found nothing. There wasn't even rubbish left behind, and the room even looked like it had been cleaned and dusted and polished.

It's almost like the school was trying to erase any proof that might be left behind that Brett/Lucas had ever been here.

I thought it was time to have another conversation with Professor Hamilton.

As everybody crossed over to Gamma building for breakfast in the Cafeteria, I instead took a longer route and went into Alpha building.

I went up the stairs to the teacher's offices, and found Professor Hamilton's office door open, with both Professor Hamilton and Nell seated inside. I suddenly felt like they were expecting me, as their eyes were immediately upon me as soon as I showed up in the doorway. They didn't seem to mind my intrusion, in fact, they were smiling.

"Elisha, come in. You're right on time." Professor Hamilton nodded to the empty chair in front of his desk, as Nell occupied the chair next to it.

"I am?" I said in surprise, taking my seat.

"You're here to ask about Lucas, are you not?" Hamilton asked me.

"Well, yeah, I am." I said in further surprise.

"We thought you would have some questions for us." Nell smiled warmly to me. "We knew you wouldn't be able to wait and find out."

"Are you saying this because of my past history for investigating things... or because you or Lucas foresaw this?" I asked them both.

"All of the above." Hamilton next smiled knowingly.

"OK..." I tried to sort my mind out to function in a logical manner and produce the first question. There was just so many things I wanted to know at once, I had to choose which one I wanted to ask first. "Where's Brett's stuff? Why is it all gone? He's not coming back for it himself?"

"Material possessions are not important to Lucas. Besides, his wardrobe and personal items that helped along his ruse as Brett are no longer required. They have been put into storage until he needs them next." Hamilton answered.

"Will he be coming back to this school as Brett to help another student out?" I asked them next.

"Possibly not. Since we won't be having a Freshmen year ever again at Hamilton's College, and since we will be closing down after the now Sophomore year then graduates after Senior year; and everybody knew who Brett is or was, there is no need." Hamilton said.

"Where is Lucas now? Back at Circulate Headquarters?" I asked them.

"Possibly. We don't know Head Council member's Hodge's itinerary. He may be there, or he may be somewhere else. Elisha, can I ask why that is important to you?" Nell asked me back.

"Because he left with out telling me more about Sophie!" I said exasperated. "I need to know!"

"What do you need to know about Sophie, Elisha?" Hamilton asked me, his smile gone and now he and Nell looked quite serious.

"Why was she so afraid of me?"

"Who told you she was afraid of you?" Nell asked me.

"Brett! No, I mean, Lucas!" I rolled my eyes in frustration and started from the beginning. "Ever since I came to this college, Brett and Sophie never talked to me. Then when Sophie left, Brett came over and started hanging out with us next. I see now that it was because Lucas was helping me out of a difficult period. But he couldn't talk to me before when Sophie was around because she was afraid of me. She had either a vision or a dream about me that made her afraid of me. I want to know what it is."

Nell and Professor Hamilton exchanged a long look, before returning back to me.

"I'm afraid we can't answer that question for you Elisha." Hamilton said.

"Can't or won't?" I replied. I had a flashback of my mother asking me that same question once when I tried to tell her once that I couldn't live with out her. *"Can't, Elisha? Or won't?"*

"Sophie has schizophrenia, which you know about. We can no more explain her delusions than we can explain what part of the brain has turned her visions of time into monsters coming to get her. Sophie is very ill, which is one of the reasons why she left this college." Hamilton told me.

"But we're learning to control these visions. Why can't we just teach her the same thing?" I asked them.

"When you first saw through time, what did you think you could see? Ghosts?" Nell asked me, knowing the answer. "But through logic, rationalization and learning, you realized that what you were interpreting as dead people, were alive people living in the past, or traveling to the past. Not even everyday people can handle this fact. Now if a person whose brain that wasn't functioning properly were given these facts, do you think that this person would understand the same conclusion the same way as you?"

"But surely in the future where the Circulate Headquarters exists, there is a cure for schizophrenia?" I asked them next.

"It's true that our medical progression in that time frame is far ahead when compared to today's standards. But unfortunately schizophrenia is still an illness that is very much in the dark in the way of 'cures'." Nell told me. "The medication we had her on here at college was working better than the medication she was on before coming here. And unfortunately since she has left college, she is no longer able to take. When Dr. Knight and myself visited Sophie in the Institution she was in to check up on her, we were both quite distraught on seeing her relapse."

"What, you couldn't keep giving her the medication she was on while she was here?" I asked her angrily.

"Not when her current doctors might ask questions about it, such as why they've never heard of it before or try to investigate the pharmacy it came from." Nell pointed out.

Bugger. She was right. But still this whole situation didn't seem right to me. "But can't we take Sophie back? Get her out of that place full of crazy people which is probably making her condition worse, and maybe even show her Circulate Headquarters, to show her the possibilities of what her future could hold?"

"Elisha, that would be like taking a possessed person on a tour of Hell. What Sophie can do is amazing, granted. But she doesn't see it that way. She thinks her ability to see and travel through time is a curse." Hamilton stated.

"To her it would be like saying to the possessed person, 'hey, we know you have a demon inside of you, and this is where you because of your demon, could end up'." Nell added.

"So she thinks she's evil, and I'm evil, and we're all evil." I sighed with resignation.

"That's correct." Hamilton said softly. "Sophie is a gifted seer, and will one day, be a powerful Circulator. Does that sound familiar to you?"

"Yeah, Lucas Hodge said the same thing to me." I said flatly, still thinking of Sophie sitting in a padded cell somewhere.

"Now both you and Sophie are actually the only Circulators known to have the ability to see things other Calculators or Circulators cannot." Hamilton informed me.

"Yeah, like what?" I asked, not really paying attention.

"The first time you Circulated with Dr. Knight and went to the Ball at Holland House and you saw your dead grandmother standing in the garden. This incident is only the second time something like this has ever been reported in Circulate history. The first time was when we were examining Sophie's delusions." Hamilton told me.

Now that caught my attention and I sat upright in the chair. "No way..." I managed out. "But there have been plenty of instances! Peter saw the ghost of a dead monk or priest or whatever hanging from the rafters, with out seeing it through a mirror or window. Nelson saw a hold up in the bank..."

"Yes, but they were images back in time of the location they were in. Your grandmother had never visited England, but she appeared to you in the gardens of the location you were in. You instantly knew of her death. You didn't have a premonition by seeing her die in her bed back in the nursing home she was in. She came to you in a vision. No member of the Circulate besides Sophie and yourself, have had visions such as these." Hamilton continued.

"Yeah, but that's nothing special!" I objected. "When I was researching hauntings I found out that plenty of people in the world who can't Circulate or Calculate or whatever have seen visions of deceased people, right on the time of death. I think they call them Crisis Apparitions or something. It's really common, so I read."

"Sophie has seen these visions on a regular basis, of people who are in no relation to her. And I believe so have you." Hamilton said softly, as if breaking some bad or important news to me.

Both of them sat there, watching me, watching for my reaction.

Mum's face entered my mind. The night I looked into the mirror, and instead of seeing the reflection of my face, I saw my mother's... and she looked dead. I had had a vision of my mother being dead, and that was before the news of the cancer came from the doctor.

I didn't see my mother lying dying in a hospital bed, or lying dead in a coffin, I just saw her face, blue, drawn, lifeless. Her eyes were closed. Her mouth slightly parted. Her hair lying flat and lifeless as her, about her ears.

"Oh god!" I suddenly gasped and I felt my eyes get tearful. "I saw my dead mother!"

Nell instantly put her hand on my shoulder to comfort me. "When was this?"

"I was 13 years old, and just started High School. I had the chicken pox. I got up late one night to put more lotion on because I couldn't sleep, and the lotion was in the cupboard under the sink in the bathroom. When I went in there, and I looked in the mirror to put the lotion on, I didn't see my reflection, I saw my mothers! She was dead! This was a few months before we got the news of the cancer." I started to cry at the memory.

"We believe that you and Sophie can see people in time with out needing to see the location they're in at the time. You can simply focus on the person." Hamilton still continued to speak softly, and he passed me a tissue box. "And I think it's related to the night of Halloween when you sensed the ripple in time caused by myself and Professor Myles changing the time-line to stop Sophie overdosing that night."

"So you've seen visions of both your mother and your grandmother." Nell established. "Have you ever seen anything else about anybody else?"

"Not that I recall." I sniffled. Isn't seeing visions of dead mothers and grandmothers enough for these people? "Other than my mother and

Gran, I've only seen things backwards or forwards in time from the location I was in."

"Not quite." Hamilton looked at me steadily, and passed me another tissue.

Now what? I looked back at him wondering what else he might know about me that I didn't. It's actually quite freaky sitting in a room with two people who know more about your own past than you do.

"The night you sat in your darkened dorm room and tried to see 18th Century England before your first excursion, but saw the darkened country side of Mars instead." Professor Hamilton pointed out.

How did he know that? Did Brett/Lucas tell him this? Or like Dr. Knight once told me, did I tell them this in a future conversation?

"What, that's the same thing?" I asked in surprise.

"Indeed it is. It may not be a person, but you were able to see a different location in a different time frame. It was so different in fact, that you didn't even know where it was, did you?" Hamilton smiled again.

"I guess not."

I guess Professor Hamilton and Nell had answered my questions… for the moment. But when I left that office this morning, I still felt unsatisfied for some reason. Something still didn't feel right. And I still didn't feel like company, so instead of trying to find either Pat or Nelson or even Maya in either the Computer Labs or Library, I returned to the dorms.

Then Diary, this is the second strange part of my morning.

I went back upstairs to my floor and walked down the hallway, and saw Brett/Lucas's door was still open. But for some reason I felt like I should have another look inside again. And what-do-ya-know… there was something different about it from the last time I looked in on it just half an hour ago.

When I opened the cupboard door again, I found an envelope sitting on the empty wooden floor. The envelope had my name written on it.

I quickly picked it up, shoved it in my pocket, and hurried out of there.

As soon as I had closed and locked my bedroom door behind me, I ripped open the envelope to find a small piece of paper with only a few words on it. I realized it was an address. It was an address for a Mental Health facility just outside of Chicago, in the U.S.

It must be the address for Sophie and it was written in Brett/Lucas's handwriting. I would recognize it anywhere after all the study sessions we had together.

So Hamilton and Nell who tried to dissuade me from trying to contact or help Sophie, are being contradicted by their Head Council Leader for the Circulate? But Brett/Lucas told me to adhere to my teacher's advice. So why is he giving me Sophie's address? Does he know how stubborn I am and that I might try in the future try to contact her anyway? But then, before he left, on our second last day in France he told me all about Sophie... he wanted to pique my interest.

Sophie and I are meant to become two of the strongest Circulators in the Circulate... are we meant to grow strong together? Am I meant to make contact with her? Then why leave her contact details so secretly for me?

===

TO: ebaker_hamiltons@evers.com

FROM: s_parson@snailmail.com
SUBJECT: Here is all I could find… and I think you bloody owe me one!
DATE: 02/ 09/ 01

Read the subject title Elisha, and read it well. If you were Scottish and we were over the age limit, in all politeness you would owe me a pretty fucking big bottle of scotch! Or even at least five pints of Guiness! But this summer was your lucky day. I went down to London to visit my friend for a week, and out of that, finding out this crap for you took me two days!

First of all, I went onto the Internet to find out where I could start looking. The National Army Museum only mentioned your boy at Plassey (which interestingly now says he lived through and scored a Medal of Honor for - I suppose thanks to you!). I came up with this list of resources, which didn't say much on the surface, but it did tell me where to look. I suggest you save these, as just in case you need to look something up yourself in future.

The British Library
www.bl.uk

The Orders and Medals Research Society
www.omrs.org.uk/

Port Maritime Information Gateway
www.port.nmn.ac.uk/

Familia (records of Anglican and County Births Deaths & Marriages)
www.familyrecords.gov.uk/

The British Library site put me onto the National Archives website which then put me onto the Familia site which was handy… until I realized I had no idea where the laddy was born, only when he was borne. So I then stumbled upon this really cool link, The Orders and Medals Research Society, that had all these other really cool links. I found out both the British Library and Royal Navy Museum kept detailed old Naval Admiralty papers and logs and personal diaries. Thinking that your boy got himself a Medal of Honor, I thought that might stick out.

Luckily for you it did. When I was in London I went to the British Library and the Royal Navy Museum and I read on microfiche and microfilm about Guy's success and daring do's… and even a couple of his logs when he had been made admiral! There were even three diary entries from the man! Which he mentioned his wife… (sorry) and in passing, where he was born… Dartford.

Now knowing where the bugger was born, then I could find out through Familia more details about him. He didn't stray too far from his home life where he was borne, as I found out heaps more through the Dartford Parish Registers at Ash near Sevenoaks on microfiche transcript who he married, how many kids, etc. So what I have to offer you is from Births Deaths and Marriages as well as the Royal Naval Museum Collections and Manuscripts section.

~Sir Guy Robertson~

4th April 1720 – Born in Dartford to father Samuel Robertson and Mary nee Ross Robertson.

August 1755 – Knighted for Bravery in Battle and made Captain of the HMS Harbinger at age 26 (and meets Elisha Baker at Lady Caroline's ball).

12th June 1757 – Fights in the Battle of Plassey in India alongside Clive of India and nearly dies but is saved (by the dashing but rebellious Elisha) at age 28.

August 1757 – Receives Medal of Honor from King George 2nd and has his 'betrothal' to Lady Elisha Durrant officially blessed by the King (and then brakes up with Elisha… am I right with this one?).

January 1758 – Marries Lydia Hume in Dartford Anglican church, the daughter of Admiral Henry Hume, who was some kind of mentor I think because when he was a Captain and before Guy was a Captain, Guy served under him. So maybe he doesn't really has a choice or he feels he owes it to him (or maybe he's on the rebound from you?).

July 1759 - Their first son, James Henry, is stillborn.

May 1760 - Son Henry James is borne (well if that's not a suck up of naming your kid after your father-in-law I don't know what is!).

September 1762 - Daughter Elisha is borne (Wow! What a compliment! I guess he never really got over you…even if he did marry that fat cow of another woman).

February 1770 - Made Admiral at the age of 41.

April 1775 - The War of Independence in the U.S starts, and Guy turns 46 years old (why do I mention it? You'll soon find out…).

August 1775 - Goes on a diplomatic mission to the court of King Louis XV. Hears Elisha's voice in Versailles gardens and decides to take it as an omen not to trust what the Minister of Defense has just told him. His ship then intercepts a French vessel sailing for the U.S. with weapons stashed on board for the Yankee rebels. (You never told me about talking to Guy in Versailles! When I read this in the Royal Naval Museum, I accidentally let out this scream in surprise, and they nearly kicked me out for it! I mean, can't you get into trouble for appearing in history?).

July 1778 - War begins (yet again… ho hum…) between France and England over the War of Independence, with the frogs taking the side of the wanks - sorry - yanks.

August 1778 - While at sea Guy is wounded in battle and is forced into retirement due to poor health.

September 1778 - Guy dies from infection (probably from his wounds - medical hygiene really sucked in those times) at the age of 49. Is buried in the little cemetery in Dartford - as I saw his headstone myself.

Well, there you go. Good news, and bad news, and then some more bad news. But you did ask me to tell you.

Look Elisha, I'm really sorry things didn't work out with you and Guy. The two of did seem like a romantic idea, even if it was a little far fetched. And it sounds like he must have been still in love with you to name his daughter after you… that's a pretty big compliment, ay?

I have a feeling you'll probably want to see the documents yourself, especially on Versailles and his reaction to hearing your voice. So expect in the mail photocopies I made of Guy's diary and log entries. But just to give you a   preview...

His Log Entry was more official and objective sounding, like he said: "after hearing the voice of an old and trusted friend, I no longer trusted the words of the French Minister of Defense, as I could trust the mistrust of my First Mate. Immediately upon returning to our vessel, we put out to sea and left France."

Then in his personal diary: "A long time ago a voice called out to me, and it has been many years since past that have been spent in yearning for that voice to return. Today that voice did just that, and I believe it came to me as an omen, to shrug off these chains of drudgery that politics has tied me down, and to regain my sea legs and the intuition that once served me as a Captain so well..."

===

03/09/01

Diary,

Today was the first day of the new semester and we started our classes as Juniors.

Everyone is still buzzing after the excitement of our trip. Not only was France the interesting point, but everyone is still talking about the Brett/Lucas revelation. I think this has invigorated everyone to learn more about the Circulate, and more about themselves.

But I felt like a ghost. Like I wasn't really present, I was just a shadow of myself making an appearance. I sat in the classrooms and I stared, but it wasn't at any of the new textbooks they handed out.

I don't think it matters anymore. I don't think I want to learn what they have to teach. I don't think I want to be in any more classes at this school.

I heard back from Sally last night and I got the information about Guy.

He died at the age of 49 of an illness connected to battle wounds. You could almost say he still dies in battle.

What do I do now? Defy school regulations once more and come running to his rescue? And then do what? It sounds like he needs the help from a modern day medical doctor and I would have to bring back futuristic medicine to bring about this miracle.

What do I do? What should I do? Should I try to help him? In our time 49 is a young age to die, but in those days... it might seem almost right. It might seem like it's his time.

He married someone else six months after our break-up. She was a Captain's daughter, apparently, and her father was the Captain of a ship that Guy served on before been given one of his own. So I guess she would have been the perfect choice, knowing the hardships connected to being a sailors wife, let alone a Captain in the King's service.

I bet she wouldn't appreciate my sudden appearance.

But I can't let Guy just die, worried about her reaction to my actions, can I?

What should I do?

Should I approach Dr. Knight and ask her to come with me? She could treat Guy's infection. But maybe she's still angry with me at my last little escapade through London from the last time I saw Guy? Should I at least try to ask her for her help?

I don't know what to do...

===

04/ 09/ 01

Diary,

After Biology today I stayed back, prepared to bite the bullet and ask Dr. Knight for her assistance.

I felt so nervous, like it would have been asking my father permission to go save the man I had been caught having sex with.

"Dr. Knight?" I timidly approached her.

"Elisha, if this is about you not doing your homework, I understand." She said, not looking at me, as she packed up her pens and books.

"You do?"

"You're probably still feeling a little shocked over the news about Lucas and feel a little displaced right now. I'll give you an extra couple of days, and you can hand it in after the weekend." She shrugged, and started to leave.

"But this isn't what this is about." I clenched my hands, trying to imagine myself building up the courage.

"Oh no? Well, Elisha? What is this about then?" Dr. Knight now turned to look at me.

"When you and Professor Hamilton said I would no longer be able to go back in time to see Guy Robertson... were you really serious? What if something happened..."

"Yes Elisha, we were very serious." Dr. Knight suddenly said crossly.

"Really?" I said in surprise. "Not even if..."

Then she cut me off again.

"Madame Coultard told us what Lucas said to you on the bus before he vanished. He told you that you would become one of our most important Circulators, am I correct?"

"Well yeah..." but what has this got to do with the price of fish?

"I hope you're not getting a big head from what Lucas has told you, or even when you abused our trust in you and our kindness when we tried to make allowances for you to continue to see Guy. You're still a student here at this school Elisha. You're still expected to hand in your homework and participate and learn in the same way as everyone else here." She said sternly.

So is that what she thinks is happening to me?

I think I was both embarrassed and angry when she said that to me... I felt my face flush as my cheeks burned bright red and I barged my way past her and left the classroom.

I couldn't believe she just said that to me!

One minute everyone here is building me up as some kind of Wonder Woman with superpowers, and the next I'm being told I'm up myself?!

They think I'm not doing my homework coz I feel it's beneath me and I don't have to anymore?!

Fuck that!

I was still fuming when I re-joined everyone else in the Caf for lunch.

I went and sat at the table with Nelson, Pat, Maya, Raj, Jordon and Numu instead of first getting something to eat.

"Not hungry again?" Pat asked me. "C'mon Elisha, you've been skipping breakfast lately, you can't skip lunch as well."

"What's up? Did you just get a detention for not doing your homework?" Nelson asked me next.

"Can I ask you guys a question?" I demanded of them. "Do I come across as up myself or special from everybody else?"

"Yes." Everyone replied.

"What?! Why?" I asked in shock.

"Well, you can phase by yourself, but we're still learning how to do it." Jordon shrugged.

"You were allowed to see a boyfriend back in time." Numu said. "We've only gone on one supervised excursion."

"You keep doing stupid things like desperately holding onto visions of a man who died two hundred years ago." Nelson said plainly.

"You jumped into the river in Paris." Pat chuckled. "Normal people don't do that."

"Oh." I said, hurt. Nelson's words just before our trip to Paris rang in my ears again..."the whole world doesn't revolve around you..."

"Thanks." I got up to leave.

"Hey, where are you going?" Nelson asked me.

"Somewhere else."

==

06/09/01

Diary,

I haven't been coming down to the Caf for breakfast or dinner, so immediately Nelson thinks I'm sulking or brooding.

Maybe they all think that.

I guess they all think that I'm upset that I only just recently learned that the world doesn't revolve around me. They don't know about Guy and I'm not going to tell them.

Maybe I am just a silly little drama queen who is upset over her Romeo dying. But I think it's unfair that I always put up with Nelson being a complete bitch, and never complained. And what about all the secrets Pat kept from us and then we started hanging out with him again... and what about Peter always being a dickhead? And Zack? Well... let's not go there.

Zack is avoiding me again. He has been since the day that Brett yelled at him that he wanted to report him for what he nearly did to me in the kitchen that night. I think he's really ashamed of himself. He hardly even looks at me in class either. I can tell it's not out of anger or bitterness, but instead it's out of guilt.

But all of this is pointless. All of this seems silly and frivolous. It's all so fucking ridiculous.

I'm tired of this life.

Even our classes with the teachers trying to impart their knowledge down to us seem useless.

I'm not interested in learning about the different era's, that's not Guy's era. I don't even want to think about traveling anywhere else. I don't want to learn how to travel, to experience, to immerse myself into different lifestyles and cultures in the history of humanity.

Why would I want to go and meet more people who are going to die, and probably in horrible ways as well?

```
===============================================
```

TO: ebaker_hamiltons@evers.com
FROM: s_parson@snailmail.com
SUBJECT: Are you OK?
DATE: 07/ 09/ 01

Hey Elisha,

I just want to check if you're OK. I haven't heard back from you. Are you angry with me or something? It's not like I killed the Guy, so don't shoot the messenger, OK? LoL.

Have classes begun again? Have you found out what are the next era's you'll be visiting next in your classes with Dr. Kell? Feel free to pass on all the goss.

Sal xo

```
===============================================
```


08/ 09/ 01

Diary,

I didn't want to watch movies for 'Fun Night'. I didn't feel like eating any hamburgers for dinner. Everyone has deserted the dorms to go watch some comedy with Ben Stiller in it. So I had the whole floor to myself so I could listen to my music really loudly with out any complaints. I sat on my bed, listening to U2's "With or Without You" over and over again.

I've already got so much homework due on Monday, but I don't care. I didn't do it during the week, so the teachers gave me an extra couple of days to get it done. I wonder what will happen in class when I still tell them I haven't done it...?

I don't care what they do to me. I don't care much about anything anymore. I wouldn't even care if they sent me home to my father.

Bring on the worst, I don't care. I wouldn't feel it. I don't feel anything anymore.

Nothing matters anymore. Nothing is real anymore. Nothing feels anymore.

Nothing nothing.... Fucking nothing.

===

10/09/01

I didn't go to class today. Not a single one. I didn't leave my room to go to the Caf and eat.

The only way I'll leave my room is if I'm allowed to go back home.

I want to go home. I want to live with Dad again. I want to be normal again. I want to go to a normal high school and live a very placid life.

No more extraordinary. I'm over it. I want to get out of this place and forget everything about it and everyone in it.

Now I fully understand why Sophie and Sally left. I didn't before, but I do now. They knew this wasn't right.

If I can't help Guy, I don't want to use my ability.

===

16/ 09/ 01

OK. Call me fickle. But I've decided to stay.

Why? Because once again, this school has shown me how much I mean to them. Drama-queen antics and all. And it wasn't just the teachers, but even my friends helped me out. Even my friend in Scotland managed to help me out from her position on the other side of the planet. Or helped Guy out, I should say...

It happened last night of the 15th. I was sitting in my room, moping, staring at my opened, empty suitcase sitting on the bed. I hadn't started packing yet. I suddenly felt really nervous about the idea of going back to live with Dad and starting at a whole new school in Wollongong. I was worried Dad might fall back into his old habits if we lived together again, or even worried that somehow my suicide attempt story might reach new ears and how I would be seen by the students at the new school.

It was 7 PM, dinner time in the Caf. But again I didn't make an appearance. I wasn't starving myself, I did have snacks at morning tea and afternoon tea, but I'd take the sandwiches back to my room and eat them there. Besides, I didn't have much of an appetite anyway.

Then there was a knock on my door.

I thought it would be Nelson or Pat or Maya, coming to tell me to get off my miserable ass and snap out of it. So I tried to ignore the knocking. But who ever it was, they were persistent.

Then suddenly both Dr. Knight and Professor Hamilton walked in, both in 18th Century period costume!

"Hallo Elisha. Would you like to take a little walk with us this evening?" Professor Hamilton smiled kindly to me. "We were thinking of taking a stroll to Dartford, in 1778."

"Huh?" I stared at the both of them in surprise.

"Here's a dress for you to put on, we won't worry about a wig this time." Dr. Knight laid the garment on my bed over the suitcase. "With it is just one petticoat and a cloak to put on over the top so you don't get cold."

When she put the clothes down, I noticed she was carrying a black leather doctor's bag that had been hiding underneath the clothing.

"Are we... we..." I stared at the doctor's bag, standing up from my chair.

"Yes we are." Professor Hamilton smiled at me again.

"Going to pay a house call." Dr. Knight added. "We'll wait for you in the hallway."

Then they turned around and left, closing my door again behind themselves.

Oh wow! Just like that... my miracle happens? How did this come about? How do they know about Guy? Who told them?

As quickly as I could, I stripped out of my jeans and sneakers and jumper, to put on the petticoat, then the dress, and then the hooded cloak. I tied my hair back in a French knot. In the space of my small dorm room, I practically ran to my door and threw it open to get underway.

I wanted to run. I wanted to run to Guy's side as fast as I could, and I think both of my teachers sensed this urgency. They led the way, and we walked at a brisk pace.

We left Beta building and headed across the oval towards Alpha building.

I realized we were doing this now, at this hour, so the former Freshmen who will now be Sophomores who still aren't entirely in the know about why they're at this college won't see our transition. Everyone in this school will all be in Gamma building, in the Caf for dinner. Now here I am, deep in secrecy, joining the conspiracy.

And just like that first night, when we saw Dr. Knight phase through the window just outside the computer labs on the second floor of Alpha building, I now phased with her, and Professor Hamilton, through the glass.

If any Sophomore in this school saw me, they would think I was a ghost.

And here I am, phasing through the layers of time like a ghost, to save a man who dies more than two hundred years before I'm even born.

Again we arrived at Dr. Knight's London Town House, to a darkened and empty Drawing Room.

I noticed it looked slightly different, with a few new portraits on the walls and a few new knick-knacks on the mantle of the fireplace.

As before on my first phase, Dr. Knight crossed over to the sideboard and rang the little silver bell to have the carriage called for us. Only different servants answered the call than when I last visited, they were new and younger. And as Dr. Knight told me, probably the most well paid servants in London, not only paid for their loyalty but for their confidentiality.

As we climbed into the carriage, Dr. Knight told the driver the destination and in 18th Century terminology, to 'step on it'.

Instead of the leisurely trot we had through London to the Fox's Ball decades ago, with only two horses, now four horses pulled us along in the fastest gallop the driver could muster.

We drove out of London to Dartford. For all I know the London in the 21st Century could have been joined to Dartford or now encompassed Dartford. But in the 18th Century, Dartford was still separate, and was on the water. There were small cottages as well as a dockside where ships were moored.

The carriage drew to a stop outside of a sleepy looking small, one story house. It had a thatched roof and a small garden, with a low hedge acting as a fence line. I wondered how Professor Hamilton and Dr. Knight knew where Guy lived? I was about to ask as we stepped out of the carriage, when something prevented it.

The front door of the house immediately opened with the sound of our arrival. A young woman dressed in modest means stood in the doorway, looking at us puzzled. Then a young man, dressed as a Naval officer also came to stand beside her, and the two talked to each other softly, while not taking their eyes off us.

I wondered if they were Guy's children? Something told me they were, and I felt my stomach go all fluttery. It's weird meeting your ex-boyfriends' grown up children. Especially when he didn't have any when I was last in his company.

Professor Hamilton opened the small wooden gate for Dr. Knight and I to pass through, before coming in and closing it behind himself. Then he walked around Dr. Knight and myself to greet the two first. I remembered protocol in this century it had to be the Gentleman to introduce first, with the Ladies second.

"Good evening. You must be Miss Elisha Robertson and Lt. Henry Robertson. My name is Dr. Stephen Hamilton, and this is Lady Vivian Dunmore, and her niece Lady Elisha Durrant. We are friends of both your father's and of Captain Greyson." Professor Hamilton greeted and took off his hat.

"Good evening Doctor. Unfortunately you have missed Captain Greyson, as he left early in the afternoon." Lt. Robertson, Guy's son, replied.

Lt. Robertson had his father's dark curly hair, but his eyes were blue and his face was a different shape, it was more rounder. Elisha Robertson had fair hair, but her father's dark eyes and his longer face shape. Lt. Robertson was also as tall as Guy, and he stood the same height as his sister. I was probably staring at them the same way they were staring at me, we were trying to make each other out by first appearances.

"The Captain informed us of your father's ill health and asked me to stop by to see what assistance I may offer. Lady Vivian and Lady Elisha, both long-standing friends of the Greyson family, both insisted on coming. Once they learned of this pressing news, they also wished to offer any help that may be possible." Professor Hamilton made out he was the medical doctor, so he could get Dr. Knight the real doctor, in to see the patient.

The brother and sister looked at each other in surprise, but then they stepped back and indicated we could pass inside.

"It's a bit funny, that. Old friends of the family, are you? Captain Greyson himself has never mentioned the two of you." Guy's daughter, Elisha said warily, staring at me, and then at Dr. Knight.

"When your father was presented at Court and awarded the Medal of Honor, it was because of the activities he participated in, in India, with Lady Vivian present." I half lied, leaving out a certain other person... myself.

"Ah, I remember that story! That was when father fought with Sir Clive, who was then Governor Clive! If I remember rightly, it also involved a Lady Elisha Durrant." Lt. Robertson looked at me next.

"She is my mother." I lied.

"Ah..." Lt. Robertson nodded. "Elisha... hmm... rather a popular name, in our small circle."

Elisha Robertson almost sneered. She didn't like sharing names with me, that was for certain. I wonder if she knows the real reason for the origin of her name?

"Shall we see the patient?" Professor Hamilton suggested, to steer the conversation away.

"This way, my Lady, Dr. Hamilton." Elisha Robertson turned and showed us the way.

We walked down a small corridor where Elisha Robertson opened a door that hid the main bedroom behind it. By 18th Century standards this room would have been called 'modest', but to modern 21st Century standards the room would have been considered to be quite small. Inside was a small fireplace, with a fire going, and the small room had a chest of draws and a small bedside table with a single candle burning on top of it and a small canopy bed.

In the canopy bed, laid a severely weakened Guy, in a nightshirt and under heavy covers.

His eyes were closed and his face looked pale and sweaty.

My stomach immediately sank at the sight of him, and the flashback of seeing him lying on the back of that one-horse cart, coming back from the battle in India instantly flashed through my mind.

"Where's his wound?" I suddenly rushed forward in a panic. "Is it his stomach?"

"The wound, my Lady, is on his leg." Lt. Robertson said in surprise at my lack of this knowledge. "Our physician says it must come off soon."

I was about to tear off the bed sheets to have a look for myself, when Dr. Knight instantly put her hand on my arm to restrain me.

"Thank you, Lt. Robertson, Miss Robertson, for kindly showing us to your sick father. Now if you would be so patient to sit outside and wait, I will examine the wound myself. That is what Captain Greyson wanted when he sent for me." Professor Hamilton tried to politely kick the kids out the door.

Elisha Robertson looked like she was about to object, when her brother then put his hand on her shoulder.

Both us Elisha's were being restrained at that moment, with the both of us eyeing each other with either mistrust or indifference.

"Then why is both the Lady Elisha and Lady Vivian staying? Why is it that the children are made to leave and the guests are allowed to stay?" Elisha Robertson complained.

"Because the guests can help your father. I understand the gravity of the situation Miss Robertson, and I will need the assistance of both Lady Vivian and Lady Elisha in my treatment of your father. I will also need your assistance, of course. As of right now, I will need boiling water. Now Miss Robertson, could you please arrange for me to have constant boiling water at hand?" Professor Hamilton spoke softly to Guy's children to try to temper the stress written all over their faces and bodies.

"Boiled in a pot, if that is convenient, please Miss Robertson. We will need to sanitize your father's bandages by boiling them. I am experienced with dressing infected wounds, which is why I believe I can assist Dr. Hamilton." Dr. Knight told her.

"Very well. I'll have Betsy boil some for you." With that Elisha Robertson turned on her heel and flounced out the door.

"If there is anything else that you require, we will be in the kitchen. Please use our home as you will and our help is at your disposal." Lt. Robertson gave a nod to all of us, before he also left the room, closing the door behind him.

What a relief that they were finally gone!

Now I could freely rush to Guy's side and take hold of his hand.

"Guy? Guy, it's me, Elisha." I sat on the side of his bed, holding his hand in my hand, and with my other I caressed the wet skin of his cheek.

His hair looked much more gray and there were a few more wrinkles about his eyes and mouth. Other than that, his illness probably added more years to his actual age. His pallor and gaunt cheeks made him look so helpless.

I was worried how he didn't come to immediately. He seemed to be in some sort of delirium that he couldn't shake himself out of. When I called his name and stroked his cheek, he moaned and turned his head in my direction, but he didn't wake up.

I looked at Dr. Knight worriedly... were we too late?

"Elisha, I need you to move please so I can examine his leg." Dr. Knight turned professional, taking her doctor's bag back from the school principal.

I stood up and Professor Hamilton pulled down the bed covers so his bandaged leg was exposed.

As soon as he did that, a putrid smell instantly hit our senses.

I exchanged another worried glance with Professor Hamilton, and he gently came and pulled me away from the bed slightly as Dr. Knight got to work.

Inside of Dr. Knight's black leather doctors bag, was a combination of both period, modern and even futuristic medical devices.

Using a futuristic scanning device, with a scanning wand attached by a cord to a small monitor, Dr. Knight waved it over his body slowly about three times.

"Low heart rate, low blood pressure. Patient's temperature is 50 degrees Celsius. The infection from the wound has spread through out his entire body. Removal of the patient's leg at this stage would be pointless." Dr. Knight announced, by the readings on the monitor.

Next she took off his linen bandages, which made the smell worse, and I gasped when I saw how hideously ugly the infected tissue was.

What looked to be like some kind of futuristic thermometer, Dr. Knight placed it against the open, weeping wound. She held it there for a minute, and then took it off and read from a small digital screen. I realized she had just taken a blood sample.

"Staphylococcus." Dr. Knight announced.

"Is that the infection?" I asked her.

"Yes." She stated, now sanitizing the blood-sampling device in a sterilizing chemical.

"How serious is that?" I swallowed.

"In our age, treatable. In this day and age, a serious threat." She sighed. "Using futuristic methods, he will recover in a day or two."

"Really?" I uttered in relief, smiling for what felt like the first time in weeks.

"I am going to treat the patient with a broad-spectrum anti-biotic that will find and attack the Staphylococcus virus, as well as raise his white and red cell count. I'm assuming by this incision on his arm the physician who has been treating him in this century has tried bleeding him." She shook her head disapprovingly. "We have to also work on getting his immune system back up to a normal level."

"Lots and lots of orange juice?" I offered a suggestion.

"Right now, we need lots of clean bandages." Dr. Knight stated. "Can you please ask Guy's family for a basin of cooled boiled water and some clean linen bandages."

I flinched. I didn't want to go and ask them for jack shit. Elisha Robertson already hates me, and I only just met her five minutes ago! I supposed if my father's ex-girlfriend just suddenly rocked up out of the blue I probably wouldn't be too warm and friendly to her either. I think she suspects something, no matter that I lied that it was my 'mother' who knew Guy and who's name I now have (when really my mother's name was Grace - which in my opinion is a much prettier name!).

"I'll go and ask." Professor Hamilton volunteered, and left the room, closing the door behind him again.

While he was gone, to get the asked for supplies and probably to do more consoling of the suspicious family, I watched Dr. Knight treat Guy.

Using a futuristic kind of injection which wasn't really a needle, but more like a compressed spray that you put against the skin and spray it at a pressurized dose, she applied the serum to Guy's system. Next she used a sterilizing chemical to clean the wound. Finally she used some kind of laser that didn't burn the skin, but rather, healed over most of the torn skin on his leg. Then she placed over the half-healed wound a special gauze-like plastic-like bandage to let the wound breathe and heal faster.

Then she went out to ask Guy's family for some clean bed sheets and a clean night shirt to change him into, to get rid of any traces of the Staph infection that might be lingering. When she went to go and ask for these things, she carried out of the room in the washbasin the old infected bandages. I would have been happy to change him, but Dr. Knight pointed out that that may look a little strange, and it should be his family made to do so. Just before Elisha Robertson and the family maid, Betsy did do so, Dr. Knight tied just one layer of clean linen wrap over Guy's leg to hide the futuristic band-aid thingy.

Next it was my turn to wait outside with both Dr. Knight and Professor Hamilton while Elisha Robertson and Betsy changed Guy's clothes and bed sheets. It felt like they were taking forever. I even wondered if they were examining Guy after we had examined him, to see if we'd done any more damage?

I paced around the small, warm kitchen, as Dr. Knight and Professor Hamilton sat at the wooden table, sipping cups of tea. Normally I would have delighted in exploring the old design of the kitchen, and maybe even the antiquated huge iron cooking stove and oven. Or I might have admired the pretty and intricate pattern on the china cups. But I felt restless and just wanted to sit by Guy's side to watch the medicine work it's magic.

"Lady Elisha, are you sure I cannot convince you of refreshing yourself with some tea?" Lt. Robertson offered a second time.

"No thanks. But thanks for your offer." I shook my head, then I returned to my pacing.

"If I may be so bold to ask, my Lady, but to which origin is your accent from? I cannot make out if it is Scottish, or Colonial?" Lt. Robertson asked me next.

That made me smile briefly, remembering these same words from both Guy and Greyson.

"Colonial." Dr. Knight answered for me.

As we waited, for what seemed nearly an eternity, I suddenly had a realization that there was a certain person missing from this house. I don't know why I only just noticed it then, and not sooner. You would think I would have, considering it was one of my worries earlier.

"Lt. Robertson." I turned to Guy's son. "If I may ask, where is your mother?" I thought she would have been here, to nurse her ailing husband and not just have his children by his side.

Lt. Robertson looked quite surprised by this question.

"My mother, Mrs. Robertson, passed away, just this last winter."

"Oh." I said in surprise, suddenly feeling a little foolish at this lack of knowledge.

"I would like to apologize for this lack of discretion, Lt. Robertson. I did not inform Lady Elisha of your mother's passing. At the time, we did not want to break the sad news of when it happened to my young niece. She thought of your mother in a very high regard." Dr. Knight tried to cover up this oversight. "She had heard some very flattering words about the kindness in Mrs. Robertson from both Sir Robertson and Captain Greyson."

"Yes. My mother's goodness and her loyalty to my father and his career was just some of her redeeming qualities." Lt. Robertson nodded at Dr. Knight's compliments.

"I am very sorry for your loss." I now sat down at the table beside Lt. Robertson. "Your mother must have led a hard life having your father away so often. And now for you to lose your mother..."

"I thank you for your kind sentiments, Lady Elisha. But I believe my sister took this loss the hardest. She and mother were quite close." Lt. Robertson smiled sadly at the memory. "And I believe that if my father did take a turn for the worse... that my sister will feel his loss deeper still."

"Don't worry, Lt. Robertson. Nothing is going to happen to your father while we're here." I said firmly.

I guess you could say my strong conviction surprised him again, as he sort of gave me funny look then.

"I'll chase death away myself if I have to." I tried to make a joke out of it to ease the tension in the room at that moment.

Guy's son had a chuckle at that last comment, and then sighed and sipped his tea.

When we were allowed back into Guy's bedroom to sit with him, Lt. Robertson brought in a couple of the kitchen stools that we could sit on.

Then the waiting began.

Lt. Robertson shortly afterwards went to bed, as Betsy manned the stove and kept boiling water on hand. Elisha Robertson also sat in the kitchen, doing needle point, but refusing to get any rest herself. Every half hour she would come in and look on her father. I could clearly see Guy's same stubborn determination shining out of her dark eyes in her head. And to keep up the ruse of our being here, Professor Hamilton in his role as physician, used an antiquated stethoscope to listen to Guy's heartbeat. Every time Elisha Robertson popped in to look on her father, Professor Hamilton played the role of the physician as he held onto

Guy's wrist to take his pulse, or put his hand on his forehead to check his temperature.

At 2 AM Professor Hamilton told Elisha Robertson that her father's high temperature had lowered dramatically after some medicine had been given to him.

As if she didn't believe him, she then put her hand on her father's forehead to check for herself. But just as she did that, her own willfulness and edgy behavior began to dissolve. The evidence was clear. Her father was beginning to heal.

"Please Miss Robertson. Your father's health is in good hands, and he is on the mend. Would you be as kind to yourself and also get some of the same rest?" Professor Hamilton suggested to her gently.

Elisha Robertson took one last look at both Professor Hamilton, Dr. Knight and myself, and finally consented to go to her bed.

Then Betsy seemed to think it was time for her to also go to bed, now that her mistress had allowed herself to catch some Zzz's.

So Professor Hamilton and Dr. Knight left me alone in Guy's bedroom to still sit by his side, as they went and had another cup of tea by the fire in the kitchen to give us our privacy.

I drew my stool closer to the bedside and continued to wait it out.

I wanted to be the first person Guy sees when he wakes up.

I fantasized about this romantic moment we would have, of him opening his eyes and seeing me immediately. I day dreamed of our reunion and me being able to apologize for acting the idiot back in London for what to me seemed weeks ago, to him, years ago. I pictured the two of us staring dreamily into each other's eyes and confessing our true feelings of love and devotion across the vast ocean of time that separated us...

"Elisha?"

Huh? What? I had been too busy staring off into space, imagining it all, that I had missed the moment! Guy woke up without me!

"Guy!" I instantly refocused my attention to my amore.

He was looking at me sleepily, with half-opened eyes, as if he thought he was dreaming me here.

"Guy, it's me. It really is me." I took hold of his hands and instantly sat on the side of his bed.

His eyes widened at my closeness, and he squeezed my hands in his a couple of times to ascertain the realness of our contact.

"Elisha... what are you doing here?" he asked confused.

"Tending to you, you idiot." I laughed out my relief to see him conscious again.

He smiled at me weakly and squeezed my hands again.

"I mean, why are you here?"

"To save your life." I said simply.

"Elisha, I am an old man now..." he began.

"If you tell me you should have died, I'll kill you." I joked again. "Besides, where I come from, there are many middle-aged men who in their 40's would be quite flattered at the attention of a girl as young as I am."

"Flattered yes... but is this a dream?" he closed his eyes for a few moments, before opening them again and staring longingly at me. "Tell me, why have you come here?"

"Dr. Knight brought me here. She gave you a medicine that saved your life. When I found out what happened to you... I thought I couldn't live... I went nuts... again." I turned tearful and pulled my hand out of one of his so I could caress his cheek.

"Elisha, my whole life has gone past..." Guy turned serious. "You must know..."

"That you married? Had two kids? I've met them. Your son is quite the gentleman. Your daughter on the other hand..." I rolled my eyes and tried to make him laugh, which he did. "I'm sorry you lost your wife though. I heard she was a nice person."

"Lydia was indeed a dear and devoted wife." Guy confessed.

"And she made the perfect Captain's wife, is that correct?" I asked knowingly.

"She was the perfect wife for ME." he said sadly, then looked up at me square in the eyes. "You know how bad tempered I am, at being the end of it twice. You know how head strong and narrow minded I can be. She was patient and kind with me. She gave me two children, and never complained at my absence. She always kept a home for me."

"Guy, I know all this. Do you really think that after my escapades in India, that out of jealousy I would just sit back and wave and watch you die? I could never do that. Your time to pass into the next life is not now... OK? Besides, your daughter would never forgive you." I jested again.

"You have met Elisha?" he asked.

"Yes. We have met Elisha. She is very devoted to you." I commented.

"She seems to think it her place in the world to take of her father now that her mother cannot." Guy sighed.

"Then hurry up and get better, so you can find a good man to marry her to. Live and make sure she ends up happy." I clasped both of his hands in mine again.

"And of course you know where her namesake comes from?" he asked me slowly.

"I think I have a good idea." I smiled.

"I must tell you Elisha... " he began. "When I married Lydia... which may have seemed so soon..."

"Guy, please, you don't have to explain yourself." I tried to stop him.

"No, I must get this off my chest." He stopped me, then continued. "I knew her father. He was the Captain of the first ship I served as an officer on board. He had become ill, and always had designs on the two of us as a couple. It was his dying wish that we become man and wife. And since I treated you so badly..."

"Guy, you did not treat me badly. It was my fault that..."

"I should not have demeaned you in such a manner..."

"Please, I was to blame..."

"And I meant what I wrote to you in my letter. Even when I took Lydia to be my bride, it was not she who consumed my every waking thought. As I laid dying not even a day ago, I thought on how I would be judged in the next life for not loving my wife as I should. There was always a kindness between Lydia and myself... but my passion laid somewhere else..."

"Did you cheat on her?" I suddenly demanded of him.

"What?" he gave me an angry look. "Certainly not!"

"Then you shouldn't worry about being judged by God. You were faithful to your wife? You didn't beat her? You didn't hurt her or your children? So don't punish yourself, Guy!"

Hearing him talk like this, it hurt me. Not by talking about another woman, well, not just by the talking about another woman... but for being so hard on himself. He was one of the most honorable men I know.

"When I named my daughter Elisha... I hoped it would be some retribution to your honor. I wanted you to see this in history. I wanted you to know that you were still in my thoughts and not so easily discarded as my actions made you out to be." Guy placed my hands on his chest, over his heart.

"I believe you Guy. I believe you." I started to cry harder. "Please stop talking like this. You sound like you're getting ready to die again."

"I do not know if this is the last time I will ever see you again." He said. I wondered if he meant my time traveling habit to pop up after long distances in his life, or that he was worried he would fall back asleep and wake up to find me gone, or maybe it was both.

"I will stay by your side until you're completely well and walking strong again." I promised him.

*****

I slept by Guy's side until dawn. Keeping to protocol, I couldn't very well snuggle up in bed beside him as I would have liked to. Instead I drew the stool close to his bedside and laid my head down on the covers. It wasn't the most comfortable position to be in, but at least it was close to Guy.

At dawn Dr. Knight and Professor Hamilton came into the room and Dr. Knight examined Guy's leg and vital signs before she would have any interruptions from Guy's family.

"His temperature is almost back to normal, and there are no traces left of the infection." Dr. Knight announced, reading off the little monitor again.

"The miracles of your modern science, never ceases to amaze me, Doctor." Guy smiled thankfully, sitting upright in bed now.

As if perfectly timed, once Dr. Knight's futuristic medical devices were returned safely inside the black leather doctor's bag, both Elisha Robertson and her brother barged their way through the door.

"Father!" Elisha Robertson cried out and rushed towards him to envelope him in a hug of relief.

"We thought we heard your voice! Thank God that you are on the mend!" Lt. Robertson laughed, and then shook his father's hand.

"Thank our visitors instead. They had a very important hand in my recovery." Guy told his children, and then shared a small smile with me.

"Your father is on the road to recovery, so our work here is done." Professor Hamilton smiled to Guy and his family.

Hamilton looked at me after he said that, and I felt suddenly a little panicky and very disappointed.

"Surely we should stay, just in case of something that might go amiss... like a relapse...?" I asked both of my teachers.

"Admiral Robertson is healing well, Lady Durrant. And I had promised your father that you would not be away for long." Dr. Knight said solemnly, as if trying to kick me with her hint.

"If I may be so bold to offer this suggestion... that perhaps Lady Durrant may stay here for a couple of days as our most welcome guest, and then I would see her return to London myself." Guy offered to Dr. Knight and Professor Hamilton.

Professor Hamilton and Dr. Knight exchanged a long glance, as if silently asking each other if it was a good idea or not.

"Please. I would feel better knowing that our old and dear family friend did make a full recovery." I pleaded with them.

Elisha Robertson and her brother exchanged a look of their own, surprised at this exchange and my insistence to stay.

"Very well. We will expect your return to our London town house the evening of tomorrow." Dr. Knight said, then looked at me long and hard. "Please keep to this schedule, as your father would worry at your absence."

I guess they were worried I'd misbehave again. So I tried to put their fears at rest. "I will, I promise."

*****

Just two hours after Dr. Knight and Professor Hamilton left in the carriage we arrived in last night, another carriage pulled up. Out of it stepped an unfamiliar middle-aged man also carrying a black leather doctor's bag, and also Captain Greyson! I saw him emerge from Guy's bedroom window that faced the front of the cottage.

"Captain Greyson is here." I smiled over at Guy.

Elisha Robertson met the two new arrivals at the garden gate and spoke to them both for a minute or two.

Captain Greyson was much more gray in hair than Guy, but not that much more wrinkled. He was out of Army uniform, and was wearing a smart suit with a long coat over it. I guessed he must have married well, telling by his appearance. His long coat was well tailored with intricate embroidery around the edges. He looked quite dashing, actually.

I instantly wondered if she asked them if they knew about the other doctor that visited last night. I bet she did... as the two men exchanged a befuddled look, and shook their heads. I hoped my ruse wouldn't be up so soon. I watched all of this from the window.

"Oh oh, here comes trouble. Your suspicious daughter just asked your oldest and dearest friend if he sent us last night." I came back and sat by Guy's side.

"Yes, Elisha was always the stubborn one." Guy chuckled. "I suppose she must get that trait from her father."

"Yes, I suppose so." I took hold of his hand again.

Then the bedroom door blew open as both Captain Greyson and the other doctor (probably the one who wanted to amputate Guy's leg and nearly bled him dry) now practically laid siege on the bedroom, expecting to accost a dangerous suspect.

"Elisha!" Greyson's boisterous voice boomed. His grin was immediate as was his recognition of me. "Come here, girl! Let me get a look at you! Let these sorry old eyes soak in a sight of beauty and of miraculous discovery!"

I stood up and went over and hugged him and kissed his cheek.

"You don't look a day older than we last met..." then he held me at arms length and eyed me closely.

"That's because I'm not." I smiled at him. "To me I only last saw you a couple of weeks ago."

Elisha Robertson looked on this exchange with suspicion, and Greyson noticed this.

"I was at her estate in Scotland just a couple of weeks ago." Greyson told Elisha Robertson. "Yes, I must have sent for their help. I made mention to Lady Durrant here and her family that their old and dear friend, your father, had been taken unwell. They must have taken it upon themselves to see to his recovery." He quickly came up with my excuse to Guy's daughter.

"Well, wasn't that good of her then." Elisha Robertson said flatly, still unconvinced.

"Elisha, please." Lt. Robertson gently scolded his little sister. "We are most grateful at the help exhibited, and the friendship you have extended, Lady Durrant."

Next we all waited in the kitchen, Greyson, Lt. Robertson, Elisha Robertson and myself, as Betsy made us some breakfast and tea, as Dr. Wilson examined Guy.

I finally sat down and let myself relax a little bit, and gratefully accepted the tea that was on offer this time. Actually, I was starving! I wished it was a proper big breakfast, like on offer in the Caf back at College. I could have eaten two plates of bacon and eggs with fried tomato and a hash brown, I was that famished. But instead I had to accept what was on offer, so I ate four scones with strawberry jam, and finished off two cups of tea.

I wanted to find out all the goss on Greyson, like who he married, and what he does with himself now. But blurting out questions like these would probably give myself away. Elisha Robertson and her brother would expect I would already know all this anyway.

"So, Captain Greyson." I put my empty cup of tea down. "How is your wife?"

"My wife Jane is quite well, thank you." Greyson got the gist of what I wanted to know. "Our two daughters, Elizabeth and Edith are well, also, I thank you."

"And how do you spend your time now?" I asked him.

"Well as you know, Jane was the daughter of the Honorable John Waynewright, a merchant banker. We spend our time between our town house in Piccadilly, and our country house in Sussex." Greyson told me.

I wanted to ask next if the old rogue enjoyed being a married man and father of two, but we were interrupted.

Dr. Wilson came out and joined us all in the kitchen.

"Your father is doing very well. In fact, I'm astonished. His state of health today is the complete opposite of the state I last saw him in, only yesterday." Dr. Wilson said, looking quite vexed.

"And his leg?" Lt. Robertson asked the doctor.

"That is healing well also. Amputation is no longer necessary." The Doctor stated, before turning to me. "I would be quite interested to know who the physician was who treated him."

"Dr. Hamilton is the physician." I half-lied.

"And where can this man be reached?" Dr. Wilson asked me next.

"I believe he may be reached in London. Sometimes it's rather difficult to get in contact with him. He spends his time in both Britain and the Colonies. In fact, when he left this morning, he said he would be sailing back to the Colonies the day after tomorrow. You see, he is one of the physician's treating the King's Army in the War." I lied again.

"It is a pity." Dr. Wilson sighed. "As I would dearly like to know the manner in which he treated the patient."

"Lady Durrant should be able to show you, Doctor. For she never left my father's side when the good doctor did apply his medicine." Elisha Robertson spoke up.

Just as she said that, I thought I caught a smirk on her lips.

Was it me, or was this young woman out to get me?

*****

Both Dr. Wilson and Captain Greyson left shortly after lunch. But before they did, Dr. Wilson told Elisha her father needed just one more day of complete bed rest to make sure he was fully recovered. I was sorry to see Captain Greyson leave so soon, as I would have liked to catch up and ask him some more questions.

As he was leaving, I got the impression he felt the same way.

"I would have liked to have spent more time in your company, my Lady, but unfortunately my business back in London will not allow me." Greyson sighed tiredly.

"Yes, married life can do that to a person." I smiled cheekily to him.

"It is not just one's wife which can be so time consuming, but managing her finances as well. I married well, my Lady, but then managing the money also can take as much attention as to managing the Lady of the House." Greyson winked cheekily back.

"I hope when you return you find your daughters are well. I would have liked to have met them." I said earnestly.

"And I would like nothing better than the same wish, my Lady. If you would allow me the pleasure of one day inviting you to my home and meeting my family, I would be honored to present them into your society." He bowed and kissed my hand, before straightening once more.

He looked at me with a serious expression on his face for a few moments, and he looked like he wanted to say something else. But instead he took a look at the window that was Guy's bedroom, and changed his mind. So he climbed inside the carriage, and closed the door behind himself.

He lowered the glass window and popped his head out.

"Farewell Lady Elisha Durrant. I hope this is not the last time we are in each other's company. Let me make good on my promise one day of having you to stay."

"Thank you Captain Greyson." I smiled, and then as the carriage started off, I waved goodbye.

I really like Captain Greyson. He has always been kind and courteous to me. And he has been a great friend to Guy. As I understood, he was paying for Dr. Wilson's services. He refused to let the family pay for any of the medical expenses of treating Guy's injury.

As I went back inside the cottage to return to Guy's side, I found Betsy cleaning up after lunch, Lt. Robertson examining a map of the colonies, and Elisha doing needle point in the sitting room by a window with the sunlight pouring through.

I was about to go back inside the bedroom, when Elisha spoke up to prevent me.

"My father is resting. If you would be so good to give him this time alone, I believe it will aid in his recovery." She said in a cold voice.

"Elisha, please. We've spoken on this matter before." Lt. Robertson looked up from the map and glared at his sister.

OK... I'll let this one slide by with out a fight, since I was a guest in their home. So I went and stood beside Lt. Robertson and looked at the map with him. I was interested to see how different it looked to the maps of the U.S. I was used to in my era.

"Will you be fighting in this war, Lt. Robertson?" I asked him.

"Indeed I will be, Lady Durrant." Guy's son stated. "I was about to set sail on my ship, the HMS Darlington for the Colonies, when my father's condition turned serious. I was granted a temporary pardon to tend to family affairs. Now that my father is on the mend again, I expect to sail out next week."

I suddenly looked at him a little afraid. Don't tell me he could die in the War of Independence? Should I warn him? Should I tell him not to bother since the Yankees will win? How old is he, maybe 18? Elisha Robertson would be my age, 17, no, hang on, she would be 16. Wow, these two actually look and seem much older.

Lt. Robertson caught me staring at him.

"Is there something the matter, my Lady?"

"You're 18, right? It seems like a really young age to go off to war." I said.

"I do not see it that way, my Lady. We have seamen as young as 14 serving on the HMS Darlington. One can never be too young to stand up for King and Country." Lt. Robertson smiled in good humor.

"But you're only 18... how did you get the promotion of Lieutenant?"

"I am a Lieutenant, Junior Grade, my Lady. I have only been at sea for 12 months. I did not start out as a yeoman or a seaman. I went to Naval college. I had to take my exam for Lieutenant. Or perhaps you feel that as my father was an Admiral, he could patronize my rank and not let me earn it?" Lt. Robertson said a little defensively.

"Please forgive me, Lieutenant. I did not mean to offend. I am uneducated and ill-advised of the ways of this world." I immediately backed off.

"Your apologies are accepted and appreciated, my Lady." Lt. Robertson nodded back to me.

Elisha Robertson, who sat listening to our conversation as she continued with her needle-point, let out a loud chortle, but did not look up.

But her brother had had enough of her behavior towards me. "Sister, since the arrival of our guest, you have been arrogant and rude. Lady Durrant has done nothing but offer her sympathies and her help, and with it came the instrumental turn in our father's health. Also with out this, Lady Durrant is a higher station than you in life. You will stand up now and make your apologies!"

"Really, it's OK." I put my hand on his arm. "I don't like your sister much either. I'm only here to help your father. I don't care if she does or doesn't like me much. I can ignore her behavior. I'm only here for one more day."

"Listen to her accent, Henry! She is no more a Lady than I am!" Elisha threw her needlepoint to the small table beside her chair and flounced upwards to take her stand. "Why have we never met her before when if she is who she says she is, and has been close friends to our mother and our father and even our Godfather, Captain Greyson? Why have we never seen her at any of the balls or hunting parties at Sterling Manor? Why has Aunt Jane or mother never mentioned her? And why does she act with such impropriety and hold our father's hand?!"

"Elisha Lydia Robertson! That is enough!"

Suddenly Guy in his bedclothes and dressing gown stood weakly in the doorway, leaning on to the doorframe for support. His body was still weak after fighting the infection for so long and for not eating or drinking properly. But his mind was strong, and at the moment, was fixed in anger at the situation he now found himself in.

"Father! Please, go back to bed and rest." Lt. Henry Robertson rushed forwards to offer his support of his weakened mentor before I could.

"I cannot believe I raised such an ungrateful, rude, sullen, immature daughter! Not only are you rude to guests in my house, not only are you not welcoming, but you are discriminating! Lady Durrant's accent comes from both the Colonies and Scotland, the two lands in which she was raised! In her home in the Colonies, her family have tended to me with such warmth and kindness when ever I have visited. It puts me now to shame to see how my family then carry on!" Guy blasted his daughter.

I suddenly felt really embarrassed and I wouldn't have to bet my cheeks were bright red again. When he said my family always showed him warmth and kindness, I assume that was on behalf of Dr. Knight's father and brother, or even the medical team at Circulate Headquarters when they brought him back to life after India. I felt a little sorry for Elisha Robertson, actually. I think she's just being over protective of her father and family.

"Guy, please. It's OK. Really." I went to his other side. "Let me help you to bed."

"Not until I witness my daughter's lament and her apologies." Guy stood his ground, not taking his eyes off Elisha Robertson.

"I'm very sorry father." Elisha said stiffly, looking down at the floor.

"Come on, let's get you to bed." I indicated to Lt. Robertson to take the lead and show the way.

Guy was limping still, from his leg wound, and I felt him put most of his weight on his son.

I actually felt a little jealous, as it reminded me of the time when Guy was shot in the stomach, and I had the pleasure of helping him walk myself, to his ship, that night in India. That one and only night we were physically together. The night that is still strong in my memory.

*****

For the rest of the day, Guy and I were very rarely alone. Betsy brought him in cups of tea or sandwiches, Elisha Robertson came in to check on his temperature and brought in his dinner, and Lt. Robertson even had an hour long discussion about the War with his father, and showed him on the map of where the English forces had planted themselves with the information he had from reading the newspapers. I just sat on the stool, this time in the corner and not so close to the bed so I would stop generating suspicion.

Lt. Henry Robertson was perfectly cordial to me. He brought in cups of tea for me, and he even remembered how I liked it, with milk and two sugars. He also brought in my dinner for me to eat with Guy, as he and his sister ate in the kitchen.

After dinner, Lt. Henry Robertson then sat in his father's bedroom and read aloud a passage from Shakespeare's Othello. He read very well, but I have to admit, there was one point I nearly laughed. This is what people did in these days when there was no TV's or the Internet or Cinema's. They made their own entertainment of reading or cards or whatever else, like needlepoint. I couldn't exactly see Henry and Guy doing needlepoint, which is when I nearly laughed, picturing it.

At 9 PM Guy closed his eyes tiredly, and Henry put down the book.

"It is getting rather late. Perhaps going to bed now would be in order." Henry said amicably. "Betsy has prepared the guest room for you. If you should need anything else, please do not hesitate to let us know. I believe even Elisha should be more hospitable now." He even joked.

"Thank you Henry." I smiled, and then caught myself. "Sorry, I mean, Lt. Robertson."

"No, please, call me Henry. As our families are old and true friends, that would mean you are like a cousin to me. Cousin's are on a first name basis. Good night cousin Elisha." He smiled at me, then left the room to go to his.

Wow. He is so nice! I even got a little fluttery in the stomach then when he smiled and said my first name! How weird is that?

"Be careful, my darling. Or you will be in very much in danger of having two men in this household worshipping the very ground you walk on." Guy opened his eyes and smiled tiredly at me.

"Yeah right." I rolled my eyes. Now that we were finally alone, and Henry had closed the door behind himself, I went and sat on the side of Guy's bed again. "You have always been quite a poet."

"What sense of romance that is lost on Elisha, Henry has inherited from me. He is not immune to your charms. And he idolizes beautiful women, as well as their eccentricities." Guy took one of my hands and kissed it. "And being of his mother's patient and kind disposition, he would be a much better romantic suitor than even his father has been."

"Guy!" I blushed, momentarily taking my hand back. "It sounds like you're trying to fix the two of us up! Yuck!"

"Living two hundred years before one's lost love, does make one imagine the future possibilities. Such as, what if one of my progeny could make a success of it where I had failed?" Guy said.

"So you're going to leave a statement in your will, and leave it with Lloyd's or whatever other company that is still open in my day, that your progeny in 2001 must meet and marry one Elisha Baker?" I laughed at the joke. "That's a good one! How about this, you also leave me some trinket or knick-knack, so by the time I come and collect it in my era, it would have accumulated so much worth in the world of antiques, that it can be my dowry as well!"

"Now that you have given me the idea..." Guy teased and I playfully slapped his chest. He caught my hand again and held it in his and then he kissed it. "Oh how much I want to see you happy in this life. You looked so sad last night. I suspect there is much going on in your era. There is so much grief hidden behind your eyes that you try to hide from me. I wish I could help you, the same way you help me. I wish I could give you something in return for all you have done for me."

"You have." I assured him. "I know it sounds cliché, but being with you, loving you, and you loving me, it has given me so much. I love being with you. It's trite, but it's true."

Guy examined me by looking deeply into my eyes for a few moments, before pulling me close to him and putting my head to rest on his chest so he could wrap his arms about me.

*****

The next morning Guy ate his breakfast in the kitchen with myself and his family. Betsy cooked a lovely breakfast of bacon and eggs and toast. It was delicious and we were all in a happy mood over the good food and the fact that we were all eating it together, with all of us this time, in excellent health.

"Henry, this morning I need you to organize a carriage to take Lady Elisha back to London this evening." Guy ordered his son.

"Yes father. I will see to Lady Elisha's journey myself." Henry nodded.

"No, I will see Lady Elisha home in the carriage. But I would like you to organize the carriage to be called at six in the evening." Guy told Henry.

Henry and Elisha Robertson exchanged a surprised glance, and both looked like they were about to object.

"But father... you have only just started to get your strength back..." Elisha complained. "I do not think that going into London and breathing in all that city air will be good for you. And the bumping and the rocking of the carriage? It simply will not do!"

"Please father, allow me the honor of seeing Lady Elisha back to her family town house in London. I must agree with my sister and protest for the sake of your health." Henry agreed with Elisha.

I looked startled back at Guy. I don't want Henry to take me home! I wanted Guy to take me back to London! I want even just a few more hours alone with him before I return to college, and maybe never see him again.

"I appreciate your concern for me..." Guy started.

"Then please show us your appreciation for us by abiding by our wishes, even if it is just this once." Elisha chimed in again. "Please father, not two days ago did you lie in this house dying!"

"I'm sure Lady Elisha will agree with us father. It is still too near the time of recovery. You cannot go on a carriage ride into London this evening." Henry said strongly.

Guy and I exchanged a helpless look.

"It looks like your children have spoken." I said simply, trying to hide my disappointment by drinking my tea.

"Very well. The plan is thus, Henry you will organize and arrange the transportation of Lady Elisha home this evening. I will keep recovering outside of London. But then to completely immerse myself in fresh air, I will take a small walk to the church and back this morning. Lady Elisha, since you have traveled all this way to see to my recovery, would you walk with me this morning?" Guy asked me now.

Elisha Robertson looked like she was about to object again, so I got in fast.

"I would love to."

"But father, your leg..." Elisha Robertson now whined.

"Yes, my daughter, my leg. It is healing well. And any doctor will tell you that some small exercise of using the wounded ligament is a way to allow it to heal strongly." Guy said to his daughter, with a warning look for no more complaints. She duly shut up.

When breakfast was finished and Betsy began cleaning up, Guy and I went for our walk.

He still did limp a lot, and he put most of his weight on his walking stick, but I at least got to link arms with him and slowly walk by his side.

This whole situation suddenly felt really weird to me.

Guy was so much older than I was now... and here he was hobbling on a walking stick. And I just had breakfast with him and his two teenaged kids. Now here we were walking down a cobbled road, past little cottages, with people in period costume giving us a good look and wondering who I am?

When we reached the Church that was just 500 meter's down the road, I was relieved when we sat in a secluded part of the cemetery, on a bench under a tree.

"Guy, this is so strange..." I suddenly said.

"I know. I am an old man now. You saw me together with my two grown children." He said sadly.

"And it's weird that you call them grown children, when in my era, they're still kids. Like I'm still a kid. And yet, here we are, walking around, trying to find a moment alone. And yet, last night, you were buttering your son up to me. I just feel really disorientated." I confessed and I even shook my head, as if scattering my brain might make everything then fall into place.

"Elisha, I had fantasized about the possibility of proposing to you before you left. I dreamed of spending the rest of my days with you. But I see now that that would be unfair. As you said yourself, you are still too young. You should be open to possibilities, but to me, unimaginable things in your future. You should be with some one young, whom you can share your adventures. I'm afraid my time has passed. Unfortunately for us, this also means that our time has passed." Guy said seriously, taking hold of my hands again.

"I know. I know all of this Guy." I sighed. "Let's change the subject. I don't want our last day together to be all sad and gloomy."

"But you must allow me to thank you for always being there. You have protected me in dangerous times, and saved my life twice. You have been like a guardian angel in times of need."

"You're welcome. Now lets change the subject." I said uncomfortably. I didn't want to start crying again.

"Would you promise me one last thing, my beloved Elisha?" suddenly he squeezed my hands very tightly.

"What is it?" I gave him a funny look at this sudden urgency.

"That you will hand over your protection to my son, Henry."

"What?" I asked him in surprise.

"No longer look over me or my life. Since I am now retired, I will lead a quiet life, safe in Dartford. I will have my daughter to look after me as I will look after her, now that her mother is gone. I would like you to look over my son, Henry. Especially now, during the war."

"Guy..." I faltered and looked away, now feeling tearful. I know how he might be feeling, since I felt it temporarily as well, yesterday, when I first found out Henry would be re-joining his ship which will be posted to the War. But being there for Guy has not always been an easy task. And what if I did leave the Circulate? I'm guessing I won't be able to just casually use their Gate to just travel whenever I want to, where ever I want to.

"Please grant this as a last wish from an old man, my love." He squeezed my hands even more tightly.

"You're not an old man!" I exclaimed. "You're an Admiral! Can't you just transfer him to a less dangerous assignment? Or change ships? Or redirect the HMS Darlington?"

"Not in my position of retirement. I have already tried. And I cannot risk rumors that might affect Henry's career, or his honor." Guy said back. "If I transferred him, he would instantly become a coward, with out even being given the chance to prove his bravery or valor."

"Guy." I said wretchedly, taking my hands back. "It's not so easy for me. I mean, I have to do a lot of research, and I have to ask a friend of a friend to find out stuff sometimes. I had a friend of a friend originally tell me you were going to die in India, then I had the friend in Scotland while she was in London visiting the said friend, find out that you died of illness. When I went back in time to India, I ran away from school and risked expulsion! My teachers brought me back in time to heal you now, because I got really depressed when I read of your untimely death and I threatened I wanted to leave school. I still don't even know if I'm going to be accepted back."

Guy looked away sadly and stared at one of the headstones.

We sat in silence for a couple of minutes.

I started to feel guilty. I know how proud he is. It probably took a lot for him to ask me to do this huge task. And what do I do? I bitch and moan.

"All right. I'll keep an eye on Henry for you." I sighed.

Guy didn't say anything, and wore his stubborn expression as he looked away from me.

"No, I mean it. I'll look out for him, for you." I took hold of his hand, but he pulled his hand back. "Guy, please. Don't be angry with me. We've already gone down that path, remember? Leaving on bad terms wasn't nice then, so it won't be nice now. I will look out for your son." I promised him.

He finally looked at me again.

I couldn't resist, my stomach melted. I just love it when he's angry! Even at the age of 49 he's still sexy when he's angry. Nelson is right. I am pathetic, but I don't care. I love his stubborn demeanor.

I started laughing at myself, which actually made Guy soften a bit too. He even shared in the chuckle, but at himself as well. Then he took hold of my hand again and squeezed it, as we shared a long look and smile.

"After all these years, we still argue." He smirked.

"Yeah, but isn't it fun?" I teased and he had a chuckle again.

*****

The carriage ride back into London took an hour longer than the ride out.

Instead of galloping the whole way like we did that first night, the horse made the way back in a leisurely trot. Also I was considering how fortunate it was that Guy remembered the address of the Dunmore Town House from my last escapade through time. I was expecting it to be me to tell Henry to tell the driver where to take us, but instead Guy told his son the address instead.

I guess this was a sign of how much he remembered me in all the years passed.

I was quiet during the ride home. I just wanted to sit back and watch the old London disappear past my window. I just wanted to think of all the things Guy and I said to each other.

I felt oddly at peace. It was like the old wounds between us were now healed. Like we both could move on. Like the both of us could now just see the future clearly, and think that it was OK, because we both had forgiven each other, and ourselves.

As we entered London city, I realized Henry was watching me as much as he was watching the view outside our windows change. This made me feel uncomfortable.

"I would just like to thank you again, Lady Elisha, for the help you rendered to my family in our time of need." Henry smiled at me.

Just then I realized he had Guy's smile. It wasn't the toothy grin that most people have, but it was the soft, small smile where his lips didn't part. This made me feel even more icky.

"It was a pleasure." I smiled shyly back and quickly looked back out the window.

"If I may inquire, what plans do you now have? Will you be staying away from the Colonies during the unrest? Will you stay in London?" Henry asked me.

"I'll probably return to Scotland." I lied.

"Lady Elisha, have you been presented into society as yet? Are your parents allowing suitors to make claim to your affections?" Henry asked me next.

I looked at him a little worriedly for a minute, trying to think of my next answer.

In this time period I would have been of marriageable age. I had been presented into society and at court. I had been passed off as a Lady connected to a great family with even a greater dowry attached to my name. But that was when I knew Guy as a 27 year old.

"I have not yet been presented at court. I have not yet attended any balls in society. I believe I may 'come out' next year, when I am next in London." I made up.

"Do you think your parents would take unkindly to the prospect of a man laying his suit at this time of your life?" Henry asked concerned.

"I think so." I only half-lied this time. I could imagine my real Dad's response at his 17-year-old daughter telling him of her engagement! This thought nearly made me crack up laughing and I quickly looked back out the window to hide this.

Henry looked a little disappointed as he then looked out the window too.

I know I was sounding discouraging, but I don't want him to try and pick me up! I've only just officially ended it with his Dad for bloody sake! I don't want to just pick up with the son where his father and I left off. It would be like going out with Zack and then having sex with Peter next, being passed on from one close acquaintance to the next. Eeww... yuck! Double yuck!

I had to quickly pretend to be really interested in a building we just passed to hide my disgusted expression.

When the carriage came to a stop at our designation, Henry hopped out first so he could then help me out.

I thought I shouldn't be a total bitch, since he had been so nice to me in his house.

"Thank you for your kindness, Henry. You were a gracious host. And thank you for remembering how I drank my tea." I smiled at him, before I let go of his hand after he helped me alight.

These words seemed to give him a new hope, as I watched his face instantly light up at my compliments.

"If you were to one day give us the pleasure of visiting with us again, Lady Elisha, it would be my pleasure to prepare your tea just the way you like." He smiled at me, taking hold of my hand again and giving me a small bow.

"I may indeed just do that." I laughed.

I turned and started making my way up the stairs to the front door when Henry called out, "Lady Elisha?"

I stopped and turned to see him looking a little anxious.

"Surely as close family friends, it would not be of any impropriety to correspond to one another. May I write to you in Scotland?" he asked.

I was about to refuse him, when Guy's request sounded in my head... "*I would like you to look over my son, Henry. Especially now, during the war...*" If Henry did write to me, then it would help me keep track of his whereabouts in history. It would make the task of looking out for him a lot easier.

"You may." I gave a nod of permission.

This made him beam, and he stayed on the footpath and watched as the maid opened the door and let me pass into the house.

I found Dr. Knight sitting in the drawing room, still in period costume for the day, waiting for me.

"Is everything in order?" she stood up upon my arrival.

"As much as it will ever be." I sighed.

She gave me a curious look on this comment. "Do you intend to make regular visitations to this place and era when you are granted permission to travel on your own?"

I looked at her and wondered what to say. I thought I should tell her the truth and have done with it. It was going to come out sooner or later anyway.

"Guy asked me to keep an eye on his son during the War of Independence." I told her.

"You didn't tell him which side would win, did you?" her eyes widened in alarm.

"No! Of course not. But if I keep just one soldier alive, I'm sure it won't cause a ripple in the time line." I retorted.

Dr. Knight didn't look too keen on this promise I'd made. "Elisha, just so you know, students aren't usually given permission to start traveling independently until their Senior year at College."

"I know." I shrugged. "I'll stick to the school rules."

"So you will be staying on at the school then?" she asked.

"I guess so." I almost said, 'I have to now', but I thought it would probably sound rude.

"Then are you ready to return to College?" she asked, looking at me closely.

"Yeah." I said hesitantly, not moving from the spot I was standing in. I wanted to ask her something first, before we went back. I really wanted to know this. "But can I ask you something first?"

"Yes?"

"How did you find out about Guy? How he got sick? And think it was related to my decision to leave?"

"You can thank your friends for that favor, Elisha." Dr. Knight now smiled at me.

"My friends?" I asked baffled. What have they to do with it?

"I believe Sally sent an email to Zack, and then Zack told Nelson and Patrick, and then the three of them this afternoon told Professor Hamilton and myself." Dr. Knight informed me. "Well, the afternoon of two days ago. But when we return to College, we will make our return to the same day, and on the same evening we left."

I was momentarily stunned.

Sally was that worried about me that she told Zack? And that made Zack worried about me that he told Nelson and Patrick? And then three of them wanted to help me out and get me to stay, that they went and asked Hamilton?

I'm sure it wouldn't have been easy for Zack, getting him to help his ex-girlfriend to save the other man in her life. But he did it. He helped me. And he got the two other people closest to me in my life right now to help him do it. And Nelson couldn't care less about Guy and thought I was weak for always focusing on him all the time, but she still helped me out.

I was really touched.

And I thought they all thought I was just some attention-seeking hypochondriac.

I can't believe I owe these wonderful couple of days to four people who I thought couldn't care less.

"Ready?" Dr. Knight now brought my attention back to the moment at hand.

"Yes." I now smiled back at her. "Definitely."

We linked hands and focused our concentration on the huge window beside us.

*****

When Dr. Knight and I passed through the window in the hallway of the second floor of Alpha Building, the time was 7.25 PM and the date was still Saturday the 15th of September. The building was empty, as everyone was still in the Cafeteria, chowing down their dinners. There were no witnesses upon our return as there were none on our departure.

Together we both crossed the oval back to Beta building and to our different bedrooms to change out of our 18th Century garb.

As soon as I had pulled up the zipper on my jeans, and pulled down the jumper over my head, I heard the voices of the returnees.

I came out of my room just as I saw Zack, Peter, Nelson and Pat all coming up the stairs.

"Hi." I smiled at them.

"Hi." They all looked surprised at my happiness.

"So Hamilton said you can go then?" Zack asked me.

"I've already gone." I kept smiling at them.

"I've been saying that all along." Peter scoffed, which earned an elbow from Nelson.

"Oy! If you hit me one more time, you psychotic bitch..." Peter raised his hand but Pat grabbed it and twisted it.

"You'll do what to my girlfriend, mate?"

"Nothing! I'm fucking kidding! Let go of me!" Peter whined. "But tell her to stop hitting me!"

Nelson and Zack removed themselves from this latest altercation and came towards me.

"So everything's OK?" Zack asked me.

"Yes. Dr. Knight healed him. He lives, apparently." I told them.

"Good. So are you staying then?" Nelson asked in her usual blunt manner.

"Yep." I nodded.

"Glad to hear it." Zack smiled back at me.

"And I heard who I'm to thank for this." I smiled at all of them as Patrick and Peter now caught up with us. "Thank you, all of you. Thank you for asking Hamilton and Dr. Knight for me."

"You're welcome." Zack said warmly. "I figured I owed you one."

I was about to ask him how he saw this, but I thought I better not in front of everybody else. I gathered it had something to do with that night in the kitchen. I guess his guilt made him repent, but he also seems honestly happy to have me stay.

"So the 49 year old lives to see another day. Are you going to keep trying to see him again? And isn't he married now?" Nelson started her lecture.

"Relax, would you? He's widowed, and no, I won't try to see him romantically again." I promised. "I won't time travel again until I'm allowed to, like the rest of you." I left out the part of me looking out for Henry, since I didn't think they really needed to know this part. Besides, I could just imagine Nelson's wisecracks on transferring my attention from Guy to his son.

"So, are you going to join us and watch 'Daredevil' in Gamma building?" Zack asked me hopeful.

"Nah, I can't. I have so much homework to catch up on." I sighed, remembering my rebelliously depressed phase.

"Actually, we haven't done our History assignment yet... you wanna go over to the Library?" Zack offered, inferring himself and Peter. Peter pulled a face at the thought of doing his homework on a Saturday night.

"Yeah, sure." I agreed.

"You wanna go too and do our Math homework?" Nelson asked Pat next.

"Yeah. Cool." Pat shrugged amiably.

So we all got our bags and books from our rooms and headed over to the Library in Alpha building.

Believe it or not, diary, that doing our homework in the Library on this Saturday night was actually one of the most fun nights I've had since coming to this college.

Since it was 'Fun Night' most of the other students were either watching videos or hanging out somewhere else. We practically had the library all to ourselves, so we didn't have to worry about being quiet. Peter and Zack kept throwing things at each others heads, and Nelson and I started singing Tori Amos songs at the top of our voices! Pat set up his Discman with these two little speakers on top of the center table and played Moby. Even Maya and Raj came and joined us at 9 PM and helped me catch up with two of my assignments by giving me their references. And in a kind gesture that was unusual in the sense that Maya took her studying very seriously, she DIDN'T ask us to shut up so she could concentrate.

===

TO: s_parson@snailmail.com
FROM: ebaker_hamiltons@evers.com
SUBJECT: Thank you Sally.
DATE: 22/ 09/ 01

Thank you Sally… Thank you for sending the email to Zack. Thank you for your help.

As you might be able to tell, Guy didn't die in September of 1778. And it is partly thanks to you. Because you told Zack, he then told Nelson and Pat and the three of them went and told Hamilton.

I did get really depressed about it, and at the thought that I couldn't use my power to help him out again. I started to wonder why I was at this school, using this ability, if I couldn't use it the way I wanted to. So I think it's kind of ironic, but really sweet, that even though you left this school, your intervention stopped me from leaving too.

I got in the mail yesterday the documents you copied and sent to me. It's so nice seeing Guy's handwriting again. It makes him seem more real to me, that even though he lived his life more than two hundred years ago, to see me mentioned in his print, makes our relationship feel more valid and special.

If there is anything I can ever do for you, please do not ever hesitate to ask it of me.

Your most humblest and grateful of friends,

Elisha xoxo

==

TO: mbaker@hotmail.com

FROM: ebaker_hamiltons@evers.com

SUBJECT: I'm all right, this is what's going on.

DATE: 09/ 10/ 01

Hey Mark,

Yeah, I've decided to stay on at the college. I hope I didn't worry you and Dad too much. Nothing here happened, I just felt really sad for a little while.

What's changed, you ask? Well, a lot has happened here lately. But this is a pretty different school, a lot different to our old High School back in the Mountains. There are heaps of new excursions coming up in the next four semesters. I'll actually be visiting Cairo, Athens, Rome, London, Beijing, and a few other places for our History class… don't worry, all expenses will be paid for by the school. But that's pretty cool, huh? I can't imagine being able to do all of this back at good ole Winmalee High.

I'm really happy for you and Jen on your engagement. And also congrats on getting the new unit in Surry Hills. I can't believe it, after two promotions you next get a mortgage and then a date to get married! And you're only four years older than me! I bet you must be making Dad very proud of you. Mum as well.

Well I better go now. I'm going to give Dad a call and catch up with him next. It's a pity I can't just email him as well. But I guess it was just a miracle in itself for Dad to learn how to use the new DVD player you gave him at Christmas, let alone the very idea of having the Internet in his house! LoL!

Lots of love from your little sister….xoxox

==

~ The Circulate Series ~

By K.R. Smith

~ Book One: Circulate ~

Elisha Baker learns something new about herself when she attends the haunted international boarding school, Hamilton's College.

~ Book Two: Circulating ~

Elisha and her friends graduate from Hamilton's and the Circulate; to begin University and SSIT – Supernatural Scientific Investigative Team.

~ Book Three: Circulation ~

Armed with degrees, Elisha and her friends continue with SSIT. However adult life isn't as straightforward as they imagined, especially when an investigation into past lives interferes with a present romance.

~ Book Four: Progeny ~

Alexandrina and twin brother Bastian, grew up without a mother and a distant father. But it's to Jarrod's chagrin that his daughter mirrors his late wife, with the fact that she too is a Circulator.

~ Book Five: Ardor & Redolence ~

Arabella joins her grandmother on a SSIT case and meets Emanuel Riverclaw. Eventually they marry and create twins Julian and Jessica; a son who will become a Lokoti Werewolf like his father and a daughter who is a Circulator like her mother.

~ Book Six: Scent ~

At first the Last Circulator can't stand the tribe's most dangerous Werewolf, then Bianca and Declan's fiery arguments turn into something else.

~ Book Seven: Sororate ~

Claws come out in the marriage of the tribe's first female Lokoti Werewolf and the world's last European Werewolf; who spend their tumultuous years together traveling the world and through time.

~ Book Eight: Small Fry ~

Declan swore he wouldn't create anymore European Werewolves like himself, so his wife's new condition has his already hot blood boiling.

~ Book Nine: Alma ~

The new girl in Alma High School called Mali Roanne, suspects there's more than meets the eye with her Lokoti friends. However Mali is hiding a supernatural secret of her own.

~ Book Ten: Heterogeneous ~

In a space age, the different breeds of Werewolves are confined to Earth because of the influence of its one moon. But there's no such holds on the separate species of Vampires or even Human/ Animal Shape Shifters.

~ Book Eleven: Cohesion ~

Parents become grandparents when their children marry and procreate; with all of the different elements of the supernatural combining into one unusual family.

~ Book Twelve: Full Circle ~

The end is nigh, with answers as to why the futuristic Circulate technology never advanced past the 25th Century; because humankind doesn't.

To find out more on the series or the author please visit:

http://onaya3.blogspot.com/

http://twitter.com/onaya3

www.storywrite.com/onaya3

www.writing.com/authors/onaya3

www.facebook.com/pages/Circulate-Series-By-KR-Smith/222260061814?ref=ts

~ References ~

- Warren, Joshua P. <u>How to Hunt Ghosts: A Practical Guide</u>. Fireside. NY. 2003

- Goldman, Jane. <u>The X-Files Book of Unexplained, Book 1</u>. Simon & Schuster. London. 1995

- Hawking, Stephen. <u>A Brief History of Time, From the Big Bang to Black Holes</u>. Bantam Books. London. 1988

- Levy, David H. <u>The Nature Company Guides, Skywatching</u>. The Five Mile Press. Noble Park. 1994

- Collins Pageant of Knowledge Series. <u>A Pageant of History: The Reigns of our Kings and Queens and Famous People and Events in our History</u>. WM. Collins Sons & Co. Ltd. London. 1958.

- Tillyard, Stella. The <u>Aristocrats: The Illustrated Companion to the Television Series</u>. Weidenfeld & Nicolson. London. 1999

- Chisolm, Jane. Millard, Anne. The <u>Usborne Book of the Ancient Worlds</u>. Usborne. London. 1991

- <u>The Berkley Guide to London, 1996</u>. Fodor's Travel Publications, inc. New York. 1996

- DK Eyewitness Travel Guides. <u>European Phrase Book</u>. London. 2001

- Pennick, Nigel. <u>Mysteries of the Ancient World: Leylines</u>. Weidenfeld & Nicolson. London. 1997

- Burl, Aubrey. <u>Mysteries of the Ancient World: Stone Circles</u>. Weidenfeld & Nicolson. London. 1997

BIN TRAVERLER FORM

Cut By: _____ Qty _11___ Date _07/17/26_

Scanned By: _____ Qty _____ Date _____

Scanned Batch ID's _____

Notes / Exceptions _____